OCEANSPACE

OCEANSPACE

ALLEN M. STEELE

ACE BOOKS, NEW YORK

OCEANSPACE

An Ace Book
Published by The Berkley Publishing Group,
a division of Penguin Putnam Inc.,
375 Hudson Street, New York, New York 10014.
The Penguin Putnam Inc. World Wide Web site address is
http://www.penguinputnam.com

Library of Congress Cataloging-in-Publication Data

ISBN: 0-441-00685-X

Printed in the United States of America

For Sir Arthur C. Clarke

OCEANSPACE

The sea may cover 71 percent of the planet. But what dominates, and does so in utter anonymity and invisibility, is the deep, which lies beyond the shallows that border the continents and in total accounts for about 65 percent of the earth's surface. This domain is so wide and so deep that by some estimates it comprises more than 97 percent of the space inhabited by living things on the globe, dwarfing the thin veneer of life on the land.

Human eyes have glimpsed perhaps one-millionth of this dark realm. Perhaps a thousandth of a billionth. No one knows, and in any case the precise number is immaterial. The truth is that our planet has remained largely unexplored, until now.

—William J. Broad, *The Universe Below*

FIRST DAY

SATURDAY, JUNE 4, 2011

FIRST DAY

ONE
Kraken

6.4.11—1024 EST

O ff the Atlantic coast of the United States, just past the edge of the continental shelf, rests a broad submarine terrace known as the Blake Plateau. Located approximately 2,500 feet below sea level, the plateau stretches from Cape Hatteras to the Bahamas, and extends nearly one hundred miles out into deep ocean before it abruptly ends at the rugged escarpment which marks the farthest edge of the North American continent; beyond that lie the vast undersea plains of the Atlantic Basin.

The Blake Plateau is a prehistoric relic of the last ice age. The same climatic shifts which caused walls of glacial ice to advance across Canada into the Midwest also dropped the average sea level to the present boundaries of the continental shelf; when the glaciers receded during the Oligocene epoch some 25 million years ago, the seas rose and the continental shelf gradually vanished beneath the waves. As it did, rivers and estuaries carried postglacial sediments across the new coastline to the Florida-Hatteras Slope, where they settled upon the leading edge of the tectonic plate forming the American continent. Thus the Blake Plateau was created.

Down here, there is no sunrise or sunset, only the eternal midnight of the abyss, pierced briefly by quick-moving sources of bioluminescence: gape-jawed anglerfish, gulper eels, and tiny squid, stalking one another in the frigid darkness. All else is dark, and still.

And then . . . something moves.

First, there's a faint sound: the gentle thrum of props, like the distant echo of a submarine earthquake, yet constant, more regular. Then a dim, horizontal row of lights ascends from unknown regions far above. As the light pierces downward, it startles the fish and eels; for a few moments they break off their deadly games to swim a little closer and investigate the source of the light and sound, until it becomes apparent even to their primitive minds that the intruder is alien to their world, and therefore dangerous. They speed away before the narrow swath of light can find them.

Downward the machine glides, the forward end of its long form backlit by thallium iodide lamps: a pair of enormous, multijointed manipulators mounted above a titanium sphere, itself connected by a slender collar and thick steel trusses to a long cylinder, on top of which was mounted an open-top cargo bed. Two barrel-shaped maneuvering thrusters are positioned along its port and starboard sides; at the aft end, recessed within a cone-shaped cowling, is the lazily rotating propeller of its main engine. There's no color down here—even within close proximity of the halogens, everything is rendered in muted shades of greenish gray—so there's no way of telling that the submarine is painted bright fluorescent yellow, interspersed with bands of reds and white.

At the front of the sphere, below and between the arms, is a single, cyclopean eye: a Plexiglas window, two inches thick. Dim light glows within the porthole, silhouetting a vague form. A creature not born in this dark universe, yet, due to a long series of evolutionary processes stretching back millions of years, a distant cousin nonetheless.

A man. A human being. Joe Niedzwiecki.

One eye on the porthole, the other on the bathymetric chart displayed on the computer screen beneath the window, Joe Niedzwiecki gently pulled back the yoke. The bottom itself was still invisible through the dish-size porthole, but the steady, high-pitched pings of the passive sonar told him it was down there nonetheless, coming closer with each passing second.

Joe inched back the yoke a little more, then found the throttle bar with his right hand and yanked it back to neutral. Gravity would take care of the rest; all he had to do was make sure the little submersible didn't crash-land. The silt stirred up by the thrusters was becoming more dense, as if he was flying through a thick green cloud. Two fathoms . . . one and half . . . one fathom . . . and suddenly the floodlights captured a flat, muddy surface just below him, strewn with small, dark brown rocks.

There was an abrupt jar as the DSV's skids connected with the seafloor. He checked the screen again, smiled to himself. Touchdown, right on the money. Joe bent over the keypad, typed in a brief message: *DSV-02 Doris. On bottom: W78.2°S29.9° 810m. Over.*

He tapped the transmit key, settled back in his chair. This far down, instant communications with the surface were impossible; he had to wait while sub's Extra Low Frequency transmitter pulsed his message to the radio buoy he had left on the surface, which in turn would relay it to Tethys. With a transmission rate of only a few words per minute, there was no room for him to send any lengthy sonnets, or even a decent haiku. Once more, he pushed to the back of his mind the fact that this information was pertinent only in the event of an accident. If the titanium hull of *Doris*'s crew sphere failed now—if, say, there was the merest hairline fracture between the porthole's glass and its frame—then nearly two thousand pounds-per-square inch of hydrostatic pressure would pulverize him so quickly that there would be no time for him to send a distress signal. So relaying his coordinates was only standard operating procedure, in the event Tethys had to send down another boat to pick up the pieces.

While he waited for the base to respond, Joe reached under his seat for the CD box. During the hourlong descent, he had listened to Miles Davis's *Bitches Brew* album on the CD player rigged beneath the sonar panel on his right side. Good music for a deep dive, but now he needed something a little less spooky. He wavered between Hancock and the Marsalis brothers, and finally settled on Coltrane's *A Love Supreme*. Cool, mysterious jazz for a cool, mysterious world.

The ELF panel above the porthole came alive as he was pulling out the Coltrane CD.

```
6.4.11/1026 EST
TETHYS TO DSV-02 DORIS
COPY LAST TRANS, PRES. COORD.
PROCD W/ SER. & RET.
OVER
```

Good. Now that the formalities were dispensed with, he could get down to serious diving. Joe slipped in the Coltrane CD, carefully turning down the volume so he could still hear the forward range sonar; every five seconds, it transmitted an acoustic pulse at 8.1 kilohertz. He found the water bottle in its nylon web next to the seat, took a slug, then spat on the deck between his knees for good luck. One more seaman's custom; only he and Mike Cilantro, Tethys's other deep-sub pilot, knew that there was an antique silver dollar taped beneath the control yoke where no one could see it, and he had made sure to place his right foot first on *Doris*'s ladder when he climbed aboard. Having a naked woman aboard might have helped, too—ancient legend had it that Poseidon liked the presence of nude women aboard ships, which was why vessels used to sport bare-breasted figureheads on their prows—but he doubted that his wife would have approved. Even if she herself was willing to make a dive with him, which she wasn't, there wasn't enough room within *Doris*'s cramped confines for him to take proper advantage of the situation.

On the other hand, even if he could have smuggled Karen aboard, he probably wouldn't have. Although a passenger seat was folded away in the back of the crew sphere, Joe preferred making these sorties by himself. It was a little less cramped that way, and besides, he enjoyed the solitude. Going down here was like visiting another world, but even the astronauts on the new lunar base didn't have the Moon all to themselves. Spit on the deck, a silver dollar, and a good onboard guidance system: that was all the assistance he needed now.

Oh, yeah . . . and a proper fix on Porky.

The electronic chart showed that he had touched down on a gentle slope about thirty nautical miles southeast of Stetson Mesa. Joe typed the robot's serial number into the keypad, then asked the computer to display its coordinates. An instant later Porky's present whereabouts appeared on the screen. Joe smiled as he studied it; the mining robot was only about a mile and a half northeast of his present position, bearing 40 degrees true North. All he had to do was lock onto its transponder signal, and the computer would navigate him straight there.

He pushed forward the throttle bar and pulled back the yoke. *Doris* lifted her skids from the muck; he turned the yoke a quarter of an arc to the right until a tiny red spot on heads-up was aligned with a yellow pointer, then he gave the main prop a little juice and off he went across the sea bottom

The *Doris* was essentially a deep-ocean truck. Although it could conceivably be used for exploration, it was specifically designed as a workhorse to service the teleoperated mining robots which prowled the Blake Plateau. As *Doris* skimmed across the sea bottom at an altitude of little less than a fathom, its floodlights caught thousands of the dark nuggets, ranging in size from golf balls to Idaho potatoes, spread so evenly over the ocean floor that they looked like a vast field of charcoal.

No one knew the exact origins of these manganese nodules. Although it was theorized that they were precipitates of dissolved metals in seawater, why they lay on the sea bottom instead of buried beneath the muck was a question which still puzzled oceanographers. Discovered during the H.M.S. *Challenger* expedition of the 1870s, they remained little more than a scientific curiosity until the 1960s, when industrialists first proposed harvesting them, for each nodule was a miniature lode of valuable metals: manganese, cobalt, copper, nickel, even trace amounts of gold. Quite valuable when gathered by the truckload, yet it wasn't until the last decade or so that the technology was finally developed which would make sea mining economically viable.

Joe followed the arrow on the screen as he homed in on the robot. The side-scan sonar pinged as it found something just ahead of him; at first he thought it was the robot, until he checked the chart and saw that Porky still lay three-quarters of a mile away. He throttled back on the main screw and raised altitude by a fathom, and presently something loomed out of the darkness just ahead: an angular, man-made shape.

He cut the main engine and used the thrusters to cautiously approach it. The DSV's lights caught the broken prow of what looked like a wooden fishing boat. No telling how long it had been down here, or where it had come from. Silt covered its battered hull, and tiny albino crabs prowled its decaying planks. The stern was nowhere to be seen. Probably a schooner which had broken apart and sunk during a storm uncounted years ago; if her crew hadn't survived, the crabs had doubtless disposed of their bodies long ago.

Another time, he would have liked to find and explore its debris field, see if there was something down here worth salvaging. Even a brass deck fixture could fetch a hundred bucks from an antique dealer. But he was on the clock, and Miles Bartlett frowned on wreck diving during company time. He reluctantly left the boat behind and continued following the GPS beacon to its source.

The sonar beeped sharply as it registered a metal contact. Joe caught sight of a pair of red strobes winking at him from far away in the darkness. No longer needing the computer to guide him, he turned the rudder a few degrees starboard as he throttled down again, and within minutes his lights found another alien object in the black depths, one much larger than the fishing boat.

"Hello, Porky," he murmured. "Long time no see."

No one Joe had met could explain why exactly the mining robot was called Porky. Certainly it didn't look like any hog he had ever seen, and Joe had been born and raised in Indiana farm country. A little larger than a

John Deere harvester, it also bore a vague resemblance to one: an enormous, rectangular machine riding on tandem caterpillar treads. The four dustpan-shaped dredge heads beneath its undercarriage scooped up nodules and fed them through semicircular tubes into its diffusers, which sifted out the silt and spat it out through vents behind the machine, leaving behind a small bin of nodules. When the onboard computer sensed that the bin was full, it shut down the robot and awaited further instructions from the surface.

Teleoperators on Tethys guided Porky during every step of the procedure, piloting the robot through a complex sequence of ELF signals transmitted from the base and downlinked through geosynchronous satellites. Porky had a companion robot—predictably named Elmer—but it was currently dry-docked at Yemaya's base of operations in Jacksonville. The big harvesters cost $20 million apiece, and although they could be operated at the same time, the company was unwilling to risk deploying both of these costly—and notoriously finicky—machines simultaneously. So Porky spent six months at sea while Elmer took a vacation, and then vice versa.

The only catch was that once the robots were down on the plateau, they were down for keeps; it was prohibitively expensive to bring them to the surface every time their bins were full. In shallow-water operations, inflatable lift bags might have been used to bring up their cargo, but that was clearly out of the question this far down; ditto for the idea of dropping ballast, since lead shot would be outweighed by the nodules. So there was only one practical solution: every two weeks or so, a DSV had to go down, pick up the load, and haul it back to Tethys.

This time, it was Joe Niedzwiecki's turn to bring home the groceries.

Porky's operator on Tethys had put the big machine on standby mode, so Porky had come to a halt, its vents clear of the cloudy silt it normally left its wake. Behind the harvester, he saw the long, shallow furrow it left along the seafloor. Once again, he was oddly reminded of the swath a combine makes through a cornfield in late September.

Now for the tricky part. Joe cut all engines, set *Doris* down on her skids. When the sub was motionless, he reached up to the low ceiling above him and pulled down the RMS hand controllers. When they were in position at shoulder height, he toggled the activator switches on the dashboard, then fitted his palms within the grips and gave the triggers a brief, experimental squeeze.

Through the porthole, he watched the manipulator claws clamp shut. He relaxed his fingers, and the claws spread open again. The remote manipulators looked fragile, but on the second day of his training course, his instructor had placed a quarter-inch lead pipe between them, then shimmied into the cockpit and proceeded to tie it into a loose knot. Graduation exercise consisted of performing the same feat, two thousand feet under water. Joe's knotted pipe presently rested on the living room floor of his Jacksonville condo; his kids were still trying to undo what their dad had done in less than a minute.

So the RMS arms checked out. Good. He left the claws open, took a moment to wipe his hands on his jeans. As an afterthought, he turned around to stab the pause button on the CD deck—too much of a distraction—and reached beneath his seat for the water bottle.

The side-scan sonar gave a loud beep as it suddenly detected something as startling in the silence of the cab as a footfall in an empty house.

He glanced up, and something moved past the porthole.

It whisked through the lights so quickly, he caught only the most fleeting glimpse of it.

Joe peered through the porthole, then turned his head again to check the sonar screen. He didn't see anything else, though, and the sonar remained blank.

He gazed out the porthole for few seconds, and finally relaxed. This far down, there was no telling what a sub driver was likely to see, and thick Plexiglas has a tendency to magnify even the smallest of sea life. Probably a cuttlefish checking him out.

Back to work. He carefully aligned the manipulators until the arms were straight ahead, the claws open. All he had to do now was maneuver *Doris* a little closer to Porky and set her down directly behind the harvester; once he was close enough for the RMS arms to reach the bin, he would detach it from the robot and empty its cargo into *Doris*'s cargo bed. Another glance at the computer screen—nope, no problems there—and he was ready to go. Once again, he reached down to pick up the water bottle.

Something slammed against the sub's port side.

The impact was hard enough to rock *Doris* on her skids. Joe's forehead struck one of the hand controllers; he yelped and the water bottle fell from his fingers and rolled across the deck as he instinctively grabbed the yoke for support. In the confusion of the moment, the harsh beep of the sonar barely registered on him.

"What the bloody . . . ?" He raised his eyes to the porthole, and felt his heart stop.

A vast gray form glided past the window.

No head, no tail. Just something that looked like a segment of a fireman's hose, except much larger: at least six feet in diameter, so close to the window that he could make out the deep wrinkles in its mottled flesh.

Powerful muscles rippled beneath its skin, and the submersible shuddered as the thing made contact again with his vehicle.

Then Joe heard the sound DSV drivers dread the most: the faint creak of hull seams under pressure. Exactly the last thing you want to hear at 2,650 feet.

That was all it took. Whatever this goddamn thing was, he wanted it off his boat. He grabbed the hand controllers and yanked them back as far as they would go, then dipped the arms and opened the claws. Then he rammed the arms forward.

The claws dug into the creature's firm flesh with as much resistance as if he was grabbing an inflated inner tube, yet for a moment he managed to get a grip. He thought he'd get a good look at this thing, but it easily writhed out of the claws and, too fast for his eye to follow, slithered away.

A long, tapering tail, with a single dorsal fin running down its back, whipped past the porthole, then it was gone.

Joe sank back in his seat. His heart beat against his chest; cool sweat drooled down the inside of his chamois shirt. All was silent, and there was nothing on the other side of the porthole.

Whatever it was, it had vanished.

Whatever it was, it was the size of a friggin' truck.

He took a deep breath, then reached for the keypad. Better send a quick squib to Tethys, tell whoever was on watch what he had seen down here. They were never going to believe—

He stopped himself. Damn straight they were never going to believe this. If fact, they'd probably send him to a shrink. So long as *Doris* remained undamaged, he'd never have any proof that . . .

The hull shuddered, ever so slightly, as something nudged the engine cowling.

Joe grabbed the RMS controllers and hauled the arms back again as he peered through the porthole. Nothing in sight, save for Porky a couple of dozen yards away, yet he had no doubt that the creature, whatever it might be, wasn't done with him yet. This time, though . . .

The camera. He remembered the 35-millimeter digital camera positioned beneath the floodlight rack, outside the sphere and under the porthole. It was seldom activated during grocery runs—you've seen one field of manganese nodules, you've seen 'em all—but it was always loaded with a film disk.

He reached to a panel on his left, snapped the toggle switch which turned on the camera. A digital readout flashed 120, indicating the number of frames available. He snapped the autofocus toggle, then found the switch which activated the motorized shutter control . . .

Beep!

He looked back at the porthole, and a pair of enormous jaws rushed straight at him.

A wide, lipless mouth filled with razor teeth slammed against the porthole. The sub rocked backward and he was thrown against his seat. In that instant he was certain he was dead; the Plexiglas would shatter, and his life would be snuffed out in a catastrophic implosion. But some assembly worker at General Dynamics had earned his Christmas bonus when he installed *Doris*'s window, because the glass held and he got to live a few moments longer.

Black and unreflective eyes, the size and shape of the buttons on his old Navy pea coat, stared through the porthole at him. He remembered the camera, and reached up to stab the shutter control switch with his finger.

Then the eyes and the evil mouth vanished, and Joe barely had time to wonder whether the camera had captured anything before the monster attacked the sub again.

This time, it hit hard enough to do serious damage. The DSV made a sickening lurch to the right, and Joe was almost hurled from his seat as one of the legs supporting the starboard landing skid buckled.

A checklist fell from its hook into his lap and CD jewelboxes skittered across the deck as *Doris* toppled to the right. The interior lights flickered and a half-dozen different alarms went off at once, yet somehow, by either miracle or damn good engineering, the titanium sphere remained intact.

Joe didn't need the buzzers or bells to tell him that *Doris* was doomed. If the sub was listing this far to the right, then the starboard thruster was probably disabled. A glance at the hydraulics panel confirmed that notion; the electrical meter belonging to the suspect thruster was flat-lined. Without it, his vehicle wasn't going to make it back to Tethys under its own power.

And that thing was still out there. If he remained here any longer, he was crab food.

The computer was showing error codes, but the red diodes on the main electrical panel left of the porthole were still lit, its meters still in the green zone. He went straight to manual. He snapped the set of toggle switches which dropped the ballast, the lead bars beneath the afterbody which he normally discarded when it was time to rise.

The deck tilted downward slightly as the DSV's rear end began to rise, but then it stopped. Dammit, the broken skid was probably mired in the muck.

Either that, or the creature itself was weighing him down.

It had been nearly fifteen years since Joe had passed his Navy tests and earned his deep-sub pilot pin. Two dolphinfish on either side of a bathyscape; he'd never worn the pin himself, though, and he had given it to

Karen as an engagement present. Now, unaccountably, the only thing in the world that he wanted was to see that pin again.

Joe hit two more switches, and the interior lights dimmed as he jettisoned the external battery packs. Now he was on emergency electrical, just enough juice for the lithium rebreather system and the auxiliary power units. Yet discarding the extra weight seemed to do the trick. The DSV began slowly to rise . . .

But not fast enough.

There was a distant thud against the afterbody; he heard a long, sickening creak, then a sudden snap as something behind him gave way. He couldn't see anything through the porthole except stirred-up mud.

"Oh, you fucking bastard!" he yelled as he jabbed another pair of switches on the hydraulics panel. "Get the hell off my boat!"

There was a dull pop from above and behind him, then the sub groaned and lurched upward. Through the porthole, he saw the RMS arms fall away, plummeting like a pair of oversize lobster claws. They raised a cloud of fine silt as they silently struck the seafloor, then they vanished as *Doris* began to ascend, a little more quickly now.

Joe glanced at the analog depth meter above the porthole. Yes, he was falling upward, but he didn't have enough juice to run the main engine, and he was defenseless without the RMS arms. Yet at least he couldn't see the . . .

A long shape moved past the porthole, farther away now, just within range of the floodlights.

Was it staying down here, or was it following him to the surface?

He cinched the lap and shoulder straps tight around himself, then flicked a look at the digital camera readout.

Yes, it had been shooting pictures all this time, one frame per second. Twelve frames left—Jesus, had this happened so quickly?—so maybe he managed to get something on film . . .

Don't worry about that now. He had to send an SOS topside, pronto.

He was reaching for the keypad again when a sixteen-wheeler slammed against the afterbody. Alarms wailed through the tiny cockpit, and he smelled ozone. Something inside the sub was on fire.

Joe reached back for the locker containing the emergency air mask, dragged it out by its hose. He clamped it against his face—now he could see only through its lenses—then he found the keypad again. No time for a complete message; he tapped in an emergency transponder code he had memorized a long time ago, then hit the transmit button on the ELF panel. Even as he did so, he was all too aware that this was probably the last act of his life . . .

No. He had a wife and two kids back home. One way or another, he was going to see them again . . .

"Oh, hell," he murmured into the mask. "Someone's going to be pissed about this."

He reached down to a candy-striped panel on the floorboards. He grasped its recessed handle, twisted it counterclockwise, wrenched it open. A red T-bar was buried within the panel. Joe took a deep breath through the air mask, then grasped the T-bar between the knuckles of his right hand and yanked it up.

This was the absolute, final resort. He had never done this before. Nor had anyone else, in all the history of deep-ocean exploration.

There was a hard lurch and a loud metallic snap, and then he was thrown back against his seat as the crew sphere detached itself from the sub.

TWO

Barracuda

6.4.11—1043 EST

T he whale pod was first spotted eighty miles off the
southern Georgia coast by an Irish freighter coming
out of port in Savannah. Its captain must have been bored
that morning, because he got on the marine-band radio
and began chatting about the sighting. In hindsight, Peter
Lipscomb didn't wonder about this; large whales were
still uncommon enough in these waters that they attracted
attention, and sailors loved to gossip; within minutes
every craft on the ocean within a hundred-mile radius of
the *Spirit of Dublin* knew about the herd.

For his part, Lipscomb got lucky. He had brought the
Barracuda up to one fathom in order to raise the UHF
antenna and radio back to Tethys when his scanner suddenly erupted with cross talk from surface traffic. He
quickly checked the heads-up display and discovered that
he was only about thirty miles southwest of the whales'
last reported position. The Barracuda still had more than
three-quarters of a tank of fuel left in reserve and he was

almost finished with that morning's test run, so he informed MainOps of his intentions, then flooded the ballast tanks, submerged to seven fathoms, and kicked in the waterjets before anyone back home had a chance to object.

Not that anyone was likely to do so. The Barracuda was still undergoing sea trials, yet this was exactly the sort of high-speed intercept for which it had been designed, although Lipscomb doubted that Yemaya's engineering division had whalespotting in mind. Fifteen feet long, with stubby inverted wings and twin vertical stabilizers mounted above high-performance inducted water jets, the prototype more closely resembled a cruise missile than a conventional submersible. But its torpedolike shape served it well, for it moved faster than just about anything else afloat. During earlier trials, Lipscomb had managed to take it up to sixty knots until its hull began to shake and he had reluctantly brought it back to lower tolerance levels.

While he was still far enough away that his side-scan sonar wouldn't interfere with the whales, Peter scanned the ocean ahead. The pod showed up clearly on the heads-up as six, sometimes eight, tiny black ellipses closely clustered together. Even before the onboard computer identified them as biologics, he knew they were sperm whales: females hosting a couple of calves, migrating south from Nova Scotia or even farther north to mating areas in the Bahamas, where some big, feisty males were doubtless waiting for them.

The sonar also picked up a surface vessel less than fifteen nautical miles behind the herd, moving south at eighteen knots. Although it was deliberately tracking the pod, it was too large and too far from shore for it to be a whale-watch boat. A cold current went down Peter's back as he realized that it was a pirate whaler in hot pursuit.

Although they were well beyond the 12-mile territorial limit, whaling ships were nonetheless operating within the 230-mile Exclusive Economic Zone established by the UN Law of the Sea Treaty. The United States had outlawed commercial whaling within its EEZ, and while most of the Atlantic Ocean nations were still honoring the International Whaling Commission's moratorium on "harvesting" large cetacean species, Norway and Japan had effectively dropped out of the IWC during the last decade. When their whaling companies didn't want to risk being caught poaching off the U.S. coast, they discreetly hired pirate operations to do the dirty work for them.

A few years ago Greenpeace might have been able to blow the whistle on these guys, yet it had recently been forced to declare bankruptcy, and now there was virtually no one left still capable of direct intervention on the high seas, and harsh denouncements from the Sierra Club and the World Wildlife Federation didn't have much effect on the pirates. There was also the fact that the news media had widely reported that global whale populations were on the rebound. This was true, to some arguable degree or another, since there had been an increased number of sightings over the last decade, yet most marine biologists believed that the data was still inaccurate, for no one knew for certain the birth rate of the great whales. However, it led to the public misperception that whales were no longer endangered, and the resultant apathy was almost as deadly as the explosive harpoons used by the pirates.

For several years now they had been making hit-and-run raids off the Atlantic coast, preying upon migrating whale pods. Once they bagged a whale or two, they towed their catch farther out to sea, beyond the 230-mile mark, where big factory ships waited to flense the carcasses. It was almost impossible to catch the trawlers; in the unlikely event that they were spotted by the Coast Guard, their crew would weight down the dead whales and drop them, then hastily dismantle the harpoon guns and hide them belowdecks. That, or else simply make a run for the territorial limit.

Despite his anger, Lipscomb found himself smiling. The Barracuda wasn't yet armed with the fly-by-wire torpedoes specified in the U.S. Navy contract, but it had a couple of other tricks at its disposal. Taking down a pirate trawler was a perfect means of testing them.

When he was within twenty nautical miles of the pod, Peter switched off the sonar. By then, he no longer needed it; through the hydrophones, he heard the staccato *click-click-click* of the whale's natural sonar, rapid fluctuations of muscle against bone which caused the oil within their enormous heads to reverberate against their blunt skulls and send out pulses. The clicking provided cadence to the mysterious, wavering pitches of whalesong, the mournful moans and ecstatic squeals familiar to every seaman who has ever gone out on the ocean.

Yet that wasn't all the hydrophones picked up. In the background, he heard the discordant, mechanical churn of a distant prop. Lipscomb rested his right hand on the keypad, asked the computer to pinpoint the source of cavitation. The Barracuda searched for and achieved a positive fix, and showed it to him on the heads-up: less than eight nautical miles from the pod. The hunters were closing in on the prey.

Lipscomb switched off the wing strobes, dimmed the cockpit lights. Diffuse sunlight formed a dark blue backdrop behind the red-and-yellow electrophoretic grid painted across the acrylic bubble canopy. The red grid beneath the crosshatch marking his position showed the presence of a thermal layer just below the minisub; he pushed the yoke forward and the Barracuda dove beneath the grid. Good, very good; the thermal layer would reflect the pirate's sonar, effectively rendering the minisub invisible.

An old sea chantey came to mind. He hummed it beneath his breath: "What shall you do with a drunken sailor? . . . What shall you do with a drunken sailor? . . . What shall you do with a drunken sailor . . . earlye in the mornin' . . . ?"

Switching on the side-scan sonar once more, he saw that the herd was almost on top of him. The whales instinctively knew that they were being pursued; they were swimming for their lives, yet since they also had to protect the slow-moving calves, there was no way they could outrun the trawler. Peter took the sub down another fathom, then throttled down the thrusters and released a few pounds of water ballast. Neutrally buoyant, the small craft hung suspended beneath the waves.

"Hooray, and up she rises . . . hooray, and up she rises . . ." Lipscomb switched off the sonar and waited.

A vast gray shape appeared above and before him, a mammoth form emerging from the aquamarine blue.

Peter stared at the great animal as it moved above his craft. A full-grown sperm, no doubt about it now. Probably a female, although he couldn't be sure. The elongated jaw on the underside of her blunt head gaped open as if in surprise, then she rushed past him like a freight train.

The backwash from her flukes pummeled his craft; he grabbed the yoke and fought for stability. An instant later she was followed by two other adults, a half-grown calf swimming between them. The hydrophones were overwhelmed with their squeals and clicks. Peter gripped the yoke and pumped the foot pedals, using the stabilizers to ride out the buffeting caused by their mighty flukes.

The calf, curious about the odd fish in their midst, abruptly dove toward the sub. For a moment a collision seemed inevitable. Peter held his breath as he braced for impact, but at the last possible instant the calf peeled away. He caught a glimpse of a wrinkled black eye regarding him with droll cetacean humor, and then the calf vanished behind him, escorted by his mother just behind him.

"Go away, kid," Peter muttered, letting out his breath. "Your mama's calling you." The Barracuda's fiberglass composite hull was capable of diving to 3,200 feet, but he doubted anyone had ever taken into account a headlong impact with a baby sperm whale, and he was lucky that none of the adults had taken his presence as a threat.

There was no need to worry, though. The rest of the whales kept their distance; they swam past the minisub like great, ghostly leviathans dimly seen through dense blue fog. He watched their stately passage until the last of the adults disappeared behind him, and then he was alone once more.

Now it was just him and the pirates.

Peter reactivated the sonar, checked the heads-up. The ship was less than four miles away, heading straight for him at thirty knots; the hydrophones captured the harsh grating noise of its screw. In a few minutes it would run right over him.

He didn't intend to wait that long. Pushing the yoke forward and throttling up the engines, he let the Barracuda push him back in his seat as it hurtled forward. Small fish scurried out of his way as he charged through the water.

A couple of minutes passed, then he caught sight of a long hull surging through the sun-dappled surface, a vast froth of bubbles churning behind it. A big old diesel, built probably forty or fifty years ago; he would have enjoyed scuttling it if he could, but then again there was already enough ocean pollution. Besides, he had a different plan in mind.

He switched off the sonar and passed the ship on its port side, then turned the Barracuda in a broad arc that cut beneath its wake and brought him around the ship's stern. Once he was along its starboard side, he jettisoned ballast and took the minisub up within six feet of the surface. When he was maintaining a steady course with the ship, he switched on the autopilot and raised the periscope from its housing behind the cockpit. He swung the fiberoptic eyepiece down from the canopy and peered through it.

The trawler was fifty yards away, yet even from this distance, it looked old. Large scabrous patches of barnacles and flaking paint pitted its rusting superstructure, and sooty fumes boiled up from its single stack. It looked like a floating slum; he had seen third-world freighters which were more seaworthy. He turned the periscope until he found the ship's name on its prow: the *Jotunheim*. Two sailors manned the harpoon gun mounted on the bow; several more stood at the railings along the weather deck, ready to grab the lines once the harpooners had killed a whale.

That wasn't what he was looking for, though. He peered a little closer, and sure enough, the trawler had a satellite transceiver dish, positioned right on top of the bridge. Even a rustbucket like the *Jotunheim* would have up-to-date GPS and satellite communications equipment; in fact, he was counting on it.

"What shall you do with a drunken sailor? . . . What shall you do with a drunken sailor? . . ." Singing softly to himself, Lipscomb used the periscope's laser sextant to get a precise sighting on the trawler's position, then he pulled out the computer's folding keyboard. Raising the UHF mast, he used the modem to open a MILSTAR satellite uplink to a commercial database of all registered ocean vessels. He typed in the ship's name; within a minute the information he wanted appeared on the flatscreen: the *Jotunheim*'s Internet address, used by its crew to send and receive information from the shore.

"Put him in a longboat and wet him all over... put him in a longboat and wet him all over..." He logged onto a commercial server, then typed in the address. A brief squeal of modem static, then he was connected with the ship's computer through its IRC function. Somewhere aboard the other vessel, he imagined that a radio operator was probably now glancing at his computer screen, wondering who was sending the *Jotunheim* an Internet relay message over the satellite link.

Time for his next trick. Lipscomb opened a window on the computer and located a nasty little program in the Barracuda's electronic warfare subsystem. He wasn't supposed to know it was there, since its very existence was still classified, but the Navy JG overseeing the Barracuda's sea trials had told him about its more exotic capabilities over a few beers at a Jacksonville bar. Lipscomb, of course, had promised him that he'd never try them, but such promises were meant to be broken.

A tap of the return key, and the program was transmitted straight into the *Jotunheim*'s computer. "Download a virus till he founders... download a virus till he founders... download a virus till he founders... earlye in the mornin'..."

He tucked away the keyboard, then pulled the periscope to his face once more. Sure enough, the trawler was already slowing down. The frothy wake in front of its bow was beginning to diminish, and through the hydrophones he heard the long, slow slush of screws winding down. The harpooners, realizing that something weird was going on, were turning to stare back at the bridge; one raised an arm and angrily gestured for the helmsman to speed up, while up on the bridge another crewman was waving his arms back and forth. On the weather deck, other crewmembers were looking at each other in confusion, then one sprinted toward the bridge ladder.

Peter grinned as he savored the confusion. Say what you will about Navy Intelligence being an oxymoronic term, but someone working for them had devised a nice piece of work. It was going to be very hard for the *Jotunheim*'s crew to get their vessel in motion again, now that its computer had totally crashed. The Navy virus obliterated all navigational and engineering subroutines while simultaneously locking out all passwords and commands. Even a cold reboot and restart wouldn't fix the system; unless the crew ripped out the mainframe entirely, their ship was utterly paralyzed. The bastards never knew what hit them, nor would they ever; the virus would soon self-destruct, taking with it all traces of its short-lived existence.

Lipscomb raised the UHF mast, then transmitted a brief, text-only message to the Coast Guard base at Jacksonville, using a PGP header to protect his anonymity. He informed them that a pirate trawler was adrift southeast of Savannah, and added its coordinates, then he lowered the periscope and the wire, submerged to ten fathoms, and throttled up the waterjets once again.

Once he was away from the trawler, he switched on the sonar once more and tried to get a fix on the whale pod. Yet the herd was gone. Just as suddenly as they had appeared, the whales had vanished; he supposed they had probably dived low to hunt squid off the Blake Spur.

Lipscomb smiled. Ah, the mysteries of the sea. Whaling ships go dead in the water for no apparent reason, and the creatures they hunt disappear unharmed. Hooray, and up she rises, earlye in the morning.

He was twenty miles south of the *Jotunheim,* still congratulating himself on his ingenuity and wondering whether he should tell anyone what he had done—Judith, at least, would keep her mouth shut about this—when the ELF chimed. He glanced at the com panel, caught the incoming text message as it slowly printed out on the screen:

```
6/4/11/1115 EST
QNC ** QNC ** QNC
DSV-02 DORIS EMRG. ASC.
29.12N/78.91W
```

"Holy smoke," he murmured.

The *Doris* was one of Tethys's deep submersibles. As its dive chief, he had cleared Joe Niedzwiecki for a grocery run down to the Blake Plateau earlier this morning, just before he had taken the Barracuda out for its sea trial. Now it was making an emergency ascent . . .

Peter checked the coordinates on the heads-up. Yes, it was coming up only about forty miles south of his present position, a little more than a hundred miles east of Tethys. Someone at Tethys doubtless would have heard the QNC; they'd send out *Amphitrite,* the base's big catamaran, but he could reach *Doris* first if he stepped on it.

Peter throttled up the thrusters to the max. This was turning out to be an interesting day.

•   •   •

The *Amphitrite* was still several miles away when Lipscomb located the *Doris*. What remained of her, at least; when he surfaced the Barracuda a few yards away, he was astonished to see only its crew sphere floating in the water, looking for all the world like an oversize fishing bob. It was fortunate that the sea was calm today: otherwise it might have been swamped by high waves.

He adjusted the radio to the VHF band, then tapped his headset mike. "*Doris,* this is Tethys SX-01." That was the Barracuda's temporary call sign until the minisub was formally christened. "Joe, it's Pete Lipscomb. Are you okay?"

He listened for a moment; when he heard nothing, he repeated the hail. From the looks of things, Joe had jettisoned everything, including the afterbody and RMS arms, before making the crash surface. No other DSV pilot had ever taken such desperate measures to escape from deep ocean. What the hell happened down there?

Lipscomb switched to Tethys's UHF frequency. "Tethys, this is SX-01. Come in, over."

A few moments passed, then he heard Miles Bartlett, Tethys's operations manager. "We read you, Pete. Your transponder shows you at *Doris*'s position."

"Roger that, Tethys. I've found *Doris*. No answer from Joe. Have you heard anything?"

"Nothing here since we received his SOS. What's going on?"

"Joe made a crash surface. Looks like he dropped everything he could. Is *Amphitrite* on the way?"

"That's an affirmative. You should be seeing her in just a few minutes."

"We copy, Tethys. Standing by for—"

An abrupt crackle of static, then another voice came over the comlink: "Pete? That you out there?"

It was Niedzwiecki. "We copy, Joe," Lipscomb said.

"I'm about twenty feet from you, on the surface. How're you doing?"

A short pause. "I'm a hurtin' puppy, chief. Think I bruised a rib or two. Say you're right outside?"

"Twenty feet from you. *Amphitrite*'s on the way. Hang loose, we'll get you out of there."

Bruised ribs. He was lucky to be alive. No one had ever come up from 2,600 feet within a jettisoned crew sphere; it was fortunate that the *Doris* was designed for one atmosphere, or Joe would have been bent for sure. Yet if he was injured . . .

"Hey, Joe, can you reach your top hatch handle?"

Another pause, longer this time. "Negatory, chief. I can barely get out of my seat."

Peter chewed his lip as he studied the craft. Tiny pressurized spheres sandwiched within the foam inside its titanium outer hull were keeping *Doris* afloat and upright, but if the hull had sustained any damage during its shotgun ascent, it might be taking on water without Niedzwiecki realizing it. And since Joe couldn't reach the inside handle, there was the remote yet nonetheless plausible chance that the *Doris* might sink while he was still aboard.

"Okay, Joe," he said. "Relax and stay put. I'm coming over to check on you."

He gently maneuvered the Barracuda closer to *Doris* until their hulls scraped together, then he grasped a red handle next to his left elbow and yanked it up. There was a faint hiss as pneumatic hinges opened the canopy like a clamshell; he smelled ocean breeze, salty and fresh, welcome after nearly three hours of chemically reconditioned air. The Barracuda was overpressurized by a few millibars, though, and Peter winced as his inner ears popped painfully. He pulled off the headset and dropped it between his knees, unbuckled his straps, and reached up to slide the canopy farther back. As an afterthought, he opened a small locker behind the seat and pulled out a first-aid kit. He tucked it into the waistband of his trousers, then he stood up, took a moment to steady himself against the gentle rocking of the surf, and jumped onto the side of the sphere.

Or tried to, at least. He meant to grab one of the vacant RMS sleeves, but missed the mark by a few inches. Peter slid helplessly down the side of sphere until he fell into the water. Dumb! He cursed under his breath, then kicked off his loafers and began swimming around the hull.

He found the porthole, and took a moment to rest a knee upon the floodlight rack and peer inside. There were some odd, angular scratches on its Plexiglas surface. Silt abrasion? Joe gazed back at him through the thick pane; he smiled painfully and gave him a thumbs-up.

Peter returned the gesture, then dropped back into the water and dog-paddled his way around the sphere to a lateral row of rung, then he climbed out of the water and on top of the craft.

The top hatch contained a recessed lock lever; he pushed at it with his right hand, then again with both hands, yet it remained frozen. Peter sat down, carefully braced himself on his palms, extended his left foot, and gave the lever a hard, swift kick. That did the trick; the lever moved, then he knelt forward, twisted the lever with both hands, and finally popped the seal. He caught a whiff of burned rubber within the stale air as he pulled the hatch open.

"Howdy, stranger," he called down.

Joe peered up at him from within the tiny space. "Hello, yourself. Thanks for the hand."

"My pleasure." The sub's interior was littered with junk: papers, a clipboard, pens, jazz CDs, a dangling oxygen mask. The only thing in place was Joe himself. "Have a fire down there?"

"Little one. Circuit panel shorted out." Joe picked up a small chemical extinguisher from the deck next to him and showed it to Peter. "Took care of it already."

"Glad to hear it." He was reluctant to climb down into the cockpit. So far, they had been lucky, but Lipscomb didn't want to give the submersible any more load than it could bear. No sign of water inside the cockpit, though; if the sphere wasn't sinking, he was not about to move Niedzwiecki from his position. His ribs could be in worse shape than Joe thought.

He gazed over his shoulder. In the far distance, he made out a large dot moving across the water. The *Amphitrite,* only a few miles away. "The cat's on its way. Hang tight, it'll be here in few minutes."

"Cool. I'm not going anywhere." Joe let his head fall back against his seat. "Man, I'm just lucky to be alive, that's all."

Peter waited for him to explain, but Joe simply stared straight ahead. "So what happened down there?" he asked at last.

Niedzwiecki said nothing. He stared out the porthole as if gazing upon something that wasn't there.

"Joe, this is serious. If it was an onboard fire—"

"It wasn't the fire." He shook his head. "Fire's the least of it."

"Then what happened?"

"You'll never believe me."

The man was in shock, but not from injury. Lipscomb gave him a moment. "Look, Joe . . . I know you're in pain right now, but you've left most of your boat a couple of thousand feet underwater, and you just said that it wasn't because of an onboard fire. In about ten minutes you're going to have a dozen guys asking you why you made a crash surface, and after that you're going to have Bartlett asking the same thing, and when they're done, a bunch of company suits are going to want to know. So I'm asking you right now, while you've still got time . . . what happened down there?"

Niedzwiecki didn't answer at once. He turned his head to study a panel to his left, then he reached out, very carefully, and flipped a switch.

"Good," he said softly. "Got it on film."

"Got what?"

"What I saw down there." Joe looked up at him again. "Hey, Pete. Isn't your wife interested in . . . ?" He hesitated. "I mean, didn't you once tell me she interested in sea monsters?"

Peter stared down at him. It must have been during a conversation he had forgotten. "Yeah," he said carefully, "she's done some research in that area. Why do you ask?"

Joe grinned. "Better give her a yell, man. I think I just saw one."

THREE
Dominica

I t was the smallest fern bush Judith had ever seen; almost hidden among the larger plants along the dirt trail, with leaves only an inch or two long, she mistook it at first for wild mint. She didn't know why Charles Toussaint stopped to kneel down next to it, but she did the same.

"Now watch this," Charles said, and then he gently tapped one of its tiny leaves. It instantly closed shut, folding in upon itself like a miniature Venus flytrap, yet so quickly that it seemed as if she was watching a time-lapse film.

"Oh, my God," she murmured, "did you kill it?"

Charles laughed. "No, no. It's simply gone to sleep. If we wait a few minutes, it will open up again. Here, you try it."

Judith reached out, touched another of the diminutive leaves. It closed immediately, just as the first one did. "Why does it do that?"

Toussaint shrugged. "Nobody knows. Evolved response to predators, I suppose. It's called a sensitive plant. Only grows on this island, nowhere else." He touched another leaf, and they watched it wilt. "We call it by another name," he added, then said something in French-African patois that, like everything else spoken in the Dominican native tongue, Judith couldn't understand. "It means, 'Missus Mary, close your door, the devil is coming after you.' "

" 'Missus Mary, close your door, the devil is coming after you.' " Judith Lipscomb absently brushed dirt off her hands on her khaki hiking shorts as she stood up. "Hard to imagine anyone fearing the devil in this place."

Indeed, the mountain trail on which they stood was as close to paradise as anyplace she had ever visited. Deep within the Roseau Valley, with Mons Anglais and Mons Nichols to the south and Mons Micotrim to the north, they were surrounded on all sides by dense tropical rain forest. Banana birds and parrots within the coconut and palm trees made sweet jungle music while cicadas and mountain chickens—giant tree frogs, really, so-called because of their taste—provided a wavering chorus. In the far distance, through the humid mist lingering between the steep ridgelines of the mountain pass, she could just make out the silver-blue expanse of the Caribbean.

"That you can owe to a strict Catholic upbringing." Charles ambled over to a small spring a few feet up the trail. He cupped his delicate hands together, filled them with water, and drank deeply. "But, no, we don't fear the devil here, or even each other. It wasn't until I came to your country that I ever locked my door when I left my house."

"Really?" Judith followed him to the spring. She had a plastic bottle clipped to the belt of her fanny pack, which she had filled from the kitchen tap before leaving

Toussaint's house, but all the mountain springs they had discovered during their morning hike had made that precaution unnecessary. "Must have been a shock, moving to Cambridge."

"It was like visiting Mars." He removed his wire-rim glasses, carefully tucked them in the breast pocket of his thin cotton shirt, then splashed more water on his creased, walnut-brown face. He hadn't shaved since they had been here, and now his cheeks and chin were covered with white stubble. "The first time I took a taxi ride—a cab, as you call it there—I failed to tip the driver. Taxis are common here, of course, but no one tips unless they've carried you a very long distance—and in that case, you take a bus. This driver only took me to Harvard Square, and if I had known it was that close to MIT, I would have walked. So I paid him only what was on the meter."

Judith pulled her long braid of blond hair out of the way, cupped her hands together. This particular spring ran lukewarm, and it had a vaguely sulfuric scent. Only made sense; they had just come back from one of the many boiling springs scattered across the island, where Dominica's eight active volcanoes brought up scalding water from deep within Earth's crust. It tasted delicious. "I imagine the driver didn't see it that way."

He chuckled as he put on his glasses again. "Oh, no. He called me something I won't repeat. Growing up here, the only time you ever heard such language, it was from Americans or Europeans. When Dominica was a British colony, there were laws which made using obscenity in public a prisonable offense."

"Really? Wow." Yet when she thought about it, it explained something she had once observed about her former academic mentor. For as long as she had known Charles Toussaint, she had never once heard him utter even the mildest of obscenities. Even when he had spilled a test tube of acid on his left wrist during a lab lecture, he merely hissed "shhhhh," without completing the monosyllabic curse, even though he had to be rushed to the Boston General ER.

"Yes, well . . ." He looked suddenly uncomfortable, as if admitting to once being offended by a Boston cabdriver was grounds for embarrassment. "I learned to get over it." He adjusted his glasses, hitched up his belt. "Care for a beer? I'll buy."

They weren't far from the tiny village of Trafalgar, where Charles had parked his Toyota in front of one of the countless open-air canteens found in every shanty-town on the island. Chickens and goats in the road, field-workers waiting for the next bus, frail wooden houses with corrugated sheet aluminum for roofs and cardboard Hillsborough Cigarette ads stapled to the walls. At first she had been appalled by the extent of poverty in Dominican daily life, until she realized that the average is-lander didn't consider himself poor unless you reminded him of the fact. And after three hours of hiking through sweltering rain forest, an ice-cold Kabuli beer would hit the spot.

"Lead on, Macduff," she said.

Charles smiled. " 'And let the first man who—' "

An electronic chirp from the satphone on his belt, as alien within this high mountain pass as a special-effects spaceship from a *Star Trek* episode, interrupted his rec-itation from *Macbeth*. Toussaint unsnapped its pouch, pulled out the phone, and unfolded it. He touched the talk button and raised the phone to his face, murmured something in patois, and listened for a moment.

"Oh, I'm terribly sorry, Peter," he said. "I thought it was a local call. Yes, she's here." Then he extended the phone to her. "Your husband."

Judith's mouth dropped open. Of course, Peter knew

how to reach her; she had given him both of Charles's numbers—his home phone along with the satphone—before she had left Tethys. Yet one of the conditions of the annual vacations they took apart from one another, agreed upon only a year after they got married, was that neither spouse would call the other unless there was a dire emergency. Peter had violated this rule only once before, when he phoned her while she was on a bicycle trip through the Smokies only to ask if she enjoying herself. She had hung up on him, then sent him a stuffed squirrel from a tourist trap in Pigeon Forge as revenge, knowing well how much he loathed those things. He got the message, and never bothered her during vacation again.

Until now, at least. She took the satphone from Charles, turned her back to him. "Hello, darling," she said with as much frost as she could muster in ninety-eight-degree heat.

"Don't hang up. Just listen. Something's come up . . ."

"This better be good. I'm a on mountaintop, enjoying the peace and quiet."

"Yeah, well, I'm aboard the *Amphitrite,* about seventy miles out from Tethys. We just rescued Joe Niedzwiecki from the *Doris*. He had to crash-surface from the Blake Plateau."

Her irritation vanished. "Oh, my God, is he okay?" Although deep-ocean dives had become fairly commonplace, everyone who worked on Tethys was nonetheless aware of the risks involved. Besides that, Joe was one of their best friends at the sea lab.

"He's fine. Bruised a couple of rubs, but that's it. Considering that he had to jettison the sphere and leave most of *Doris* on the bottom, he's pretty lucky."

"Joe evacked in the sphere?" Judith sat down on the trail, crossing her bare legs under her. That meant Joe's ascent had been uncontrolled; he must have breached the surface like an ICBM. "Lucky's not the word. He could have broken his . . ." She shook her head. "What did he do that for?"

"That's the weird part. He says . . . hold it a sec."

Pause. In the background, she heard a dim, sliding sound: the closing of a cabin door. She guessed that Peter must be somewhere belowdecks. His voice returned a moment later: "Judith? Still there?"

"Right here." She glanced up, saw Charles watching her. "What's going on? Why did Joe crash-surface *Doris*?"

She heard him take a deep breath. "He claims he saw a sea monster. No, correct that . . . he said it was a sea serpent, quote unquote."

For an instant time itself seemed to come to a stop. For an instant everything around her simply froze, as if caught in stasis: the jungle breeze, the birdsongs, the mountain spring. Judith stared at the dusty trail without really seeing it, and after a moment she remembered that she had to breathe in order to keep her heart beating.

"A sea serpent," she said softly. "Did I just hear you correctly? He said he saw a . . . ?"

"That's exactly what he said. And he also says . . . Judith, he thinks he managed to get it on film."

"He got pictures?" She surged to her feet so quickly she almost lost her balance; Charles grabbed her shoulder before she fell over. "Goddammit, Lipscomb, if you're pulling a prank of some kind, I swear to God I'll—"

"Honey, sweetheart . . ." She heard him laugh, and for an instant she thought it was a practical joke. He'd done this once before, during their engagement, when he was still in the Navy and off at sea; he gotten a couple of his SEAL buddies to rig together a seven-foot replica of the Loch Ness monster from chicken wire and painted scraps of neoprene, which they held erect from beneath the water while he shot several out-of-focus pictures. When he emailed them to her from the *Kitty Hawk,* claiming that the shots had been taken in the Mediterranean just off the coast of Israel, she was ready to drop everything and catch the next flight to Tel Aviv before she glanced at a wall calendar and realized what the date was.

Funny the first time. Not so funny the second. She was ready to hurl Charles's phone into the underbrush when her husband spoke again. "No, babe, it's not a gag. Scout's honor. Joe says he saw a sea serpent, and he says he caught it on *Doris*'s camera. At least he thinks he did."

"What's this about a sea serpent?" Charles was still holding her left shoulder. "Judith, what's . . . ?"

She placed a hand over the phone. "I'll tell you in a minute," she whispered, then uncupped the phone again. "Have you seen the film? Have you looked at it yet?"

"Haven't had a chance. The sphere's still down in the slipway. No one's entered it yet. Joe's in trouble over this one. I mean, he left most of his boat down on the plateau. The company's going to ream him for this, and if he tells them that he junked a ten-million-dollar sub because he saw a—"

"Peter . . . Peter, listen to me." She took a lungful of moist air, slowly let it out. God, this was coming too fast; she needed time to think. "Okay, first thing . . . how many people has Joe told about this?"

"'Um . . . just me, I think. He's pretty shook up about this. I mean, it really scared the shit out of him. That's why I believe him. Somebody this frightened doesn't make this—"

"Okay, good. Keep it that way." She ran a hand through her short-cropped bangs. "Get back to him and tell him to keep his mouth shut. Not a word to anyone, okay?"

"I'll tell him, but . . . Judy, he's going to have to explain to someone why—"

"I know, I know. Just try to keep a lid on this until I get back." Even as she said this, she knew that her vacation had just come to a premature end. She glanced at Toussaint and pursed her mouth in an apologetic frown, and he nodded his head knowingly. Good old Doc . . . "Second thing, get the disk out of the sub and don't let anyone else see it. Do you understand me? Get the disk, Peter."

"Why can't anyone else see it?"

Because one of the problems which had vexed investigators of any short-lived phenomenon, whether it be UFOs or sea serpents, had been accusations of tampered evidence. The skeptics were right, of course: in this era of desktop computer imaging, it was all too easy for someone to perpetrate a hoax. Judith had been studying cryptozoology for as long as she had been a marine biologist, but she had been fooled by Peter's little April Fool's Day hoax. In this instance, the fewer hands laid on the film disk, the less chance anyone had of claiming that it was a fraud.

No time to explain that, though. "Just do it, okay? Trust me on this one."

"No sweat. I'll retrieve it from the camera soon as we arrive at Tethys. Anything else?"

Was there anything else? She shut her eyes, trying to think of something she was missing. A couple of dozen different details she was overlooking, no doubt, but for the moment there was nothing else she could—"Oh, goddammit! Oh, shit! Shit goddammit!"

Charles flinched at her outburst. "What?" Peter snapped. "What did you—?"

"Andrea! Your niece! When is she coming?"

Long silence. "Oh, hell," Peter said at last, his voice barely audible. "I forgot about her."

Judith closed her eyes. No, she didn't need this. Not now, of all times. "Call Jack.You've got to call Jack. Get your brother to cancel the trip."

"No can do. Andie's left K.C. this morning. She's flying to Jacksonville, then catching the afternoon VTOL from Yemaya to Tethys. She's due to come in around four o'clock."

She let out her breath. Already she was feeling a headache coming on. "Peter, this is a bad time. A really, really bad—"

"I know. I couldn't agree more." An expansive sigh. "Look, you want to call the Yemaya suits and try to explain things to them, after we went through hell getting Andie a visitor's pass? And then explain to Jack and Dorothy why we have to send Andie back after we promised to—?"

"Okay, all right. Yeah, yeah, yeah. I understand." Judith fumbled through her fanny pack for the tin of Tylenol she routinely carried with her for emergencies. "Just try to keep her out of the way, okay?"

Another dry laugh. "Hey, lighten up, willya? It's just my niece . . ."

She winced. "Correction. It's *your* niece. Leave out the 'just' part." That was unfair, of course. She liked Andie, thought she was a pretty good kid. But, God, could she be a handful . . . Where the hell was that Tylenol?

"So when are you coming in?"

Good question. She glanced at her watch. It was a quarter after one, Atlantic Standard, which made it a quarter after twelve Eastern. If she hurried, she could still catch the daily turboprop out of Melville Hall, on the other side of the island. That would put her in San Juan by four o'clock; if she nuked her company credit card, she might be able grab a seat on the next jet to Jacksonville. She ticked off the travel time on her fingers, subtracted an hour for the difference in time zones . . . "Call it eight, nine o'clock. I'll call you when I've got it worked out. Look, do me a favor and call Yemaya. Ask them to arrange a chopper flight to Tethys from Jacksonville."

She felt a nudge at her elbow, looked around to see Charles silently raising two fingers. "Doc's coming in, too," she added. "Better that way, don't you think?"

Another long pause on the phone. "Yeah, right. You and Doc, coming in together."

There was an unmistakable edge of jealousy in his voice. "Peter . . ."

"Never mind. I'll call the company and arrange the details. Anything else?"

"Only more thing . . ." she began.

"What? A limo from the airport?"

Boy, was he rubbing it in. "If you want. I just wanted to say—"

"Look, I gotta go. See you tonight topside."

"Thanks, Pete. I love—"

Click. The line was already dead.

She thumbed the satphone's off button, her ear sore from its pressure. She was still staring at it when Charles extended his hand.

"I take it that your holiday's over," he said quietly.

Judith folded the phone and gave it back to him. Once more, she stood on a mountain ridge overlooking the Roseau Valley of Dominica. Until ten minutes ago she could have been sipping latté in a Paris café, hiking the desert canyons of Utah, photographing glaciers in Antarctica, playing blackjack with a Tanzanian teenager. The miracle of point-to-point global satellite communications: in the words of Buckaroo Banzai, no matter where you go, there you are.

Which means that your husband could phone you from a catamaran off the coast of Florida while you're hiking through a mountain rain forest in Dominica, and you can still get in a fight over nothing.

"Better skip the beer." She allowed her gaze to linger upon the peaceful valley surrounding her. "Time to go find a sea serpent."

C harles Toussaint's home was a tan stucco cottage on the outskirts of Roseau, surrounded by tiny, immaculate gardens and a high stone wall. Modest by American standards, it was a veritable mansion in Dominica's capital city, as Judith discovered the first time she had gone for a stroll and found herself, within less than two blocks, walking past windowless shanties. The house once belonged to one of the countless British expatriates who had moved away after England allowed its former colony to peacefully declare independence thirty-three years ago; like many other former British residences, it had gradually fallen into ruin until "Doc" Toussaint, as he was widely known on the island, purchased the place and restored it. When he wasn't teaching at MIT or working on Tethys, this was where he returned.

They stopped by the house in order to pack their bags. As soon as they came through the door, Toussaint went into his office to call the airport. He found Judith in the guest room and informed her that he had booked two seats on the 3:30 TWA Express flight to Puerto Rico. This gave them plenty of time to catch a taxi to Melville Hall.

Judith felt sticky after their long hike in the mountains, so she took the opportunity to take a fast shower and change into a dress for the flight. When she came out of the guest room, she found Mary, Charles's matronly housekeeper, placing his suitcase in the foyer. "Doc's in his office," she said as she hobbled over to take Judith's bag. "I'm so sad to see you go so soon, Missus Judith."

"I wish I didn't have to go, either." Judith didn't resist Mary's insistence upon taking her heavy bag, even though she could have carried it the few extra feet by herself. Indeed, it had taken nearly three days for her to get Mary to stop addressing her as Missus Lipscomb; Missus Judith was an unspoken compromise, but it still gave her a twinge of white person's guilt. "You've been so gracious these last few days."

"Likewise, ma'am. Make sure Doc brings you back to see us." Mary hauled the bag into the clay-tiled foyer and carefully placed it next to Charles's luggage, then she excused herself and returned to the kitchen, where she spent her days reading her Bible and listening to reggae music on the local radio station. Like her employer, Mary Bond was widowed; although she had a dozen children and grandchildren scattered across the island, she preferred to live in the Toussaint house.

No wonder. Although Judith was sure he didn't earn more than the average corporate research scientist in the States, Doc was nonetheless one of the wealthiest men on Dominica. And one of the most revered, from the way she had seen him respectfully treated wherever he went: everyone in Roseau knew his face, everyone regarded him highly. No small wonder, when you knew his background. Born and raised in a small village outside Roseau, educated in a Catholic convent school while cutting bananas and sugarcane in early morning and late afternoon, finally managing to earn one of the island's government scholarships which enabled him to travel to the United States and, after many more years, earn his Ph.D., and eventually becoming first a full professor at MIT, working in the Department of Earth, Atmospheric and Planetary Sciences, then a consultant for Yemaya Ocean Resources. It was a record which was impressive even by American standards; here on Dominica, he was the eastern Caribbean's answer to Robert Ballard, with a bit of Horatio Alger thrown in for good measure.

She found Charles in his study in the back of the house. Its garden door was open, allowing in, along with the summer breeze, a couple of the banana birds which haunted the date trees Mary tended. They feasted upon the crumbs Charles had left for them from the croissant he had brought from the kitchen; as always, he put the plate on top of a bookshelf near the door, where they could easily find it.

Charles was seated behind his old oak desk, shoulders bent forward, his back turned to her as he studied something displayed on the screen of his computer. "Yes . . . leaving at 3:30 from Melville Hall," he murmured. "Yes, we will . . ."

The banana birds cheeped in alarm and fluttered away as Judith came in. Charles looked up sharply, noticed Judith for the first time. She now saw the phone in his hand. "Yes, that's fine," he said quickly, raising a finger to her. "We'll be there . . . goodbye."

"Sorry to interrupt," she said when he hung up. "The company?"

"Yes. I called in, let them know we were coming." He scribbled a note on a yellow pad, then tore off the sheet, folded it, and shoved it in the pocket of the linen sport coat he now wore. He had taken a few minutes to clean up and change as well, and even run a razor across his face. "Seems there's more than one good reason for us to end our holiday," he added. "Look at this."

The computer screen displayed a multicolored topographical map which, when Judith walked closer, she recognized as a real-time topographic map. Another aspect of Charles's house which made it stand out in Roseau was the satellite transceiver dish mounted on its slate roof; through it, he was able to link with the global information net, independent of Dominica's third-world phone lines.The header at the top of the display showed that it had been downloaded from Woods Hole.

"New SOSUS data," he said. "Received just this morning. Major seismic activity in the Mid-Atlantic Ridge south of the Azores."

"No kidding." Judith walked around the desk and bent down to study the chart. "A marine earthquake?"

"Could be, yes." Charles pointed to a tiny, fractal-generated white splotch resting in the center of a long, serpentine curve of yellow-red hues surrounded by shades of blue. "However, the epicenter appears to be located in the central rift valley, somewhere between the Oceanographer and Atlantis rift zones. Given the location, it may be a new hot vent."

SOSUS was an acronym for Sound Surveillance System. Secretly developed by the U.S. Navy during the cold war, it was a global network of hydrophones deployed in various locations along floors of the world's oceans, linked by undersea cables to receiving stations on the shore which, in fed, transmitted the data to the United States. The initial purpose of SOSUS had been to track Soviet submarines, but in 1993 the Navy made the technology available to civilian scientists. Since then, it had been used for all manner of marine research, everything from tracking the movements of whale populations to—as in this instance—listening for major tectonic events in deep ocean which might signal the eruption of the deep fissures in the ocean floor commonly known as hot vents.

Charles's research for Yemaya involved finding and classifying hyperthermophiles, the mysterious microorganisms which had been discovered within black smokers, the plumes of superheated water which boiled up out of hot vents on the ocean floor. Because these organisms thrived, against all odds, in temperatures which would normally kill land-based bacteria, the biotech industry had great use for *Thermus aquaticus,* or "taq" for short. Yemaya Ocean Resources had already discovered several new strains of hyperthermophiles; once cloned, they could be patented and sold to biotech companies, which in turn used them as a source of enzymes for a variety of industrial processes. The company had already reaped over $2 billion in profit from such bioprospecting; Charles Toussaint's job was to help his employers earn even more.

"If that's a new vent, it's the first one we've seen in the North Atlantic in many years." He moved the trackball cursor to the top of the screen and toggled a button; the laser printer next to his desk purred as it began to produce a hard copy. "Most of them tend to pop up in the Pacific or the Indian Ocean. This one's right in our backyard." Charles smiled as he glanced over his shoulder at Judith. "If we move quickly enough, we might be able to stake a claim before the competition does."

"If we don't move quickly enough, we're never going to catch that flight." She glanced at the wall clock. "Mary's already put our bags by the door. Have you called a taxi?"

"No need. There's a stand only a couple of blocks away. We'll carry our bags there."

"Charles! Why didn't you call a—?"

"A week on Dominica, and you still don't understand the meaning of Caribbean time." He pulled the sheet of paper from the printer tray, carefully folded it, and tucked it within his linen sport coat. "When you call a taxi here, the operator has to get up and walk over to the dispatcher, who's having a cold drink and reading his newspaper. He takes a few minutes to finish the article he's reading, then he picks up the mike and calls one of his drivers. The driver is having a cigarette and having a chat with a couple of his friends. If he's diligent, he picks up the mike as soon as he hears the dispatcher, but even if he does, he has to finish his smoke first and hear the rest of the story his friend was telling. Then he gets back in his car, checks his map, and then—"

"Okay, okay, you're right. Caribbean time." She remembered how long it took them to get dinner at a hotel restaurant the other evening. It wasn't as if Dominicans were lazy; they just didn't see any real reason to do anything in a hurry. And Charles didn't want to leave his own car at the airport, for he never knew how many weeks, or even months, would pass before he returned home again. "It'll be faster if we carry our bags to where the taxis are."

"You always were a bright student." Charles shut down his computer, then stood up. "Very well, let's be off."

A quick hug for Mary, a final check to see if they had everything, then they picked up their bags and marched out the door, down the front walk, and through the wrought-iron gate to the street. A brief afternoon shower, one of many which occurred every day during rainy season, had rinsed off the crumbling cement sidewalk and cleared the air, leaving fresh puddles of water within the potholes which dotted the narrow cobblestone road. Judith followed Charles as he turned right and headed toward the center of town.

As always, she found it difficult to believe that she was walking through a nation's capital. Roseau was no larger than Bangor, Maine, her hometown; the tallest building here was no more than five stories in height, and most of the city looked as if it had been frozen in time since the mid-1940s. On this side street, there was almost no vehicle traffic at all. An old lady pushed a broom across the front step of her fruit shop. A feral dog with mange rooted through garbage in an alley. A handful of teenage boys wearing T-shirts of American rock bands kicked a soccer ball around a vacant lot. In the distance, she heard a bell tolling from a nearby church. Yet the air was fresh, the days calm and placid; if there was poverty here, then there was also powerful and sublime beauty. More than once over the last week she had entertained fantasies of retiring here . . .

Not that Peter would accept that. Judith shifted her heavy bag from her right hand to her left. Would her husband willingly leave behind shopping malls, multi-screen movie theaters, twenty-four-hour convenience stores, two-hundred-channel Internet TV, Big Macs, and the latest toy the Navy wanted him to test-drive? Only if he was strapped into a wheelchair and—

A battered Nissan minivan, racing at the usual break-neck speed Dominican drivers seemed to prefer even in the city, came up from behind them and pulled up to curb. Hearing it, Judith turned around gratefully. Dominican taxis were almost always Japanese-made minivans, and their drivers were always on the lookout for white Americans who looked as if they were in need of a lift.

"Hey, look," she called out to Charles. "We got lucky. Here's—"

Then the rear passenger door slid open, and two skinny black men launched themselves from the van's backseat onto the sidewalk.

For an instant Judith thought she was being attacked. She froze in place, her mouth open in a breathless, silent scream, but then the nearest one simply cast her a cold glance as he joined his partner in an assault on Doc Toussaint.

Charles didn't see them coming, though, and wasn't even aware of their presence until they were upon him. He turned only when the one of the thugs grabbed him from behind, and even then there was disbelief in his face. He shouted something in patois and hefted his heavy suitcase as a shield.

"Get off him!" Judith found her voice. "Get away from him!"

The two men ignored her. One grabbed Charles's suitcase, yanked it out of his grasp and flung it into the street. Its catches popped open and clothes spilled out onto the filthy cobblestones. Then they were all over him, grabbing his arms. From the van, the driver yelled something in harsh broken French.

"Get off him!" Judith screamed.

Charles dug in his heels against the battered sidewalk. His face briefly appeared between the shoulders of the men trying to abduct him. "Run!" he shouted, trying to tear his arms free. "Run! Get out of—!"

One of the men punched Charles in the face. Blood spurted from his nose and he staggered backward, then the attackers began dragging him toward the van.

That's all it took. In that instant adrenaline surged through Judith's veins; suddenly, forty pounds of luggage felt light as a sandwich bag. Hauling it back with both hands, she dashed forward, then brought up the bag in a long, wide sweep.

It caught the nearest man in the back of his neck. She couldn't have done better if she had used a tire iron. He let go of Charles and crashed against the cinderblock wall behind them, then staggered and fell to his knees.

"Get away!" she yelled. "Leave him alone!"

His accomplice turned just in time to receive her backswing. He released Charles, tried to bring up his hands, but she was faster than he was. Judith swung the bag into his groin; he groaned as he doubled over, grabbing at himself.

Free once more, Charles lurched away, clutching his bloody nose with both hands. Judith wanted to run to him, but she didn't have enough time. The first man was already staggering to his feet, dark malevolence in his eyes . . .

"Get out of here!"

She whipped the bag back around and slammed it into his ribs.This time the zipper broke; in an abstract way, she was horrified to see a pair of her underwear tossed out into plain view. But the blow was enough to give her opponent second thoughts; he yelped as he toppled against the van's open door, then he lurched half inside, leaning over an armrest to dry-heave.

His partner scrambled to his feet, glared at Judith, then at Charles. For a moment he seemed indecisive. Then the driver shouted something, and that was enough for him. He darted across the sidewalk and plunged headfirst into the van, hauling his accomplice the rest of the way into the vehicle

"Get the hell out of . . ." She charged after them, wildly swinging her bag around herself.

"Judith, for God's sake!"

She barely heard Charles, but it stopped her nonetheless. Just as well; the two men were giving up.

The passenger door slammed shut; the minivan's clutch coughed and its balding tires squealed against decaying pavement as the driver tore away from the curb and down the lonesome street. Two children leaped for the sidewalk as it made a hard turn to the left at the next intersection, and then it was gone. Judith was helping

Charles to his feet when she heard car horns blaring a couple of blocks away.

Just like that, as suddenly as it begun, it was over.

Once more, the street was peaceful. The old woman who had been sweeping her shop doorway stared at them. The children regarded her and Charles with adolescent puzzlement. From somewhere far off, she heard the low, distant bellow of a cruise ship's horn as it left port from the waterside. No other cars, no other pedestrians. For all intents and purposes, nothing ever happened here.

"What was that all about?" she whispered.

FOUR

Tethys 1

6/4/11—1539 EST

S he had never been aboard a VTOL before, so she was
sure it should have been totally fascinating, but after
the first five minutes or so it was not much different than
the plane trip from Kansas City, only the cabin was
smaller, there weren't any peanuts or in-flight magazines,
and—oh, yeah—the ride was bumpier. A lot bumpier.

Turbulence didn't bother Andie Lipscomb; you just
hold on tight and pretend you're on the Screamin' Eagle
at Six Flags. At seventeen, there isn't much left in the
world that can scare you. She peered through her window
across the engine nacelles at the sun-specked blue waters
of the Atlantic and worried about whether she was going
to get any beach time, because it would be a major bum-
mer if she went home without a decent tan to show that
she had just been to Florida, as the fuselage trembled and
stuff in the overhead compartments rattled around and
the woman seated across the aisle from her clutched at
her armrests and closed her eyes every time the plane
lurched.

"Sorry for the chop, ladies." The pilot, who looked a lot like Terrance DiAmico, Andie's favorite movie actor, spoke to them over the ceiling speaker although she could clearly see his broad shoulders through the cockpit hatch. "Nothing we can do about it. If it's any consolation, we'll be touching down in about ten minutes, so just make yourself comfortable and . . . um, enjoy the ride."

Like, if she was going to barf, she was going to do it in his presence. No way. But the woman sitting across from her didn't look like she was doing so well. In fact, Andie was certain she was going to blow her cookies any minute now. Not that Andie particularly cared, because she had ignored her from the moment they met on the helicopter pad at Yemaya's corporate campus and had said very little to her since then. But her knees were practically touching Andie's, which meant that if she was going to hurl, there was a good chance Andie would catch some of it. Better do something before she turns green . . .

"It's going to be all right," Andie said. "I hear these things are really safe."

Lame, but what else was she supposed to say? Did that suit come from Lord & Taylor or JC Penney? But it got her attention. The woman opened her almond eyes to regard her with cool disdain. "Do you know the safety record of this aircraft?" she asked softly.

"Uh . . . no, not really."

"The test models tended to crash." She swallowed hard. "One of them killed everyone aboard."

The hunk in the pilot's seat turned his head slightly, as if he overheard that. The V-22B Osprey lurched again, and suddenly the sea below them looked a lot closer. Okay, wrong subject. "Sounds like you know a lot about this kind of thing.What are you, an engineer?"

"No. Just interviewed someone from the FAA once."

Her dark skirt was riding up over her knees; she self-consciously pulled it down, then shut her eyes again.

"Oh, yeah. The FAA. Right." Andie was suddenly glad that she was wearing jeans. Easier to wash. "So . . . what do you do?"

No less lame, but it got her attention again. She opened her eyes, even sat up a little straighter. "I'm a journalist. Working on assignment for *Millennium*."

"Really? No kidding?" Andie didn't have to pretend interest this time. Her school library carried *Millennium;* she had picked it up a few times, and not just when she had to do a paper for her geography class. Sort of like *National Geographic,* but a lot hipper. Articles about rock stars trekking the Himalayas, stuff like that. "You write for them?"

"That's what I do." In an instant the woman looked as if she had taken an intravenous shot of Dramamine. "I've written several articles for them, mostly about ocean research. Now I'm—"

"Hey, did you write the one about—?"

"Salmon overfishing in the Pacific Rim?" She smiled expectantly.

Actually, Andie was about to ask if she had written the story about the new James Bond actor swimming with pilot whales off the coast of Jamaica, because that guy had great buns. "Oh, yeah, I read that one," she lied. "It was really good."

"That was mine." Once more, the Osprey hit a pothole; this time, though, the woman didn't seem to notice. Andie was reminded of something her high-school newspaper adviser had once told her: people love to talk about themselves. "I was nominated for an award for that piece. I didn't win, but—"

"So what's your name?"

"Leslie. Leslie Sun." She said this half-expectantly, as

if anticipating name recognition. "And you're . . . ?"

"Andrea Lipscomb . . . Andie."

Leslie held out her hand. "Pleased to meet you, Andie. And what brings you out here?"

Well, you see, Ms. Sun, my parents, two of the nicest people you've ever met unless they're in the same room together, are going through a really nasty divorce, not the least of which involves a knock-down-drag-out battle over my custody, if not my immortal soul. I got tired of being caught in the cross fire, so Dad asked if I'd like to spend a week with Uncle Peter and Aunt Judy. Since they live in Florida, I thought this meant I'd go to the beach. Sunbathing, learning how to surf, maybe finding a summer boyfriend . . . y'know, that sort of thing. But it turns out that they're working on Tethys for the next three months, and since Uncle Pete has arranged for me to come visit them there, I get to help Aunt Judy count fish instead. Lucky me.

"I'm doing research," she said instead, shaking her hand.

"Oh, really? Of what sort?"

"My aunt's a marine biologist. She's studying game-fish populations in the North Atlantic. I'm supposed to be assisting her." That didn't sound very impressive, so she quickly added, "And I'm working on a project of my own. A film."

Leslie smiled slightly. She glanced up at the luggage compartment above their heads. "I was wondering why you're carrying camera gear. Is that what you want to be when you—?"

The aircraft took another violet lurch, which mercifully cut short that patronizing question. Leslie Sun winced and gripped her armrests more tightly; Andie found herself hoping that she'd get sick. Lay off the kid stuff, bitch, she thought. I'm almost a senior in high school.

"You're not ill, are you?" she asked sweetly.

Leslie Sun glared at her, but said nothing. A few seconds later there was a hollow noise from somewhere below them, and the floor beneath their feet trembled as the landing gear opened. "We're coming in, ladies," the pilot announced. "If you'll look out your right window, you can see Tethys."

As he spoke, the VTOL began to make a slow left turn. The floor canted beneath them; Leslie Sun remained rigid in her seat, leaving Andie to peer out the window by herself. The aircraft's altitude had dropped to about a thousand feet; for a moment all she saw was shimmering blue horizon titled at a sharp sideways angle, then the craft leveled off and there, just ahead, lay Tethys Oceanographic Research Station.

Tethys 1, to be exact. The undersea part of the station, Tethys 2, was hidden beneath nearly 330 feet of water. The top half floated on the surface like a gargantuan white cork made of concrete and steel, faintly resembling an offshore oil rig, with red-painted scaffolds and platforms encircling its outer hull. On one side of the hull was painted the corporate logo: a woman's silhouette, artfully framed against a fan shell; the company took its name after a Santarian sea goddess, Andie recalled from the stuff her uncle had emailed her. An enormous derrick crane ran along tracks across a broad upper deck crowded with sheds, red-painted tanks, radio masts, satellite dishes, and a tall central tower through which thin white vapor escaped. A large catamaran was moored alongside a pier, next to a couple of smaller boats. Tiny figures wearing hard hats walked along the pier and the catwalks.

Boss tech, new cent, way cool, all that stuff. Boring. A few nerds she knew back home—none of them her friends, thank God—would be wetting their BVDs right now, but nothing down there looked even remotely like a cabana or a beach shop, and even if she found someplace up here to lie out—oh yeah, right—she was damned if she was going to try out her new string bikini with all these old guys around

"Thanks, Uncle Pete," she murmured. "You're a real pal."

Then they were almost directly above the base, less than a few hundred feet above an elevated helicopter pad. She caught a glimpse of a painted triangle with the letter *H* in its center; someone wearing ear protectors was waving a pair of white sticks back and forth, up and down. The Osprey's tilt-rotor turboprops angled upward, and there was a thin whine from the nacelles as the aircraft shuddered and slowly lost its forward momentum. Leslie Sun's eyes were tightly shut; her fingernails dug into the upholstery as she opened her small mouth and gasped, and Andie idly wondered if that's what she looked like when she was having sex, then the aircraft began to descend. The ocean gradually disappeared as the pad rose around them, then there was a hard thump as the wheels met the surface.

Leslie opened her eyes. "Are we down?"

"We're down," Andie said. "Was it good for you, too?"

She gave her a puzzled look. Andie bit her lip and made a show of searching for the buckle of her seat belt. Bitch.

"All right, ladies, we're here," the pilot said as he unsnapped his harness and stood up. Stooping forward a little, he left the cockpit and walked back to release the bar on passenger hatch. "Sorry for the bumps back there. Hope you enjoyed the ride."

He pushed open the hatch, and the mixed scent of salt

air and aviation fuel rushed into the aircraft. "Oh, yeah!"
Andie said enthusiastically, trying to catch the pilot's eye.
"It was really great! I mean, I thought it was—'

"Thanks. Appreciate it." He gave her a quick, fleeting
smile that made her instantly forget three guys from
school who had been trying to ask her out, then he turned
his full and undivided attention to Leslie Sun. "You
okay? You looked like you were having a tough time
back there."

"Me? No problem." She had already unclasped her
belt. "Thanks for the lift."

"My pleasure. Let me give you a hand." The pilot
opened the luggage bin; the first thing he pulled out was
Leslie's black nylon flight bag.

"That's all right, but if you—"

"Not a problem, Ms. Sun. Not a problem."

"I'm Leslie."

"Mike Jacobs."

"You should have seen her, Mike," Andie said as he
set the bag down on the seat next to her. "She was about
to—"

"Oh, yeah. Sorry, Miss Lipscomb . . . almost forgot."
Mike barely looked at her as he hauled the aluminum
case containing her camera out of the bin and set it down
in the aisle. "Got a radio call as we were coming in. Your
Uncle Peter is supposed to meet you as soon as he gets
done with something, and your Aunt Judy is coming in
later this evening. If you want, we can get someone to
take you down to the commissary, buy you an ice cream.
Okay?"

She could have fried an egg on her face. "Okay . . ."

"Good." He leaned forward to take Leslie's hand, help
her out of her seat. "All right, easy does it . . . watch your
head . . ."

In a last, desperate measure to prove that she was the

better woman, Andie hastily stood up. The top of her
head smacked against the underside of the luggage bin;
Mike didn't notice as she yelped and collapsed back in
her seat, but Leslie cast her a brief, condescending glance
as she gracefully rose and, with the pilot's gallant assistance, picked up her flight bag.

God. This trip was really beginning to suck.

P eter Lipscomb found his niece on the Level 2 scaffold
just outside the commissary, drinking a Diet Coke
and watching the activity down on the pier. *Doris*'s crew
sphere had been wrenched up from the slipway between
the *Amphitrite*'s double hull. It now rested on the pier,
and a couple of engineers had crawled down the top hatch
to inspect its interior. Peter wondered how much Andrea
had seen, then reminded himself that she probably didn't
have a clue as to what was going on.

She looked up as he came up the ladder, and for a
moment it seemed as if she didn't recognize him. No
wonder there; the last time they had laid eyes on each
other was nearly two years ago, when he still had the
shoulder-length hair and beard he had cultivated after he
left the Navy. The ponytail and beard were gone now,
replaced by a butch cut and long sideburns; it seemed to
take her a second to match his new face with his old one.
Then she gave him the radiant smile that she had inherited from Jack's wife—soon-to-be former wife, actually—
and nearly dropped the half-empty soda as she rushed
across the steel-mesh catwalk.

"Uncle Peter!" she yelled, and an instant later his arms
were full of hyperactive teenager. "Wow, it's great to see
you!"

"Nice to see you, too." Damn, but the kid had grown
up fast. Of course, he was still a freshman at University

of Alabama when she was born, and had missed most of her childhood while he was in the Navy and, later, working on his master's at MIT. Nonetheless he had been anticipating a plump fifteen-year-old with braces on her teeth, not an eye-catching young woman just shy of adulthood. "I thought someone was supposed to be taking care of you."

"They were, but I let 'em go. Jeez, you think I can't take care of myself." She released him from the bear hug and glared at him. "Hey, whose idea was it to have me taken down here for ice cream? I mean, c'mon . . ."

"Mine. Sorry." He felt his face turning red. "I was thinking . . . never mind."

That was enough. The apology brought back the smile. "It's okay. I'll let you go . . . this time, at least." She pointed toward the pier. "I thought I saw you down there, but I couldn't be sure. What's going on?"

Didn't miss a trick, did she? She might have inherited Dorothy's looks, but sharp eyes was something that ran in the Lipscomb family. "Had a little trouble out on the water today," he said, trying to sound as casual as he could before changing the subject. "So, how was the flight? How's your folks?"

Her expression darkened, and she glanced away. Too late, Peter realized that he had picked the wrong subject. "Hey, y'know . . . what can I say?" she said softly, nervously taking a sip from her soda. "Dad wants to kill Mom, Mom wants to kill Dad, and baby makes three."

She was trying to be funny—indeed, Peter wondered how Andrea had cribbed a line from a song so old that her grandparents might have danced to it—but the joke fell flat. Peter had witnessed his share of separations and divorces, but the one his older brother was going through was the most hostile he had ever seen, even from a distance. Twenty-one years of marriage, apparently as solid and happy as the one enjoyed by their late parents, then all of a sudden Jack was sending him email, telling him and Judith that he had temporarily moved into an apartment and was filing for divorce. Peter still hadn't learned the root cause of the breakup, but whatever it was, Andrea was caught in the middle.

"Sorry, Andrea," he murmured, uncomfortably aware that this was the second time in as many minutes he was apologizing to his niece. "Didn't mean it that way. I just—"

"Andie."

"Huh?"

"I'm not Andrea anymore. It's Andie now."

"Oh. Right." One more change. Jack had called her Andrea when Peter called to ask if he and Judith could take her in for a week while he and Dorothy went to divorce court; Peter wondered if his brother was aware that his daughter had altered her name. Probably not. "Okay, so it's Andie now. Any more surprises?"

"Not unless you got some for me." She looked around. "Where's Aunt Judy? She's usually with you."

"She's in Dominica, but—"

"Dominica? Where's that?"

"An island in the Caribbean. She's been down there the last few days with an old friend of ours. Taking a vacation, that sort of thing."

"She's gone on vacation by herself?" The sea breeze wafted a lock of her long brown hair across her face; she absently tucked it behind her face. "Why aren't you with her?"

No point in telling her that her uncle and aunt often took separate vacations. Poor girl had seen enough of that sort of thing already. "More of a working vacation, really," Peter said. "She's with our old MIT adviser. He's from Dominica, and she wanted to see the place. Do a little reef diving, see if there was anything she might learn for her research. But I talked with her a few hours ago and she's coming home early, so she should be getting in later this evening. I'm sure she wants to—"

"Uncle Peter?"

"Yeah?"

"When we made this trip—I mean, when you and Dad set this thing up, y'know, for me to visit you—Aunt Judy said that she wanted me to help her with her research. Now I get here, and she's not around, and . . ."

Goddammit! Judith must have told Andrea—Andie!—something, then forgotten all about it. The plan was for Andie to spend time with them while Jack and Dorothy and their lawyers duked it out in court. Since Andie herself had suggested Florida, he and Judith had gone along with it, with the intent of putting her up in the VIP quarters aboard Tethys 1.

This had been successfully arranged with the company. As it turned out, Yemaya had a low-key student program which allowed high-school kids to visit Tethys, one of those line-item things which helped make the company eligible for federal research grants, but which had never been utilized until now. Judith and Charles Toussaint had pulled a few strings and managed to get Andie into the program, even though she had no previous experience, let alone much interest, in oceanography, on the grounds that she would be assisting her aunt with her research. Yet this had been done a couple of months ago; in the meantime Judith had accepted Charles's invitation to visit Dominica, with the understanding that Peter would take care of Andie until she got home.

Now everything had changed. The whole plan was falling apart even as they spoke, and once again his niece was caught in the middle. Bad timing all around. Yet if there was a seventeen-year-old girl who didn't need to be given an ice cream cone and shunted aside, it was Andrea.

Peter let out his breath. "Okay, kiddo, I'll be straight with you. Something . . . well, pretty unusual occurred this morning." He gestured to the pier below them. "I can't tell you exactly what it is just yet, but it happened to the guy who was driving that sub."

"That's a sub?" Andie peered closer at the salvaged sphere crew. "I didn't even recognize it. Aren't they . . . y'know, a lot bigger?"

"Usually, yeah. That's just the part that came up. He had to leave most of it on the ocean floor, but before he did, he captured the event on video. Or at least he thinks he did. That's what I was doing down there . . . retrieving the disk." Peter reached into the breast pocket of his shirt, pulled out the disk case, showed it to her. "When we replay this, we'll find out whether he was seeing things or not."

"Well, hey, what are we waiting for? Let's go find a player and—"

"Not until Aunt Judy gets back." He slipped the case back in his pocket. "She should be getting on the flight from Dominica just about now. Until then, the only people who know about this are Joe—that's the sub pilot— you and me, and Judith. And it's got to stay that way, understand?"

"Yeah, sure, I guess. I just . . ."

Her chin and lower lip trembled a bit, then she abruptly turned away from him. She went to the railing and rested her arms against it, dangling the soda can between her fingertips as she gazed out at the horizon. Peter was confused. What did he just say?

He walked over to the railing, leaned against it. "What's wrong?" he asked softly.

"I dunno." She ducked her head, letting her hair cover her face. "Forget it. Nothing."

"No, c'mon, really. What is it?"

When she raised her face again, she was blinking rapidly, as if forcing back tears. "Look, Uncle Pete . . . you don't have to treat me like a kid. I don't need a babysitter. If you want me to get lost, I'll get a ride back to the mainland and catch the next flight back to K.C. Dad'll be pissed, but I can stay at a friend's house or something."

It was tempting to say yes. The last thing in the world he needed right now was to be shepherding a teenager around Tethys. Yet he simply couldn't send her home. He might be Tethys's dive chief, but he was also Andie Lipscomb's uncle, and right now she needed her Uncle Pete.

"No, no, I'm not going to do that to you," he said, shaking his head. "You're here, and I'm not about to send you off. Besides, this whole thing might blow over." He glanced around to make sure that they weren't being overheard, then added quietly, "But things might get hairy around here if it doesn't blow over, and . . . well, let's just play it by ear. Okay?"

Andie snuffled a little, slowly nodded. "Okay. So . . . I mean, y'know, what do you want me to do?"

Good question. "Well, you were supposed to be assisting Judith with her research, so I guess you'll still be doing that." Then he smiled. "But I think it's going to be different than marine census. Judy's been studying something else for the last several years. Sort of a side project the company doesn't know about."

Andie's eyes brightened. "A secret project?" she whispered, and practically jumped up and down when he gravely nodded. "Oh! What is it, what is it? C'mon, you can tell me!"

"I better let her explain it herself, but here's the deal ... it may mean that we'll have to go down to Tethys 2." He took a deep breath. "We weren't originally planning to do that. The idea had been for you to remain topside the whole time you were here, and stay in the VIP quarters. If you saw Tethys 2, it was only going to be on video feed."

She nodded solemnly. "And you aren't going back to Jacksonville?"

"Nope. We've only got a one-bedroom apartment there anyway, and it's ten miles from the beach. We only use it when we're not out here. A few days every six weeks or so. You didn't know that?"

She shook her head; there was a disappointed look in her eyes, which told him, in a flash, that she had been expecting something else. A beachside condo: two bedrooms, large deck, ocean view, clambakes every night. The stuff of teenage fantasy. She probably wasn't even aware that he and Judith spent the winter in a rented house in Buzzard's Bay, Massachusetts, which was even less inviting than an apartment complex in Jacksonville. His damn brother probably hadn't told her that either ...

Well, never mind that now. "So it may be that we'll have to go down to Tethys 2," he continued. "We might be able to take you along, but I gotta tell you, kiddo, going below is serious business. It isn't anything like being up here."

Andie looked puzzled. "How come? I don't understand."

He took her hand. "C'mon. I better show you something."

Andie started to follow him, then stopped. "Hold it. Lemme grab my stuff." She turned and ran back to where she had been standing. A canvas duffel bag and an aluminum camera case were parked next to the commissary door. Peter almost told her that she could leave her luggage there—if there was anything no one aboard Tethys had to worry about, it was theft, unless it was a six-pack of beer—but when he saw her pick up the camera case, that thought disappeared. Perhaps his niece would come in handy, after all . . .

He took the duffel bag from her, then led her down the scaffold to an open hatch and into one of the passageways that curved around the inside of the floating island, so narrow that they had to step aside to allow a crewman to walk past. The riveted steel walls echoed faintly from a faint thrumming noise from deep within the base; the nylon-carpeted floor vibrated beneath their feet. It was like walking around the inside of a massive concrete drum.

Peter escorted her down the corridor until he found an unoccupied briefing room. He flipped on the fluorescent lights, placed her bag on the cheap folding table, then turned to a large cutaway chart within a glass case on the wall. "Okay," he said, "here's the layout of the place."

He pointed to the squat cylinder at the top of the chart. "That's where we are, Tethys 1. You've seen the top deck already, of course, and these decks down here and here. But those are just the outer layers, like the hallway we just passed through, the commissary, and this room." He moved his finger to the cutaway segments farther within the base. "This is the OTEC power plant. That means—"

"Ocean Thermal Energy Conversion." She pointed to the maze of intake and discharge pipes, condensators, separators, evaporators, and electrical generators deep inside the base's core. "Cold water moves up the main pipe, meets warm water on the surface, runs turbines here and here, produces electricity. The cold water is then desalinated before it runs back down the main pipe to Tethys 2. Right?"

Peter was impressed. "You read the material I emailed you."

She gave him a withering look. "What do I look like? C'mon . . ."

He tapped a forefinger against the middle pipe of the three which ran down from the bottom of Tethys 1. "Okay, smart guy, then what's this one do?"

She peered at it closely. "Um . . . that's the snorkel, I think."

"Give the girl a cigar," he said, and she made a face. "Okay, another Coke then. Yeah, that's the snorkel. It pumps in fresh air from the surface for Tethys 2." He ran his finger down the cluster of color-coded conduits beneath the drum-shaped topside half of the installation. "Air, fresh water, electricity . . . everything moves in a closed-loop system. At least until we get down here."

He stopped his finger at a row of spheres positioned on the roof of Tethys 2's main habitat, a squat drum positioned in the center of a cluster of four smaller cylinders. "What are those?" he asked, then placed his hand over the legend so she couldn't cheat.

"Uh . . . the washing machines?"

"Zaaak! Sorry, no trip to Hawaii for you. Those are the helium storage tanks." She giggled a bit, but Peter didn't let her go easily. "Here's where we get serious. The reason why we mix helium with oxygen and nitrogen is because this part of the base is exactly 328 feet below the surface, and that means it's under higher pressure. Nearly ten atmospheres, in fact. But nitrogen becomes toxic once you get below 180 feet, and since it's dangerous to work in a pure-oxygen atmosphere, we have to add helium to the breathing mix. Follow me so far?"

Andie nodded, and he went on. "Now, the habs could have been designed for one-atmosphere pressure, just like submarines, but that would have meant that they would

have had to have really thick walls and no one could exit
the base except in JIM suits." He indicated the air locks on
the lowest of the main hab's three decks. "That's incon-
venient, though, because those suits are a bitch to handle,
and since we've got people going in and out all day
long—"

"Like, to work at the manganese plant."

"Uh-huh, and to do maintenance and basic research,
stuff like that. No sense in building an undersea base if
you can't go outside in scuba gear, right? So we're working under ten atmospheres down there." He pointed to
the topside half of the base again. "We launch most of
the subs from up here, where the drivers can get in and
out quickly, but all the major work goes on down—"

"Yeah, okay, sure. So what are you getting at?"

"You didn't read everything I sent you, did you?" he
asked, and she glanced down at the floor. "Okay, here it
is. Going down is easy enough. You take one of the shuttle subs, and when you get down you enter the hyperbaric
chamber for a couple of hours." He pointed to the diving
bells. "But coming back up isn't so simple. Once you get
topside again, you have to decompress for nearly sixty
hours, which means that you have to spend two and half
days in another hyperbaric chamber. It's like a college
dorm . . . bunks, books to read, TV, all that stuff . . . but
you have to stay there until you're ready to come out, or
you'll get bent."

She smirked when he said that, and put a hand over
her mouth to hide a mischievous smile. No doubt the
phrase meant something different to her than it did to
him. At her age, everything had something to do with
sex. "As in, getting the bends," he added solemnly. "Believe me, it's nothing you want."

He waited patiently until she was over her giggling fit.
"So that's where it stands," he went on. "If you go

down—I mean, if you decide to go to Tethys 2—you'll have to learn how to live under pressure. Like I said, things are different down there."

"How different is that?" She was still grinning.

He looked around, spotted the Diet Coke she was still drinking. "Through with that?" he asked, and took it from her hand when she nodded. He chugged the last of the soda, then held the can in front of her face. "This is what ten atmospheres would do to this can," he said, then he crunched it within his fist. "If it was still full, it would explode, because of the carbonation. Your body can get acclimated to this sort of thing pretty fast—that's why it's called saturation diving, because your body cells get saturated with helium—but that's only on the way down. When you come up, you've got nearly three days of decompression, with wearing an oxygen mask for sixteen hours each day. I've done it a few times. Believe me, it's no fun."

Andie wasn't laughing now. It had gotten through to her. "What do you mean, things are different down there? I mean, I get the point about the Coke can, but—"

"Everything. It's just . . . everything." He shrugged. "It's not all that bad, once you get used to it, but—"

"Can I take my camera along with me? Will it still work?"

"Does it use disks?" She nodded. "Sure. That's what they use down there."

"And you'll be there, and Aunt Judy?"

"Judy will, most likely. I might go down, too. Most of my work is up here, though."

Andie mulled it over as she gazed at the chart. Peter crossed his arms and rested against the table, stepping back to give her a little room to think. Truth to be told, he was just as reluctant as she was, although for different reasons. This was Jack's only child, after all: his brother the criminal lawyer, whose idea of high risk was walking into a courtroom to argue a pro bono case. Yet there was a certain wild streak in the family which couldn't be denied. This was his niece's chance to break away from Midwestern suburb culture. He couldn't push her, but he could offer the chance.

"I think I'd—" she began.

She was interrupted by a sharp beep from the phone on Peter's belt. "Hold that thought," he murmured, then he pulled the phone out of its pouch and flipped it open. "Lipscomb," he said.

"Pete, it's Miles." Miles Bartlett was Tethys's general manager; Peter had seen him only a couple of hours ago in MainOps, shortly after he had returned the Barracuda to the sub pen. "We need you up here. We've got a problem."

Great. Someone must have discovered that the film disk was missing from the *Doris*. Miles probably figured out that he had filched it, and now Miles wanted it back. Of course, if Peter got to a computer first, he might be able to download it into a password file before he had to surrender it.

"Can it wait?" he asked "I've got my niece with me, and I can't get away right—"

"It's Judy. Look, I don't want to alarm you, but she's run into some trouble on Dominica."

In an instant the disk was forgotten."What's going on?" he snapped.

"Calm down. She's okay, but we've just heard that she and Charles Toussaint were attacked on their way to the airport. From what we've been told, it sounds like someone tried to kidnap Doc."

"Where is she now?"

"On her way here. The company's sent a jet down to

pick them up. Peter, she's fine, and so is Doc, but we need to—"

"I'm on my way." Peter stabbed the off button.

Andie was staring at him, her mouth open in puzzlement. "Is it Aunt Judy?" she asked. "What's—?"

"Something's come up. Don't worry, it's nothing major." He didn't like lying to her, but neither did he want to send her into a panic. As it was, it took every bit of self-control to remain calm, if only to keep up appearances. "I've got to head up to MainOps. Do me a favor, will you, and stay here until I come back. Okay?"

"Sure. Okay." She hesitated as he turned toward the door, then added, "If it makes any difference, but . . . I'd like to go down. To Tethys 2, I mean."

For a moment he had forgotten what they had been discussing before Miles called. He glanced over his shoulder and smiled at her. "Good. I'll see what we can do."

Then he was out the door. He carefully closed it behind him, then set out running for the nearest ladder.

FIVE

Interview

Leslie Sun's interview with Miles Bartlett was originally scheduled for four o'clock. She didn't mind when it was pushed back to 4:30, because she was still getting over the nausea she had suffered during the flight, yet when she arrived at Bartlett's office, located just down the corridor from the Main Operations Center on Tethys 1's second deck, no one was there. Her escort— an earnest young woman in her mid-twenties whose name escaped her, but who had informed Leslie that she was a summer intern from Duke University—surmised that Bartlett was probably running a little behind schedule. Would she like some coffee while she waited?

Leslie politely declined, then as an afterthought asked for some water instead. The intern smiled and nodded, then left her in Bartlett's cubbyhole, carefully shutting the door behind her. Leslie had just unpacked her notebook and minirecorder when the girl came back with a bottle of Evian water and an apology. Mr. Bartlett was terribly sorry, but something had just come up; would she mind waiting a little while longer? No, Leslie didn't mind, so the intern left again, once more closing the door behind her, and Leslie settled down in the only other chair in the tiny office.

There was a novelty clock on the faux-wood-paneled wall above the file cabinet: Elvis Presley's knock-kneed legs swung back and forth, keeping metronomic time with the soft ticking of the second hand. Elvis shook his hips about nine hundred times before Leslie got tired of gazing at the photos of tube worms and basking sharks framed on the walls and the folders, spiral notebooks, and computer printout piled in untidy heaps on the small desk. She gave him five more minutes, then she decided to find the general manager herself.

The door to the operations center had a keycard lock, yet the knob turned when Leslie tried it. No real wonder there; she had learned from past experience that people who worked in high-security areas often jimmied automatic locks because they were a nuisance. Leslie hesitated a moment, then carefully opened the door and stepped inside.

Tethys 1's Main Operations Center—MainOps, as the intern called it—faintly resembled the bridge of an oil tanker. A room whose low ceiling was jammed with conduits, AC ducts, and fluorescent lamps, its circular walls were lined by consoles densely crowded with toggle switches and illuminated buttons, dials and digital readouts, keyboards and flatscreen panels. An electronic mapboard in the center of the far wall depicted a cross section of the entire installation; suspended from the ceiling were a dozen TV monitors, each displaying a different image, some of which were underwater. Four men and women wearing T-shirts and shorts were seated in front of the consoles. Late afternoon sunlight, toasty-warm and unobstructed by the furled venetian blinds, streamed through wide bay windows overlooking the ocean.

Two men stood near a desk in the center of the room. They appeared to be arguing about something, but since their backs were turned to the door, neither of them noticed Leslie when she came in. She eased the door shut behind her, then quietly stood against the wall and pretended to be a coat of paint.

". . . the hell do you mean, pulling that disk? If it's got something we can use, I need to see it." The first guy was in his mid-fifties. Thin gray hair, permanent desk slouch, something of a gut, wearing a faded-out blue jumpsuit.

"It's got something, but Judy's got to be the first one to look at it. She might be able to . . ." This from the younger one. Dark brown hair, stylish retro-seventies sideburns, athletic build, just an inch or so under six feet. Nice tush.

"Maybe she will. I'm not arguing that. But I've got Jacksonville climbing all over me right now. If there's something on the disk we can—"

"Just wait, please? Judy will take a look at it as soon as she gets here, and then she can tell us what—"

"What makes you think we can't figure this out? Chrissakes, Pete, I was doing research at Scripps when she was—"

"I promised her she'd have first the first look."

"I could just order you to give it up. You know that, don't you? It came from a company sub, so it's company property."

"Right. You look at it, and then you get someone else to look at it just to be on the safe side, and they call someone else, and the next thing you know, some joker's calling his wife and kids to tell them . . ."

"Tell them what?" the older man asked. "What's the big deal?"

Pete sighed, rubbed his forehead with his fingertips. "Joe says he saw . . ."

Then he glanced aside, spotted Leslie standing near the door. He turned away and muttered something under his breath. The older man looked around sharply, saw her. "Hey, who are you? How did you get in here?"

Busted. "Pardon me," she said, feigning innocence. "The door was open, and I was searching for someone, so—"

"Who are you looking for?"

"Uh . . . Miles Bartlett. I'm Leslie Sun, from *Millennium* magazine. I was supposed to have an interview with him about an hour ago."

The operators stopped what they were doing to peer over their shoulders at her. The younger one hid a smile behind his hand as the older gentleman winced. "I'm Miles Bartlett," he said. A little less truculent now, he stepped away from the desk, walked across the control center. "I'm sorry, Ms. Sun, I didn't recognize you."

"I'm sorry for intruding, but—"

"We were supposed to have a meeting at four, yes. I didn't forget you. It's only that we've had an . . ." She could tell that Bartlett almost said "emergency" before he caught himself. "An unforeseen occurrence," he said instead. "Something's come up that we had to deal with. I hope you understand."

There was a questioning look in his eyes; he didn't know how long she had been standing there, and was wondering how much she had overheard. Enough to raise her curiosity, but she wasn't going to tell him that. Behind him, Pete leaned against the desk, arms crossed, sizing her up.

"I certainly understand you're busy, Mr. Bartlett," she

said, "but I've been waiting in your office for the last hour, and this visit was arranged almost two months ago. If you can't see me now, please say so. That way I can call my people in New York and tell them I'm not going to be able to—"

"Go ahead and take care of this, Miles," Pete said. "I think we can handle everything here."

There was a canny smile on his face, one which disappeared when Bartlett glanced back at him, but was replaced by a sly wink in her direction when Bartlett looked away once more. He was taking advantage of her presence, she realized. And what was this about a disk . . . ?

"I think I may be able to give you a few minutes," Bartlett said reluctantly, surrendering to the inevitable. "Let's go back to my office."

"Thank you, Mr. Bartlett."

Bartlett nodded, then walked past her to the door. She turned to follow him; as he opened the door for her, she glanced over her shoulder, caught Pete's eye. *Thank you,* she silently mouthed, and he gave her the faintest nod in return.

Sweet, she thought. Wonder if he's available?

Not that this had ever made much difference before . . .

"So," she asked, ever so casually, "what sort of problem were you dealing with just then?"

Perhaps it was rash to throw a curve so early in the interview. Leslie usually preferred to wait a bit longer before she started slinging hardballs. Yet she had just spent the last five minutes warming up the subject—in this case, questions about Bartlett's professional background as Tethys's general manager, although she already knew most of that stuff from the press kit Yemaya had sent her—and she was curious about the exchange she had overheard in MainOps.

Bartlett shifted uneasily in his chair. "Nothing to speak of, really," he said, his gaze briefly wandering to the minirecorder on his desk. "We . . . uh . . ."

"Do you want me to turn it off?" Leslie gestured to the recorder with her pen. "We can go off record, if you like. I'm just interested in what sort of problems you normally encounter out here."

Bartlett hesitated, then silently nodded toward the recorder. She reached forward and clicked the pause switch. "We lost a submersible on the Blake Plateau this morning," he said. "It's not something that happens every day. In fact, this is the first time for us."

"Oh, my! Was anyone hurt?"

He quickly shook his head. "Oh, no, no. The driver escaped with only minor injuries . . . but like I said, it's a first for us, and we're still trying to figure out why."

"Any idea what could have caused it?"

"We're still investigating."

"Was it equipment failure?"

"No comment," he said tightly.

"Okay. Fair enough." When they resort to that, it's time to back off. No sense in rushing things, and she wanted to get him on her side. Leslie glanced at the question list in her notebook, picked the most innocuous one. "Let's backtrack a little. What's Tethys's purpose? I mean, what do you intend to accomplish out here?"

"Are we back on the record?" She nodded and released the pause button, and he continued. "The company—Yemaya Ocean Resources, I mean—has a long-term interest in commercial undersea exploration . . ."

The rest was standard corporate spiel: Yemaya Ocean Resources was an independent subsidiary of ICR International, a multinational corporation which had begun as a builder of nuclear power plants and, during the last three decades, had diversified into industrial electronics and aerospace. Six years earlier it had formed Yemaya with the intention of exploring and developing deep-ocean resources; although its emphasis was on seabed mining, it was also involved in other projects: renewable energy sources, advanced marine technology, bioprospecting, aquaculture, and so forth.

"So Tethys is a multipurpose installation," he went on. "Although its main job is to serve as an offshore mining facility, it's also the largest undersea habitat yet built, able to accommodate up to forty people below, about a quarter of whom are involved in basic scientific research. Its electrical supply is derived from the world's first fully functional OTEC plant, which also doubles as a pilot desalination facility. We're actively testing new technologies which were only on the drawing board a decade ago, everything from teleoperated robots to advanced rebreathing systems to experimental submersibles . . ."

Leslie felt her eyes beginning to glaze over. It was much the same stuff she had read already in the press kit. Ten minutes of tape lost to stuff she could have cribbed from company literature, and Bartlett sounded like he could continue in this vein for the next hour. "So why do everything out here, thirty-five miles from shore?" she asked. "If this is a research facility, wouldn't it be easier and less expensive to do most of it from the company's headquarters in Jacksonville?"

For a moment Bartlett looked nonplussed. "Well, I wouldn't know about it being less expensive . . ."

"According to . . . um . . ." She took a moment to check her notes. "According to *The Wall Street Journal,* ICR has invested nearly $2 billion in R&D alone, and another estimated $8 billion in construction costs. So this site had set the parent company back by $10 billion the day it opened nine months ago, and every analyst with whom I've spoken says that it'll take at least ten years, if not more, for Yemaya to achieve any sort of profit."

She had to give Bartlett credit; she had thrown him a fastball, and he didn't even blink. "I can't comment on *The Wall Street Journal*'s figures, but it will undoubtedly take some time for the company to recover its overhead costs. But you have to understand that deep-ocean exploration is as much of a new frontier as outer space . . . even more so, if you take into account the fact that we know far more about, say, the surface of Mars than we do about what lies on the ocean floor between here and Europe. Another company sent men back to the Moon last year for about the same cost. Everyone regards this as a major accomplishment, and rightly so, yet I could name a thousand places in the North Atlantic which haven't yet been visited by either ROVs or manned submersibles."

He stood up and walked over to a cutaway chart of Tethys framed on the office wall. "You're used to the idea of space stations and lunar bases. Everyone is by now, but when I was kid, all that was science fiction stuff no one took seriously. Well, think of this as a space station of a different sort . . . a station in oceanspace."

Here it comes, she thought. The corporate line.

"A lot of folks thought it was a waste of time and money to explore outer space," Bartlett went on, "and they were proven wrong. Now we're intending to do much the same thing out here. Sure, the company might be able to do some of these things by taking ships out on the ocean, but eventually you have to return to shore. There's some things you can't do on the beach. Eventually you have to get out in deep water, and stay there."

Leslie was impressed. It was possible that Yemaya had sent Bartlett through a PR seminar—companies often did that for their upper management, in order to prepare them for handling the press—but even if so, he spoke with more heartfelt conviction than any other white-collar stiff she had ever interviewed. Even so, everything he had just said sounded canned; a couple of great quotes, sure, but nothing that would make the reader stop eating his Cheerios. She needed to get under his skin.

"Those are admirable ambitions," she said, stealing another glance at her question list, "but I understand there's been some opposition to Tethys."

"Of what sort?"

"Various environmental organizations have gone on record to oppose deep-ocean mining. They state that it could it could destroy vital aquatic habitats."

"Our operations, or deep-ocean mining in general?" She started to check her notes, but he was already rushing on. "You're probably talking about past statements regarding dredging on the continental shelf. Yes, that was condemned in the past . . . and rightly so, to tell the truth. The first time private companies attempted to mine manganese nodules, back in the seventies and eighties, they used vacuum hoses and mechanical scoops lowered from ships on the surface. That was a kind of brute-force approach, and it tore up the sea bottom and ruined natural habitats. It prompted lawsuits and, eventually, proved to be unprofitable."

She already knew where this was leading. "But now you're using robots."

"Right. Our machines—we've got two, but we only use one at a time—operate via Extra Low Frequency signals downlinked via satellite from the operations center you just saw. This means the controllers can guide the 'bots along the seafloor and precisely select which areas they wish to harvest. So we're not just blindly groping in the dark. A couple of environmental interest groups

were initially opposed to what we were doing and filed
lawsuits in federal court to stop us, until we demonstrated
our system to their representatives. They've subsequently
dropped the lawsuits."

"Why do you think they did that?"

He shrugged, smiled a little. "Why fight a battle you
know you can't win?"

Good answer. She could always do a little research,
find out later whether he was telling the truth or just
blowing smoke. Right now, though, she wanted to keep
him on the hook. "There's also been some questions
raised in the United Nations, in regard to possible American violation of the 1982 Law of the Sea Treaty."

"We haven't violated any UN treaties." Bartlett sat
down and folded his hands together on his desk, regarding her with the blandest of gazes.

Leslie checked her notes. "Pardon me, but in 1982, the
Reagan Administration issued a proclamation which established a two-hundred-mile—"

"Two hundred nautical miles," he corrected. "That's
230 statute miles."

"Two-hundred-nautical-mile Exclusive Economic Zone
around the United States coastline. This was in accor-
dance with the UN Law of the Sea Treaty."

"That's correct, yes."

"And in order for a country to mine the ocean floor
within that zone, it would have to pay a user fee of
$500,000, and half the claims would be turned over to
the UN nonprofit corporation Enterprise for dispersement
among the nations of the world, on the principle that the
world's oceans belong to everyone." She looked up
again. "Yemaya Ocean Resources hasn't done this."

"That's because neither Reagan, nor any White House
resident since then, has formally signed the Law of the
Sea Treaty." Bartlett remained unflappable. "The U.S.

has stated that it will accept the two-hundred-nautical mile rule, but not ratify the remainder of the treaty. Yemaya is an American-owned company, so it abides by the American interpretation of the treaty."

"Then why—?"

"Because it's a stupid law. It would mean that my company, along with any other U.S. company doing business in the deep ocean, would have to pony up half a million dollars just to stake a claim upon something the UN itself concedes to be American territory, then pay half of the money it makes developing those claims to countries which otherwise have no interest or investment in deep-ocean exploration. As you yourself noted, it may take several years for ICR to earn back the money it's put into this project. If half that money automatically went to the UN, then Yemaya would go broke even before it got started. It's crypto-socialist bullshit, pure and simple."

That's a quote, she thought, but Bartlett wasn't through yet. "Look, let's try it another way. English is the language commonly used by most of the nations of the world, right? It may not be their official language, but it's become the one most often used in industrialized countries. Aircraft pilots, diplomats, business travelers, scientists, sign painters, so forth and so on. Even children in third-world countries are taught English, because that's what most of what the rest of the world uses when they want to talk to one another. Like the sea, you could make a case that the English language is the common heritage of mankind. Okay, so how would you feel if, every time you wrote an article, you had to pay royalties to the UN?"

"That's not the same thing."

"Perhaps not exactly, no. Nonetheless, the UN is trying to eat their cake and have it, too, much same way they did with the Moon Treaty back in the early seventies. When third-world countries realized that there were fortunes to made in space, but only by countries willing and able to commit their resources to development, they tried to use diplomacy to make a grab for free cash. Let someone else make the effort and take the risks. When they show a profit, we'll say it half of it belongs to us and—"

Bartlett stopped himself. "I'm sorry. I'm getting carried away. What was the question again?"

"Never mind. I think you just answered it." She pretended to study her notes, but her next question was already framed. She had managed to get him on a roll; now it was time to see if she could keep the momentum going. "Isn't there a certain element of risk to all this? Beyond the financial aspect, I mean. What about the human factor, the fact that you're working in such a hostile environment?"

That seemed to amuse him, because he laughed out loud. "Hostile environment? Hey, lady, don't talk about your mother that way!" Bartlett caught her perplexed expression and shook his head. "Sorry. Look, the sea may seem hostile to you—and yeah, I guess you're not alone, because many people feel that way—but for those of us who've worked on the water all our lives, it's our mother. It's no more or less a hostile environment than anywhere else in the world. Hundreds of millions of people live in Southern California. They put up with earthquakes, brushfires, and severe drought, not to mention smog, traffic jams, and road rage . . . and most of them wouldn't live anywhere else. The worst we have to deal with out here is hurricanes, and we've handled one of those already."

"I was curious about that. How did—?"

"This installation was designed to withstand hurricanes up to force five. Tethys 1 is secured by titanium-alloy bridge cables leading down to four thousand-ton seabed anchors. When we learned Hurricane Amelda was going to hit us, we just gave the cables a little more slack and temporarily disconnected the OTEC feedpipes along with the snorkel, power lines, and freshwater pipes leading down to Tethys 2. We sent the surface boats ashore and sent the subs down below. Down there, of course, they hardly noticed a thing, except for a temporary power brownout and some bottom silt being stirred up. Some of us up here got seasick and we lost the radio mast, but otherwise we fared a lot better than the mainland did."

She jotted down another note—*H. Amelda—sidebar?*—and went on. "That's good to know, but I was thinking more about the risks of working at extreme depths. I mean, after all, you had an accident of some sort today. Doesn't that imply that some of the things you do down here are inherently hazardous?"

"Oh, sure, there's an element of danger," Bartlett said easily. "No question about it. And we do everything we can to minimize the risks. But you've got to understand that deep-ocean exploration is a frontier, and with any frontier there's always—"

The phone on desk chose that moment to purr. Bartlett held up a finger, then picked up the receiver. Leslie inwardly cursed. So close! Another few seconds and she might have had him talking about whatever happened down on the Blake Plateau that morning. She tried not to look impatient as she shifted her legs and pretended not to eavesdrop.

"Bartlett," he said, then listened for a moment. "Uh-huh . . . okay, good . . . yeah, please, bring her down to A-12." He glanced sideways at Leslie. "I'm almost done here. See if you can find someone to show Ms. Sun around . . . yes, Rachel will do."

Rachel. Leslie's heart sank. Rachel whatshername, the

intern who had escorted her from the helicopter pad. Bartlett was handing her off to a college kid. She stole a glance at her watch. Thirty-five minutes, and the interview was practically over.

"Tell Pete I want to see him down there, too," Bartlett continued. "Oh, yeah, and get Joe, if he's feeling up to it . . . okay, good . . . thanks. Bye."

"Work never ceases," she said as he hung up.

"'Fraid not." He made a show of looking up at his absurd Elvis clock. "I'm afraid I'm going to have to cut this short. But I've asked Rachel Lewis, the woman who—"

"Met me when I came in. I remember."

"Right. She's going to give you a walk-around while I'm gone, then show you to the VIP quarters." He smiled politely and stood up. "I'm sorry to rush off like this, but . . ."

"I understand." Leslie reached over to pick up her recorder. "There's just one thing."

"Yes?" He was already around his desk and halfway to the door.

"The arrangement I made . . . that my magazine made, rather . . . with the company was that I'd get to spend few days down below." She paused. "On Tethys 2, that is."

That stopped him. "You did?"

"That's the arrangement. And as much as I find Tethys 1 fascinating"—an obvious lie; topside was as stimulating as an oil derrick—"the real focus of the article I'm writing is about the undersea operations."

Bartlett gave her a polite, icy smile. "Well, I'm sure that's true, Ms. Sun—"

"Call me Leslie, please."

"I'm afraid I have to check with the bottomside operations manager to see if there's a berth available. Like

I said earlier, Tethys 2 can only accommodate forty people at a time, and there's . . ."

He went back to his desk, moved aside a stack of paper, found a thick logbook, and opened it. Bartlett flipped to a page in the middle, ran his finger down the list. "According to my list, we've got thirty-five people down there already, and we're expecting to send down at least three or four more this evening. That's running it a little tight."

"But you should have space for at least one more. And I was told that you'd have a place for *Millennium* magazine."

She deliberately referred to herself by her magazine's title; as expected, that brought him up short. *Millennium* had a paid circulation of just over 700,000 readers, with almost as many in newsstand sales and secondhand readers, not to mention the millions who logged onto the magazine's website. Everyone from high-school punks like the girl on her flight from Jacksonville to senators and congressmen bought it every month. Coldshouldering a *Millennium* writer was just as unconscionable as the Schwag booting a *Rolling Stone* reporter off a summer tour. It just wasn't done. At least, not if you wanted good press.

"I'll see what I can do," Bartlett said.

"Please. And thank you for the interview."

He gave her a formal nod, then opened the door and fled from his own office. Leslie hummed to herself as she packed away her minirecorder and notebook. She had little doubt that she'd get a ride down to Tethys 2; that's when the real fun would begin.

However, she wasn't about to wait for her Duke princess to arrive. The guided tour of Tethys 1 could wait; right now the game was afoot, and she wasn't going to win it by tagging along with a college intern. If she tried to follow Bartlett, though, he'd find a way to shake her. Maybe if she wandered around a little on her own . . .

Slinging her bag over her shoulder, Leslie stepped out into the corridor. A couple of crewmen walked past with no more than a curious glance in her direction. From what she had just overheard, it sounded as if someone else was arriving. If she backtracked to the landing pad, perhaps she could see what the fuss was about.

She had just passed MainOps when the door opened behind her. She looked over her shoulder, saw the guy who had been arguing with Bartlett a few minutes earlier . . . Pete, right.

"Oh! Hi!" she said brightly.

He did a little double take when he saw her, then smiled and walked over. "Hello yourself. Lost again?"

God, but was he good-looking. "Yeah, well, sort of. Your boss left me in his office, and I got tired of waiting for someone to come find me."

"Yeah, well . . . it's not the best place to be wandering around by yourself, y'know . . ."

"I know, I know, but . . ." Change the subject, dammit! "Hey, I didn't get a chance to thank you. I might not have gotten that interview if it wasn't for you."

"No sweat. Just don't go in there alone again, okay? It's not—"

"Right. Not a public area. I didn't catch your name."

"Peter Lipscomb." He formally offered his hand. "I'm the dive chief around here."

"Leslie Sun, from *Millennium* . . . but I guess you know that already." As she took his hand—crap! he wore a wedding ring!—she remembered something she had heard earlier. His name rang a bell. Lipscomb, Peter Lipscomb . . . "Say, do you have a daughter? Or a niece, maybe . . . ?"

"Andrea. Yeah, that's my niece. Why, have you—?"

"We rode in together from Jacksonville, yeah. Nice girl." So this was her Uncle Pete. Which meant that her Aunt Judith—oh ho!—was the same Judy everyone was waiting for.

"Glad you think so." He released her hand, glanced over his shoulder in a distracted sort of way. "In fact, I'm on my way right now to find her."

"Well, hey," Leslie said quickly, "what a coincidence. Miles told me I could go to the same place."

A blatant, bald-faced, and utterly unscrupulous lie. It wasn't the first one she had told in her career, though, and she was getting better at it all the time. "Miles told you this?" he asked, faintly incredulous.

"Sure. Why not?"

He looked down at the floor, muttered something obscene beneath his breath. For a second Leslie wondered if she had overstepped her boundaries. Probably so, and sooner or later she would get caught. Yet there was something going on here . . .

"Okay," he said reluctantly, "c'mon. Let's find Andie, then we'll get this straightened out." Then he turned and began marching back down the corridor. Leslie fell in behind him, with a last glance behind her to see if anyone had seen them.

Yes, she was definitely onto something here, big time. Now all she had to do was follow the story.

SIX

Video

Peter was surprised to see that the Osprey which shuttled Judith and Charles over from Jacksonville wasn't the one belonging to Yemaya, but a similar aircraft bearing an unfamiliar corporate logo, a large, stylized *W* set against a globe. He glanced at Bartlett as it clattered into view, and the operations manager crooked his finger for him to come closer.

"Belongs to a private security firm," he said quietly when they were out of earshot from Andie, who stood nearby on the balcony overlooking the weather deck. "Sort of like Pinkerton, only more corporate. They protect businessmen traveling overseas. Soon as our people heard what happened, they called these guys. They mobilized an emergency team from their San Juan office and extracted Judy and Doc from his house, then flew them straight back to Puerto Rico. Nobody's been allowed near them except a doctor and American customs officials."

"No one else knows about this?"

"Not unless you've told that reporter." Bartlett shot a dark look at Leslie Sun. She stood at the railing about ten feet away, the evening breeze whipping her dark hair around her face. "What's she doing up here, anyway? I thought I left her in my office."

"She told me you said it was okay for her to come up here. I brought her along after I found Andie."

Bartlett's mouth tightened. "She spent the whole interview trying to get me to talk about what happened to the *Doris* this morning," he murmured angrily. "Of all the times for the press to come calling . . ."

"So? Get rid of her. You're in charge around here."

"I'm tempted, believe me." But he shook his head. "Can't do it, though, much as I'd like to. The front office would have my scalp. Just keep her out of my hair . . . and your niece, too, for that matter."

"Hey, lay off the kid. She hasn't done anything."

Bartlett shook his head and said something which sounded like an apology, but his voice was lost in a loud surge of prop wash as the VTOL came in for a landing. Peter raised a hand to shade his eyes against the setting sun and watched the Osprey settle down on the chopper pad. Two men rushed in to chock the landing gear as the tilt rotors began to wind down; a few moments later someone inside the craft popped open the passenger door and cranked down the ladder.

Peter turned away from the railing and headed for the stairs leading down to the weather deck. "C'mon," he murmured to Andie, tapping her on the shoulder. "I think your Aunt Judy needs family right now."

Andie nodded and followed him. Without being invited, Leslie Sun fell in behind them. Peter was annoyed, but he couldn't think of a polite way to ask her to stay back.

The first person to emerge from the aircraft wasn't

either his wife or Charles Toussaint, but a large black man with a linebacker's build, wearing jeans and a Hawaiian shirt. He studied Peter as he crossed the deck and ran up the landing pad gangway, then stepped in front of him. "I'm sorry, sir," he rumbled, holding out his left hand, "but you can't go this way."

Peter noticed the holstered Glock .45 sticking out from under the man's shirt, its handle only a few inches from his right hand. "It's okay. I'm Peter Lipscomb, Judith's husband." He glanced over his shoulder at Andie. "That's my niece. We've been waiting for her."

At that moment Judith emerged from the aircraft. She caught sight of Peter and yelled his name. Observing this, the bodyguard silently nodded and stepped aside to let him and Andie pass.

"Stop the lady behind us," Peter murmured as he slipped by him. "She doesn't belong here."

The security man remained taciturn, but nodded ever so slightly. He stepped in front of the gangway like a human gate, preventing Leslie Sun from coming onto the platform. "Sorry, ma'am, but you're going to have to stay back."

Peter barely noticed. In another instant Judith was in his arms, hugging him with a ferocity that went far beyond marital reunion after a few days' absence. "Oh, God, Peter," she whispered, "I'm so glad to see you! I was so . . . !"

"Shh . . . shh . . . it's all right, it's okay." He held her against him and stroked her hair, and was startled to find that she was trembling, her face wet with tears. She was frightened, all right; in fact, she was scared half out of her wits. She had managed to keep her fear locked down for the several hours, but now it was all coming to the surface. "Everything's going to be all right, everything's fine . . ."

Behind her, Charles Toussaint descended from the aircraft, helped down the ladder by a second bodyguard. There was a bandage across the bridge of his nose, but otherwise he looked unruffled. Spotting Peter, he smiled broadly, then strode across the deck to him and Judith.

"You neglected to tell me you had trained your wife in the martial arts," Charles said. Lipscomb didn't get the joke, but it broke Judith from her weepy fit; she laughed out loud and wiped tears from the corners of her eyes. "Seriously," he added, "if it wasn't for her, I probably wouldn't be here now."

"I don't know what you're talking about," Peter said as Judith released him.

"Neither do I," Andie said. Momentarily forgotten, she stood nearby. "I mean, is there something I should know?"

"Hi, Andrea!" Judith noticed her niece for the first time. "God, but you've grown up!"

Andie's eyes rolled in embarrassment. "Oh, God . . ."

"Our niece, Andrea . . . Andie, I mean," Peter said to Charles. "She's visiting this week."

"So I've been told." Charles stepped forward, gallantly offered his hand. "Ms. Lipscomb, I'm very pleased to meet you. I'm Dr. Charles Toussaint, an old friend of your uncle and aunt."

"Uh . . . likewise." Andie seemed to be momentarily put off by Charles's formality, but shyly took his hand anyway. Charles clasped it with both hands and gave her his warmest smile; Andie's face turned bright red and looked away. "Um . . . someone want to tell me what's going on here?"

"Andrea," Judith began, "you wouldn't believe what—"

"Uh, honey? Hold that thought." Peter stole a glance at the gangway. Leslie Sun stood on the top step; although the bodyguard was preventing her from coming any closer, she could hear every word that was being said. At the foot of the stairs behind her, Bartlett was making gestures with his hands: *Ten minutes, inside, got it?*

Peter gave him a swift nod, then turned back to the others. "Ixnay on the alk-tay," he said softly, huddling a little closer. "See the woman behind us, on the ladder? She's a magazine writer. Came in this afternoon."

"A reporter?" Judith's face darkened. "What's she—?"

"Company PR thing. The point is, she's been all over us like a coat of paint."

"Coat of slime, more like it. She's a real creep." Andie glared at her. "I think she likes you, Uncle Pete. Eeeww . . ."

"Really? Hadn't noticed." He tried to ignore Judith's hard-eyed expression. "Seriously, we need to get past her. Miles wants to see us ASAP."

"Do you have the disk?" Judith whispered.

Man, was she focused, or what? Assaulted in a third-world country, and all she cared about was the contents of a mini-DVD. "Right here," he said softly, tapping his breast pocket. "I've been holding off everyone till you got here."

"Then we should . . ." Charles began.

"Hello?" Andie interrupted. "Phone call from the Burger King Kids Club. . . ."

"Don't worry, you're coming with us," Peter said. Judith and Charles cast him sharp looks. "She's in on this. I promised her."

Charles gave an indifferent shrug, but Judith raised an eyebrow. *Are you out of your mind?* she silently mouthed.

The second bodyguard was hauling their bags out of

the Osprey; the wind was beginning to pick up as twilight set in. Nothing was being accomplished here on the chopper pad; time to go below and get everything straightened out. Peter pointed to the second set of stairs on the other side of the landing pad. "You guys go that way. I'll hold off the posse until you're clear."

"Why don't you just throw her overboard?" Andie asked.

Not a bad suggestion, yet for some reason, Peter couldn't see himself following it. He stole another glance at Leslie Sun, and found her smiling at him again.

Joe Niedzwiecki was already in the conference room next to MainOps by the time they arrived. He had a pair of crutches propped against the table, and Peter noticed that his T-shirt was stretched over elastic bandages wrapped around his chest. He smiled painfully when everyone came in but didn't get up from his chair, and he took Andie up on her offer to fetch soft drinks for everyone from the commissary. Bartlett took her departure as an opportunity to address the first order of business.

"I don't think it was a random street crime," Judith said, once she had given the others a blow-by-blow account of what had happened in Roseau. "I've never been mugged, but it didn't seem like robbery was the motive. They went after Charles and totally ignored me until I fought back."

"You're lucky they didn't pull a gun." Bartlett had taken a seat at the head of the table, his back to the door. "It sounds like these guys meant business."

"That's rather unlikely," Charles said. "There aren't that many privately owned firearms on Dominica, and assaults against foreign visitors are extremely rare."

"Then they could have pulled a knife." Peter shook his head. "Jeez, Judy, you could have gotten yourself killed."

"What was I supposed to do? Stand by and let them take Charles?"

"I think you touched on it right there," Bartlett said. "From the way you've described things, it sounds like a botched kidnapping."

"Yeah, that's what I thought, too, but if that was it, then why not grab both of us? That way they would have had two hostages instead of one. More money that way."

"Maybe it was too much trouble. You said there were only three guys . . . the two who jumped you, plus the driver. They would have had trouble controlling both of you, especially if they were unarmed, and if they had to grab one or the other, they would have done better—"

"That doesn't make sense either," Peter said. "Given the choice between a white American female and a black Dominican male, which one would have gotten them a higher ransom?" He glanced at Charles. "Sorry if that sounds racist, but that's the way it seems to me."

Charles shook his head, but said nothing. He gazed pensively at his folded hands on the tabletop. "I'd agree if it was random kidnapping," Judith countered, "but it wasn't like they just happened to be driving past, saw us on the sidewalk, and decided right then and there to grab someone. We were on the street only a minute or so when it happened. That makes me think they were waiting for us to leave Charles's house . . ."

"Then why didn't they make their move as soon as we were outside my front gate?" Charles asked, still not looking up.

"You remember what happened when we got back to

your place. Mary said she hadn't seen or heard anything.
I bet—"

"Who's Mary?" Bartlett asked.

"Mary Bond, my housekeeper. But she doesn't sit at
the window all day, waiting to see if someone's going to
get kidnapped." Low chuckles from around the table. "If
I know Mary, she probably changing the bedsheets as
soon as we left."

"But they wouldn't have known that," Judith said,
"even if they had been planning this in advance. All they
would have known was that Mary was there, and that she
could have been a reliable witness when the police arrived. So they waited until we were further down the
block before they tried to make the snatch."

"Which brings us back to square one," Peter said.
"Why grab Charles and not you?"

"Charles is well known. He's . . ." Judith glanced apologetically at her mentor. "Okay, let's face it . . . he's one
of the wealthiest men on the island. From what I saw,
he's as famous as the president or one of the local hip-
hop stars. And he lives right in the middle of Roseau and
doesn't have any bodyguards."

"Never thought it was important to hire any." There
was a trace of irony in Charles's voice. "Believe me, I've
never felt any reason to distrust my fellow countrymen.
It isn't as if I live in America, you know."

Bartlett coughed uncomfortably. "Charles, those guys
were your fellow countrymen," Judith said in a low
voice. "You can't claim they were Haitians or black
Puerto Ricans. I saw them up close, heard them speak.
They used patois. Like it or not, they were—"

The door opened, and everyone looked up as Andie
came in, bearing an armload of Cokes. She stopped and
looked around the room. "Uh . . . don't let me stop you
guys. Did I miss something important?"

"Nothing really," Peter said. "We were just talking." He glanced around the table at the others, and everyone silently nodded. No sense is letting Andie know that her aunt had almost been abducted in Dominica this morning. At least not yet. "Thanks for the drinks."

"No problemo, señor." She grunted as she bent down to unload the cold soda cans in front of Bartlett. "I hope nobody wanted anything else except Coke, but I had to guess, so . . ."

"Coke's fine, thank you." Peter reached forward and snagged a can rolling down the tabletop. "Did you see your friend Leslie while you were gone?"

"Um . . . matter of fact, yeah. I did." There was an uncertain hesitancy in her voice. "To tell the truth, she's right outside."

Stone silence. Everyone glanced at each other. "Right outside?" Bartlett asked. "What do you mean?"

"Uh . . . I found her outside the door when I came back. She wasn't there when I left, but she was hanging out when I came back." Andie handed Cokes to Joe, Charles, and Judith. "She asked me to ask you if it was okay for her to come in."

"Aw, shit," Peter muttered.

"Who is this woman?" Joe Niedzwiecki asked in a low voice.

Bartlett pushed back his chair. "Let me handle this. It's time we established some ground rules."

He had just stood up when Leslie Sun appeared in the door. "Don't blame Andie," she said. "It was my idea. Sorry."

No one said anything for a moment.

"Nobody's blaming her," Miles said. "You're the one we've got a problem with."

"Look, I promise you, I haven't been eavesdropping, if that's what's bothering you." Her attitude had become more demure; standing just outside the room, she looked like a wallflower scorned on the dance floor. "I just got here a couple of minutes ago. I've been waiting for someone to come out so I could ask what's going on."

Joe made a flatulent noise with his lips. "I'll be only too happy to do so later," Bartlett said, sitting down again, "but this is an executive meeting. You'll have to wait until—"

Peter raised a hand. "Just a moment," he said, then he looked at Leslie. "Ms. Sun, why is it so important that you know everything that goes on here?"

"Because I—" She stopped, took a deep breath. "Look, I've been assigned to write a major article about Tethys . . . its purpose, the people who work here, the challenges they have to meet, so forth and so on. I can't do that with a handful of press releases. My editors want me right in the middle of things. If I go back with only a few interviews and some notes from a walk-around tour . . ."

"You'll lose your job?" Peter asked.

She shook her head. "I'm a freelancer, so they can't fire me per se. What they will do is pay me a kill fee, then reassign the story to a staff writer. But they won't let the story go, and I don't think they'll be very sympathetic when they learn that you haven't cooperated."

"That sounds like extortion," Bartlett growled.

"I'm sorry if it seems that way, but try to look at it from my side. Your company agreed to let *Millennium* send a writer—me—out here for the express purpose of researching an in-depth piece. Everyone knew in advance that I was coming, and what I was going to be doing once I got here." She shrugged. "So what happens? My interview with you happens an hour late, and gets interrupted after barely thirty minutes. I'm denied access to almost every place except the commissary, and when I

try to ask straight questions, I'm either stonewalled or
given vague answers."

"And then we find you lurking outside . . ."

"I wasn't lurking anywhere, Mr. Bartlett." She turned
to Andie. "Andie, when you found me out here, where
exactly was I? Did I have my ear pressed up against the
door?"

"No . . . no, you didn't," Andie said quietly. "She . . .
I mean, you were leaning against the wall about five, ten
feet away."

Leslie reached into her bag, pulled out her minirecorder. "Did I have this in my hand?" Andie shook her head.
Leslie extended the recorder to Bartlett. "If you want, you
can rewind the tape and listen to it yourself. You'll find
nothing on it except our interview. That should settle the
question of whether I was eavesdropping."

Now it was Bartlett's turn to look embarrassed. "I
didn't mean to imply that you were."

"Yes, you did." Leslie's voice remained even. " I don't
blame you for wondering, though. I was in the wrong
place at the wrong time, and I apologize for that. But if
I'm going to do my job right, then I'm going to need to
get you to trust me. Otherwise, you can put me on the
next flight back to the mainland, and I'll have to tell my
editors what happened here. So it's your call."

The room was very quiet for a few moments. Bartlett
leaned back in his chair and absently touched a forefinger
to his lips, then looked at the others, posing a silent question. Peter nodded; so did Charles, after a guarded moment. Judith hesitated, then reluctantly nodded as well.
Only Joe Niedzwiecki shook his head; Andie apparently
realized that her own status was slippery, because she
didn't offer an opinion either way.

Bartlett let out his breath. "Okay, you're in, on two
conditions." He held up a finger. "First, everything you

see or hear in this room is strictly off-the-record. That means no notes, no tape recordings. Understand?"

Leslie nodded. "Good. Second, if you want anything from any of us—an interview, say, or to be shown someplace, or anything like that—you ask permission first. No skulking around, no shadowing my people. Understand?"

"I wouldn't have it any other way."

"Glad to hear it, because I won't either. Those are the ground rules. Break 'em, and I'll throw you over the rail, and toss you a life preserver if I'm feeling generous." Leslie nodded again, and Bartlett motioned to an empty chair. "Okay, you can come in now. Have a seat."

"Thank you." Leslie meekly walked into the conference room and took the chair Bartlett had indicated. She pointedly placed her bag on the floor behind her where everyone could see it, then smiled to the people seated around her. Judith noticed that her gaze lingered upon Peter for a few extra moments.

Bartlett got up to close the door. "Okay, people," he said, "let's get onto the next order of business. Joe, you're on. Tell us what happened this morning."

Joe winced as he sat up a little straighter in his chair. "Well, okay, here's how it is. I took *Doris* down to the plateau, past Stetson Mesa about a hundred miles due west from here . . ."

The first image they saw was nebulous and indistinct: a horizontal blur of mottled gray against dark black, with off-white specks floating in the background. It could have been almost anything—a thumb pressed against the lens, a squid passing too close to the camera, a UFO—but it made Joe sit bolt upright in his chair.

"There it is!" he shouted. "There's the fucker!"

A couple of polite coughs from Peter and Miles.

"Sorry, ladies," Joe said from the other side of the table. "Don't mean to be crude."

"That's okay." Judith peered at the digital frame projected on the flatscreen rolled down from the ceiling on the far side of the darkened conference room. "Uh . . . what are we looking at, exactly?"

"That's the sucker that attacked my boat." Joe said this as if it was obvious.

Peter closely studied the image. "Joe, that could be . . . I dunno, a basking shark, a reflection on the porthole, some sort of afterimage . . ."

"Let's try the next shot." Bartlett touched a stud on the remote in his hand, and the DVD deck beneath the flatscreen flashed to the next image on the disk.

Again, the same gray blur, only slightly different this time. The digital frame counter at the bottom of the screen showed that this shot had been taken only a second later. "There it is again!" Joe exclaimed. "You see it this time?"

"I don't see shit," Andie muttered.

Peter snorted behind his hand. "Try the next one," Judith suggested.

The next shot was nearly identical to the first two, save for the shape and size of the blur. Now it seemed just a little smaller, the area of darkness surrounding it a few inches larger. This time Joe wisely stayed quiet.

"Let's go forward a few more frames," Bartlett said.

The next several images whisked past them on the screen as time-lapse photos, each taken a full second later than the last. Had this been a motion-picture film, each elapsed second would have held twenty frames, but since *Doris*'s onboard camera was capable of photographing only one frame per second while in autofocus mode, the result was much akin to an old-style kinematograph, an effect increased by the flat, greenish-gray monotones of each frame.

As the object became smaller, though, its details also seemed to become sharper. After ten frames, it was no longer blurred. Now they could see that it was an elongated, tubular mass, rather like an elephant's trunk except much wider.

"Slow it down," Charles murmured. Bartlett touched the remote again, returning to manual select. In the eleventh frame, they could make out one of the RMS arms in the foreground. "Look at that," Charles said, pointing to a shadow of its claw cast upon the object by the searchlight beams. "It has to be at least six feet in diameter."

"That's not all." Judith stood up, walked closer to the screen. "See that?" she said, pointing to a sharp edge on the object's upper surface. "What does that look like to you?"

Charles got out of his seat to inspect the image more closely. "It seems to be . . . it looks like a dorsal fin."

"That's what I see, too," she said quietly. "Next frame."

The next picture was almost the same, except that the fin was more distinct, and the left end of the object—or creature, whatever it might be—seemed to be tapering down. "Could it be an oarfish?" Charles murmured.

"A what?" Andie asked.

"An oarfish. *Regalecus glesne*. A very rare species, sometimes seen in tropical waters . . . but very seldom, and never around here." Judith shook her head. "They can grow up to fifty feet, so it's about the right size, but they dive down to only about six hundred feet, and their dorsal fins don't look like that." She glanced at Joe. "Besides, they're very shy. Only two or three times have they ever been photographed alive. I've never heard of one attacking a boat."

"I guess you believe me now," Joe said, rather smugly.

"Belief was never an issue," Bartlett said. "Okay, next shot . . ."

He clicked the remote again, and everyone in the room gasped, for there on the screen, half in the shadow of the RMS claw but distinct nevertheless, was the creature.

"Holy shit," Andie murmured. Caught in profile, it had a sharp, almost angular snout above a long, fleshy mouth, its jaws lined with dagger-shaped teeth. A single black and unreflective eye, set deep within the side of its almost iguanalike skull, seemed to regard the camera with dark malevolence. It didn't appear to have any gills, but they could see the beginning of its dorsal fin along the top of its skull.

"Goddamn!" Peter exclaimed. "It's a moray!"

"Can't be!" Judith snapped. "Moray eels don't grow this big, and they live in reefs, near the surface! That's not a moray."

"Well, that's sure as hell what it looks like!"

"Ease down!" Bartlett yelled. "Both of you, put a lid on it!"

"Whatever it is," Joe said, "it's the same bastard that nearly killed me this morning."

Everyone looked his way. They were only studying pictures, after all; he had seen this thing close up. "I agree with Peter," Charles said quietly. "And with you, Judith. Yes, it's definitely an eel, but no, it can't be a moray."

"Maybe it's Godzilla," Andie said. "Y'know, a giant, radioactive moray." She hesitated. "What's a moray?"

That broke the tension. Everyone laughed out loud. "So you're saying it may be a sea serpent," Leslie Sun said, then darted a glance at Bartlett. "Off the record, that is."

"Not strictly speaking, no," Judith said. "Eels and serpents are different species entirely. But in generic terms . . . yes, you're looking at a sea serpent." She couldn't take her eyes off the screen. "I've been looking for this baby all my life," she added softly.

Everyone was quiet for a moment, then Charles politely cleared his throat. "There's only one problem," he said. "Eels live in reefs. This thing was nearly 2,500 feet down."

Judith let out her breath. "I can explain that, but . . . look, I've got some ideas, but not any hard evidence." She pointed at the screen. "Not until now. Not until this. We need to send a sub back down there. Whatever this thing is, we might be able to find it again."

"Okay," Bartlett said. "We'll see what we can do."

"Miles, c'mon . . ."

"Judy, I know this is important, but . . ." He sighed and rubbed his eyelids. "Look, I've got more important things to worry about right now. The suits have been crawling my ass all afternoon, wanting to know what happened to *Doris*—"

"Show 'em the pictures!" Joe yelled. "Send 'em the disk, let me tell them what happened . . . bing, bang, boom, case closed! What do they want, *Eyewitness News*?"

"That's what I'm afraid of," Judith said. She glanced across the room at Leslie Sun; the other woman pretended not to notice.

"They could say that we faked it," Peter said quietly. "I've tried to protect this thing as much as possible, but the fact of the matter is, there's nothing here that couldn't be done with a good CGI program."

"Exactly," Judith said. "Which is why we need to send

down another sub. I mean, if even we didn't spot this thing again, there might be something in the wreckage which would help substantiate Joe's story."

"Fuckin' A," Joe muttered.

"Couldn't we put in a request for the *Galatea*?" Peter asked.

Everyone looked at him sharply. The *Galatea* was a nuclear research sub, capable of traveling nonstop across the Atlantic without surface support ships and descending to ten thousand feet. Built a few years ago by Yemaya as an advancement upon the Navy's NR-1, the company frequently made it available to oceanographic research institutions.

Bartlett shook his head. "I don't think so. It's still on loan to WHOI." He pronounced it as *whooey*. "It was making a dive off the Georges Bank, last time I checked."

"It returned to Jacksonville last week," Peter said, "and isn't due to ship out again until late this month, for a Navy salvage operation. And it's supposed to be our boat, after all . . . the company just rents it out."

"Right." Miles folded his arms. "And what am I supposed to tell the front office? We want the *Galatea* to go hunting for sea serpents? I don't think so."

Judith opened her mouth, then closed it again. Like it or not, Miles was right. No one said anything for a moment.

"Actually, there's another reason," Charles said.

He reached into his jacket, pulled out a folded sheet of paper, spread it out, and passed it across the table to Bartlett. "That's new SOSUS data I received this morning, just before . . . um, before we left Dominica. It appears that a new hot vent has erupted in the Mid-Atlantic Ridge, just south of the Azores."

Bartlett pulled a pair of reading glasses out of his shirt pocket as he leaned forward to examine the printout. He whistled low under his breath, then picked up the sheet to look at more closely. "A new vent? And it's not the Lucky Strike?"

The Lucky Strike was a vast field of hot vents discovered on the Mid-Atlantic Ridge by Woods Hole; since the mid-eighties, it had been extensively explored by American, French, and Russian deep-ocean submersibles. "I haven't completely analyzed the data yet," Charles said, "but no, I don't believe so. It appears to lie somewhere in the central rift valley between Lucky Strike and Broken Spur."

"Think it's a smoker?"

"I'd say the possibility is quite large, but we cannot possibly know until we go out there." Charles pointed at the printout. "But if we know about this from SOSUS, then there's no doubt in my mind someone else does as well."

With the exception of Andie Lipscomb and possibly Leslie Sun, everyone in the room knew what he meant by that remark. Yemaya wasn't the only company interested in harvesting hyperthermophiles from black smokers, and since this particular region of the Mid-Atlantic Ridge lay beyond any of the economic zones claimed by France or Portugal, it was legally a no-man's-land; any company in the world was free to explore it as the first move toward deep-ocean bioprospecting. And if new taq life-forms were discovered down there, the payoff was potentially worth billions of dollars. It was all a matter of who would reach the new vent first.

"Yeah, that might be a reason to put in a priority request for the *Galatea.*" Bartlett absently ran a finger down the printout. "And, of course, since it's on the way, there's always a chance you might make a quick detour to the *Doris,* just to see if there's anything of interest."

"I was thinking the same thing myself," Charles replied. Judith was hardly able to disguise the smile on her face.

"We'll cross that bridge when, and if, we get there." Miles took off his glasses and leaned back in his chair. "It'll be a tough sell, I kid thee not . . . but I can talk to the company, see what they have to say." He looked around the table. "I'm sure everyone wants dinner as much as I do. Anyone else have any new business?"

Peter raised a hand. "Who's going down, and when?"

"Bottomside?" Bartlett carefully tucked away his glasses. "Judith, Charles, you have business down there, of course. We've already got bunks reserved for both of you. Peter, you can go, too, if you want to."

"I can take"—he coughed in his hand—"y'know, my side project . . . it's scheduled for another round of low-depth tests." He meant the Barracuda. With Leslie Sun in the room, it wasn't wise to be openly discussing its existence.

"Of course," Bartlett said, nodding in agreement. "And I'm sure you want to spend some time with Judy." He looked at Niedzwiecki. "Joe, needless to say, I'm grounding you topside, at least until those ribs heal."

"Not if you're sending down the *Galatea*, you're not," Joe said. "I'm the only guy here who's Navy certified for it."

"And you're not the only DSV driver, either." Bartlett held up a hand before Joe could argue further. "We'll hash this out later. Besides, we don't have a ride yet, so until we do it's a moot point." He turned to Andie and Leslie. "Ladies, my guess is that neither of you are PADI-certified."

"Pardon me," Leslie said, "but I am." She smiled when Bartlett registered surprise. "I can show you my card, if you don't believe me."

She started to reach for her bag, but Bartlett shook his

head. "That's okay, I'll trust you on that score. The question is, will you continue to behave yourself? That is to say, would you be willing to abide by the same terms of our agreement?"

"I can do that, yes."

"Good. I'm going to hold you to that." Bartlett looked at Peter again. "Would you be willing to shepherd Ms. Sun for the next few days?" Peter nodded. Judith said nothing, but there was a dark look on her face. "Okay, then, you've got permission to go down." Miles acknowledged Leslie's smile with a brisk nod, then turned to Andie. "So that leaves you, Ms. Lipscomb."

"Andie," she corrected him.

"Andie . . . Andie, you've got as much business going below as a tadpole at a roller derby. No PADI card, no previous experience. The first doesn't matter, realistically speaking, so long as you don't put on diving gear . . . but the second does. I'd have to be crazy to let you go down."

"I understand, sure." Andie meekly stared into her lap. "I guess I can find something to do here for a few days."

"Miles, c'mon . . ." Peter began.

Bartlett held up a hand. "On the other hand, your aunt and uncle have applied to the company for you to spend some time aboard as a student researcher, and your aunt wanted you to assist her in her work." He grinned. "Hell, I wouldn't be where I am today if my father hadn't smuggled me aboard his ship when he was in the Royal Canadian Navy. So here's the deal . . . if you still want to, you can go below with your aunt and uncle, with the understanding that you do everything they tell you to do, and nothing that they tell you not to do. You don't behave yourself and I hear about it, you'll be back up here quick as a whistle, and I'll have the TV removed from the hyperbaric chamber before you arrive. Understood?"

Andie hastily nodded. "Sure. Anything you say. Rock on . . ."

"Not so fast. It's a very different world down there. A lot of things you take for granted—"

"I told her already," Peter said. "She knows."

"Just so she knows. Okay, kid, you're on." Bartlett glanced at his watch, then pushed back his chair. "Now let's go get dinner before the gravy turns cold. Everyone eat and bunk out. Next boat leaves at 0700 tomorrow morning."

SECOND DAY

SUNDAY, JUNE 5, 2011

SEVEN
Descent

6.5.11—0658 EST

A high-pressure system had drifted over northern Florida during the night, pushing ahead of it banks of towering cumulus clouds; by early morning the sky was the color of slate, the sea whitecapped and choppy. In a couple of hours the patchy fog which lay over the water would gradually dissipate, but for now the floating dock below the station was shrouded in thick, humid mists.

Judith stood at the end of the dock, watching as the boat crew loaded the last few plastic supply crates through the open hatch of the shuttle sub. It bobbed next to the dock like a misplaced storage tank, its yellow-striped hull the only trace of color in the gray, dismal morning. The paper cup of coffee in her hands warmed her more than the oversized sweatshirt she had borrowed from Peter; there was an unseasonable chill in the air that reminded her more of New England than Florida, and although she hadn't bothered to check the daily meteorological report, the reddish tint on the horizon and the dull snap she felt in the back of her throat when she swallowed were as reliable indicators as any barometer reading. A storm was coming.

"Penny for your thoughts?"

She turned, found Charles Toussaint standing behind her. He had on the same sport coat he had worn yesterday when they left Dominica, but this time over a T-shirt and a pair of jeans. Like her, he had been counting on more summerlike weather. "Only that I'll be glad when we've gone below," she replied.

He shrugged offhandedly. "Give it a few days, and you'll take even this."

"Maybe so, but not now." She took another sip from her coffee, then impatiently glanced toward the stairs leading down from the station's lowermost platform. "Where the hell is she?"

"You're expecting a teenager to be on time?" Charles tucked his hands in his coat pockets. "No wonder you and Peter don't have—" He caught himself and stopped. "Sorry."

Judith nodded silently and looked away. Three years ago she and Peter tried to have a child, but she miscarried a few weeks into her first trimester, and that was the end of that. Probably just as well; the nomadic nature of their careers didn't give them the liberty of even owning a dog as a surrogate child. Perhaps they might try again, one day, when their jobs didn't—

"We're ready to go here." Alan Hughes, the submersible's pilot, appeared waist-up within the open hatch. "Have you got your people together?"

Doc was there, of course, and so was Leslie Sun. In fact, she had arrived before anyone else, as if afraid that being late would provide someone with an excuse to leave her behind. She had just handed her flight bag and laptop computer to one of the boat bums, who took the opportunity to be overly courteous, just in case she remembered him seven days later when she emerged from the hyperbaric chamber. God, Judith hated women who managed to look good under any circumstances; casually dressed in a knit sweater—how did she know it was going to get cold?—designer jeans, and North Face hiking boots, her straight black hair carefully tied back, she could have posed for a fashion spread in her own magazine.

But that wasn't all there was to it, was it? Judith couldn't quite put her finger on it, but there was something about Leslie Sun which she instinctively didn't like. Not that the other woman hadn't bent over backward to ingratiate herself with the rest of her family. Last night over dinner, she had spent a considerable amount of time chatting up Andie, asking her all about the journalism classes she was taking in school, until little by little the kid warmed up to her. And the looks she kept giving Peter . . .

"We're still waiting for someone," Judith called back. "My niece. She's supposed to be here."

Hughes glanced at his watch. "Five minutes after the hour, Judy. I've got a schedule to keep."

Leslie Sun turned away from the sub. "Would you like for me to go find her, Dr. Lipscomb?" she asked, perhaps just a little too helpfully. "She was in the next room last night."

"No, thanks, that's okay. I'll go." Judith tossed the rest of her coffee into the water and began walking down the pier, then stopped when she heard rapid footfalls on the metal stairs. She couldn't make out their source through the sullen fog, but she heard a low voice in harmony with each step.

"Shit, shit, shit, shit, shit . . ."

"Hark!" Charles exclaimed. "I hear the morning call

of *Adolescentus americanus*... the Wild American
Teenager in full flight!"

The boat crew laughed and Judith gave him a foul
look, then Andie's sneakers hit the bottom step and she
emerged from the fog, charging down the pier with little
attention paid to the slippery condition of the planks.
"I'm sorry, I'm sorry, I'm sorry," she gasped. "I woke
up late, and then I had to take a shower and put on my
clothes, and then I went to get some coffee . . . and then
I went back to get . . . and then I couldn't find—"

"Okay, all right. Slow down, take it easy." Judith
stopped her before she slipped and fell off the pier. Typical teenager, sure enough; not only was Andie late, but
she was also inappropriately dressed. Wearing cutoffs
and a *Simpsons* T-shirt over a bikini bra, she looked as
if she was ready for a day at the beach. "Aren't you
cold?" she asked.

"Um . . . yeah, I guess." Her chest rose and fell as she
let the straps of her duffel bag and camera case slide off
her shoulders. "I was just afraid . . . I thought you were
going to . . . leave me . . . and I didn't want to—"

"Calm down. Nobody's going anywhere." Judith
glanced over her shoulder at Hughes. The pilot had his
chin propped in his left hand as he impatiently drummed
the hull of his sub with the fingers of his right. She raised
a hand, silently begging his indulgence for another minute or two; his eyes rolled up, but he said nothing. "Let's
see if you've got something warm in here."

She knelt down and started to unzip Andie's bag. "No,
really, that's okay," Andie said, even as she rubbed her
hands across her goose-pimpled shoulders. "I'm fine, really . . ."

"Maybe we can find a long-sleeve shirt." The bag
wasn't packed so much as it was stuffed; everything inside looked as if it had been wadded together at the last

minute. Shorts, T-shirts, jeans, more shorts, underwear, two or three different swimsuits . . . "Well, you're not taking this," Judith said, pulling out of tube of toothpaste and tossing it on the dock. "Or this either," she added as she fished out a spray can of mousse and a plastic bottle of shaving gel. "And this has definitely got to go," she continued, contributing sunscreen to the pile.

"Hey, I'm going to need those!"

"Not where you're going, you're not. No sun down there, so you won't need sunscreen." Judith picked up the toothpaste. "As for this . . . we're sending you down to ten atmospheres. Want to see what happens to this under high pressure?" She flicked off the top with her thumb, then clenched the tube within her fist. Blue-white toothpaste jetted out of its top. Judith wiped off her knuckles on the knees of her jeans before she picked up the mousse can. "This is worse . . . aerosol cans explode like cherry bombs." She added it to the pile, then held up the shaving gel. "This won't, because it's not under pressure, but it'll squirt all over the inside of your bag and make a mess. Besides, when was the last time you shaved your legs?"

"Uh . . . yesterday morning."

"Then you're okay for the next week or so. Body and facial hair grow very slowly in high-pressure environments. You won't need it. Now, anything else you want to show me?"

Irritated, Andie dug into her bag and pulled out a couple of cellophane bags of cocktail peanuts she had taken off the plane from Kansas City. "Are these going to blow up, too?" she asked sarcastically.

Judith smiled. "No, but . . . well, go ahead and take 'em. You'll see." She found an oversize Royals sweatshirt and tossed it to her, then zipped the bag shut again.

"We've got everything you'll need down there. C'mon, now. We're holding up the boat."

She picked up Andie's bag and carried it to the gangway, where it was passed hand to hand among the boat bums until it was loaded into the sub. The men climbed off the vessel, save for one seaman wearing a wet suit, snorkel mask, and fins who waited next to the open hatch. "Okay, we're ready," he called down to the pier. "Right foot first when you step aboard, please."

Andie gave Judith a querying look. "Old tradition," she murmured. "Don't ask, just do it."

"At least no one here has red hair," Charles said as he gallantly stepped aside to allow the women to go first. "That's considered bad luck as well."

"But if anyone cares to go aboard naked," said one of the crewmen standing ready near the guy ropes, "I'm sure we won't object."

That brought laughter from the other sailors and a withering glare from Leslie as she stepped onto the gangway. "Funny, guys," Judith said sourly. "Real funny."

Andie, though, wasn't about to let them have the last laugh. She turned to the boat bums just as she set foot on the gangway, gave them a lascivious smile, then grabbed the bottom of her T-shirt and yanked it up. The quick flash of a well-fed bikini top made their eyes grow wide. They hooted in glee, then Andie dropped her shirt, smirked, and flipped the heel of her palm beneath her chin.

"Dream on!" she yelled back. "That's the best you'll ever get!"

The men were still groaning as Judith hastened her across the gangway. Leslie was laughing so hard, she slipped and almost fell off the sub before the diver caught her. "Six points for class, eight for delivery, ten for style!" she shouted. "Girl, you go!"

"That was . . . exceptional," Charles said quietly, grinning as he brought up the rear.

Great, Judith silently fumed as she watched her niece high-five the journalist. This is going to be a long week.

The sub's interior was no larger than that of a minibus and far less comfortable. They sat close together in tube-frame sling chairs which folded down from the cylindrical bulkhead, the tops of their heads nearly touching the riveted ceiling, their baggage jammed within nylon nets in the rear of the compartment. It was like climbing into a giant beer can, and as almost as cold.

"Everyone comfortable?" Hughes ignored the grunts and mutters which answered that question as he reached up to secure the hatch and twist its lock wheel. "Okay, then we're off."

"Aren't there any seat belts?" Andie groped around Judith's left knee, searching for a safety strap. Across from her, Leslie was doing the same, while Charles sat silently, arms tightly crossed above his chest.

"Don't need 'em." The pilot banged the back of his fist twice against the bottom of the hatch, signaling to the seaman still squatting on top of the sub that the hatch was secure from his end. He waited until he heard two dull knocks on the other side of the hull, then he bent his head and shoulders and brushed past Judith and Charles. "Going down's so smooth, you'll swear you're on an elevator."

The cockpit was only slightly less cramped than the aft end of the compartment, but its forward port made it seem far more spacious. The shuttle's bow was a transparent hemisphere composed of eight pie wedges of two-inch acrylic glass sealed together by narrow strips of aluminum alloy. Through the window, they saw a split image: the top half, cloudy sky above the floating dock; the bottom half, blue water, with the pressurized barrels supporting the dock magnified by several degrees.

"If anyone here's claustrophobic, now's the time to say so." Hughes settled into the low-slung pilot's seat; he glanced over his shoulder at his passengers as he pulled on a headset. "No? All right, then, time to roll." He turned to the console positioned in front of his knees, turned a knob. "Tethys one-ten, this is DSV two-zip-two. Hatch sealed, ready to flood tanks. Request permission to descend, over."

Leslie fidgeted nervously. Judith peered at her. "You okay there?" she asked quietly.

"Sure. I'm fine." But her mouth was taut, her knees trembling slightly.

Charles noticed as well. He shared a quick glance with Judith. "It's easy," he said softly to the journalist. "I've done this a dozen times. Just relax. Enjoy the ride."

There was a loud hiss within the compartment. "What's he doing now?" Andie asked. There was more curiosity in her eyes than alarm.

"Bringing up the internal pressure a few millibars to stop any hull leaks. You may hear your ears pop a little, but don't worry . . . we'll remain at one atmosphere all the way down, until we reach the hab." He dug into his shirt pocket, pulled out a pack of Juicy Fruit. "Want some? Helps a little."

Andie pulled a stick out of the pack; after a moment, so did Leslie. "Roger that, one-ten," Hughes said. "Thank you. Lines off. DSV two-zip-two beginning descent."

They heard a faint gurgle from deep within the hull, as if they were within a bottle slowly taking on water. "That's the ballast tanks opening," Charles said, putting the gum pack back in his pocket as they felt a slight jar.

"The diver's just jumped off," he added. "Look, there he is."

Through the forward port, they could see the seaman who had helped them aboard. The sub was completely immersed now; he swam just ahead of them, kicking the water with his fins as he peered through the cockpit at them. Bubbles rose from his snorkel as he glanced either way, then he raised a hand and gave Hughes an okay sign before he swam upward.

"That's it?" Andie asked. "That's all there is to it?"

"It gets a little more complicated after this," Judith said, "but that's all you have to worry about right now. We're going down."

For the first eighty feet, the sub descended alongside Tethys 1. Hughes used the sub's thrusters to avoid the massive flotation tanks arranged along the vast hull below the waterline, then moved outward a little more as they passed the OTEC discharge valve. Schools of small fish, silhouetted by spotlights ringed around the hull, haunted the warm water bubbling from the valve, scurried away as the sub approached them. Then the lower hull disappeared entirely, and the view through the forward port became progressively darker as the sub slowly fell downward, passing from translucent aquamarine to dark blue. All they heard was the rhythmic ping of sonar, the gentle thrum of the props.

"Let's throw a little light on the subject," the pilot said, and reached up to snap a couple of switches on the ceiling console. Floodlights on either side of the port flashed on; through the blue haze, they saw a taut vertical cable only a couple of dozen yards away, tangled with gossamer strands of seaweed, encrusted with the tiny shells of zebra mussels.

"That's one of the mooring cables." Hughes gently pulled back the left plane control next to his thigh as he pushed the right one forward. "I'm going to take us down in a spiral so you can see everything as we go down."

Andie's forearm rested on Judith's knee as her niece leaned across her to get a better view. On the other side of the compartment, Leslie Sun was hastily jotting down notes. "What are those big pipes?" she asked. "Way back there, behind the cable?"

The lights caught four metal shafts, two as wide as the sub itself; they came out of the gloom like slender sky-scrapers. "The big ones belong to the OTEC plant," Hughes replied. "The one on the far right is the intake pipe . . . it runs all the way down past the habs to the edge of the shelf, and then goes further down to the Blake Plateau, where the cold water is. Pressure pumps the water up to the surface, where it enters the generator. The one on the far left is the freshwater pipe. After the water runs through the turbines and desalinators, what's left drains down to Tethys 2, so there's no shortage of drinking water."

Judith caught Charles's eye, and they gave each other a knowing smile. Bartlett must have informed Hughes that he would playing tour guide. "The two smaller ones are the snorkel—that brings in fresh air from the surface—and the main electrical conduit." Hughes orbited the pipes, carefully staying away from the mooring cables. "Bottomside depends on topside for just about everything . . . air, power, water, you name it."

"I thought Mr. Bartlett told me that Tethys was self-sufficient," Leslie said.

"Well, so it is," Charles said. "Everything we need to survive, we can get out here."

"What about food?" Andie asked, then corrected herself: "Oh, I get it . . . you do a lot of fishing."

"Yeah, well, sure, we eat a lot of seafood," Hughes replied, "but we still get stuff flown in from the beach. I think there's some prime rib in those crates back there." He chuckled to himself. "I like lobster, but you get pretty sick of them if you eat 'em all the time."

Not to mention that they're a protected species, Judith silently added, although the handful of Atlantic lobsters Tethys divers caught for their own consumption hardly put a dent in the population. Yet there was no sense in pointing that out; this was one bit of information Leslie Sun didn't need for her article.

As the submersible completed its orbit around the pipes, its lights caught a pair of narrow cables which slowly moved upward. "Oh, here's something you oughta see," Hughes said, then he carefully moved the sub until it was only forty feet away. The cables crawled past the them, then a large steel sphere came into view. Lights on its upper half illuminated its yellow checkerboard paint pattern and the narrow, cake-box-shaped structure attached to its bottom.

"That's one of the diving bells," the pilot explained. "We've got two. They're like . . ."

"Elevators to the surface," Andie said.

"That's right." The pilot glanced back at her. "Hey, you've done your homework. Go to the head of the class." Resenting the patronizing, Andie glared at him, but Hughes didn't seem to notice. "We don't normally transfer people down this way, only up, because they lead straight to the hyperbaric dorm topside. That's probably a dive crew heading home. When you leave, you'll go back this way, and spend about three days—"

"She's been told about this already," Judith interrupted. "Why don't you take us the rest of the way down, Al?"

"Okay, sure." Hughes pushed forward his yoke, and

the deck tilted forward slightly, just enough to roll a marble down the aisle if one was so inclined, as the forest of cables and pipes hove away from the glass cockpit.

Now they could only see deep, dense blue, broken only by bubbles and snowlike flecks of plankton. The outer hull creaked as the sub descended farther into the darkness. Judith felt her sinuses beginning to swell; she clasped her nostrils between a thumb and forefinger and gently blew her nose, and felt her head clear when her ears popped. Andie did the same, and grinned a moment later. The kid was catching on fast.

Down they fell, the laws of gravity and hydrostatic pressure compensated for by the sub's engines and atmospheric regulators, the sonar's echo return becoming less metronomic, steadily moving ever closer together. Judith didn't need to see the depth indicator to know that they were now beyond the limits of scuba divers from the surface; past 280 feet, even with pony bottles attached to an ascent line to allow for gradual decompression, no diver could safely rise from this dark, cold place. They had entered the realm of the shark and the octopus, the lobster and the crab. Davy Jones's locker, where a thousand undiscovered wrecks still lay hidden from sonar and lasers and satellites. Men and women were walking on the Moon again, and within a few years they would doubtless set foot on Mars, yet for all the miles of extraterrestrial territory soon to be explored, humankind had charted only a relative few inches beneath the oceans of their home world.

"Depth, forty-one-point-eight fathoms," Hughes said. "Range to bottom, twelve-point-eight and closing. Look sharp, we should be seeing the base about . . . ah, there we go."

Everyone craned their necks to peer over his shoulder. At first they saw nothing, save for an indistinct pale blue glow rising from the bottom. Then it slowly resolved itself into a broad *X*, with a large ring of white lights at its center and four smaller rings at the end of each leg. Red-and-blue fireflies, some larger than others, moved slowly around the cruciform as if transfixed by its light, while the pipes and cables leading down from the surface were backlit by its ethereal shine.

As the sub dropped farther, shapes and sizes became more apparent: a large, drum-shaped central habitat, about sixty feet wide and three stories in height, surrounded by four smaller cylinders, each about thirty feet in diameter and only slightly shorter. The smaller habs were connected to the central core by horizontal tubes suspended from overhead cables; all five habs were raised above the seafloor by thick steel girders sunk into concrete pilings. Light gleamed through thick circular portholes in the walls of the habitats like firelight through the windows of a lonely farmhouse on a moonless winter night.

"Looks like a keg surrounded by beer cans," said Andie. "Not that I know anything about that," she quickly added, glancing at her aunt.

"I should hope not," Judith murmured.

"Not even close," Hughes said. "The habs are made of concrete, not metal. They were built in dry dock in Savannah, towed out here one at a time, then sunk."

"Concrete floats?" Andie asked.

"Sure. Anything can float, so long as it's filled with enough air to give it buoyancy." He leveled off the submersible at two fathoms from the bottom and began to circle the habitats. "The real trick was getting them to all come down in exactly the right position. Like trying to drop a cement block from a thirty-story building and have it land on a dime. Here, let me show you the rest."

He steered away from the hab, began following a long

pipeline laid out across the seafloor. "There's the intake shaft again. It goes out about another half mile or so until it reaches the drop-off at the edge of the continental shelf, then"—he lifted his right hand from the elevator stick, flattened out his palm, then sharply dipped it down— "straight down the Florida-Hatteras Slope. About 5,800 feet to the bottom of the canyon. That was even more fun to build, believe me."

"You had people doing this?" Leslie asked.

He shook his head. "Naw. They used ROVs most of the time, except when things got hung up and they had to send a man down." He glanced over his shoulder at her and grinned. "Sometimes it was me. I could tell you some stories about that."

Judith raised a hand to hide her smile. Al was trying to find a way into Leslie's story. Probably imagined his face on the cover of *Millennium*. "Why does the ground . . . I mean, the . . . uh, whatever you call it . . . look so shiny?" Andie asked.

"I noticed that, too," Leslie asked. Indeed, large sections of the seafloor seemed to dully reflect the lights of the submersible as it passed over it.

"We've pegged down plastic sheets around the base," the pilot said. "We've got a lot of traffic passing through here, and when the silt gets stirred up, it tends to get in everything. This way we've stabilized the sea floor. Makes for cleaner working conditions."

"Doesn't that damage the environment?" Leslie asked. "I mean, wouldn't that kill a lot of bottom feeders?"

Judith and Charles cast each other sharp looks—what was she trying to get at?—but Hughes shrugged off-handedly. "Probably, but we've hardly covered a few acres with this stuff, and there's a lot of ocean left. You're from the Big Apple, aren't you?" She nodded, and he went on. "Well, you want to see severe environmental damage, go look at the New York Bight just off Long Island. That's where Manhattan's been dumping its garbage for the last hundred years or so."

Judith coughed in her hand to disguise her laughter. Good for Al. He might have just blown his chance to get in *Millennium,* but at least he had set the record straight. Leslie Sun wrote something in her notebook and said nothing.

"That's the manganese plant just ahead," Hughes said, pointing to a smaller ring of floodlights about fifty yards from the habs before he pulled back on the sticks. "Sorry I can't take you any closer, but we try to keep traffic to a minimum out this way. That's where we bring in the nodules we've brought up from the plateau and refine them before we send them to the surface."

"You have a lot of activity out here?" Leslie asked.

"Yes, ma'am. About three-fifths of the crew work here . . . six men each shift, six hours per shift, with four shifts a day, round the clock. It comes out to one shift on the clock, three off. Our rockhounds spend a month on the job, then get two off. Tough work, believe me."

"Who does this stuff?" Andie asked. "I mean, Jesus . . . who'd be crazy enough to live down here for a month?"

Leslie smiled like a shark catching the scent of chum in the water, and Judith put her hand over her eyes. Oh, Andie, that was a bad question . . .

But Hughes rescued the moment with a laugh. "I know, I know . . . you gotta be crazy to do this sort of thing, right? But, y'know, you ought to meet some of these guys. Some of 'em are ex–Navy divers who left the service a few years ago . . . like me, for instance . . . and some are guys who've been specially trained for this job, but it's the same thing, really. You do it for two or three years, earn some serious money and stash it away in the bank, then you get out and go do something else with your life. Buy a charter boat and take businessmen on fishing trips, or go back to school and earn a law degree. Start a little business of your own. Maybe send the kids through college. Something like that."

"Can you earn that much money doing this?" Leslie asked.

"Ms. Sun, not to be rude, but . . . how much did you earn last year? Before taxes, I mean."

She hesitated. "Forty thousand dollars."

Judith sensed that this was an exaggeration, but if Hughes did, he didn't show it. He brayed laughter. "Forty grand! Hell, lady, I earned twice that last year . . . and you can get three times that much if you're a rockhound for more than a year, once the bonuses and risers kick in."

"But with not as much risk," she said.

"Where do you live in New York?"

"Queens."

"Emilio's Deli still open?" he asked, and she dumbly nodded. "Grew up in Queens. Don't miss it much, to tell the truth. Got a nice place in Key Largo now."

Leslie opened her mouth. "Let it go," Judith said quietly, "unless you want to hear about his new sailboat."

The sub made a wide, semicircular turn and came back around toward the habitat. Hughes dropped altitude to less than a fathom; now they were skimming only a few feet above the ocean floor. As they approached Tethys 2, they saw a diver crouched on his knees directly in front of the central habitat, bubbles rising from his helmet as he waved a pair of fluorescent light sticks over his shoulders, guiding the sub into a broad opening between the support beams beneath the hab. Speaking quietly into his headset, Hughes gradually reversed prop as the main hab loomed before them, and allowed the sub to coast gently between the support beams as the diver kicked his legs and swam out of the way.

Then the hab passed directly above them. Crusted with barnacles, the concrete hull looked much older than it actually was. They caught a glimpse of the shark cage positioned beneath a wide opening in the hab's center, then they felt a hard thump as the sub mated with the docking collar protruding from the bottom of the hull.

"Okay, we're here," Hughes said. "Hope you enjoy your stay."

Andie let out her breath. " Now what?"

Judith stood up, careful not to bang her head on the ceiling. "Hope you brought a book," she said, then she remembered that she hadn't seen one while she was sorting through her niece's bag. "How are you at blackjack?"

"Uh . . . okay. Why do you ask?"

"Because you're going to be playing it for the next two and half hours."

EIGHT

Tethys 2

"C'mon, Charles," Andie begged. "One more time . . ."

"No." Arms stubbornly folded across his chest, Charles sat next to her on the folding cot and waited for the hatch to open. Through the hyperbaric chamber's small porthole, they could see a crewman standing just outside. "Absolutely not. It's beneath my dignity."

"Oh, c'mon," she pleaded, rocking back and forth on her knees. "Pleeeease? For me?"

Toussaint glanced at Judith. "Shouldn't we check the breathing mixture? I'm afraid the nitrogen levels may be too high."

Judith barely looked up from the pair of cards in her hand. "Hit me," she told Leslie, and hissed under her breath as the journalist drew a ten of clubs from the shoe and placed it faceup on the card table between them. "Down for the count," she said as she put a queen and a two of diamonds on the table. "The air's okay. I checked the trimix levels just a few minutes ago. It's not nitrogen narcosis you're dealing with . . . just a teenager."

"Just one more time . . . c'mon . . ."

Charles sighed, glanced again out the porthole. The crewman finished examining the gauges on the panel outside the chamber; he turned to the hatch and rapped on it twice, the customary signal that he was about to open up. "Very well, then, but only this last time. Ready?"

Andie nodded brightly, then reached up to pull off her wireless headset. "You don't have to do that, remember?" her aunt said as she picked up the cards and shuffled them. "Just say, 'Juan, Andie Lipscomb off-line.' "

"Right, right . . . Juan, Andie Lipscomb off line." Andie waited until she heard a double-beep through her headset. "Okay, I'm ready."

Charles closed his eyes. " 'Comrades, leave me here a little, while yet 'tis early morn . . . leave me here, and when you want me, sound upon the bugle-horn. . . .' "

Properly delivered in his eastern Caribbean accent, "Locksley Hall" should have been melodious and dramatic; in a trimix environment of helium, nitrogen, and oxygen, it sounded like Tennyson as recited by Donald Duck. When Charles had first done this while the chamber was being slowly pumped up to ten atmospheres, it had reduced Andie to a quivering, teary-eyed heap on the floor. Judith hastily shut down the valves to make sure that her niece wasn't suffering high-pressure nervous syndrome, but it wasn't HPNS at all; Andie simply thought it was the most hilarious thing she had ever heard.

" ' 'Tis the place, and all around it, as of old, the curlews call . . .' " Charles couldn't help but smile as the girl next to him rolled over on her back, holding her ribs as she giggled hysterically. Judith grinned as she watched Andie get her kicks. Leslie remained stoical; she took the cards from Judith's hand and tucked them into the frayed

Bicycle pack they had found on shelf next to the emergency manual.

" 'Dreary gleams the moorland flying over Locksley Hall,' and that's enough for you, young lady," he finished. "Juan, put Andie Lipscomb back on-line. Andie, can you hear me now?"

"Yeah, sure. Loud and clear." Andie was still chuckling as she caught her breath. "God, that's funny," she gasped, letting Charles help her sit up. "I won't ask you to do that again, I promise."

"If you do, it'll have to be from someone else," Charles said. "But I can safely guarantee that no one else aboard has memorized Alfred."

"Seriously, that's the last time," Judith warned. "You keep your headset on whenever you're not sleeping or in the shower, and when you're wearing it, you keep Juan online. Otherwise you won't understand anything people are saying. That's—"

"Rule number one. Gotcha."

Actually, there were much more important rules aboard Tethys 2, but keeping one's comlink active at all times was near the top of the list. Juan was the name given to the station's neural-net AI, so called because of the channel it occupied—one—on the cellular communications network hardwired through the habitats. One of Juan's primary functions was to filter out vocal distortions caused by the high helium content of the atmosphere; when someone was in a compartment with another person within the station, Juan would automatically detect their presence through the headsets everyone wore and feed their voices through a digital voice processor which removed the cartoonish effects helium rendered upon the vocal cords. This made everyone sound normal, more or less, although if they carefully watched each other's lips, they could detect the slightest half-second time delay between what was actually being spoken and what was being interpreted by Juan, much as if they were in a Japanese monster movie.

Judith had encountered Juan's first-generation prototype when she was at MIT, while it was still under development by the Artificial Intelligence Lab. Although Juan was nowhere near as sophisticated as the talking computers on *Star Trek* its designers tried to emulate, she was grateful to have the technology aboard Tethys 2, if only because it saved everyone the hassle of trying to understand exactly what the other guy was saying, a problem frequently encountered aboard early deep-water habitats like Sealab and Conshelf.

Yet it also meant that Juan was capable of tracking one's movements through the station; that was one subtle aspect of the system which Judith didn't relish. No matter where you were within the fifteen decks scattered among the five hab modules, if you were wearing a headset, Juan could always locate you. Only if you were diving off the station did you have any real assurance of privacy, and although you could voluntarily take yourself off-line, there was a well-known bug in the program—as Charles had just demonstrated—which allowed another user to put you back on the comlink, and even eavesdrop on you so long as you were both in the same compartment.

Judith pondered this as the crewman outside turned the lock wheel and pulled open the hatch. The system wasn't quite Orwellian enough to amount to electronic surveillance, yet nonetheless she always made a point of going off-line, say, when she was in the head, or sneaking a little quality time with Peter.

And speak of the devil . . .

"I was wondering when you'd get here." Peter folded shut the electronic book he had been reading while waiting for them outside the compression chamber. "How was the card game?"

Peter had left Tethys 1 a couple of hours before they had departed in order to bring down the Barracuda, so he had already cycled through. "Fine," Judith said, dropping her bag to give him a quick hug. "I think she cheats," she added as a whisper in his ear.

Behind them, Leslie Sun was pulling her bag and laptop computer from beneath her cot. When Andie finally got bored with blackjack, Judith had reluctantly taken up the game with the writer. Losing two out of every three hands to Leslie hadn't helped her mood very much, and despite sharing close quarters for the last two and half hours, neither woman had warmed to the other very much.

"Now, now," Peter murmured. "Don't be a sore loser." He stepped past Judith to help Andie out of the chamber. Although she had pulled on her sweatshirt, she was briskly rubbing her arms. "How you doing, tiger? Don't tell me you're cold."

"I'm freezing," she muttered through chattering teeth.

"It's the helium." Peter massaged her arms to warm her up. "Plus, you're in the wet room, so it tends to get a little drafty in here, so to speak."

Deck CC was the largest compartment within Tethys 2. Shaped like a large *D* with a flat bulkhead across from a semicircular wall, it had a low ceiling from which dangled pulley-mounted chains and grappling hooks. Scattered around the room were wetsuit lockers, racks of oxygen bottles, air compressors, shelves holding tools and spare machine parts. A cement tub of fresh water containing diving equipment lay next to a tile-floored shower stall. A large circular pool dominated the center of the compartment, floodlights beneath the surface lending it a rippling aquamarine glow. Seawater seemed to be dripping from everything, and the air tasted of salty brine.

"This is where we send the divers out. " Peter pointed to the moon pool. "Once they're suited up, they go out that way. Believe me, once you come back in, it feels warm as toast."

"It'd be a lot warmer if you'd heat the place," Andie griped.

"No point in it. We'd only lose it to the pool." He pointed to a man-sized hatch in the bulkhead across the compartment. "That's the minisub bay. If you think sitting in there was tough, you should have been where I was. Even after the water was pumped out, I had to wait in the sub until it was brought up to pressure before I could pop the hatch."

Leslie seemed to perk up her ears. "I understand you came down in an experimental sub. Mind if I see it?"

"Sorry, no can do." Peter looked a little uncomfortable. "It's something the company's developing for another client."

"Oh, c'mon. I can keep a secret." She cast him a sly wink, then started to walk toward the minisub bay. Peter started to reach for her, but Leslie was already out of reach. He was about to say something when the crewman who had opened the hyperbaric chamber stepped in front of her.

"Sorry, ma'am," he said, blocking her way. "If the chief says no . . ."

Leslie stopped, then turned to glare at Peter. "I mean it," he said solemnly. "Remember, you made a promise . . ."

"Nowhere without permission. Right." She sighed. "I hope this isn't going to be how everything goes the next few days."

You better believe it is, sweetheart, Judith thought,

smiling to herself. A little flirtation might be one thing, but letting a reporter get close to a classified Navy test program was quite another, and her husband wasn't about to cross that particular line. Score one for the home team.

"It won't," Peter said. "There's not too many secrets we keep down here . . . but that's one of them." He turned away to bend down and pick up Andie's camera case. "It's a little warmer upstairs," he said to his niece.

"God, I hope so." Andie hugged her shoulders as she followed Peter to a nearby ladder. "I'm freezing my little fanny off."

Gathering their bags, the others fell in behind them. Peter stepped aside to let Andie climb up first; he shoved her luggage up the manhole behind her, then waited for Leslie to reach the bottom of the ladder. "Let me take that," he said, reaching out to relieve Leslie of her flight bag. She smiled as she surrendered it to him, and caught a dark look from his wife.

"Knock yourself out," Judith murmured, and shouldered her own bag as she scaled the ladder.

The manhole led to a short, narrow corridor. The ceiling was lower than the one in the wet room, and crowded with pipes, conduits, and electrical fixtures, yet the bulkheads were lined with wafer-thin wood panels, the floor carpeted. The air was slightly warmer up here.

"Level CB." Peter closed the floor hatch, then rose and gestured down the corridor. "Middle level of C Hab. Here we've got the operations and communications, the operations manager's office, and the briefing room, along with access tunnels to the four adjunct habs." He placed a hand against a closed wall hatch next to the manhole. "This one leads to Tunnel B, which takes you to Hab 2.

If you go further down the corridor, you'll find the tunnels to—"

Charles politely cleared his throat. "Pardon me, but I believe this where I'll leave the tour." He nodded toward Tunnel B. " I think my business is this way."

"I think I'll join you." Judith pushed past her husband, all but carelessly allowing the bag under her shoulder to swing into his midriff. "There's stuff in my lab I want to check out." She paused at the hatch to look back over her shoulder. "Do you know where we're bunked?"

"I think we're in 3B," Peter said. "These two are in 1A. Or at least that's what Jared told me."

"Okay. See you there later." She pushed down the hatch lever and pulled it open. "Be good," she added as Charles ducked through the opening, then she followed him.

Peter pushed the hatch shut behind her, then turned back to his charges. Leslie seemed to be giving the ceiling work a close examination. "What's different about 1A?" Andie asked.

What the hell was Judith's problem? Sure, yesterday had been an ordeal for her, what with the attack on her and Charles in Roseau. But she sure was being bitchy about—

"Uncle Pete? What's—?"

"VIP quarters," he replied. "We keep it open for visitors. Company reps, university scientists, that sort of thing." He picked up Andie's camera case again. "C'mon, I'll show you."

He led past the control room to the entrance to Tunnel A. "Whenever you go through one of these things," he said as he opened the hatch and ducked his head to step through, "it means you're entering a watertight compartment. All the habs are designed to operate independently in case of an emergency, but that'll only work if the hatches are closed. So after you go through, you shut it behind you and dog it tight. Okay?"

Andie nodded, ducking her head a little as she stepped through. "But what happens if there is an emergency?" Leslie asked. "Aren't we then stranded down here?"

"Nope. There's a way out. I'll show you in a minute." Peter waited until she and Leslie had come through, then he carefully shut the hatch behind them and twisted the lock lever. "We've never had an emergency down here, so it's just a precaution. But we have drills once a month, just to be on the safe side, so if anything does go wrong, find the nearest crewman and get them to show you what to do."

"Sounds comforting," Leslie said dryly. It was hard to tell whether she was being sarcastic or not.

The access tunnel was a concrete tube about fifteen feet long, with rubber skids on the floor and caged sodium bulbs in the low ceiling. Peter opened the hatch at the opposite end and closed it behind them when they were past. Now they were within a small vestibule. On the bulkhead across from the hatch was a stencil-painted sign—1B—along a placard displaying a schematic diagram of the module. More pipes and conduits ran down the walls, and next to an ordinary door marked MESS was a chemical fire extinguisher. A narrow spiral staircase led through manholes in the ceiling and floor.

"We're in Hab 1 now," he said. "We'll go upstairs first so you can park your bags, then I'll give you the nickel tour."

"Can I bring my camera?" Andie asked.

"Sure, why not?" Peter gestured to the staircase. "Ladies first. Watch your heads going up. It's pretty steep."

An almost identical vestibule lay at the top of the stairs, except here the door was marked BERTHS 1-10. Before they entered, Peter pointed to a darkened light panel next to the door. "Rule two . . . check the privacy light before you go walking in. If it's on, it means that someone's sleeping. In that case, if you need to enter, keep it quiet."

"Doesn't everyone go to bed at the same time?" Andie asked.

Peter shook his head. "We've got four shifts going twenty-four hours a day, so someone's always catching some shut-eye. You've really got to be careful when you go to Hab 3, because that's where most of the berths are located."

"You've got thirty people living in one hab?" Leslie was horrified. "Where do they all fit?"

Peter smiled as he opened the door. "Welcome to the sardine can."

The dorm was no more than thirty feet in diameter, and not an inch of space had been wasted. Double-decker bunks, each six and a half feet long by three feet wide, were fitted into the bulkheads, with two-drawer lockers tucked beneath each one. Each berth contained an overstuffed mattress; fabric curtains were folded against the sides, and reading lamps, electrical outlets, and miniature computer terminals were recessed into the ceiling and headboards. No windows here; there simply wasn't enough room.

The women gaped at the tiny compartment. "Oh, gaawd," Andie whispered, "I don't believe this."

"I thought you said this was the VIP quarters," Leslie said.

"It is," Peter said. "You don't have to share it with the dive crew. Right now you've only got . . . um, eight other people living here, I think. You'll get to meet them later."

"But it's . . . so small."

"Yes, it is."

"Are there guys here, too?" Andie asked meekly.

"Probably." He shrugged apologetically. "Sorry, but the female-only quarters on Deck 3C are booked up right now, and we've even got some women cohabbing in 3A."

"But how are we supposed to . . . ?" Leslie hesitated. "You know . . . girl stuff. "

Peter walked over to a sleeve door between two of the bunks and pushed it open. A ceiling panel automatically lit, exposing a bathroom not much larger than one found on a commercial airliner: a small commode, a tiny metal sink beneath a miniature mirror, recessed cabinets in the bulkheads. The only major difference was the tiny shower stall placed next to the commode; it was possible for someone to enter the stall from the door in a single step.

"You gotta be kidding," Andie whispered, appalled.

"Sorry, but that's the way it is." Peter shut the door again. "Personal space is at a premium here. If it makes you feel any better, everyone lives the same way. No one has private quarters."

The two women looked as if they had both been struck with hammers. He felt sorry for them, but there was no way that he could soften the blow. Everyone who came down here the first time had much the same reaction unless they were former Navy seamen; the guys who once served aboard ballistic missile subs were ecstatic over not having to hot-bunk with another sailor. Compared with that experience, this was the lap of luxury. But there was no sense in pointing this out to these two; the sooner they got used to it, the better.

Peter gestured to a couple of bunks on the opposite side of the deck. "You can have those two, up and down," he said, then went over to spread open the curtain of the lower one. "In fact, you're in luck . . . you get spring mattresses."

"That makes a difference?" Leslie asked.

"Sure it does." Peter pushed down on the cushion, let it rise beneath his hand again. "They put futons in here when the place was built. They might be comfortable topside, but down here it's like sleeping on a table. It's hard to haul spring mattresses down here, though, so a lot of guys in Hab 3 are still sleeping on the old cushions. Consider yourself lucky."

"Overwhelmed." Leslie walked over to it, tested it with her hand. "Okay, kid, you get the top bunk."

"No problem here." Andie had noticed a circular pressure hatch in the center of the ceiling, a folding ladder fixed next to it. The hatch was painted with black and yellow candy stripes, with a red arrow marked EMERGENCY pointing straight to a lock lever. "What's that, the attic?"

"That's what I said I'd show you a few minutes ago," Peter said. "Put down your stuff, now, and pay attention." Leslie dropped her bag on the lower bunk; Andie laid her own on the floor. "If we get orders to evacuate, here's what you do."

He reached up to pull down the ladder and gave it a hard kick to lock its elbow joints in place. He stepped up on the first two rungs, then reached up to yank the lock lever. The hatch fell open and a light switched on from inside. "This here's the lifeboat for this hab. There's one mounted on top of each of the others, except for C Hab. There's not much up there, so don't bother to climb up, but it'll hold up to ten people."

"So if there's an emergency, we head here," Leslie said.

Peter shook his head. "Wrong. If there's an emergency, the first thing you do is sit tight and wait until someone in Operations issues an evacuation order. We've had other emergencies down here before, but we've never come close to launching the lifeboats. This is the last resort." He patted the ladder. "But if we do have to evac, you get into this thing, and when you're ready to go, you seal the hatch. There's a glass panel up there with a red bar inside—you'll see it next to the hatch—and you break it and pull the bar down. That'll blow explosive bolts that'll detach the pod from the hab's roof." He raised a hand. "Boom. You'll float right up to the surface."

"Won't we have to decompress first?"

"Nope. The pod's designed to hold internal pressure. Whoever rescues you won't open it at once, but will tow you to the nearest decompression chamber—presumably the one on Tethys 1, since you'll come up right next to it. The upper hatch is designed to mate directly with it, and then you'll climb inside. Just to be safe, though, the pod has sufficient air supply to hold ten people for twelve hours, plus fresh water, a first-aid kit, and a radio."

"Everything except a deck of cards."

"Bring your own." He shut the hatch, then came back down and let the ladder fold back against the ceiling. "Don't worry, you're never going to have to use it while you're here."

"That's what they said on the *Titanic*," Leslie mused.

"No, that's what they didn't say on the *Titanic*." Andie had opened her bag and was digging through it. "What they said was . . . hey, what happened to my peanuts?"

"I don't think I've heard that punch line before," Peter said. "Want to explain it to me?"

"No. I mean the peanuts I put in here. The ones I got on the plane yesterday." Andie held up two cellophane baggies of cocktail nuts. Or at least what used to be cocktail nuts; now they contained nothing but brown dust. "They're all broken!"

"They disintegrated under pressure." Peter took one of the bags from her, tore it open, sifted a little peanut dust into his hand. "Things like that happen to stuff we bring down here. Soda goes flat, canned food explodes unless we punch holes in the tins first, glass jars shatter. And the high helium content tends to make everything taste bland."

"So what are we going to eat down here?" Leslie asked. "Food sticks?"

"Hey, Uncle Pete?" Andie interrupted. "Not to make a big deal about it, but I gotta change into something warmer."

"Sure . . . but you better get used to getting undressed in front of other people. Things get pretty tight in here sometimes, and there's always someone using the head when you want it."

Andie grumbled something under her breath as Peter turned his back to her and Leslie did the same. "No, you'll be surprised how good the meals are here," he went on. "Our cook used to be master chef at a four-star restaurant on Fisherman's Wharf in San Francisco. He's learned how to spice up everything so we can taste it. A culinary genius."

Leslie raised a skeptical eyebrow. "Oh, c'mon. How did you get a four-star chef down here?"

"The company recruited him." Peter shrugged. "He's a diving nut . . . and how many chefs get a chance to go out every morning to speargun fresh fish?"

"Not many, I suppose." Leslie walked to the nearest bunk, tested the mattress with her hand. "Seems comfortable enough. A little small."

"Yeah, well . . . you get used to it after a while."

"Only large enough for one, though. I like a little more room."

"Well, you . . . um, you find ways to adapt."

There was a coy smile on her face when she looked back at him. "Really? Any tricks you care to share?"

He felt blood rush to his face. "Uh . . . well, you can try moving the pillow a little bit, and—"

"Okay, ready," Andie said.

For once, Peter was grateful for his niece's interruption, although he couldn't help but note the irritated expression which briefly crossed Leslie's face. He turned around, saw that Andie had pulled on a pair of baggy jeans. The bikini and shorts she had worn when she left topside earlier this morning lay in a heap next to the bag. "Good choice," he said, perhaps a little too quickly.

Andie said something in unintelligible duck talk before she remembered the headset she had discarded along with her T-shirt. She picked it up and put it back in place. "Sorry . . . yeah, but they're the only jeans I brought with me, except the ones I wore on the plane. Didn't think I was going to be cold."

"Like I said, it's the high helium content. Absorbs more heat. If we were at sea-level pressure, you'd be sweltering by now. When the base first opened, we had the thermostats cranked up so high, we were all stripped down to our underwear."

"That must have been interesting," Leslie said, utterly straight-faced.

There was a fraction of a second in which no one said anything, but everyone knew exactly what was meant. Andie and Leslie glanced at each other, and for a moment Peter wondered if the two women were going to bare their teeth to expose fangs and grow fingernails into inch-long claws.

"Better get out my camera," Andie said, then she bent over to open its aluminum case.

"Excuse me. I need to powder my nose." Leslie retreated into the head, firmly shutting the door behind her.

Peter slowly let out his breath, then walked over to the nearest bunk and sat down. Its present occupant had left its curtain open. The bedsheets were unmade, a paperback copy of *20,000 Leagues Under the Sea* lay open and facedown on the crumpled blanket; color photos of manta rays and tiger sharks were taped on the wall above the pillow. A visiting scientist doubtless rented this space. With any luck, he was bald, fat, had five kids at home, and snored in his sleep.

A cultural stereotype, to be sure, but Peter hoped he fit the description. The poor damn fool had no clue as to who would be sharing his humble quarters for the next several days.

NINE

Analysis

H ab 2 was entirely given to lab space, with Marine Bio occupying Decks 2A and 2B and Marine Geo taking up Deck 2C. The fact that no more than eight people at any given time had exclusive dominion over three entire decks was a source of no small envy among the rest of the crew, especially since the scientists were able to suspend hammocks within the labs when they didn't want to return to their cramped bunks. What was often neglected was the fact that they frequently worked longer hours than the divers or the support staff, and that their job pressures were of a considerably different nature.

For one thing, there was no permanent science team aboard Tethys 2; the average length of stay for a visiting researcher was usually three or four weeks, often much shorter. The longest stretch anyone had stayed below was four months, and that was the geologist hired by Yemaya to lead the survey team which mapped the manganese fields on the Blake Plateau shortly after the base was built. For another, many of the scientists who spent time aboard Tethys 2 weren't employed by Yemaya Ocean Resources, but instead worked for other concerns: smaller companies, universities, various nonprofit research foundations, even the U.S. government. Yemaya made a small profit leasing out its facilities and charged its users accordingly, for everything from bunk space and meals to use of ROVs. The rent didn't come cheap, so researchers were often under pressure to produce the maximum results in the minimum amount of time; it wasn't uncommon for a visiting scientist to spend eighteen hours a day in Hab 2.

Judith Lipscomb and Charles Toussaint, on the other hand, were Yemaya employees; collectively they had logged nearly six months aboard Tethys 2. This meant that they rated treatment slightly better than the norm, including preferred use of Deck 2A. Their passwords were permanently encrypted into the computer terminals, and a pair of locked cabinets beneath the wraparound worktable contained their private files. Best of all, they were allowed to have their own coffeemaker. This didn't seem like much of a perk at first glance, until one spent a few days working in Hab 2 and discovered that the only other sources of fresh coffee were in the mess compartment and the operations center.

"Last of the pot," Judith said, holding up the small four-cup carafe. "Want some?"

Charles didn't look up from his work. He had been hunched in front of one of the two computer terminals for the last few hours, completely absorbed in his work, undistracted by the reggae music playing on the CD deck. *Rastaman Vibrations,* his favorite album. Judith reached over to turn down Bob Marley. "Want some more coffee?" she repeated. "I'll have to make more after this."

"Um?" He glanced over his shoulder at her. "Coffee? What about it?"

She let out her breath. "Coffee. Yes or no?"

He gave her a sheepish smile. "Sorry. No, thanks anyway. Do we have any lemonade left?"

"I don't know. Lemme check." She put down the carafe, walked over to a small refrigerator marked with a spiked biohazard trefoil, and opened it. Racks of sealed test tubes filled with seawater samples and glass jars containing formaldehyde-preserved sea creatures vied for space with various noncarbonated soft drinks. "Sorry, no lemonade left. Got some iced tea, though."

"The canned stuff?" he asked, and made a face when she nodded. "I'll settle for water," he said, then stood up and stretched his back. "Thought we put an off-limits sign on the lemonade."

"We did. You thought someone might pay attention." She grinned. "I told you to mark it as urine samples."

"Then I wouldn't touch it either." Charles pulled a paper cup from the dispenser, filled it from the spigot on the center island. A triggerfish swam lazily past a bubble window, paused for a curious moment to peer inside, then disappeared with a flick of its tail when Charles moved past the porthole. "Making any progress?" he asked, gesturing to the other terminal where she had been working all afternoon.

Judith scratched the back of her head as she gazed at its screen. "Not sure. There's a lot of fresh data here, but you could infer almost anything from it."

The bar graphs on the screen represented recent estimates of marine fauna for the eastern seaboard, everything from large mammals like whales, dolphins, and manatees to major predators like sharks and manta rays, down through pelagic game fish like tuna, swordfish, and tarpon, to various species of crab and lobster. Despite radio tagging and satellite remote sensing, keeping track of these populations was still largely a matter of monitoring commercial catches and what washed ashore.

Yet Yemaya made money from Judith's research, by selling the information she collected to commercial fishing operations so that they could remain within the letter of the various federal laws passed during the last decade to prevent overfishing and protect endangered species. Meaningful environmental legislation had almost come too little, too late; by the time Congress awakened to the crisis, entire species of game fish had nearly been driven to extinction as everything from blue marlin to grouper to snapper wound up in seafood restaurants and grocery stores. The fishing industry had vigorously lobbied against the new laws until the rapid decline in catches demonstrated that the continental shelf was on the verge of becoming a desert; it was a hard call, but even the skeptics came to agree that it was better to place moratoriums on certain species and accept short-term losses of jobs and profits than to lose everything over the long run by continuing to use deep-ocean seine nets and long-lines until nothing remained. Now, only a decade later, cod, haddock, and flounder were off the critical list, shrimp and halibut were once more plentiful, and schools of yellowfin and skipjack tuna were being spotted off the Atlantic and Pacific coasts.

For once, though, Judith wasn't looking at the most recent data as an end in itself, but as a clue to a larger puzzle.

"Here's what we've got from the last two months for the northern Florida coast," she said. "We've got a slight decline in catches for most deep-ocean species, except benthic crustaceans. Lobster, crab, and scallops remain about the same."

"Maybe it doesn't like bottom feeders."

"Yeah, well . . . maybe." She absently gnawed the fingernail of her left thumb until she realized what she was doing. An old childhood habit she had never completely overcome; she deliberately tucked her hand in her pocket. "Maybe not. If it's got anglerfish and squid to prey upon, why settle for the crunchy stuff? Anglers are garbage fish, so trawlers throw them back when they find them in their nets. Squid's never really been endangered, so a major decline probably wouldn't be immediately noticed." She nodded toward the screen. "If you looked at this one way, you'd say that we've got something big down there with an appetite to match."

"Then why doesn't it come closer to the surface to eat?"

"Maybe it does, from time to time. In fact, there've been many reliable sightings over the last couple of hundred years. Look."

Judith picked up the electronic book she had laid down next to the terminal. Earlier in the afternoon she had downloaded *Exotic Zoology* from Juan's online library. She had first read Willy Ley's book when she was an undergrad at the University of Maine—indeed, this was the book that had roused her interest in marine cryptozoology—and once again she found herself referring to it. She opened the ebook's plastic cover and pressed one of the bookmark tabs.

"Between August 10 and 23, 1817," she began, paraphrasing the text, "a large unidentified creature was spotted several times in the Massachusetts Bay off Gloucester, according to sworn depositions taken from various seamen, including several U.S. Navy officers." She tabbed another page. "On August 6, 1848, a large serpent was spotted by the captain and crew of the HMS *Daedalus* off the Cape of Good Hope in the Indian Ocean." Another page. "And then on December 4, 1893, the captain and first mate of the S.S. *Umfuli* spotted one off the west coast of Africa when it rushed their ship."

"I've heard all that before." Charles shrugged, unimpressed. "Sea stories. Tales bored sailors make up to tell their wives and children back home."

She knew what he was doing: playing the devil's advocate by challenging her findings. "These weren't hoaxes, Doc. All the men involved had their professional reputations at stake. You don't tell an official board of inquiry that you've seen a sea monster unless—"

"Then they might have been illusions. You've been out on the water enough to know how the eye plays tricks on you. Dolphin schools, oarfish, loggerhead turtles . . ."

She flipped to another page. "In 1905, two British naturalists, E.G.B. Meade-Waldo and Michael J. Nicoll, reported a sea serpent off the coast of Brazil while spending their vacation on the Earl of Crawford's yacht. They went so far as to publish an account of their sighting in the *Proceedings of the Zoological Society*. Again, reliable eyewitnesses, only this time they were trained scientists. Kinda hard to dismiss, don't you think?"

Charles said nothing. He leaned against the island, folding his arms as he listened. "On May 22, 1917," she continued, "an armed merchant cruiser southeast off Iceland, the *Hilary*, encountered a sea serpent. This time, someone aboard ship actually opened fire on the thing, and the captain reported hitting it on the fifth round. It thrashed around in the water for a while before it sank from sight. And that's not the only time one of these things has been killed."

She tabbed the next page. "On September 30, 1947, a steamship out of New York, the *Santa Clara*, reported running over a large creature on the high seas due east of Cape Lookout. It left blood on the water before it sank.

Both times the captains of these ships made the final reports, based upon their log entries."

"A bit more credible, I'll grant you that, but what does it add up to?"

"A couple of things. In all of these accounts, the description of the creature remains consistent. A long serpentine body, approximately sixty feet long, with a large head—the first mate of the *Umfali* described it as resembling that of a conger eel—and scaleless skin varying in color from dull gray to black. And"—she raised a finger—"a long, slender dorsal fin running along its spine. Sound familiar?"

Charles raised an eyebrow. What she described sounded very much like the creature which had been partially photographed by Joe Niedzwiecki aboard the *Doris*. "But all these creatures have been seen on the surface."

"Right, and that's another thing. In all these instances, no matter where they were, the conditions were nearly the same. Calm seas, sunny weather . . . optimal conditions for feeding. And even when they've occurred on high seas, they've never been very far from continental shelves. And the Blake Plateau is a nice in-between point for—"

She stopped herself. "What?" Charles gently asked. "Spawning?"

"Possibly. Why not?" She closed the ebook, dropped it on the counter. "Maybe that's part of their life cycle. Back in 1930, a leptocephalus larva was caught by a Danish research vessel off the coast of South Africa. It came from nearly one thousand feet deep, and was six feet long. Since when do moray eels give birth to six-foot—"

"So I've heard, from a reliable secondhand source."

"Doc . . ."

"Hey, I believe you!" He laughed, raising his hands

defensively. "Really, I do! Everything you say makes perfect sense!"

"But?"

He stopped laughing. "But you don't have any proof. No evidence."

"The disk! What do you call that?"

Charles shook his head. "No reputable journal would accept that as hard evidence. If you wish, we can notify the *Weekly World News*. I'm sure they'd pay good money for it."

"All right, okay." Judith sat down heavily in her chair. "You've made your point."

"Besides, you still haven't explained why this creature would attack the *Doris*."

"I don't know." She closed her eyes, rubbed the bridge of her nose between her fingers. "If it was spawning, maybe the *Doris* was getting too close to where it had laid its larva . . . larvae, whatever. That's the only thing I can figure."

"Even so, it doesn't hold up. If that were the case, why haven't other deep submersibles seen these things?"

"There's been a couple of instances. The first happened in 1934, when the oceanographer Charles Beebe spotted a large, unidentified creature while submerged in a bathysphere off the coast of Bermuda. And in the late sixties, the *Deepstar 4000* spotted something at four thousand feet, on the bottom of the San Diego Trough. The two men aboard guesstimated that it was thirty to forty feet long, and they caught one good picture of its midsection before it vanished. Most people think it was a whale shark or a giant grouper, but—"

"But you think it might have been a sea serpent."

"I don't know what to think, except that the name itself is probably a misnomer. Despite their appearance, they can't be reptiles . . . if they live at that depth, then they can't be warm-blooded. And, no, I don't think they're long-lost plesiosaurs or any other kind of extinct dinosaurs." Judith let out her breath. "But there's definitely something out there, and now we've got one in our own backyard."

Toussaint turned to refill his paper cup from the spigot. "Well, you've gone far to explain your theories to me. I'm only sorry that I haven't paid much attention before now. I've always considered it to be . . ."

He hesitated. "An undergraduate fantasy?" Judith asked, frowning.

"A hobby." He sipped the water. "If you hadn't proven yourself to be an accomplished researcher, I'd dismiss it as such." Charles crumpled the cup in his fist and tossed it in a nearby waste can. "But why this? If you want sea monsters, you could always study giant squid. We now know they exist, but no one has yet to photograph a living specimen. But sea serpents, or whatever they are . . . well, you know as well as I do that 99 percent of the marine science community still regard them as myths. Hardly a safe way of establishing a reputation."

Despite herself, Judith found she was smiling. "A few decades ago everyone believed giant squid were myths, too. Then we found a few dead specimens, and now every Ph.D. candidate is doing dissertation work on them. They've become hip. But sea serpents—"

"Aha! So you think this may be a way to make a name for yourself." Charles pointedly checked his watch. "Wonder if I can still get lunch. Want anything from the mess deck, Dr. Darwin?"

"Doc . . . !"

"Hey! Anyone up there?"

A familiar voice, faintly echoing against the metal bulkhead, rose from the stairwell on the other side of the room. Charles raised a finger to his lips and shook his head. "Nobody here but us mad scientists," Judith called back. Or at least one angry one. "C'mon up."

Two pairs of footsteps ascending the spiral stairs from the deck below; a moment later Jack Sheldon came through the manhole: a slender young man in his mid-thirties, with the mustacheless Abe Lincoln beard favored by divers. "Thought you guys would still be up here," he said, "but I wasn't sure."

"No, no, we're here."

"Hope we're not interrupting anything." A few steps behind Sheldon was Jared Hilliard, Tethys 2's operations manager. Thickset and bull-necked, with a broad, flat face, he resembled the generations of Massachusetts merchant seamen from which he had come.

"Nothing but the usual bull session." Charles extended his left hand to Hilliard. "Good to see you again. My apologies for not stopping by when we came in."

"No offense taken." Hilliard used his only remaining hand to shake with Charles. He had lost his right forearm many years earlier, so the story went, during a brief but nasty encounter with a great white while diving off the coast of New Zealand. Physicians had fitted him with a serviceable prosthetic arm, but he wore it only when he was on the surface. "Sorry to hear that your vacation got cut short. I heard what happened."

"Any clue why they tried to grab you?" Sheldon asked. Judith and Charles had met up with the geologist shortly after they entered Hab 2. He and Charles had worked together in the past, and since his lab was located on the lower deck, he frequently came upstairs to scrounge a cup of coffee. "I mean, of all the places in the world . . ."

"I know." Charles shook his head. "It's a mystery to us, too, I'm afraid."

"You think it was just random street crime?" Hilliard
asked.

"That's a possibility, yes."

Judith gave him a sharp look. Although Doc wasn't
lying, neither was he telling the entire truth; they had
discarded that idea last night during their meeting with
Bartlett. Yet Charles could be reticent at times; if he har-
bored any theories of his own as to why someone might
have attempted to abduct him, he was probably keeping
them to himself.

Jared was regarding her with curious eyes. He was
quick to pick up on things like that; he was naturally
empathic to begin with, and being in charge of forty people in an enclosed, high-pressure environment tended to
make him sensitive to the slightest nuances of expression.
"I was just going to brew some more coffee," she said,
turning away to pick up the carafe. "I take it you guys
want some."

"Bring back any beans?" Sheldon asked. He was fond
of Dominican black mountain coffee, unavailable in any
stores in the States.

"Yeah, but they're still in my bag. Haven't had a
chance to grind 'em yet." Grateful for the distraction,
Judith poured the rest of the last batch down the drain.
"You'll have to settle for Maxwell House, sorry."

"Thanks, that'll do." Hilliard pulled a stool from beneath the bench and sat down, resting the stump of his
right arm on the table. "Look, I know you guys have
gone through a lot lately, but we need to discuss something."

"Our request for the *Galatea*, I suppose," Charles in-
quired. "We were just talking about that."

Judith was glad her back was turned, so Hilliard
couldn't see her face. That hadn't been the topic of discussion at all. She pulled out a filter bag of coffee and

dropped it in the basket, then rinsed out the carafe and began to fill it with fresh water.

"Good guess," Hilliard replied. "Miles has put in a priority request for the sub, but the company's still sort of iffy about it. I got a call from Jacksonville just a half hour ago, asking for my two cents. I wanted to get your side of it."

Great. Now she was going to have to explain sea serpents to one of the most unimaginative individuals working down here. Hilliard was a top-notch administrator, to be sure; when he was taking his six-week duty tour, the mining operations met their quotas, the food was served hot, the quarters were kept tidy, and any problems large or small were dealt with in a quick and efficient manner. But Hilliard was a company man; despite his abiding interest in sharks, he was a bureaucrat at heart. He was no Captain Bligh, but neither was he the next Jacques Cousteau.

"Well," she began as she poured water into the coffeemaker, "it seems we've discovered something rather interesting—"

"Indeed we have," Charles said. "A new vent field has opened in the Mid-Atlantic Ridge. Want to take a look?"

Judith nearly dropped the carafe. She had completely forgotten about that.

"Yes, please." Hilliard turned around on the stool as Toussaint walked over to his terminal. "Jack's told me a little, but I want to get the big picture."

"Juan flagged it for me yesterday when the new SO-SUS data came in," Sheldon said. "I sort of thought it was interesting, but . . . well, I was busy with new samples from the Blake, so I didn't get a chance to examine it closely."

"Quite all right," Charles said. "That's more in my area at any rate." Not entirely true, either; hydrothermal vents were principally a matter for geologists to investigate, with biologists taking a piggyback ride. Yet basic research wasn't Jack's forte; his principal task aboard Tethys 2 was analyzing random samples of the nodules brought up from the plateau. "I've been sorting through the raw data. Here's what I've found so far."

Charles sat down at his terminal and opened a file he had encrypted earlier. The screen changed to display a multicolored Geosat radar altimeter map of the North Atlantic; he moved the trackball until a small square was positioned over a region midway between Florida and the West African coast. "Juan, overlay chart coordinates and put this on the wall."

"Yes, Dr. Toussaint," the AI said in their headsets. "Reproducing image on wall screen."

The same image on Doc's terminal appeared on a rolldown flatscreen above the coffeemaker, large enough for everyone to examine it easily. It depicted a magnified image of a rectangular region of the Mid-Atlantic Ridge. The ridge itself was easily seen as a rugged, yellow-reddish area against the dark blue of the Atlantic Basin. Superimposed over it was a map grid, with coordinates running along the margins: 35 degrees to 25 degrees North on the sides, 50 degrees to 30 degrees West at the top and bottom.

Charles stood up and walked over to the screen. "Here's the central rift valley," he began, pointing to a slender, slightly darker line running southwest through the center of the ridge. "Throughout this whole area are previously discovered hydrothermal fields . . . Juan, display map names, please."

The AI added lines of type to various positions on the chart. "The major fracture zones are Oceanographer, here, Hayes, here, and Atlantis, here," Charles continued, pointing to large submarine valleys running horizontal across the ridgeline. "Up to now, the major fields have been Lucky Strike—here, above Oceanographer—and Broken Spur, just south of Atlantis, with the Trans-Atlantic Geotraverse and Snake Pit lying further south. All these places were found during the eighties and nineties by Woods Hole, and they've been subsequently explored by American, French, and Russian expeditions."

He pointed to an area of the chart just south of the Hayes Fracture Zone, midway between the Lucky Strike and Broken Spur hydrothermal fields. "Nothing was found here during those dives, even though this entire region is known to be geologically active due to the shifting of tectonic plates. But then, just a few of days ago, SOSUS registered a series of seaquakes epicentered in this area. Seismographs in the Azores have registered tremors of 4.0 and above. That's the sort of geological activity which tends to signal the opening of a new vent. Juan, find and overlay the USGS bathymetric chart for this region, please."

A bathymetric chart was superimposed over the Geosat map; now the wall was an information-dense sprawl of colors, lines, and soundings. "At 33 degrees North latitude, the average depth ranges from about 2,200 meters to 3,000 meters, signifying a minor latitude rift. That's the sort of terrain where we're likely to find hot vents."

Hilliard peered closely at the chart. "So what's the bottom line?"

"The bottom line is that we've got a major seismic event in an area of the Mid-Atlantic Ridge where past vent activity has already been documented. Indeed, this may the most significant since the Juan de Fuca Range event of—"

"Repeat, please?" Juan said, obviously misinterpreting Charles's utterance of its name as a verbal command.

"I wasn't talking to you, Juan," Charles said loudly. Everyone else chuckled quietly, and his eyelids flickered with annoyance before he went on. "If that's the case, then there may be new hyperthermophiles in this region. Earlier dives have already established that the biota can be markedly different from one vent field to another in just this region."

"So you believe we may find something different here." Jared rubbed his chin with his fingers.

"It's entirely possible, yes. And if—"

"If we don't explore it first, someone else will," Judith interjected, then caught the look on Charles's face. "Sorry," she added quickly. "Didn't mean to interrupt."

Charles shook his head, then gave her an approving nod. "No, go on, please. You've made a good point."

"You were saying . . . ?" Jared asked.

"Well . . . I was just thinking . . . if we know about this, so does everyone else. And it's early summer, after all. Sailing conditions in the North Atlantic are excellent. That area could be swarming with ships within a few weeks."

"Which is why we need to send down the *Galatea*," Charles finished. "The sooner the better. It's your call, Jared."

Hilliard mulled it over for a few moments. He glanced at Sheldon, who quietly nodded. "Okay," he said at last, "you've got my vote. We'll get you the *Galatea*."

Charles and Judith shared a quick grin. With both operations managers in their court, there was no doubt that they could get the company to send them the research sub. "It'll be tough," Jared hastily added. "It might help if I can tell them who's going to be on the team. If we can get people who are already here, that'll help me sell the trip." He turned to Sheldon. "We're going to need a geologist, for starters. Jack, are you interested?"

"Wouldn't miss it for the world." A broad smile spread across Sheldon's face; Judith couldn't blame him for being pleased. Endless weeks of examining manganese nodules could drive anyone nuts, and this trip was a marine geologist's dream. "Bags packed and ready to go."

"Okay, there's one." Hilliard turned to Toussaint. "I assume you're interested as well."

Charles coughed in his hand. "Begging your pardon . . . and I'm glad that you've asked . . . but if it's all the same to you, I'd prefer not to go."

If he had just announced that he was turning down a Nobel Prize, Judith couldn't have been more surprised."Charles! This is your discovery, for God's sake!"

Charles nervously shifted from one foot to another. "I've been thinking about this since the possibility was first raised," he said reluctantly. "I've seen the *Galatea* up close, and . . . well, to tell the truth, I'm a bit leery of making a long trip in it."

"It won't be that long, Doc." Jared pointed at the map. "The site's nearly a straight shot due east from here. Twenty hours or so to get to the ridge, a day exploring the site, then another twenty hours back . . . if it leaves tomorrow morning, you'll be back here by dinnertime Wednesday night."

"Leaving tomorrow?" Judith was astounded. "Gee, someone's in a hurry. Can we send out an expedition that fast?"

"Well . . . yes, and yes." Jared smiled at them. "To tell the truth, the company's been ready to move on this for a couple of days now. Someone in Jacksonville saw the SOSUS data when it came in and alerted the top office. They've been working round the clock since yesterday morning to prepare *Galatea* for a sortie. That's why we need people who are already out here . . . no time to fly in someone new. We were just waiting to hear Doc's opinion on the matter." He looked at Charles. "I'm just surprised that you're not interested in seeing the new field for yourself."

"I understand," Charles said, shaking his head, "and I appreciate it, but I'm a bit long in the tooth for such adventuring." He glanced at Judith. "If you don't mind, dear, I think you should go instead."

Judith's mouth dropped open. "What . . . me? You want me to . . . you think I can . . . ?"

"Certainly. You know as much about this sort of thing as I do." Charles chuckled. "Unless you were dozing during my lectures, that is."

"But I don't—" She took a deep breath. "Look, sure, I know all about hot vents and taq, but I've never operated an ROV before."

"You won't have to," Jared said. "Joe Niedzwiecki has volunteered to go along as second mate. He's fully rated to fly the ROV. All you'll have to do is tell him where to go."

"I can monitor the operation from back here," Charles said. "I understand we can do that, can't we? Even without a surface support ship?"

"Sure. All the pilot has to do is deploy a buoy, and we'll have a real-time satellite link." Hilliard looked back at Judith. "Nobody can make you do this, Judy, but if Doc's not up to it . . ."

"We could always see if Harry Chang's willing to go," Charles quickly added, "but, to tell the truth, he's not nearly as qualified to do this as you are." Then he favored her with a sly wink. "Besides, you have that little side project of yours. You may be able to check that out on the way."

Judith shot him a look: *Shut the hell up!* "I'm not sure I know what you—"

"Pardon me, but if you're referring to"—Hilliard tactfully cleared his throa—"the interesting fauna Joe spotted on the plateau yesterday . . . yeah, well, Miles has briefed me on this. That's another reason Joe's coming along. We're allotting a few extra hours for the *Galatea* to make a quick dive to *Doris*."

"You know about it?" Judith was appalled. "How much else has Miles told you?"

"What are you guys talking about?" Jack asked.

"I'll fill you in later." Jared held up his hand. "Hey, Judy, look . . . I know you've got your niece down here, but Peter can take care of her for the next few days. The main thing is, one, we need to check out this thing ASAP, and two, the company's breathing down our necks about what happened to *Doris*. We need a good—no, an excellent scientist to check these things out, and you're the—"

"Knock it off, Jared." Judith let out her breath. "You want me, I'm in. I'm going."

She wasn't about to admit it to anyone here, except perhaps Charles and only then in private, but deep inside she was ecstatic. A chance to journey to a place on Earth no other human had ever visited: this was just the sort of adventure that makes little girls from Bangor, Maine, want to become scientists in the first place. She had met marine biologists twice her age, many of whom had been actively studying deep-ocean life when she was trying to get a date for the senior prom, who had fruitlessly applied for NSA research grants that would allow them to dive to hot vents in the Galápagos Islands or in the western Pacific. If she had been an astronaut, it was as if someone had just offered her a seat on the first Mars expedition. Only an idiot would pass up this sort of opportunity.

"Good. Then it's settled." Jared slapped his hand on the table. "I'll call upside and tell them to pick up three passengers tomorrow morning." He turned and started to head for the stairs.

Three passengers? Judith did a quick mental count. "Hey, wait . . . Jared, hold on. If there's me and Jack here, who's the third guy?"

"Oh, hell . . ." Hilliard snapped his fingers, then stopped and turned around again. "I forgot . . . didn't I tell you? That journalist you came down here with . . . Leslie Sun, the writer for *Millennium*? We're sending her along, too."

Judith couldn't say anything for a moment. She simply stared at him.

Jared's smile vanished when he saw the expression on her face. "Why, is there a problem?"

TEN
Secrets

6.5.11—1756 EST

I f one ignored the fish swimming past the windows, it
was almost possible to mistake the mess hall on Level
1B for an office cafeteria: round tables with seating for
six, walls paneled with fake mahogany, indirect fluorescent lighting, muted classical music from the ceiling
speakers. You picked up a tray, a paper plate, and plastic
flatware at the head of the serving line and pushed it
down the rack past steam trays filled with this evening's
menu: roast beef *au jus,* garlic mashed potatoes, roasted
corn, turnip greens, and apple strudel, with dispensers at
the end offering ice tea, milk, water, and coffee. The chef
moved in and out of the compact kitchen—out of a sense
of pride, he refused to call it a galley—with replenish-
ments; when he was on duty, he wore a mushroom cap,
as if to assert his claim that he was no galley drudge but
a culinary *artiste.* People seldom complained about his
food, but when anyone dared to do so, they were treated
to a cold stare and told that they were welcome to visit

Tethys's other employee cafeteria. It was only 328 feet away, straight up.

When Peter heard the door swing open, he didn't need to look up to know Judith had just arrived, and that she was righteously pissed off. There was no other person in the world who could enter a room with a mad-on the way she did. No melodramatic slamming of doors, no stomping around, no yelling. It simply seemed as if the temperature had suddenly dropped twenty degrees.

On the other hand, perhaps it was only the sort of familiarity which comes with marriage, because no one else seemed to notice. The handful of divers at the next table barely glanced up from their conversation, nor did the trio of German oceanographers seated across the room. Leslie and Andie were absorbed in an animated discussion of weird web sites. Only Peter seemed to notice the brief, cold look which Judith cast in their direction before she picked up a tray and began moving down the serving line.

Oh, Lord, Peter thought. She must have heard about the crew selection for the *Galatea*. He picked at the turnip greens on his plate and waited for the fireworks to begin.

Judith was quiet when she brought her tray over to their table. "Hi, Aunt Judy," Andie said brightly as she sat down next to him, then she looked back at Leslie. "So, anyway, you click to this page, and you've got a flycam following this truckstop waitress around. I mean, it's really bizarre, 'cause she takes the footage and edits it so it's, y'know, like her own private sitcom, with—"

"So I hear you're going on the *Galatea*," Judith said to Leslie, unapologetically interrupting her niece.

"Yes, I am," she replied. "I understand you're going, too."

"I certainly am." Judith picked up her knife and fork

and carefully trimmed some fat away from the slice of beef on her plate. "I was rather surprised to hear that you were picked. They usually save the passenger berths for scientists."

"Yeah, well . . ." Leslie wiped her mouth with her napkin. "Someone thought it might be good idea to send along a reporter, and—"

"Goodness, really?" Judith raised her eyebrows. "And all this time we've been doing research without having one before. How lucky that you just happened to be around at the right time."

Leslie said nothing. "Judy . . ." Peter began.

"I wish I could go." Typical of a teenager, Andie wasn't picking up the wavelength of the conversation. "I mean, it sounds really cool."

"I wish you could go, too." Judith was speaking to her, but her gaze never left Leslie. "You'd probably be just as useful as Ms. Sun—"

Peter raised a hand to his face as he faked a cough. "Cut it out," he whispered behind his palm.

Judith ignored him. "I mean, you've really got some chutzpah," she continued, still watching Leslie. "You didn't even know about the vent until last night, but then you find out there's something else happening, and . . ." She shook her head. "I'm impressed. Really. You must be one world-class con artist to pull this off."

Peter moved his hand over his eyes. Oh, hell, here it comes . . .

"For the record, Dr. Lipscomb, I didn't con anyone." Leslie's voice, soft and calm, was nonetheless frosted. "After last night's meeting, I contacted my editors and informed them that there was a potential story here—"

"After Miles specifically told you that everything we talked about was off the record."

"Off the record, yes . . . but not off background."

"Aw, Jesus!" Judith slammed her fork down on her plate. Gravy splattered onto the table. "Talk about splitting hairs!"

The compartment had gone quiet, save for the Vivaldi wafting through the ceiling speakers. Peter peered over his shoulder; all around them, divers and scientists were staring in their direction. Even the cook had walked out from behind the serving line, wiping his hands on his apron as he listened in.

"I'm not splitting hairs," Leslie said evenly. "I kept to the letter of our agreement. Nothing I heard was recorded or used without prior permission. All I did was contact my people and inform them that—"

"You got your magazine to lean on the company. Put our writer on this expedition, and we'll give you good press." Judith smiled humorlessly. "I didn't know what that phrase meant till now. Pretty well sums up the nature of the relationship, doesn't it?"

"Aunt Judy . . ." Andie was embarrassed.

"You can interpret it any way you want." Leslie remained cool and professional. "I'd prefer if you'd lay off the cheap innuendo, though. It's beneath you."

"Yeah, right . . ."

"The fact remains that your people and my people reached a certain understanding. Your company gets favorable PR, we get a cover story. What's so terrible about all that?"

Judith glared at Leslie, her dinner forgotten and growing colder by the moment. From her unwanted position between them, Andie nervously glanced back and forth, as if wondering whether she should throw herself under the table. The Vivaldi concerto faded out, followed by dead silence.

"What's so terrible," Judith said finally, "is that there's a hundred guys who've waited years for a chance to make the trip, and they're far more qualified than—"

"I'm sorry you feel that way, Judith. I really am. I was hoping we could work together, but—"

"Bullshit." Judith angrily pushed back her chair and stood up.

"Dr, Lipscomb, please . . ."

Judith placed her hands on the table and leaned closer until she was looking Leslie straight in the eye. "One more thing," she whispered. "Stay the hell away from my husband."

Peter felt the blood rush from his face. "Judy, goddammit . . ."

But she wasn't hearing anything else. Judith turned away from the table and marched across the room, leaving her meal untouched. Everyone watched as she yanked open the door and stormed out.

For a moment no one said anything. Then Andie jumped up and ran toward the door, leaving behind the camera gear she had carried around the station all afternoon. She paused to look back at her uncle, and Peter was stunned to see tears brimming in the corners of her angry eyes. Then she followed her aunt out of the mess room, slamming the door shut behind her.

Peter started to rise, then stopped and slowly sat down again. Even if he caught up with Judith, he wouldn't know what to say. He felt eyes drilling into his back from all directions; everyone in the room was staring at him. Leslie seemed just as mortified as he was, if not more.

"I'm sorry," she said softly. "I think I've gotten myself in the middle of something."

"No, you haven't," he lied. "It's just . . ."

His voice trailed off; he didn't know how to explain it, either. Sure, Judith became snappish when she was under pressure, and she never liked not having things go exactly her way when it came to a major project, yet he had never seen her confront another person in this way before. And the last thing she had said to Leslie . . .

"You don't have to explain." She hesitated, then pushed back her chair and started to stand up. "Look, maybe I've gotten out of line here. I better go see Jared, have him take me off the expedition—"

"No, no. Don't do that." Peter grabbed her arm. "Look, it's not you. She's gone through a lot lately, and . . . well, it's not you. Don't worry about it."

It was a lie, of course, and a rather transparent one at that, but Leslie seemed to take it at face value. She seemed relieved as she sat down again. "Thanks," she said quietly. "Look, maybe I shouldn't have gotten my editors to pull strings for me, but I really do want to go on the *Galatea*. It would be really embarrassing if I had to go back to them now and tell them I've changed my mind."

"Yeah. I can imagine it would be."

She picked up her coffee, took a sip, made a face. "Too bad you don't have any liquor down here. I could use a drink right now."

"Well . . ." Peter hesitated. "That's not entirely true. There's some bourbon stashed in the rec room. The divers keep it for after-hours. I'm not supposed to know about it, but . . ."

"But you know about it." She smiled a little. "I'm supposed to stay away from you, though, remember?"

"It's in the DVD cabinet, behind the movies. Just look—"

"I hate to drink alone." She shook her head, then she gave him a little smile. "We could always meet later, of course. After things have calmed down a bit."

"Well . . ."

"Well . . . ?" He felt her foot brush against his beneath the table. "Care to buy me a drink, sailor?" she asked.

Peter felt his heart skip a beat. He could always pretend otherwise, yet there was no denying the essential fact. From the moment they met yesterday, there had been all the small talk, all the coy smiles: a subtle dance as old as time itself.

Get out of here. Get out now. Be polite about it, though. Don't rush off. Thank the nice lady for her invitation, but remind her that you're married . . . no, no, don't do that, she knows this already. Just leave, before . . .

Before Judy finds out? What's she going to do even if she does? Right now she's too angry to do anything except snarl. Besides, it's just a goddamn drink . . .

"Sure," he said. "How about 2100 hours, Deck 1C—"

"No, no, no." Leslie pouted. "I don't do navy lingo. Ask me again, like a gentleman."

Jesus, you've got to be crazy . . . "Nine o'clock, in the rec room. How's that?"

"Much better." She rose and picked up her tray. "See you then."

He fought the urge to watch as she carried her tray to the recycling bins, even though every other man in the mess deck eyed her covetously as she sorted out the paper and plastic items. He made himself try the dessert while she sashayed across the room; out of the corner of his eye, he saw divers murmuring to one another. Even the stoical German oceanographers seemed distracted when she walked past on her way out to the door.

But she was good. She never once glanced back in his direction.

A though Tethys 2 had four shifts which operated around the clock, at certain times there was very little activity. The dinner hours were one of those; because the mess deck was open between 1700 and 1900, everyone who wanted to eat that night had to grab a bite during that two-hour stretch. So the laboratories tended to be vacant around 1800; if there was ever an opportunity for someone to have privacy in Hab 2, this was it.

On the pretense of searching for a notepad, Charles Toussaint visited the two lower decks, just to make sure everyone was gone. Satisfied that the hab was deserted, he returned to Deck 2A. He sat down again at his terminal and, with a last glance over his shoulder, signed onto the station's commercial Internet server. He logged on under his own name and entered his password, and once the modem had buzzed and whistled its way through cyberspace, he opened his mailbox and checked for messages. There were nine new letters, mostly from colleagues at various universities and research foundations; he would eventually get back to them, but right now he was looking for one bit of email in particular.

As anticipated, he found it under the header *Hi Cutie ;)* and it came from *Pattie@hot.com*. According to the time stamp, it had been sent yesterday morning at 1830. Charles checked his watch; it was almost 6:30. He opened the letter:

XXX GIRLS GIRLS GIRLS XXX
Totally outrageous pics—ALL NUDE!
CUM Visit The HOTTEST SITE ANYWHERE!!
*** ADULTS ONLY ***
Toggle HERE For Your *Secret Password*

Charles slipped the cursor over the bottom sentence and tapped the trackball key. The screen changed; now it displayed a silhouetted nude.

```
XXX GIRLS GIRLS GIRLS XXX
    Your Secret Password Is
           BEAVER
    *** ADULTS ONLY!! ***
```

He grimaced in distaste, then closed the window and deleted both it and the original email. Then he opened the IRC function, paused to check the time again, and entered *Pattie@hot.com* into the address bar. He typed *Beaver* into the message bar, then moused the send button.

A couple of minutes passed, during which he ran down his list of bookmarks and selected the American online edition of *Nature*. He was beginning to read the synopsis of an article on serotonin levels in freshwater crayfish when the terminal chimed and a small window opened in the upper left corner of his screen:

```
You have received an Instant Letter
through
the Internet from Pattie@hot.com.
Accept?/Refuse?
```

He toggled the accept button. A moment later another message appeared in the window:

```
Hi, cutie! Got something for me? ;)
```

Charles typed:

```
I've never done this before.
```

A moment passed, then someone who doubtless looked very much unlike any Pattie he might imagine came back:

What happened yesterday?

He typed:

Friend interfered. Didn't expect this.
Sorry.

He sent the message, waited for a response. Unlike email, Internet Relay Chats weren't stored in the computer's memory buffer, and since he was using an elaborate system of cutouts disguised as spam, it was highly improbable that anyone who might later care to investigate his past activity on the server would tumble to the exchange of passwords.

"Pattie" replied:

Need to arrange new pickup time/place
ASAP.

Charles frowned. He was afraid this might happen. His connection was becoming impatient. On the other hand, perhaps it was just as well . . .

Delay pickup. New info coming soon, i.e.
data from new MAR site.

He sent the message, then settled back in his chair and waited for Pattie to respond. He imagined that two or three men sitting in a decrepit hotel room somewhere in Havana were bent over a laptop computer wired to a portable satellite dish. At least one of them would be French, an employee of the biotech firm which had secretly contacted him in Roseau three months ago.

Charles Toussaint didn't consider himself to be an evil man. His motivations weren't guided by politics, revenge, or even greed, or at least as he defined the latter. The simple fact of the matter was that he had grown up poor, and the major motivating force of his life had been a single-minded desire to have so much money that he would never have to worry again about returning to the shantytown existence he had known during his first two decades.

Intelligence, hard work, a talent for scientific inquiry, and not a little bit of luck had taken him far in life, yet in recent months he had gradually come to realize that he would never achieve the level of wealth he desired by teaching at MIT and working for Yemaya Ocean Resources. Perhaps he had more money than almost anyone else he knew on Dominica, but that wasn't where he wanted to retire. A place in southern Italy, perhaps—he often fantasized about living in a large house overlooking the Mediterranean, where he could snorkel every day— or maybe just a modest bungalow on the coast of Belize.

He hadn't intended to betray his employers, though, until opportunity presented itself in the form of a gentleman from France who visited him in Roseau early last spring. The Paris-based pharmaceutical firm he represented was interested in the same genus of hyperthermophiles Yemaya had earlier discovered at hot vents in the Atlantic and Pacific. However, the industrial enzymes developed from the *Thermus aquaticus* found at those sites had been long since patented, and the company for which he worked didn't have Yemaya's technological resources. Without deep-ocean submersibles of their own, it was effectively out of the competition. Aware that Yemaya was constantly searching for new strains of taq, it had sent someone to Dominica to offer Toussaint a lucrative proposal.

Charles listened to the Frenchman, whose name was Hilaire Benoit, then told him about a promising new taq strain Yemaya had recently discovered at a hot vent near the Galápagos Islands, one which was still being tested and thus hadn't yet been patented. For a certain figure, he was willing to obtain a raw sample from the company's Jacksonville headquarters and deliver it to him. Benoit named a figure for his services, Toussaint countered with a higher figure, and after a few minutes of polite haggling they reached a compromise: $1.5 million American, with a 15 percent retainer fee deposited in a serial-numbered bank account in the Grand Caymans.

The only problem was, the French company needed his knowledge as well. Simply delivering a sample of seawater wasn't enough; it also had to have Toussaint at their lab outside Paris while they isolated the taq strain. This presented a major stumbling block, for Yemaya would surely become suspicious if Toussaint abruptly went to Europe for several weeks, then returned shortly before the French company suddenly announced that it had developed a new polymerase-base enzyme. Toussaint could be arrested on charges of industrial espionage, and Yemaya would sue its rivals for theft of proprietary information

The solution was crude, yet ingenious: Charles would be kidnapped while on vacation in Dominica. A previously unknown far-left extremist group, Caribbean Dawn, would then announce that it was holding Toussaint hostage in exchange for the release of ten felons presently serving time in Labass State Prison. Since Judith Lipscomb would have witnessed the abduction, she would unwittingly provide his alibi; meanwhile Charles himself would have been spirited to Paris, where he would deliver the stolen taq sample and secretly assist his associates in having it cloned. Once this was achieved, Toussaint would be brought back to Dominica, where he would be released in a remote mountain village, considerably shaken by his experience but otherwise unharmed. Caribbean Dawn would vanish without a trace—since Toussaint had been blindfolded the entire time, he never had seen their faces—and it would only be a matter of coincidence when, a few weeks later, a French pharmaceutical company publicly announced that it had developed a new product.

Stealing twenty cc of Pacific seawater hadn't been difficult. Toussaint had an all-access keycard to the Jacksonville lab, which he visited on a routine trip just before he left for Dominica with Judith. Smuggling it through customs at Melville Hall had been child's play, since the inspectors were more intent on searching for drugs than a small glass vial concealed in his eyeglass case. Yet Charles hadn't anticipated Judith successfully fighting off his "abductors" during the prearranged kidnap attempt outside his home; although he tried to remain docile during the fight, the Dominican youths hired to make the snatch had apparently been deterred by their strict instructions to leave the American woman unharmed. Nor was there any way for them to make a second attempt: Judith had called first the Roseau police, then the company, as soon as they returned to his house.

Yet neither had he anticipated new SOSUS data from the Mid-Atlantic Ridge. There had always been a certain risk associated with stealing taq samples from the Galápagos site; if the MAR dive panned out, though, and he played his cards right, this was something from which his French contact might benefit even more . . .

A new message from Benoit appeared on the screen:

Q: Vent at MAR at 30 N?

Charles smiled. It appeared that the French company was aware of the recent eruption on the Mid-Atlantic

Ridge. SOSUS data wasn't secret to anyone who knew where and how to look for it, like so much other American military technology made publicly available after the end of the cold war. Yet while third-world governments sought satellite photos of the borders of their neighbor countries and entrepreneurs were able to access accurate GPS coordinates of possible real estate, only a relative handful of people were aware of the potential of undersea remote sensing. The oceans were the next great frontier, in more ways than one.

He typed:

Yes. Y to send Galatea to MAR site 6/6 AM.
ETA 6/7 PM. Expect new taq sample 6/8 PM.

He sent it and waited.

Interested. Delivery of new taq frm u?

Ah, but that was the question, wasn't it? He had already been paid a substantial sum for the Galápagos taq; it hadn't yet been delivered, but that could always be rearranged at their convenience. However, now he had a line on fresh goods; even if no one yet knew what was down there, a sample of seawater from a brand-new North Atlantic site had considerable value, potentially even more than the Galápagos taq.

Benoit would be aware of that; during their previous conversations, Toussaint had been impressed with the other man's intellect. He was no scientist, to be sure—in fact, Charles rather suspected that he was a high-priced mercenary of some sort—but he seemed to have a good grasp of the issue. And since Benoit was acting as the intermediary between Toussaint and the pharmaceutical company in Paris, Charles knew that he was empowered to make important decisions.

That being the case, how much more was he willing to pay for the new MAR taq? As the Americans liked to say, he was selling the sizzle, not the steak. yet it was a big, juicy steak all the same. Absently drumming his fingers against the table, Charles thought about it for a few moments. Then he typed:

```
Delivery w/ G. taq guaranteed. $3M U.S.
for both.
```

The reply came almost instantly:

```
No. Same price as before.
```

Charles smiled. He had been expecting just such a response. He sent:

```
New price stands. All or nothing.
```

On the deck below, he heard a hatch open and shut. Someone had just entered the hab from the access tunnel. He listened carefully, heard faint movement down on Deck 2B. Charles hissed under his breath, then glanced toward the screen as it chimed again.

```
Accepted. Need to make new arrangements,
re: delivery of both samples.
```

Footsteps on the staircase; someone was coming up. He hastily typed:

```
Contact again later. Must go now.
```

"Is someone up there?" Judith called out. Her voice sounded odd. "Doc, is that you?"

"I'm here," he said as he sent the message. He closed the message window just as Judith appeared in the stairwell. "Just getting in a little—" he began, then stopped when he saw her face.

Judith's eyes were red-rimmed and swollen, her cheeks moist. Somehow she had managed to dislodge her headset; it dangled loose around her neck, tangled among her disheveled blond hair. When she saw him, she started to say something, but it caught in her throat and all that came out was a wretched sob.

"Judith!" Fear of discovery vanished immediately. He shoved back his chair and was across the deck in two steps, catching her just as her legs buckled and she collapsed against the stair railing. "Judith, what on earth . . . ?"

"Oh, Christ, Doc . . ." She fell against his shoulder and buried her face in his chest. With her headset mike out of place, her voice sounded absurdly high-pitched; at any other time it might have been funny, but not now. "I can't believe I . . . goddammit, I just made a fool out of myself in front of—"

"Shhh . . . easy now. Take it easy." Charles led her to his chair, gently lowered her into it. "Everything's going to be all right."

"No, it's not going to be all right." She clung to him, breathing hard against her tears. "I went down to . . . down to the mess deck and . . . God, I shouldn't have, but I so pissed off, and—"

"Wait. Hold on. I can barely understand you." He carefully untangled the headset from her hair, then gently put it back in place again. "All right, now you won't sound like . . . what's her name, the Disney character? Donald Duck's wife?"

"I don't . . . you mean Minnie?"

"No, no, I don't think it's that."

"Daisy." Despite herself, she managed a halfhearted smile. "Her name's Daisy. Minnie is Mickey's wife . . . girlfriend, whatever . . . and Daisy was Donald's . . ." Her smile became a little larger, if not even less humorless. "I wonder if they ever swapped partners."

"Frankly, my dear, the thought has never occurred to me."

Judith giggled hysterically, as if it was best joke she had ever heard. Charles took the opportunity to turn to the center island and run a cup of water from the spigot. He ripped a paper towel from the roll beneath the table, then he knelt down next to her. "Here, drink this," he said softly. "Just a little . . . easy now . . ."

"Daisy doing Mickey . . . what a hoot." Judith's hand shook a little as she took the paper cup from Charles and drank deeply. "It'd be funny if it wasn't true."

"You said something happened in the mess deck . . ."

The wan smile vanished as quickly as it had come. She gulped down the water, took a deep breath that rattled in her throat. "I was pissed off when Jared told me she was on the *Galatea*—"

"You mean Leslie Sun . . ." Of course he knew; he had been present when Jared had broken the news to both of them, witnessed the heated argument which finally sent Judith barging out of the lab. "I take it you went to confront her."

"No . . . I mean, not at once, I didn't . . ." Judith took the towel from Charles's hand, wiped her eyes. "I tried to calm down first. Went for a walk to cool off, that sort of thing. Then I asked Juan where she was—"

"And you found her in the mess deck."

"Uh-huh." She blew her nose into the towel. "I thought I was ready to discuss this with her . . . calmly, I mean,

just the two of us, like adults . . . but then I get down
there, and . . ."

She sighed deeply. "Peter was with her."

Something cold ran down Charles's back. He had been
witness to the relationship between Judith and Peter from
the very beginning, when they had both been his students
at MIT. Although Judith was his protégé, he had always
been fond of Peter as well, so he wasn't shocked when
they eventually became lovers, if only because they were
so very much alike, at least in their interests. Yet he had
been surprised when the campus romance lasted beyond
graduation ceremonies and unexpectedly became a marriage. While Judith, as pretty as she was, had always been
somewhat bookish, Peter was indisputably a lady's man:
a handsome former Navy SEAL who turned girls' heads
every time he walked into a classroom. Charles had never
been overly impressed with Peter's intellect, but he
thought they made a nice couple. He had attended their
wedding in Provincetown, and when they returned from
their honeymoon a week later, he had given them his
wedding present: a matched pair of job interviews with
Yemaya, the same company for which he himself had
only recently been hired as a consultant.

He loved Judith like the daughter he never had, and
accepted Peter in much the same spirit, as a surrogate
son-in-law. The fact that he was surreptitiously selling
company secrets to a European rival was none of their
business.

"What were they doing?" he asked.

"Nothing. I mean, they were talking . . ." Judith
daubed her eyes with the crumpled towel. "No, that's not
right . . . Andie was doing all the talking, and she was
listening to her, but—"

"But he was paying attention to her. Leslie, I mean."

Judith raised her head. "Doc, I've seen that look in his

eyes. And he really didn't want me to sit down with them when I came in."

"Judy, you don't know that. He was supposed to—"

"Show them around the base . . . I know, I know." She raised the towel to her eyes again, self-consciously gazed at it, then dropped it to the floor. "I dunno, but something just snapped in me . . . I got stupid, and I yelled at them . . . and everyone saw me yell at them, and . . ."

She glanced at the screen beside her. "Hey, somebody's sent you something."

Charles stared past her at his terminal. The message window had opened again, and within it read:

```
Next contact 6/7 1800 frm Pattie
Expect update re: MAR site
```

He felt the blood rush from his face. His French contact must have sent this final message while he was distracted with Judith; he hadn't heard the terminal chime when it came in.

"Who's Pattie?" Judith asked, reading the identifier at the left margin of the window.

"One of my grad students," Charles replied, thinking quickly. "She's doing an internship at Scripps this summer."

"You've told her about the new site?" Judith gave him a look. "Better watch out . . . the company doesn't like us disclosing information."

For a moment Charles wondered if Judith had guessed what he was really doing. Yet there was no way she could, from so little evidence. She was very intelligent, certainly, but there were limits to even deductive reasoning. "She doesn't know anything she couldn't figure out from reading the SOSUS data," he replied as he reached across her to close the window. "I'm hoping that she finds similar Scripps data from the Juan de Fuca sites that might help us, that's all."

He picked up the discarded cup and stood up. "Look, I don't think there's anything going on between Peter and that woman, if that's what's bothering you. And you can't afford to let it affect your work."

"Yeah, I know." She snuffled a little, then picked up the towel and used it to dry her face. "You're right. I'm just being foolish . . . but, Charles, the way she's been looking at him . . ."

"She's probably just flirting." He was relieved that the subject had been changed. "How does Andie feel about this? Have you spoken to her?"

"Yeah. She was there when I . . ." Judith grimaced. "I talked to her afterward. She was with them all afternoon, and she says nothing happened between them. But Andie's starting to like her, so . . ."

"Perhaps you ought to do the same. After all, you're going to be aboard the *Galatea* together for the next three days."

Judith didn't look pleased at this prospect, but she nodded. "Maybe you're right." Then she stood up and looked around. "Where do we stow the hammocks?"

"Over there. Bottom shelf." He pointed to a supply cabinet on the far side of the compartment. "You're going to sleep here tonight? You've never done that before."

"I've got some more work to do before we leave tomorrow." Judith snuffled again, then walked over to the cabinet. "Besides, when I'm mad, I stay mad. I think I should be alone for a while."

"Hmm . . . well, suit yourself." While her back was turned, Charles quickly made sure he had deleted everything from memory. Satisfied that his tracks were covered, he shut off the computer. "I think it's time to get some dinner myself," he said, pushing back his chair. "If I see Peter, should I tell him anything?"

Judith had just pulled the folded hammock out of the cabinet. She thought about it a moment, then shook her head. "No. If I want to talk, I'll page him."

"Do what you will." He stood up and headed toward the stairs. "See you in the morning. Try to get some sleep."

"Good night, Charles." She smiled at him. "And . . . thanks."

"Think nothing of it," he replied, returning the smile. "Good night."

Then he tramped down the stairs and let himself out of the hab, shutting the hatch behind him. It wasn't until he was out of sight that he stopped in the access tunnel to let out his breath.

So many secrets . . .

THIRD DAY

MONDAY, JUNE 6, 2011

ELEVEN

Galatea

6.6.11—0850 EST

"**R** eady for the pack?"

"Hold it a sec." Peter snapped shut the plastic buckles of his buoyancy control vest, then picked up the yellow diving helmet and checked the regulator valves and dataport socket to make sure they weren't salt-corroded. They were clean and shiny, but the faceplate was smudged on the inside; he reached over to a roll of tissue paper on the nearby bench and tore off a small wad, spit in the faceplate, then used the paper to clean the visor. He put the helmet back on the bench, then lowered his arms to his sides. "Okay, I'm ready."

The crewman standing behind him grunted as he hefted the rebreather and held it against Peter's back. Peter bent forward and took its weight on his hips while simultaneously slipping his arms through the dangling shoulder straps. He straightened up, found the waist belt, and snapped it shut while Meyer attached an air hose from the unit to the BC, then yanked the straps tight. He shrugged a little; good, the rebreather rested firmly between his shoulders.

"Any critters in the water this morning?" he asked as he pulled on his gloves.

"Nothing serious." As dive assistant, Meyer had been in the wet room since 0530, so he had heard reports from the rockhounds returning from the overnight shift at the nodule processing facility. "Someone spotted a couple of sharks out on the eighteenth hole, but they were just playing through."

"So long as they're not loitering around the clubhouse, that's fine by me." Golf talk was popular among these guys, since that tended to be their preferred hobby when they were back on dry land. Peter pressed a rubberized button on the back of his left glove, was satisfied to see a small red diode light. He cinched the BC and rebreather straps a little tighter. "Juan, I'm about to go EVA," he said. "Transfer comlink to"—he glanced at the helmet, read the serial number above the faceplate—"18-Texas David."

"Transferring comlink to 18-TD," the AI responded. "Have a safe dive, Peter."

"Thank you, Juan." He pulled off his headset and dropped it on the bench next to his watch and wedding ring. Meyer would put them in his locker along with his clothes. "Ready back there?" he asked, speaking carefully so that he would be understood.

"Whenever you are," said the talking duck behind him.

Peter picked up the helmet, took a deep breath, then shoved his head through the elastic collar until his neck popped through the helmet on the other side. His vision was warped by the concave Plexiglas plate pressed close against his face, his ears squeezed by the foam-padded built-in headset. For the briefest instant there was an instinctive moment of panic as his brain told him he was about to suffocate, then Meyer attached the hoses leading from the rebreather to the regulator. The crewman twisted the recessed knobs on the right side of the back, and Peter heard a long, low hiss as cool air rushed into the helmet.

Meyer handed him the rubber-coated communications cable; Peter plugged it into the socket next to the regulator. *"Hear me okay, chief?"* the assistant asked, his voice no longer sounding silly.

"Loud and clear, thanks." He raised his left hand again, stabbed another tiny button on the back of his glove. Scarlet letters and bar graphs flashed upon the heads-up display on the top half of the faceplate. Peter scanned the suit-stat readout and checked it against the handheld dive computer tethered to the BC as a backup, then he pushed the glove button again to make the HUD disappear. Some divers liked to keep it on all the time, but Peter remembered the good old days of masks and mouthpieces. Constantly having a electronic billboard in his face was too much like playing a video game.

"Okay, caddy," he said, "let's go." Personally, he hated golf.

"Right with you, boss." Meyer picked up a pair of frog fins and fell in beside Peter as he slowly marched, shoulders hunched forward, to the edge of the moon pool.

Peter held on to the ladder rail as he first took one fin, then the other, and slipped them over his dive shoes. One last pat-down to make sure everything was properly in place, then he walked away from the ladder. He turned around and gave the crewman a thumbs-up. Meyer smiled and responded in kind, and then Peter jumped backward.

He felt a hard, cold jolt as he entered the water. The BC automatically inflated and promptly brought him to the surface, until he reached up to a broad orange button on the vest's right shoulder and pressed it. The vest deflated and he began to sink again.

"Radio test, one two," he said. "Juan, I'm in the water."

"I understand, Peter. Tracking."

"Thank you, Juan." He was already beginning to warm up as the suit reacted to the sudden temperature drop by releasing thermoreactive chemicals into tiny capillaries honeycombed through the neoprene. Peter moved his arms and legs to speed up the process. "Patch me through to MainOps topside, please."

The rebreather was nearly weightless now, its mass compensated for by small ballast tanks which took in water according to buoyancy levels given by the suit's internal computer. From the moment he jumped into the moon pool, Peter had become a miniature, self-sustained submarine; several generations of technology separated him from the relatively primitive scuba equipment which Jacques Cousteau and his associates had developed sixty years earlier. No wasted air bubbles and lessened threats of hyperthermia meant longer dive stays underwater; gone were the days when divers had to use chalkboards to communicate, and although it was still prudent to dive with a partner, the increased safety factor of the new equipment no longer made the buddy system an imperative.

He fell past the floodlights which ringed the pool's concrete walls into the circular shark cage beneath the main hab. There was a plastic sign attached to the bars next to the cage door:

LAST CHANCE TO CHECK!!
ARE YOU SAFE TO DIVE?

The warning was followed by a six-step list which principally involved double-checking tank levels, emergency gear, and radio equipment. Shortly after the sign had been posted, some joker had used a marking pen to add a seventh question to the bottom of the list:

CAN YOU SWIM?

Since the sign was his own idea, he switched on his HUD. He was giving himself a final checkout when Juan came back online: *"Peter, Miles Bartlett is online."*

"Thank you, Juan. Put him on." He waited until he heard a double click. "Hey, Miles! How's the weather up there?"

"Had some storms yesterday afternoon, but we're better now." Bartlett's voice was thin, filtered by the usual acoustic phone static. *"How're you?"*

"Clear as can be. Not a cloud in the sky." He kicked over to the cage door, pulled it open. A horseshoe crab stirred up a small cloud of silt as it scuttled out of the way. "I don't see the sub. Is it on the way?"

"It should be there any minute now. They're pressurizing on the way down, so it's taking a little longer than usual."

Peter shut the cage door behind him, then dog-paddled in place as he turned and looked around. No one else was in sight, and he couldn't detect any lights moving beyond the main hab. This was an unusual procedure, having the *Galatea* rendezvous directly with Tethys 2. In fact, it had been practiced only once before, in a trial run just after the sub was commissioned. Most of the time it either went straight out to ocean from its port in Jacksonville, or took on passengers and cargo topside at Tethys 1. "Just as well," he said. "I've got to rig the docking hatch for it."

"Sounds good." There was a short pause. *"Listen, Pete, I got a call from your wife. It's about Leslie Sun."*

Peter was suddenly glad that Bartlett couldn't see his face. "I know all about it. She doesn't want her on the expedition. I've already talked this over with Judith."

"Really? When did you have this discussion?"

"Last night, during dinner." No point in telling Miles that it hadn't been much of a discussion, nor that Judith had been so angry that she stormed out of the mess deck and spent the night by herself in the bio lab. He switched on his helmet lamp, then began belly-stroking his way toward the docking collar. "She's pretty upset about this, but she'll calm down."

"I don't think so. She called me just a half hour ago. You mean you haven't talked to her since last night?"

Peter had to bite his lip to keep from swearing out loud. What did Judith think she was doing? It wasn't bad enough that she didn't want to speak to him; now she was trying to go over Jared's head. "I haven't seen her this morning," he admitted. "She's a little pissed at me. What did she tell you?"

The docking collar was on the bottom of a short turret protruding beneath the barnacle-crusted hull of the main hab. He swam up to it, then adjusted the pressure in his BC so that he floated stationary just below it. The outer hatch was shut; he twisted its lock wheel and pulled it open, pinning the cover against the hull so that it was out of the way.

"She wants Ms. Sun off the expedition," Miles continued. *"Says she isn't qualified to make the dive."*

"I know that," Peter said. He opened a utility pouch on his left hip, pulled out an adjustable socket wrench, and fitted it against a cross bolt outside the collar. "I had a talk with Leslie last night in the rec deck," he continued as he began to widen the collar aperture by ten inches.

"She's aware that she isn't qualified. In fact, she's rather ashamed that she might have bumped off a scientist. But her case is that . . ." He grunted as he twisted at the frozen bolt. "Her position is that she's qualified as a journalist, and that makes her essential to this trip."

"And you're taking her side, and not Judith's?"

He muttered an obscenity under his breath, and not just because of the recaltritant bolt. "It's not an either-or thing. I mean, it's not like Judith is the one who's been bumped. Doc doesn't want to go, and Harry Chang's doing beach time. It isn't like we've got a waiting list down here."

The bolt finally gave way; Peter pumped at the wrench handle, carefully watching the inch marks within the collar to make sure he got the alignment right. *"Sounds like you're taking another woman's side against your wife's,"* Bartlett said. *"That's dangerous territory, man."*

Just for once, Peter wanted to tell Miles where to go, and which train to take. But he wasn't about to discuss his marital problems while he was at 328 feet. "Look, just let me handle this, okay?" he said. "I've got stuff to do."

There was a long pause. Peter took the moment to pull the wrench off the bolt. He glanced to one side and was startled to see a barracuda hovering only a few feet away, its sharp-toothed jaws agape. Apparently it had been attracted by the reflective glint of stainless steel. More of a nuisance than a threat, the damn things were always curious about bright, shiny objects. He carefully placed the wrench in his pouch and swam in place, trying not to make any sudden moves. After a few moments the ugly fish lost interest and turned away, disappearing as quickly as it had come.

"Whatever you say," Bartlett said at last. *"Talk to you later. Over and out."*

"Copy that, Tethys. Over and out." Peter sighed, then flooded his BC a little more and sank away from the docking collar. Christ on a broomstick. The last thing he wanted to deal with this morning was . . .

Pale greenish-yellow light washed over his right shoulder, casting his elongated shadow against the sea bottom. A school of small fish rushed past him, then Juan's calm voice spoke his headphone:

"Peter, the Galatea *is on final approach."*

Peter turned to see an enormous shape just beyond the habitat's support beams, backlit by its forward searchlight. Dazzled by the cyclopean glare, he raised a hand against his visor. "Juan, tell him to kill the light!"

"Sorry about that, diver," a new voice said. *"Didn't know there was someone down there."*

Peter recognized the voice. "Hey, Mike, is that you?"

The searchlight blinked off, leaving a hazy afterimage imprinted on his retinas. *"Is that Pete Lipscomb?"* the voice asked. *"Whoa . . . sorry about that. Didn't think I was going to get a reception committee."*

"It's okay. Just give me a second." If Peter could have rubbed his eyes, he would have done so. Instead, he closed them for a few moments, waited for the spots to fade. "I've just been getting the collar adjusted. Are you in position?"

"Right in the alley. Ready to guide me in?"

"Will do." Peter opened his eyes again, then reached into another pouch on his right hip and pulled out two chemical light sticks. He bent their plastic shafts within his fists and carefully looked away as they glowed to life, then took one in each hand. "Okay, follow me in," he said as he held the sticks apart and swam backward from the docking collar. "Easy does it . . ."

He heard the dull mechanical thrum of cavitating screws, then the shape slowly surged forward. As it passed beneath the lights along the habitat's hull, for a few seconds it vaguely resembled a whale shark Peter had once glimpsed while sport-diving off Mexico's gulf coast. Then it came farther into the light, and now he could see that it was a submarine.

Ninety-three feet long, twenty-two abeam, with low handrails mounted on either side of its squat sail, it vaguely resembled a hybrid of a U.S. Navy attack sub and a WWI-vintage German U-boat. This was where any similarity to wartime submersibles ended. Beneath its blunt prow, below and behind the searchlight, was a large ovoid blister containing a circular porthole the size of a dinner plate; below the porthole were the recessed lenses of two stereoscopic TV cameras. On either side of the forward hull, along a wide yellow stripe running down from the sail, were a pair of broad diving planes; mounted behind the planes were two gimbal-mounted maneuvering thrusters. Welded to the lower hull were a pair of tiger-striped landing skids; just forward of them, behind the blister, was a double-door hatch leading to the ROV bay. A vertical rudder rose above the main-engine screw.

"Twenty feet . . . fifteen feet . . ." Peter gently coaxed the submersible forward, guiding it with his light sticks. "Raise your altitude two feet . . ."

"Crash my boat, son," the pilot snarled, *"and I'll nail up your hide and throw the rest out for chum!"*

"If you keep distracting me," Peter responded, "there won't be enough left of your boat for you to go home in."

This wasn't far from the truth, for there was barely enough room beneath Tethys for the *Galatea* to dock. Its skids were coasting only a few feet above the sea bottom, and although its aft end would stick out from beneath the sub bay, the top of its rudder would almost graze the side of the habitat. It was like trying to park a semi in a chicken coop.

"Easy does it," he said, swimming backward. "Ten feet to go . . . okay, reverse prop . . ."

The thrusters churned water as they slowed the enormous craft. There was just enough momentum left for *Galatea* to glide in the rest of the way. The docking hatch on top of the sail slid beneath the collar. "Hold position!" Peter snapped, crossing his sticks together. "You're under the collar. Now bring it up slowly . . ."

Bubbles rose from the ballast vents as the sub slowly ascended, a few inches at a time. Peter fought the urge to hold his breath—a serious mistake when you're on regulator—as he waved the sticks up and down. "Three feet . . . you're doing fine . . . two feet . . . just a foot to go . . ."

There was a muffled clang as the hatch connected with the collar, then its flanges snapped shut around the ring surrounding the hatch.

"Okay, you're in," Peter said, then he swam over to the sail to give it a quick inspection. No problems there. The connection was watertight. "You're solid, Mike."

"Thanks, partner."

"Okey-doke," he replied. "See you inside."

He swam away from the sub and headed for the shark cage.

Judith was standing outside the hyperbaric chamber when she heard a rusty rasp from within. Looking around, she saw the lock wheel on the floor hatch begin to turn.

"There's our ride." Jack Sheldon picked up his duffel bag, moved it a little farther away from the chamber's open outer hatch. "They'll probably want to get out, stretch their legs a bit."

Judith absently nodded. Since the *Galatea* pressurized to ten atmospheres during its descent, there wasn't any need for its crew to cycle through. She gazed around the wet room. A few crewmembers leaned against bulkheads or sat on the plastic supply crates they had hauled down from the storeroom. Andie hovered nearby, her camcorder positioned on her right shoulder, ready to record her aunt's departure. Jared Hilliard leaned against the chugging air compressor, quietly observing everything.

As for Leslie Sun, she was seated on a bench a few feet away, her feet propped up on her bag as she took notes. She happened to glance up just then; for a moment the two women found themselves regarding one another. Then Leslie gave Judith a catty smile before, ever so casually, she returned her attention to her work.

Bitch, Judith thought. You really think you're getting away with something, don't you?

Judith knew all about the little rendezvous Leslie had with her husband last night. After Charles left the bio lab, she asked Juan to locate Peter. When the AI told her that he was in the rec deck, she almost went to see him; although she was still angry, she thought it was important that she apologize for her outburst in the mess deck. But just as she was about to leave, on sudden impulse, she asked Juan to locate Leslie as well.

When Juan informed her that she, too, was in the rec deck, Judith felt as if she had just been punched in the heart.

A second confrontation was out of the question. She had made a fool out of herself once already; there was no way she was going to make that mistake again. Yet neither could she stand the thought of being locked in a sub for the next three days with that woman. She waited to see if Peter would voluntarily come to her, but when he hadn't appeared by 2400, she queried Juan once more, and discovered that he had returned to his bunk. It wasn't until then that she unrolled the nylon hammock she had fetched from the storage cabinet. She slept uneasily that night, fully clothed, all alone in the bio lab.

The next morning, feeling cramped and uneasy, she returned to the deck where she and Peter were berthed, only to discover that he had already left. Once again, Juan provided his location; he was in the wet room, getting suited up for a dive. Judith took a long, hot shower, during which she weighed her options, then she went to her bunk, untouched from the night before. After closing herself inside, she put on her headset once more and had Juan patch through a couple of phone calls.

Okay, so Ms. Leslie Sun knew how to play dirty. Fine by her. She had a few mud pies of her own to sling.

Judith gazed at the still surface of the moon pool. No sign of Peter, but he should be coming up any minute now . . .

Her thoughts were interrupted by the metallic squeal of the hatch cover being raised. Out of the corner of her eye, she saw Leslie lower her notebook.

They heard a pair of steps on the ladder, then a tall, muscular black man with a shaved head and a gold ring in his right ear climbed up through the manhole. Seeing him, Judith was reminded of Queequeg, the Polynesian harpooner from *Moby-Dick*; all he needed was a beaverskin top hat and a shrunken head. He adjusted his rimwire glasses as he peered through the exit hatch, then he quietly sat down on a bench within the chamber, making room for the person coming up the ladder behind him.

A short, barrel-chested man climbed through the manhole. Balding scalp with a fringe of gray hair around his ears and neck, handlebar mustache, deep-set eyes. Moving past the silent black man, he stamped across the hyperbaric chamber to the hatch, where he stopped to gaze around the room. His flinty eyes settled first Leslie, then Andie, and finally Judith.

"One of you ladies call a cab?" he growled.

"I don't know," Judith replied. "I was looking for one, but maybe I better wait for the next ride."

He favored her with glare so hostile that she involuntarily stepped back. "You got a problem with my driving, lady?" he demanded in a harsh whiskey-and-cigar rasp, then he stamped down the ladder to advance on her. "You think you know someone better, huh?"

Out of the corner of her eye, Judith caught a glimpse of Leslie Sun smirking at her. "I might," she said, staring back at him. "If he's sober, I'll take anyone."

"Why, you snotty little . . ." Then he pounced on her. "Judy, you bitch, how the hell are you?" he yelled as he wrapped his muscular arms around her in a rib-crunching bear hug. "Haven't seen you in ages, baby!"

"Watch it," she gasped, gently pushing him back. "You're going to break something." She ran her hand across his scalp. "When did this happen? Last time I saw you, there were still enough left to count."

Even within the rarefied community of DSV pilots, Mike Cilantro was something of a legend. While in the Navy, he had served for a short time aboard ICBM boomers before being trained as a DSRV driver; later, during the waning years of the cold war, he had been a second officer aboard the NR-1 while it was still undertaking classified CIA missions. After leaving the service, he had moved to Woods Hole and piloted the *Alvin* during more than thirty deep-ocean dives, before being lured away from WHOI by Yemaya. In the course of his long career, he had located a sunken Russian sub, explored both the *Titanic* and the *Bismarck,* charted deep-ocean vents in

both the Atlantic and Pacific, and assisted in at least one
covert Navy operation.

"What can I say? Wife number three took the rest in
divorce court." When he grinned, she was able to count
the gold caps on his molars. "The new girlfriend thinks
I look better this way, so what the hell."

"You broke up with Eve? Oh, jeez, Mike, I'm
sorry . . ."

"Don't be. She hated my guts, and I didn't like her
much either." As he stepped back, she felt his hands
lightly brush her buttocks. She didn't mind; Mike had
always been a dirty old man, and the one and only time
he had made a serious pass at her was while they were
on a WHOI expedition to the Cayman Trench. She turned
him down, of course, but only because she was engaged
to Peter. For his part, Cilantro had taken it like a gentleman, but she had no doubt that she was always welcome
to be his next girlfriend. Some of them were young
enough to be his daughter; Mike might be bald, fat, and
pushing fifty, but nonetheless he was one of the sexiest
men she had ever met.

He turned away from her, surveyed the rest of the
bystanders. "Okay, the boat's ready to go, and I'm told
we've got two more passengers. Who are they?" Before
anyone could respond, he pointed to Andie. "You with
the camera. You going?"

Andie was squinting through the eyepiece when he
said that. Her eyes widened and her grip on the unit wavered. "Who, me? . . . uh, no . . . I mean, but . . ."

"That's my niece, Andrea," Judith said quietly. "She's
not going."

"Hmm. Nice to meet you. Andrea. Sorry to leave you
behind." Cilantro turned to Jack Sheldon. "You. Are you
with us?"

"Uh . . ." Sheldon glanced both ways, as if Cilantro

might be addressing someone else. "I'm going, sure." He stepped forward to offer his hand. "Jack Sheldon, marine geologist. I'm really happy to meet you, Captain. I've heard much about—"

"Thanks, but don't call me Captain. Left the Navy while you were still in kindergarten. Skipper will do." Cilantro briefly shook with Sheldon, then he turned to Leslie Sun. "And who may you be?"

Leslie smiled radiantly as she extended her hand. "I'm Leslie Sun, from *Millennium* magazine. It's a pleasure to meet you, Mister . . ."

"Put it away, sister. I'm not impressed." Cilantro glowered at her, and didn't deign to shake her hand. "Let's get two things straight. First, you're a reporter, which makes you more worthless than lead shot as far as I'm concerned, because at least I can jettison lead if I have to. Second, I don't like being told who I have to be take on my boat, and I was told that I had to take you. That makes you an uninvited guest. So you've got two strikes against you from the git-go."

Leslie dropped her hand, her smile remaining frozen on her face. Despite herself, Judith had to admire her poise; another woman might have wilted under such a verbal onslaught. "I'm sorry you feel that way, Mr. Cilantro," she replied evenly. "I'll try to convince you otherwise."

"You're going to have to try real hard, sweetheart." He turned to the others. "Okay, listen up now, because here's the ground rules. It doesn't look like it on the outside, but *Galatea* is a small boat on the inside. You'll see how just how small it is when you get in there. Since we're going to be operating at ten atmospheres, this means we're going to remain submerged the entire time. No coming up to surface unless there's an extreme emergency, and even then we won't be able to pop the hatch.

So everyone has to do everything exactly as I say it, when I say it. No discussion, no debate. This is not a democracy. I give an order, you follow it, case closed. Are we clear on that?"

Judith and Jack nodded; Leslie's eyes widened a bit, but she reluctantly nodded as well. "Good," Cilantro said. "Now, I see that you're all carrying bags. We don't have much storage space, so I'm going to have to ask you to leave a lot of your gear behind. One change of clothes, including a sweatshirt and a pair of trousers, and that's it. Same goes for toilet supplies. A toothbrush is okay, and I'd appreciate it if you brought some deodorant, but forget everything else." He glanced at Judith and Leslie. "Ladies, if either of you are having your periods or expecting them to begin in the next three or four days, bring what you need, but only that much. Understand?"

As he spoke, Leslie knelt down next to her bag and was unzipping it. Judith guiltily looked at her overstuffed duffel bag; most of the stuff in there would have to be left behind. She bent down and started to untie the drawstring when she heard something splash within the moon pool. She looked up to see Peter emerging from the far side of the pool; although he was in full diving gear, she instantly recognized him from his height and build. A crewman helped him climb up the ladder; when he was out of the water, the other man went around behind him to disconnect the hoses from the rebreather unit on his back.

"I'm going to have you board the sub one at a time," Cilantro was saying. He pointed to the tall black man waiting by the manhole within the hyperbaric chamber. "This is my first officer, Dale Schuster." Schuster silently nodded to them. "He's going to help you climb down the ladder, one at a time. Our second officer, Mr. Niedzwiecki, I think some of you have already met. He's waiting inside to help you get settled in. He's recovering from a mild chest injury, so please follow his instructions, because he's going to need all the help you can give him."

Judith watched as Peter tugged the helmet from his head. It dripped seawater as he carefully placed it on a nearby bench. He pinched his nose to equalize the slight difference in pressure, then, still bent over from the weight of the rebreather, he began to unsnap the pack's buckles. So far, he hadn't spotted her on the opposite side of the compartment.

"Ms. Sun," Mike said, "you look like you're ready to go, so you're first."

Leslie had removed most of her belongings from her nylon bag and placed them in a pile on the bench where she had been sitting. "Someone will take these to my quarters, won't they?" she said, speaking in the general direction of the crewmembers lounging nearby. One of them nodded indifferently and Jared gave her an okay sign. Andie quietly stepped around her, right eye glued to her camcorder, filming her every move.

Leslie noticed the camera's presence, and grinned at the lens. "Here we go," she said. "Wish me luck." Then she picked up her half-empty bag and walked up the ladder into the chamber.

Judith glanced across the wet room again. Peter had finally looked up to see the small crowd on the opposite side of the room. He caught sight of Judith and briefly held up a hand, then turned his head to say something to the crewman removing his breather. The other man grabbed the unit in his arms and hauled it off Peter's back while he scrambled to pull off his BC and fins.

Within the chamber, Leslie was climbing down the narrow manhole. Schuster waited until she disappeared from sight before he carefully handed her bag to her, then he glanced back toward Cilantro.

Cilantro nodded, and then Schuster bent down, picked

up the hatch cover, and lowered it shut above the manhole.

Cilantro looked at Judith. Without saying a word, he gave her a wink.

Judith smiled back at him, then looked once more around the room. Andie had lowered her camera and was examining the film meter. Jack was still pulling stuff out of his bag. Jared was checking his watch. Everyone else was quietly talking among themselves.

She heard a wet, sloppy sound behind her, and turned to see Peter walking across the deck toward her. He had unzipped the front of his wet suit and taken off his fins, but he had neglected to put on his headset.

"Hey, you didn't come back last night," he said. "What's going on?"

Despite his hydrogen gargle, Judith understood him perfectly. Nonetheless, she cupped a hand against her ear. "Come again? I didn't hear you."

Peter started to repeat himself, then stopped. He made an impatient gesture to a nearby crewman, and the other man surrendered his headset to him. Peter pulled it on, adjusted the mike, murmured something to Juan. A moment later his voice came through her earpiece: "I said, you didn't come to bed last night. You stayed in the bio lab. What's wrong?"

Jack and Jared looked up when he said this. "Juan, private line to Peter Lipscomb, please," she murmured, and waited until the AI double-beeped its compliance. Now no one else could hear them unless they happened to be standing nearby. "You were out on a date," she continued. "I didn't want to bother you."

She had the pleasure of watching Peter's face go pale. "It wasn't a date," he said quietly. "She wanted to have a drink, so I took her to the rec room. We had a drink, threw some darts, talked some . . . that was it."

"Sounds like fun.Wish I could have been there. Why didn't you call me?"

"You were pissed off. I figured you wanted to be left alone."

"I was pissed off, sure, but that didn't mean I wanted to be left alone." A small lie, but why should he know that? "Besides, isn't that what a husband's supposed to do?"

Peter's face darkened. "What are you trying to get at?"

"That's funny. I was about to ask you the same thing."

He stared back at her, and for a moment she saw a flicker of suppressed anger in his face. Then he glanced away, and as he did, he raised a fist to his mouth and coughed meaningfully. Judith followed his gaze; Andie stood only a few feet away, her camera lowered from her shoulder. How long she had been standing there, Judith had no way of knowing, yet there was a terrible look in her eyes.

"Hey, kiddo," Peter said. "How're you . . ."

Without a word, Andie turned on her heel and stalked away.

"You're not fooling her, either," Judith murmured.

Peter looked back at her, and was about to say something—what, she couldn't imagine—when they heard the harsh clang of the floor hatch banging open.

Everyone turned to see Leslie Sun hastily climb up from the sub. Her face was flushed, and she appeared to be breathing hard. She reached down to pull up her nylon bag, then she hurried past Schuster and stalked out of the chamber.

"Uh-oh," Judith murmured. "Looks like we have a little trouble here."

Mike Cilantro met her at the foot of the ladder. She said something to him in a voice so low that no one could hear her; Cilantro nodded and said something to her in return, then Leslie pulled the bag strap over her shoulder and walked away. She paused briefly to gather the clothes she had left on the bench; then, avoiding everyone's gaze, she silently marched across the wet room to the ladder leading to the upper decks.

"Looks like your friend just copped out," Judith said softly.

Peter watched the journalist as she climbed up the ladder. "But she told me—"

He was interrupted by Mike Cilantro. "Seems we're having a slight change of plan," he said, addressing the others. "Ms. Sun doesn't think she can make the trip after all. She just found that the sub is a little tighter than she expected. Happens from time to time."

Judith had to fight to keep from smiling. And indeed, so it did; people who didn't think they were claustrophobic were often rattled when brought aboard a deep-ocean submersible. For this reason, sub drivers made a point of testing passengers before departure by taking them into the sub and carefully observing their reactions once the hatch was shut.

"You tipped him off, didn't you?" Peter asked quietly.

Damn. He must have seen the look on her face. "I gave him a call this morning, sure," she replied. "I saw how nervous she was in the shuttle sub yesterday . . ."

"So you thought he should know." Peter shook his head. "Got to hand it to you. You're pretty slick when you want to be."

"Better go see how she's doing," she said. "I don't think she ought to be alone just now."

Peter glared at her, but didn't reply.

"So it looks like we've got an empty seat," Cilantro continued, "and since Ms. Sun isn't going with us, we need someone to document this trip. Any takers?"

He gazed expectantly around the compartment. Judith

caught his eye and jabbed a finger in Andie's direction.
Cilantro faintly nodded back, then turned to her niece.
"You there . . . the one with the camera. What's your
name again?"

"Me?" Andie's mouth dropped open. "You're talking
to me?"

"No, I'm talking to Robert De Niro." A couple of
crewmembers chuckled as Cilantro grinned at her. "Your
name's Andrea, right?"

"Uh . . . yeah, but people call me Andie."

"You know how to handle that thing, Andie?"

"This? " She looked at the camcorder on her shoulder.
"Uh . . . yeah, sure."

"She's good, Mike," Peter said. "I've seen some of
her work."

Andie glanced uncertainly over her shoulder at her uncle. "Go on," he said, giving her an encouraging nod.
"Chance of a lifetime. Go for it."

"The seat's yours," Cilantro said, "provided you can
stand five minutes in the sub. And we need a camera
operator."

"Go on, do it." Judith stepped closer to whisper in
Andie's ear. "I'll be with you. It'll be great. Trust me."

Andie hesitated, then lowered her rig from her shoulder. "Can I grab some clothes first? And the rest of my
equipment?"

Cilantro glanced at his watch. "You've got five
minutes, Camera Girl. Run."

"Thanks! Don't leave without me!" She carefully
placed the camera on the floor in front of Judith. "Watch
this for me, willya?" she said, then she bolted for the
ladder, pushing a startled diver out of the way.

"Do you think this is smart?" Peter said quietly. "I
mean, maybe I should call Jack first."

"Your brother doesn't know the Mid-Atlantic Ridge

from his butt." Judith crossed her arms as she watched Andie take the ladder two rungs at a time. "That's not who I'm worried about."

"Andie?" He shrugged. "Hey, it's your idea, so it's your problem. I'm—"

"Staying behind. Right." She lowered her voice once more. "And you'll have company, too."

For a moment Peter said nothing. Then he turned around to look her square in the eye. "Judy, there's nothing going on between us, I promise."

"That's all I need to hear." She picked up her bag and hefted it over her shoulder. "If you're lying, though . . ."

"What is this, a test?"

"No . . . no, it's not a test." Judith thought about it a moment. "Let's call it what it is," she said finally. "An expedition."

She stood on tiptoe to give him a quick buss. It was meant to be a polite goodbye, but when she stepped back and saw the wounded expression on his face, she felt her heart melt a bit. "Be good," she whispered, then wrapped her arms around his neck and gave him a much longer and more meaningful kiss. "Be here when I get back."

"I will," he murmured. "Trust me."

"I guess I'll have to," she said as she released him. Then she turned and walked toward the waiting sub.

TWELVE

Plateau

6.6.11—1042 EST

Like some great beast emerging from an undersea grotto, the *Galatea* slowly backed out of its temporary berth beneath Tethys 1, its thrusters churning frothy water as divers waved light sticks to guide the pilots within the sub. The craft moved gradually, a few feet at a time, until its bow was clear of the support beams, then it made a gradual turn to starboard until its stern was parallel to the main hab. One diver swam out of the way while the other positioned himself just ahead of the sub; after making sure that the way was clear, he signaled the pilot to come forward, then he, too, kicked away as fast as he could.

Its forward light casting a broad oval across the seafloor, the *Galatea* moved away from the station. A few bubbles rose from its ballast valves as it ascended to cruise depth; when it was forty feet above the bottom, the thrusters slowed and stopped. There was a short pause, then the main prop was engaged, and the *Galatea* surged forward. It made a port turn as it picked up speed; after another minute its forward searchlight was extinguished, and now the sub was surrounded by darkness, the pale blue glow of Tethys fading in the distance.

The sub headed due east, out to deep ocean and the abyss beyond.

"Hey, kid! Want to bring me some coffee?"

At first, Andie didn't realize that Cilantro was addressing her. In fact, she could barely hear him, even though he was speaking through her headset. The constant engine noise seemed to vibrate through the soles of her shoes and echo off the steel casing surrounding her; every few seconds it was interrupted by a sharp *pong!* from the depth-finding sonar, clearly heard from the forward control room.

She sat on the edge of her narrow bunk, her head between her knees as she tried to cram her camera case into the tiny space which had been given to her. However hard she wiggled and shoved, though, the case kept sticking out into the aisle between the bunks, so narrow that only one person could walk through at a time.

"Hey! Camera Girl! Coffee, on the double!"

Hearing her new nickname, she jerked her head up. Too fast, too hard; the top of her skull smacked against the tubular frame of the bunk above her. She winced and cursed under her breath, and reached back to feel the bump on her scalp.

"Okay, okay," she muttered. "Just gimme a sec." She rose to her feet, and it was at that moment when the deck tilted sideways a couple of degrees. It wasn't much of an incline, but just enough to throw her off balance; the camera case slid out from under her bunk and caught her in the shins, and Andie yelped as she pitched forward.

She caught herself on the frame of the upper bunk across the aisle just before she fell across Jack Sheldon. The geologist was sitting cross-legged on his own bunk, studying the screen of the notebook computer perched in his lap. He immediately reached up to steady her. "Whoa, watch your step . . ."

"Sorry." Andie regained her balance, righted herself by holding on to the bunks. Dale Schuster, the second officer, lay on the bunk above her. He barely glanced away from the paperback thriller he was reading. "Where's the . . . y'know. Where they keep the coffee."

"The galley." Sheldon nodded aft, through a narrow hatch in the bulkhead just past the four tiered bunks. "Back there. Want some help?"

"No, no, no . . . I can get it myself." She kicked her camera case back underneath her bunk, then baby-stepped down the aisle. She had to bend almost double, while raising first one foot, then the other, to make it through the four-foot hatchway.

As confined as Tethys had been, it was practically a luxury liner compared with the *Galatea*. The ceiling was only a few inches above her head; in some places, she could tuck in her forearms, raise her elbows to shoulder height, and touch either side of the casing. Conduits, pipes, valve wheels, consoles, and airducts filled every available inch of space. The bunks were fold-down steel slabs with a miniature pillow and a wafer-thin foam mattress, with only a curtain to separate them from the control room. As she clambered through the hatch, she spotted the head: a closet containing a dwarfish metal commode, a tiny sink, and a mirror the size of a snapshot frame.

No wonder Leslie Sun flipped out. Enclosed spaces didn't make Andie nervous—she had no problem when Joe Niedzwiecki brought her aboard shortly before departure—but apparently Leslie had a touch of claustrophobia. Andie didn't mind taking her place; she was getting the adventure of a lifetime, not to mention bragging rights when she returned to Kansas City. Yet she sensed that her aunt had something to do with this; there was something going on between her, Uncle Pete, and Leslie . . .

She found Aunt Judy in the galley, a small compartment about the size of a walk-in closet. Fresh coffee was dripping into a small carafe tucked above a microwave oven. "I thought Mike and Joe would want some," Judith said as she pulled a pair of travel mugs from a cabinet. "Gimme a minute, and I'll let you run them up front."

"Yeah, okay. Sure." Andie walked a little farther down the passageway. Next to the galley was a small wardroom, not much larger than a restaurant booth. A Formica-top table was folded against the wood-paneled bulkhead between two Naugahyde-upholstered couches, and a TV and DVD deck were built into the bulkhead behind them. "This place was made for munchkins," she said when she came back to the galley.

"No worse than any other ship I've been on. You'll get used to it." She pointed farther down the passageway. "The lab's down that way. Seen it yet?" Andie shook her head, and Judith stepped out of the galley. "C'mon, I'll show you."

They reached the end of the passageway, where a round metal hatch was fitted into the aft bulkhead. The hatch was painted with yellow and white stripes, with a radiation trefoil stenciled in the center. "That's the way to the engine room and the reactor space," Judith said. "Don't even think about going in there."

"Wasn't planning to." Andie pointed to a small pocket door next to the hatch. "Is this it?"

Judith nodded and slid the door open. The lab was

about the same size as the galley, but even more crowded: a computer terminal, a couple of TV monitors, racks of test tubes, a miniature centrifuge, a microscope. Her aunt pointed to a small glove box built into the wall. "We can bring in samples from the ROV bay through here, run tests and so forth. Can't do a full workup, of course, but enough to let us know if we've got anything worth the effort while we're still on-site." She pointed to the monitors. "Jack will be back here when we're over the vent. Joe will fly the ROV from the control room."

"Where am I going to be?"

"With me, down in the blister. You'll get a chance to rehearse your act with Joe when we reach the plateau." She glanced at Andie. "Think you can handle it?"

"Sure, I guess." Cilantro had already announced that the first stop would be a trip to the Blake Plateau, to the spot where Joe Niedzwiecki had abandoned the *Doris* two days earlier.

Judith smiled. "Don't worry about it. I wouldn't have recommended you if I didn't think—"

"I don't remember that part," Andie said. "When did that happen?"

Her aunt turned to the microscope. "Well, I . . . y'know, I had a feeling that Leslie wouldn't be able to make the trip, so I talked to Mike this morning, and—"

"You got her bumped, didn't you?" Andie felt her face flush. "You told the captain that you didn't want her aboard, so you rigged things so that—"

"I didn't rig anything." When Aunt Judy looked back at her, her face was hard, her eyes cool. "You saw how nervous she was in the shuttle yesterday. Someone like that could crack at any minute during a deep-ocean dive."

"She did fine in the hyperbaric chamber."

"That was different. She knew she was in a larger place, with plenty of people around. And, no, I didn't have her bumped. I simply told Mike that her frame of mind was questionable, and recommended that they take you instead if she couldn't pass the—"

"Yeah. Right." Andie squeezed past her aunt. "I better get that coffee before he starts yelling again."

"Andie, wait . . ."

She felt her aunt touch her elbow, but she ignored her. Tears stung the corners of her eyes; she ran the back of her hand across her face. For a little while there, she had believed she was a member of this expedition because of her talent. Now she knew better. Aunt Judy had pulled strings on her behalf, and only then to deny Leslie Sun a berth.

God, that hurt . . .

Andie walked back to the galley. The carafe was full; she poured coffee into the travel mugs and fitted their lids in place, then carried them out into passageway. She saw her aunt leaning against the lab door. The expression on her face was unreadable; when she opened her mouth to say something, though, Andie turned away to duck through the hatch leading into the forward section.

Maybe they could talk later. Right now, though, she was too pissed off. Dammit, why was she always getting stuck in the middle?

"Bearing ninety-two-point-two, depth eight hundred meters." Cilantro glanced at the Ship Internal Navigation System's digital readout, then matched the SINS coordinates against the bathymetric chart displayed on the small flatscreen above his aircraft-style yoke. "Coming up on Stetson Mesa."

"Copy that, skipper." Joe Niedzwiecki took a last sip from his lukewarm coffee, then placed the mug in a plastic holder above his station. "You going to take it from here?"

"Got it. Taking it off autopilot now." Cilantro reached up and flipped a couple of toggle switches which reverted control from the sub's computer to the helm station. The TV monitors above the console showed only matte-black darkness. "I'll get us over the mesa, then down to the bottom. Why don't you and the kid go below and make yourselves comfortable."

"Sounds like a plan." Joe unbuckled his seat belt, then stood up from the plastic chair within the instrument-jammed compartment and slid past Mike's right shoulder. Schuster waited until he was clear, then inched his way into the left-hand seat. "Okay, kiddo, you're on."

Standing in the back of the control room, holding on to ceiling rungs, Andie watched as Joe knelt next to a small floor hatch cover not much larger than the lid of a kitchen trash can. He twisted its lock wheel counterclockwise, then pulled it open. "Ladies first," he said, looking up at her with a sly grin.

"Um . . ." She swallowed nervously. "Maybe you should go first."

Joe glanced at Mike, and the commander gave him a nod. "Okey-doke," he said, then he stepped into the manhole, holding on to the hatch cover for support. As he climbed down, one step at a time, he raised both arms above his head; Andie noted that he sucked in his gut, and he had to squirm a little to get his shoulders through. She was reminded of magic tricks she had seen where someone would disappear into a box little larger than an orange crate.

"Okay," he called up, "hand me down your rig."

Andie had already removed the camcorder from its case and inserted a film disk. Dangling it from its shoulder strap, she carefully lowered the camera through the hatch. Joe reached up and took it, then placed it off to the side. "Your turn," he said. "Watch your head."

Andie took a deep breath, then squatted on her hips and, one leg at a time, shimmied down into the hole. She was skinnier than Joe, so she didn't have any trouble until she got to her shoulders, but then she raised her left arm straight above her head and dipped her right shoulder, and the rest was easy.

The blister was no larger than the backseat of a car, and shaped like the inside of an egg. There was no room for chairs; instead, two foam pads rested on the floor in front of the porthole, Joe lay on his stomach, a small pillow bunched up under his chest, his legs raised in the air. "Right here," he said, patting the pad next to him, and grinned when she visibly hesitated. "Don't worry, I'm not going to get fresh. I've got a daughter nearly your age."

Andie laughed uneasily, but she got down on her hands and knees and crawled forward until her shoulders were rubbing against his. Another pillow was waiting for her, and she rested her chest and shoulders against it. "There you go," Joe said. "You're getting the hang of it."

"Why is so tight in here?"

"You think this is tight? You should have been aboard the old *Alvin*. Makes this look like a limo." He reached up to switch on a small ceiling lamp; now she could clearly see the small control panel set in the floor before them. "Okay, lemme show you how this works."

Joe went down the panel, showing her all the buttons: interior lights, outside floodlights, ceiling fan, the voice recorder. "We've got a couple of still cameras, too," he said, pointing to a pair of shutter controls beneath video viewfinders the size of postage stamps, "but they're mainly for backup. We get more mileage out of someone handling a camcorder down here. That's where you come in."

"Uh-huh." Andie glanced back at her camcorder where it lay between their legs. "You want me to shoot the entire time?"

"Uh-uh. Save your film until we get to the bottom." He hesitated, then he lowered his voice. "Look, kiddo . . ."

"Joe? No offense, but—"

"You don't like people calling you that?" She shook her head. "Sorry. Won't do it again." She smiled and he went on. "Okay, Andie, here's the deal. We might see something down that's a little scary—"

"Your sea serpent, right?"

He gaped at her, then smacked his forehead. "Jeez! I forgot. You were at the briefing a couple of nights ago."

"Yeah, I was there. Saw the film and everything."

"And you're not worried?"

God! What did she look like, a five-year-old? "No, I'm not worried. I really want to—"

She was interrupted by Cilantro's voice in her headset. "Okay, blister team, we're fifty fathoms from the bottom, ten miles from site. We're going to make a slow sweep of the western area before we home in on *Doris*. Ready down there?"

"Ready, skipper." Joe nodded toward her camera. "Get your rig. Time to go monster hunting."

W ithin the control room, Judith knelt on the deck be-hind Cilantro and Schuster, her elbows resting on the backs of their chairs as she watched the ragged lines of the sonar screen. *Galatea* had cleared Stetson Mesa, the broad sea mount just past the narrow canyon between the Florida-Hatteras Slope and the Blake Plateau. Now the sub was taking on ballast and descending to the plateau itself.

"Forty fathoms to bottom," Schuster murmured. His hands gripped on the helm yoke, deftly manipulating the sub's rudder and elevators. "Seven miles from target."

"Got a transponder fix yet?" Cilantro asked.

Schuster pointed to a computer screen above the sonarscope. "Right here. Weak but steady."

"Very good. Give me a SINS fix and close in."

Judith absently nibbled the thumbnail of her right hand. "Are you guys still using the main engine?"

"Of course," Cilantro said. "Cover more ground this way."

"No good." She shook her head. "Cut the prop and use the thrusters."

Cilantro glanced over his shoulder at her. "That's going to take more time, Judy. We're on a deadline here."

"I know, I know." Once again, she was reminded that this was a side trip; the major objective was the Mid-Atlantic Ridge, and this was supposed to be a brief stopover. "I'd prefer to make this as quiet as possible. If there's something down here, we want to sneak up on it."

Cilantro thought about it a moment, then nodded to Schuster. "Okay, cut the prop and go to lateral thrusters." Then he glanced at Judith again and raised a finger. "One hour, no more. We get pics of *Doris* and take a quick peek, then—"

"Chrissakes, Mike. You think this thing keeps a schedule?"

"No, but we do. One hour, tops, then we're out of here."

"Ah, c'mon . . ."

"Take it or leave it." He paused. "Look, if we have

enough time after the MAR dive, we'll swing back here on the return leg. Fair enough?"

As if she had any choice. "Okay"—she sighed—"fair enough."

The view through the blister porthole was like a window into another universe, mysterious and awe-inspiring. Andie forgot all about her camera and stared through the Plexiglas pane, transfixed by the alien beauty. Hand-size squid jetted past like miniature torpedoes, their rubbery flesh pulsating with color as they raced away from the sub; anglerfish, resembling monsters from a bad sci-fi movie, gaped at her before vanishing back into the darkness. Plankton scintillated in the floodlight beam like snowflakes on a wintery Midwestern morning.

"God," she whispered, "it's so weird down here."

"I know what you mean." Lying on his stomach next to her, Joe Niedzwiecki nodded. "I've been down here so many times, I've lost count, and I'm still not used to it."

"Two fathoms to bottom," Hughes's voice said in their headsets. "Coming up on the site."

Through the porthole, they began to make out the nodule field, black potatoes resting in the fine gray silt. "There's Porky's track," Joe said, pointing to a long, broad furrow leading through the field. "You see that, Al?"

"Got it, Joe," Mike replied. "Dale's going to follow it to *Doris*."

Sediment floated up from the seafloor, stirred by the *Galatea*'s thrusters. "Picking up some muck," Joe said. "Recommend that we stay at this altitude." He glanced at Andie, saw that she was still staring out the porthole. He gently nudged her shoulder with his elbow. "Hey, next James Cameron . . . look alive over there."

"Um? Oh, right. Sorry." Andie picked up her camera, propped it up on the pillow, and steadied it with her hands as she peered through the viewfinder. "Damn, I'm getting a reflection from the glass."

"Easily taken care of." Joe reached up and flipped off the interior lights. "Better?"

"Yeah. Thanks." The abrupt darkness caught her by surprise. She felt a chill race through her, and not just because of the low temperature within the blister. "Uh, Joe?"

"Yeah, kiddo—sorry. Andie."

"Not to make a big deal about it, but . . . what if this window broke? What would we do then?"

"Don't worry about it." He reached forward and gently tapped a fingernail against the pane. "That's three inches of optical acrylic, same stuff they use in the president's limo. It could stop a bullet."

"Yeah, I know, but still . . ."

"If the window broke, you'd be dead so quick, you'd never know it." He gently patted her shoulder. "It's never happened, though, so don't worry about it."

"Don't worry about it. Right." She swallowed hard, took a deep breath. It was hard to keep the camera still; her hands wouldn't stop trembling. Cut it out, she thought. You don't want to wimp out in front of these guys. And you're seventeen, for heaven's sake. Nobody dies at seventeen . . .

"Any sonar contacts?" Joe asked.

"Nothing except *Doris*," Schuster replied. "It's straight ahead, two hundred feet. You should see it any minute now."

Galatea cruised low over the nodule field, following the eroded tracks left by the mining robot. Albino crabs and spiny lobsters scuttled away as the floodlight touched them; after a few moments Andie felt wonder overcoming her fear. "Man, I'm going to ace film class next fall," she murmured, focusing the camera on the crustaceans. "They're never going to believe—whoa!"

"Throttle it back, Dale," Joe said quietly. "We've found *Doris*."

Captured by the floodlight, the submersible loomed out of the darkness like an automobile abandoned on a country road. It lay on its side, landing skids thrust outward. There was a gaping hole forward of the afterbody where the crew sphere had once been attached; severed electrical lines lay limp in the sediment. Crabs scuttled along the wreckage like looters, searching in vain for something digestible.

"Look at the port skid," Joe said, pointing to the upper one. "See how it's bent inward?"

"We see it, Joe." Now they heard Judith's voice through their headsets. "Is that where it rammed you?"

"I think so, yeah. Get us in a little more, will you?" As the *Galatea* moved closer, he prodded Andie. "Zoom in on that. Make sure you get it."

"I'm getting it." Andie nibbled her lower lip. It was difficult to focus, though, while the sub was in motion; the camera bobbed in her hands, and she impatiently shoved the pillow out of her way so that she could brace her elbows against the cold deck. "I just wish we'd stop jiggling so much."

"There's a clear space on the other side," Schuster said. "Looks like that's where Porky was. If it helps any, I can put it down over there."

For a moment Andie didn't realize he was speaking to her. "Yeah, okay," she said, feeling a sudden rush of authority. She was telling the driver where to park. "That would be great. Thanks."

The bottom floated away as *Galatea* ascended a few

feet; they watched as the wreckage passed beneath them. "Check out that dent in the afterbody, upper left side," Joe said quietly. "You catch that, Andie?"

"Got it." She managed to zoom in on the dent just as the floodlight passed over it. "Is that where . . . ?"

"It hit me the first time, uh-huh, I think so." His voice was low. "Christ, that fucker was—oops, sorry."

"Don't worry about it." She was about to add that she had heard far worse in gym class when Joe snorted in amusement. She glanced at him and saw the broad smile on his face, and she suddenly realized that she had echoed exactly what he had said to her a few minutes earlier.

They were still chuckling over this when Cilantro spoke to them again. "Joe? Andie? You guys paying attention down there?"

"We're here," Joe said. "Sorry. We just—"

"We've got a sonar contact."

"Holy shit," Judith whispered. Hands braced against the seatbacks, she hunched forward to peer at the side-scan sonar. A fuzzy, S-shaped image appeared at the upper left side of the screen, at the limit of sonar range. There was another sharp *beep* from the return pulse, and as everyone in the control room watched breathlessly, the screen changed. Now the object had moved a few degrees closer, and its shape had altered to an reversed S.

"Bearing forty-two-point-five degrees, distance 390 feet," Schuster said calmly. "Still approaching."

"Put us down!" Judith grabbed Mike's shoulder. "Anywhere you can, put us down!"

"Ow! Cut it out!" Cilantro swatted her hand away as Schuster turned the yoke hard to starboard, bringing the sub around to directly face the incoming object. "Dammit, Judy, this ain't a helicopter. I can't make it land on a dime." He glanced up at the TV monitors. " 'Sides, we're too close to *Doris*. If I bring it down now, our back end will smash into her."

Judith hissed under her breath. He was right. *Galatea* was over ninety feet long, and it was still above the wreck of the *Doris*. If they landed here, there was a good chance that *Galatea* would collide with the downed submersible; such an accident might or might not damage the larger vessel's titanium hull, but it would almost certainly screw up the main prop. If that happened, it would be the end of the trip; Mike would have no choice but to blow tanks and make an emergency surface.

She stared at the sonar screen. The object was still closing in; the latest image showed that it had become a proper S again. "Then get us away from *Doris*," she said. "Put it down over there." She pointed to the right TV screen; it displayed the cleared area where the mining robot had once rested. "That's far enough away for us to go dead boat."

Schuster and Cilantro gave each other uncertain looks. Dead boat was a sub pilot's term for landing on the bottom and shutting down all nonvital systems: engines, lights, sonar, the works. Submarine captains had devised it as a wartime strategy, in more shallow waters, to play possum in order to evade surface vessels searching for them; deep-ocean pilots sometimes did it when they wanted to conserve battery power while taking a break to eat lunch, or perhaps just to take in the dark silence of the deep.

Cilantro shook his head. "No," he murmured to Schuster. "Hold present position. We're going to see—"

"Goddammit, Mike!"

"No argument." He gave Judith a sharp look, which shut her up. "It's probably just as curious about us as we are about it," he added. "Let's just see what happens."

Judith bit her lip. She didn't like Mike's decision, but *Galatea* was his ship.

She checked the sonar again.The object was still on the same bearing, and was now less than three hundred feet away.

"D amn, damn, damn . . ."
Although she continued to peer through the viewfinder, Andie glanced out of the corner of her eye at Joe. He was crouched forward, his face nearly touching the blister porthole, fists clenched against the pillow. "What's wrong?" she asked softly.

"We're going about this all wrong," he murmured. "We should be dead boat, like I was when I—"

"Two hundred feet," Cilantro said. "Stay sharp down there. It's coming right for us."

Through the porthole, they saw a floodlit, mono-chrome expanse: dark manganese nodules against silt and sand, broken only by the broad swath left by the mining 'bot. Beyond a fifty-foot radius, though, lay only impenetrable darkness. Nothing moved, save for the ever-present snow of detritus. Strange. Even the crabs seemed to have disappeared . . .

"For chrissakes, Mike," Joe snapped, "put us down and cut the sonar! It's never going to come closer if we're still active!"

A long pause. Andie touched a stud on the camera, checked the digital readout within the viewfinder. Still plenty of time left on this disk; she could stretch it out more, but that would mean losing resolution.

"Mike . . ." Joe said.

"Hang on," Cilantro replied. "It's at 120 feet and closing."

She heard Joe mutter an obscenity, but she dared not look away from the viewfinder. The porthole was much too small; all of sudden it seemed as if she was trying to film a football game through a knothole in a wooden fence.

"One hundred feet," Cilantro said. "Stay cool, everyone."

She felt Joe move restlessly against her side. "Are you scared?" she whispered.

"Not a bit. You?"

She recalled the footage she had been shown in the briefing room two nights ago, the long wall of flesh and muscle captured by *Doris*'s camera, the gaping jaws in the wedgelike head. It wasn't so much what she had seen, though, as what she hadn't. Indeed, it was all too easy to imagine the rest. All at once she wanted to drop her camera, scurry out of the blister, head for her tiny bunk, and curl up beneath the blankets. Seventeen wasn't too young to die, was it?

"Me?" she murmured. "Naw . . ."

"Eighty feet," Cilantro said. "Seventy . . ."

Something flashed into the light. She jerked, moved her camera to track it, caught the briefest glimpse of a small object that appeared and vanished within a second. A fish of some sort, racing away. Fleeing from . . . something.

She caught her breath, turned the camera back to its original point of focus. For an instant it seemed like plankton and sediment was being stirred toward them, as if swept into the light by something just beyond floodlight range. Her heart trip-hammered against her chest as she fought to hold the camera steady.

"Okay, okay . . ." she whispered. "C'mon . . ."

She heard Joe's breathing, the subtle creak of pressure against the hull, muted movement along the deck plates above her. Through the viewfinder, though, she saw nothing save lunar landscape.

They waited, and watched, as the seconds trickled slowly past.

And they saw nothing.

After a minute Joe slowly let out his breath.

"It's gone," he said. "Goddammit . . . it's gone."

THIRTEEN
Thresher

6.6.11—2003 AST

"I don't get it," Andie said. "How could it have just disappeared?"

Chin cradled in her palm, she picked at the plate of sweet-and-sour chicken which Judith had brought her from the galley; like almost everything else in the larder, it was a prepackaged meal, in and out of the microwave with the minimum of preparation. With typical teenage fussiness, Andie had spent ten minutes trying to decide between it, Yankee pot roast, and roast turkey, even going so far as to study the ingredients stickers to make sure nothing contained lactose or MSG. Now that it was on the table, though, she had apparently lost all interest.

"It didn't just disappear," Judith said from the galley as she waited for her own dinner to heat. "I told you . . . when it was about seventy feet away, it suddenly turned and took off in another direction. Just like that—"

"It was gone. Sure. That's what everyone says." Her niece absently stirred the gooey broccoli and chicken with her plastic fork. "So why didn't we go after it? That's what I don't understand."

"Because it . . . hold on." An instant later the microwave chimed; Judith opened the door, carefully removed the hot plate, and put it on the counter. She peeled off the cellophane cover and prodded the food with a fingertip. The turkey was reasonably warm, although the mashed potatoes and stuffing were still a bit on the cool side. Altogether, it was as appetizing as the TV dinner it closely resembled. It would have to do, though; she was ravenous, and pretty soon the others would be coming back for dinner. Someone had slipped a CD into the deck up front, and Beethoven's *Pastoral* drifted in from the control room.

"It was going too fast," she continued. "At least ten knots." Fast as a barracuda, she thought, still amazed at how something so large could move so quickly. "Even if the skipper had chased it, we couldn't have possibly caught up."

"Yeah, well . . ." Andie didn't look up when her aunt carried her plate into the wardroom and sat down on the other side of the small table. "I'd just like to know why we didn't—what did you call it? When we sit down and do nothing?"

"Go dead boat." Judith shrugged as she spread a paper napkin across her lap and picked up her knife and fork. "I agree. Maybe that's what we should have done. That's what I told Mike, but—"

She heard footsteps coming down the passageway, and caught herself when she saw the embarrassed expression on Andie's face. "Eat up," she said. "Don't let your food get cold."

"I can't taste anything," Andie whined. "And there's no soy sauce."

"Sorry. None aboard." Mike Cilantro stopped in the

doorway, resting his broad hands on its frame. "Wouldn't do much good anyway. Breathing helium does that to you."

"I could taste the food on Tethys," Andie said. "Must be this junk."

There was just a trace of insolence in her voice, and Judith shot her a warning look: *Be nice, or I'll pull you over my knee.* If Cilantro caught the gibe, though, he chose to disregard it. "That's because we don't have a master chef aboard to spice everything up." He nodded toward Andie's plate. "If you don't want that, though, I'll take it. We've got some granola bars, if that's what you'd rather have."

Andie made a face. "No, no . . . this is great." She stabbed a chunk of chicken with her fork and shoved it into her mouth. If Mike was practicing a bit of late-adolescent psychology, Judith mused as she sliced into her own tasteless entrée, he was doing a damn good job.

"Oh, well," he said. "Maybe I'll just settle for some coffee. Mind if I join you ladies?"

"Please. By all means." Judith pushed her plate around to the other side of the table, then scooted over until she was nearly rubbing elbows with Andie. "Aren't you going to eat?"

"And aren't you supposed to be driving?" Andie added, speaking around a mouthful of food.

"First question, no," Cilantro said from the galley. "Not hungry. I've been nibbling all day." They heard him moving around on the galley: taking a fresh mug from the cabinet, removing the carafe from the hot plate, pouring coffee, opening a cabinet beneath the microwave. "Second question, no. I'm off duty now. Joe's on watch until oh-dark-one, then Dale gets graveyard shift until 0600. I'm off till then."

"What if there's an emergency?" Andie asked.

"Then whoever's on watch sounds the alarm and wakes everyone up. That's probably not going to happen, though. We're at about a hundred fathoms, and not following any major shipping lanes, so there's not a helluva lot we can run into down here."

Judith had almost forgotten that the *Galatea* was submerged nearly six hundred feet below the surface, and had been ever since it ascended from the Blake Plateau almost six hours ago. The continental shelf lay far behind them; the sub now cruised above the uncharted depths of the Atlantic Basin. A tiny metal lozenge, traveling through oceanspace somewhere halfway between the twilight waters above and the lightless desert below. And here she was, sitting in reasonably comfortable quarters, having dinner with her niece, much as if they were in the back of an RV on a summer trip to the Grand Canyon.

"So what are you going to do till then?" Andie reached up to the shelf above her head, grabbed a handful of DVDs stacked beneath the TV. "Got some good movies here. *The Sorcerer's Apprentice, The Long Goodbye,* a couple of *Star Wars* films . . ."

"Seen 'em all. I carry them for the passengers." Cilantro emerged from the galley, carrying a mug of hot coffee. "You can put one in if you want, so long as you keep the volume down. Dale's sacked out, and I'm going to do the same after I have a nightcap."

Have a nightcap? Then Judith noticed the aluminum liquor flask in his left hand. Mike caught her look. "Captain's prerogative," he said with a wry grin as he settled into the booth across from them. "I get a shot each night before I go to bed. Helps me sleep." He held up the flask. "Want some?"

"What is it?" Andie asked.

"Jack Daniel's. Genuine Tennessee sippin' whiskey."

He unscrewed the cap and extended it to her. "Here. See if you can smell that."

Andie hesitated, then leaned forward and took a sniff. "Whoa!"

"Sorry, but a whiff's all you get. Come back when you're out of school." He offered it to Judith. "Care for some, m'lady?"

"Maybe another time." She was tempted, but it wouldn't be fair to indulge herself in anything that her niece wasn't allowed . . . although she had little doubt that Andie hadn't already sampled some of her dad's liquor on the sly. She certainly had, when she was her niece's age.

"Suit yourself." Mike smiled knowingly as he added a modest dose to his coffee. "So . . . the subject's sea monsters, right?"

All of a sudden Andie seemed engrossed in her food. Judith swallowed the bite she had just taken, then picked up her napkin and wiped her mouth. "I take it you heard us talking."

"Maybe I did, maybe I didn't." The skipper shrugged as he picked up a spoon and stirred the whiskey into his coffee. "You should be aware, though, that voices tend to carry pretty well in here. Even if you switch off your headsets, you can hear stuff all the way across the boat. Isn't that right, chief?"

Although he hadn't raised his voice above conversational level, they clearly heard Dale Schuster's sleepy voice from the next compartment: "Right, skipper."

Judith and Andie stole a glance at each other. So much for sharing secrets in the wardroom. "Of course," Mike added, "if you need a little privacy, all you have to do is close this." He grasped the recessed handle of the pocket door and slid it out a couple of inches. "In fact, you may want to keep this in mind when you're changing. A little easier than trying to dress in your bunk."

"Thanks for the tip," Judith said. The bunk alcove was a tight fit, and although the bunks had curtains, they were a little too cramped to double as boudoirs. She knew that Andie would appreciate being able to change into fresh undies without worrying if one of the guys was going to sneak a peek, and the smile on her face confirmed this. "Anyway, you were saying something about sea serpents?"

"I wasn't . . . you were. I just happened to overhear, that's all." He took a sip from his makeshift Irish coffee. "I take it you're disappointed that I didn't go dead boat, and still wondering why I ignored your advice to do so."

"You're half right." Judith laid her fork down and pushed her plate aside. "This was only supposed to be a side trip. Since we're on a tight schedule, we could only spend a few minutes down there. The main purpose was to get some pics of the *Doris* to send back to Tethys, and that was it." Cilantro nodded, and she went on. "What I still don't understand is why, when we got a positive sonar contact, you ignored my advice, and Joe's, to set down and stop all engines. That was the condition the *Doris* was in when the serpent—"

She stopped as Mike chuckled and shook his head. "So you don't think we're dealing with a sea serpent," she said, her eyes narrowing.

"Oh, no! God, no!" The skipper laughed out loud. "Hey, I'll admit, I was a little skeptical before, but when I saw Joe's sub, and then the sonar . . ." He took another sip. "I just can't believe, after all these years, that I would find myself chasing Bennie and Cecil."

"Who's Bennie and Cecil?" Andie asked.

"Before your time. Never mind." Judith didn't want to get distracted with talk of a children's TV show that was in syndicated rerun when she herself was a child. "I understand that, but why didn't you put down? We had a good landing site . . . all you had to do was move a little further away from the wreck. If you had, we might have been able to catch a glimpse of the thing before our props scared it off."

"Yeah," Andie said. "I mean, it must be attracted by light, so if we had just . . . y'know . . ."

Her voice trailed off in self-conscious embarrassment, yet Judith found herself intrigued by her niece's remark. Why hadn't she thought of that earlier? Of course something that lived that far down would be photoreactive; this was how most benthic predators tended to lure one another, through self-emitted light. This could explain why the creature had attacked the *Doris* in the first place; its lights had attracted it.

"I'm aware of that." Mike absently ran a fingertip around the edge of his mug. "I'm sorry for not doing that when we had a chance. But you have to be aware that, as skipper of this boat, I'm not at liberty to take any unnecessary risks with the lives of its passengers and crew. I had just seen what happened to *Doris,* and keeping that in mind, I believed that it was remotely possible—"

"Mike, this isn't the *Doris.*" Judith sought to keep her temper in check. "*Galatea*'s at least three times larger, and it's built like a tank. If we had gone dead boat . . ."

"I don't do dead boat." Cilantro shook his head. "And I don't take unnecessary risks."

He picked up his mug again, raised it to his lips. Judith couldn't help but notice that his hand trembled slightly. "That's an odd thing to hear from a deep-sub driver," she said quietly. "I thought you guys were all into macho."

Cilantro glared at her over the rim of his mug. He took a long drink, then carefully and deliberately set the mug down on the table. He said nothing for a moment; his lips pursed into a tight line as he toyed with the mug's handle. When he finally spoke again, his voice was low.

"I know something about risk," he said quietly, "and I know a little about monsters."

When it was commissioned at the Portsmouth Naval Shipyard on August 3, 1961, the U.S.S. *Thresher* was the pride and joy of the United States Navy. Two hundred and seventy-eight feet in length, with a surface displacement of 3,500 tons, it was the first of a new class of nuclear attack submarines, specifically designed for the purpose of stalking and destroying Soviet ballistic missile subs. It was the most advanced sea vessel the world had ever seen, and on the day that it was launched, no one dreamed that it was doomed.

For the next year and a half the *Thresher* underwent a series of shakedown cruises in the North Atlantic and the Caribbean. During that period it experienced a couple of accidents. While the sub was in harbor in Puerto Rico with its nuclear reactor scrammed, its standby diesel engine broke down, causing a long brownout which, in the tropical heat, sent temperatures within the engine spaces soaring above 140 degrees. During a visit to Port Canaveral on June 3, 1962, a tugboat collided with the *Thresher*'s port side, opening a three-foot gash below its waterline. Yet the Navy remained confident in its creation; the sub eventually passed the shakedown phase, and after a long overhaul at the New London shipyard, the *Thresher* went to sea once again, this time for the first of its last set of operational tests.

Early in the morning of April 9, 1963, the *Thresher* set out from Portsmouth, New Hampshire, to undergo a series of short test dives to cruise depth six hundred feet below the surface. Aboard were twelve officers, including its captain, Lieutenant Commander John W. Harvey, and ninety-six crewmen, along with military and civilian representatives from the shipyard, the Navy, and various private contractors. Four crewmen were forced to remain behind: a lieutenant who had suffered a household accident the night before, a communications electrician who was still in navigation school, a machinist's mate who had flown to Washington, D.C., for an interview with Vice-Admiral Hyman Rickover, and a torpedoman's mate sent ashore for what was delicately described as a "nervous condition." In hindsight, they were the lucky ones.

The following morning, the *Thresher* was off the coast of Massachusetts, two hundred miles due east of Cape Cod. Escorting her was the U.S.S. *Skylark*, a submarine rescue ship containing, as its primary emergency equipment, a diving bell capable of submerging to 850 feet. This was adequate for saving the lives of World War II–vintage submarines, as had been done when the U.S.S. *Squalus* sank at 240 feet in 1939, but when the *Thresher* slipped beneath the waves for the last time on April 10, 1963, it was in 8,400 feet of water.

To this day, no one knows exactly what happened down there. At 9:12 A.M., the *Skylark*'s captain and a radio officer heard a brief, distorted voice message from the *Thresher* through the acoustic telephone:

"Experiencing minor problem . . . have positive angle . . . attempting to blow."

The *Skylark*'s captain picked up the mike and asked the *Thresher* if there was a problem. No answer. He made this call over and over for the next several minutes, until he finally received one last faint, garbled message:

". . . test depth . . ."

And then he heard the sound of a hull imploding.

"That was the last anyone heard of the *Thresher*," Cilantro said. "One hundred and twenty-nine men died that day, just like that."

When he snapped his fingers, the sound was almost lost against the background engine hum, yet Judith and Andie both jerked as if he had fired a pistol. "They said that when the end came, it must have quick and painless," he continued, not looking at either of them, "but since the *Thresher*'s crush depth was a lot lower than six hundred feet, I reckon the guys aboard had four or five minutes to live before the hull gave in."

"Gave in?" Andie's voice was soft. "But if they had that long, couldn't they have . . . I dunno . . . done something?"

Cilantro picked up his mug, sipped his spiked coffee. "I'm sure they must have tried, but whatever caused the accident must have happened too fast for anyone to handle it. The *Thresher* wasn't designed to blow the tanks and hit the roof like later subs were. So when it hit crush depth . . ."

He laid back his head, gazed up at the double row of rivets joining plates together along the low ceiling. "Well, Judy, maybe you know your sea monsters, but I know mine. You get past crush depth, and the pressure . . . well, it's like a huge dragon has grabbed your boat in its jaws. No way you can escape something like that. It just . . ."

He shook his head. "Anyway, it took several months for the Navy to locate the wreckage. The only deep sub at the time was the *Trieste,* the bathyscaphe Cousteau built to explore the Mariana Trench, and that old thing was as maneuverable as a freight elevator. They didn't have any other DSVs back then. Didn't think they were necessary. *Thresher* was the wake-up call. Anyway, when they finally found the crash site . . ."

He chugged down the last of his coffee and hissed

between his teeth. "Well, there wasn't much of anything. Pieces of hull plate. Broken pipes. Part of an anchor. Nothing but junk."

Cilantro picked up the whiskey flask, gazed at it for a moment, then unscrewed its cap. "So here's to Henry T. Cilantro, machinist's mate third class," he said solemnly as he raised the flask. "My old man. May he rest in peace."

Judith stared at him, unable to speak. She waited until he put down the shot and screwed the cap back on the flask. "You've never told me this," she said.

"Of course I didn't." Cilantro shrugged and deliberately pushed the flask across the table. "Not exactly something you bring up during casual conversation. Besides, you'd be surprised how many people have never heard about the *Thresher*. Talk to anyone who was around in '63 about what they remember from that year, and they'll tell you about the Kennedy assassination, the Beatles, Vietnam, whatever. The *Thresher* seems to be something that just slipped through the cracks."

"But you remember—" Andie began.

"No, I don't." Cilantro raised a finger. "My mother was seven months pregnant when my dad went out on the *Thresher* that last time. I was born two months later. Never got a chance to meet my father." He smiled wistfully. "I've got some pictures of him. We look a lot alike. Or least we used to . . . I'm now almost twice as he old was when he died."

"But . . ." Andie started to say something, then hesitated. Her eyes flitted nervously from one side to another, as if she was afraid to meet Mike's gaze. It suddenly occurred to Judith that this might be the first time her niece had ever met someone whose father had died under tragic circumstances. She had grown up in a rather sheltered environment, after all: a privileged child from an upscale Midwestern neighborhood, too young even to remember the last major war her country had fought.

"It's okay," Mike prompted. For once, he seemed uncommonly patient. "It happened a long time ago. You can't hurt my feelings."

"I just . . . I dunno." Andie shrugged. "I was just wondering . . . if your father died on a sub, then what are you doing here?"

A damn good question, Judith had to admit, and it was just as well that Andie asked it, because she wouldn't have dared pose it herself. Yet Cilantro didn't seem at all insulted. Instead, he smiled as he propped his left foot up on the bench next to Judith. "Curiosity, really," he said. "As soon as I was old enough to understand—I guess I was about four or five—my mother sat down with me and told me what happened to my father. She was about to get married again, but she wanted me to know that the guy with whom she was engaged wasn't my real dad, even though I had been seeing him around almost as soon as I could walk. So she showed me pictures of my dad in his uniform, and some snapshots she had taken of the commissioning ceremony, and explained as best she could how he died."

"But didn't that . . . I mean, wouldn't that have frightened you away from submarines?"

"I think that's was what she wanted." Cilantro smiled a little. "If it was, though, it didn't work. Just the opposite, because I got fascinated with subs. Dad left behind some operations manuals, and as soon as I learned how to read, I was taking them down off the shelf and hiding them under my bed so I could look at them after she and my stepfather went to sleep." He chuckled and gazed up at the ceiling. "Y'know, when I began Navy training for submarine service, I had to go through psychiatric evaluation—strictly routine stuff, just to make sure I wasn't some wacko who'd pull a knife on someone—and when I told the shrink about this, he told me that I was sub- consciously searching for my dad."

"Were you?" Judith asked.

"Maybe I was, deep down inside." Mike shrugged. "But that wasn't it. I just got hooked on subs, that's all. First subs, then the sea. Like father, like son . . . maybe that's Freudian as hell, but that's the way it works out sometimes."

"And your mother?"

"She didn't object. Not much, at least. Maybe she saw in me the same thing that shrink did." He picked up his mug, took a sip from the cold coffee, grimaced, and pushed it aside. "At any rate, to make a long story short, I did my time in the Navy, then left to go civilian with Woods Hole. After I completed my training for the *Alvin,* I had to make a test dive with my instructor, just to make sure that I knew how to handle the boat. So I had them take *Alvin* out to the place where the *Thresher* went down, and I made my first solo to the place where my father died."

The wardroom was very quiet now. The Beethoven symphony had long since ended, and no one up front had bothered to replace the CD. Even the mechanical back- ground noise had faded into near silence; for a moment it seemed as if even the sea had stopped to listen. "The night before I made the dive," Mike went on, "I took a ballpoint pen and used it to sketch a little picture of my father, as I remembered how he looked from those photos my mother showed me when I was a kid, on a paper foam coffee up, along with a little message of my own. The next morning, just before the crew lowered *Alvin* into the water, I attached the cup to one of its manipulators."

"A coffee cup?" Andie shook her head. "I don't . . . I'm sorry, but I don't get it."

Judith felt warm tears stinging the corners of her eyes, but she didn't say anything as she wiped them away with the back of her hand. "When you make a deep dive," Cilantro explained, "the pressure crushes everything equally, from all sides at once. The Woods Hole guys found out that if you put a foam coffee cup outside the hull of a submersible and go down gradually, as we did on *Alvin*—and on this boat, too—then all the air bubbles get forced out and the foam cup is reduced to the size of a shot glass. It's hard as rock by the time you reach bottom, but everything you've drawn on the outside stays legible."

"But why didn't you take down a wreath or . . ." Andie's eyes widened she seemed to grasp the concept. "Oh, I get it. A wreath would have been crushed."

"Right. Nothing would have been left except some wire and a few twigs. I didn't have enough money for a bronze plaque, so the coffee cup was the best I could afford." Mike picked up the whiskey flask again, but only played with it in his hands. "It was enough for me. There wasn't much left of the *Thresher* by then . . . most of the wreckage was covered over, and in the end I had to settle for placing the cup next to a broken piece of hull plating I found sticking out of the mud . . . but that's how I finally made peace with my old man."

He sighed expansively. "Anyway, to answer your question, Judith . . . that's why I don't take unnecessary risks. To this day, no one knows exactly what killed the *Thresher* and its crew. I'm not saying that her CO was rolling the dice, or even that the Navy was playing long odds with a new boat that already had an accident record. But nevertheless, I've been down a hundred times, and I've always come back up, and that's because—"

"You don't tempt fate."

"Right." He tapped a forefinger against the tabletop.

"You don't go screwing with Mother Ocean, and there's stuff out here that's more scary than your sea serpent. A lot more scary."

Judith slowly nodded. Andie had lost all interest in her unfinished meal; instead, she seemed to regard Mike Cilantro with newfound awe . . . even fear, as if she had just learned that he was the Ancient Mariner.

"Anyway, that's the story." Cilantro picked up his flask, then pushed himself out from behind the table. "We've got a long day ahead of us tomorrow," he added as he stood up and stepped back out of the wardroom. "You can stay up long as you want, but I suggest you get some sleep. Good night."

Then he left, pausing only to return the whiskey flask to its hiding place in the galley. Neither Judith nor Andie spoke until they heard him move to the front of the sub. There was a short, murmured conversation from the control room. A brief bit of subdued laughter, then silence.

Save for engine noise, and the low music wafted back through the passageway. A Brahms string quartet, strange and mysterious, like a ghost drifting through the depths of the haunted ocean.

FOURTEEN

Guilt

6.6.11—2317 EST

C harles Toussaint found Jared Hilliard in the operations center. Apparently Jared had also been in bed,
for he wore a terrycloth robe over a pair of sweatpants,
the right sleeve hanging limp past his elbow. At this time
of night, there were only a couple of crewmen on duty;
the ceiling lights were turned down low, the narrow room
chiefly illuminated by the pale blue glow of TV monitors
and computer screens.

"Were you in bed?" Jared asked apologetically when
Charles arrived. He was seated in front of the communications console, sipping a mug of hot chocolate someone had fetched. He gestured with the mug to a vacant
chair parked nearby.

"Yes, but only reading." Charles was about to doze
off when Juan summoned him from his berth in Hab 3;
he had obligingly pulled on a sweatshirt and jeans.
"What's the problem?"

"Don't know." Hilliard stifled a yawn behind his hand

and shook his head. "Jacobi here says we got a priority call about fifteen minutes ago. Someone topside wants to talk to both of us." He glanced at a younger man sitting behind him. "Ty?"

"All I know is that there's some sort of emergency." The duty officer had his right hand poised above the console trackball. "They've also patched in Jacksonville. I've got them both on hold. Anytime you're ready, chief."

Jared placed the mug on the counter, then pointed to the digital minicam positioned on top of the nearest computer monitor, which displayed a random fractal pattern. "We're going to conference-call this," Jared explained. Charles gave him a puzzled look as he sat down next to him, which the operations manager returned with a shrug. "Don't look at me," he added. "I don't know either. Okay, Ty, put 'em on."

Jacobi murmured into his headset as he palmed the trackball. The fractal pattern vanished and Miles Bartlett appeared on-screen. In the background, they could see one of the windows within MainOps; it was nearly midnight up on the surface, as if anyone down below needed reminding. "Jared?" Bartlett asked, peering closer at the screen. "I've got you, but I don't see Charles. Is he there?"

"I'm here, Miles." Toussaint pulled his chair a little closer so that the minicam could pick him up. "Juan, patch me into the active com channel, please," he added. "Can you hear me now?"

"Loud and clear, Charles," Bartlett replied. "Sorry to get you guys out of the sack, but a couple of things have come up."

"That's okay, Miles. Neither of us were sleeping." Jared glanced at Charles. "Or at least Doc wasn't. At any rate, we're here. What's the story?"

"I'll tell you in a sec, but we've got someone else here

who wants to introduce herself first." Miles's gaze shifted to the left as he checked his own screen. "Helen?"

A moment later, the screen split in half and a woman appeared on the right side. Middle-aged, with silvered brown hair and a broad fleshy face, she alone seemed fully awake. The digital readout at the bottom of the screen told them that she was calling in from Yemaya's corporate office in Jacksonville, yet Charles couldn't recall ever having met her before.

"Thank you, Miles." The illusion of closeness was shattered when it took a half second for her to visibly respond; when she did, it was with only the faintest of smiles, and a no-nonsense one at that. Her voice had a deep Southern accent that hinted at a childhood spent in Louisiana or Mississippi. "Gentlemen, I'm Helen Blanchard, head of corporate security for Yemaya. Believe me, I'd rather be asleep myself right now, so I'll try to get through this as fast as I can."

Charles felt himself wake up a little more. What business did the company's security chief have with them at this hour? "Good to meet you, ma'am," he replied. "I hope it's not serious, whatever it is."

"I'm afraid it is, Dr. Toussaint." Again, there was a momentary delay between her voice and the change in her facial expression. "But Miles has some important business to cover first, so we'll get to that in a minute. Miles?"

"Thanks, Helen." Bartlett nodded. "Doc, I take it you were already asleep when the new SOSUS data came in, otherwise we'd probably be hearing from you instead of vice versa. At any rate, we've been getting readings of significant seismic activity on the MAR. It appears to be coming from the same area where we've sent the *Galatea*."

"What are you getting there?" Hilliard instantly became alert; before Bartlett could answer, he turned to

Jacobi. "Ty, patch into SOSUS and get me the latest MAR data. Put it on this screen." Looking back at the minicam, he said, "Hold on a moment, we're pulling it up."

The younger man's fingers were already dashing across his keyboard. A few seconds later a small window opened on the screen between Bartlett and Blanchard, depicting a bathymetric chart of the region of the Mid-Atlantic Ridge southwest of the Azores. It was much the same display Charles had shown Jared the previous evening, except now there were concentric circles painted over the topographic whorls.

"At about 9:30 tonight," Bartlett continued, "seismographs on Flores and Ponta Delgada in the Azores registered a series of tremors between 4.2 and 4.8 on the Richter scale, with lesser aftershocks since then. At the same time SOSUS listening posts in the North Atlantic detected seaquakes in the MAR, with the probable epicenter being the central rift valley between the Lucky Strike and Snake Pit vent fields."

As he spoke, a larger version of the same data appeared on the monitor above Jacobi's station. Jared and Charles turned to peer over his shoulder at the screen. "Given the latest data," Bartlett went on, "we've reason to believe that the hydrothermal vent *Galatea* is scheduled to visit tomorrow has become active."

"But it's always been active, Miles," Charles said patiently. "In fact, that's the very reason why we insisted on getting out there as soon as possible. An inactive site—"

"Is less valuable. Yes, I understand." Bartlett stared back at him. "But this degree of seismic activity signifies more violent eruptions. That increases the risk posed to the *Galatea*. If it's down there when—"

"Miles, you know Mike Cilantro as well as I do." Jared remained calm. "He's one of the best pilots in the world. The last thing he's going to do is put anyone at risk. If he sees that there's a unacceptable risk involved here, he'll abort the dive and . . ."

"Just wait a minute." Bartlett held up a hand. "The problem isn't that clear-cut. I know Mike would abort . . . *if* he saw that this was a dangerous situation. But you know as well as I do that when you're that far down, you can't see anything until you're right on top of it. So Mike might not know what's going on until it's too late."

Charles absently rubbed his unshaven chin. Miles had a good point. If the new MAR vent was in eruption, there would be little indication to anyone aboard the *Galatea*. Unlike dry-land volcanoes, deep-ocean vents didn't emit light, and the temperature of the water surrounding them remained just above the freezing point until one entered the thermal plume rising from the vent. "We're planning to monitor the operation through real-time satellite link," he pointed out. "*Galatea* will leave a communications buoy on the surface before it dives. If we keep an eye on SOSUS, we can give Mike some advance warning if there's another major tremor."

Out of the corner of his eye, he caught Jared giving him a skeptical look. They both knew that it wouldn't be so simple. New data from SOSUS would necessarily be delayed by satellite transmission time between the listening posts and Tethys 2, and further complicated by the time it would take for someone on Tethys to alert the *Galatea*. True, they were only talking about a matter of seconds, yet by comparison, an uplink between Earth and the Moon would be instantaneous.

"I know you can do this," Bartlett said, "and I appreciate the fact that we've got a safety factor. But there's a lot at risk involved here, and . . ." He hesitated. "I dunno, guys. I think we should call the whole thing off."

In that instant Charles Toussaint saw $3 million evaporate. If the *Galatea* dive was postponed, he would have little to offer his French connection; he instinctively knew that their interest had waned in the hyperthermophiles from the Galápagos site, and that they were counting on him delivering new taq samples from the MAR. They would simply wait until another company—American, Japanese, even Russian—made plans to explore the new vent, then cut a similar deal with someone else.

"I don't agree," Jared said, and Charles almost sighed in relief. "I think we can still do this without putting anyone in danger."

"I agree," Charles said.

"And what do we tell Cilantro?" Bartlett asked.

"Everything!" Jared laughed out loud. "Jeez, Miles, you think I'm saying we should keep him in the dark? Look, *Galatea* arrives at the dive site at about 01100 tomorrow. That's when they deploy the buoy before they go down, and they'll report in then." He looked up at the set of world clocks arranged above the console. "That's twelve hours from now, Atlantic Standard. We can apprise them of the situation then and let Mike make the final call."

Bartlett appeared to mull this over. Charles glanced warily at Helen Blanchard's image on the split screen. Although the security chief had listened attentively to the entire discussion, never once had she offered her own opinion. Again, he found himself wondering why she was there.

"Okay, Jared." Bartlett let out his breath and sat back in his chair. "I'll sign off on this one, but only so long as we're in agreement that Mike gets the final say."

"Wouldn't have it any other way." Jared smiled and nodded. "It'd be a shame to send those guys all the way out there, just to come home empty-handed." He picked up his mug and took a sip of hot chocolate. "Is that it?"

"Sorry, no. That's just the first item." Again, Bartlett glanced to his right, as if looking at a different monitor. "Helen?"

"Thanks, Miles." Blanchard sat forward at little farther. "I know you've got a long day ahead of you tomorrow, guys, so I won't keep you much longer. But since I happened to call Miles about this when he was getting ready to call you about that, I asked if I could share the link with him so I could make sure of catching Dr. Toussaint."

She was calling specifically to speak with him? Charles felt an uncomfortable itch on the nape of his neck. "How may I help you, ma'am?" he asked.

She laughed easily. "Oh, don't be so formal, Doc . . . can I call you Doc? I know we haven't met, but I'm a big fan of your work. Sort of an armchair oceanographer myself . . ."

"Glad to hear that, ma'am. Didn't know I had any fans."

"Call me Helen. Please." Even through the minicam linkup, Helen Blanchard seemed to radiate Southern warmth. "But hey, that's beside the point. Look, I know you're tired, but something came up that I thought you might want to know about. You know that thing that happened yesterday, down in Dominica?" As typical of an American, she mispronounced the island's name. "Well, the private security company we hired to get you and Dr. Lipscomb out of the country has been keeping on top of the case, and they had a break earlier today. It seems the police down there just arrested one of the goons who tried to kidnap you."

The itch became a long, cold wire running down the middle of his back. "Really?" Charles said softly, forcing himself to smile. "They found one of the men?"

"Surprised?" She raised an eyebrow. "Hey, it shouldn't have been all that hard. There's only about—what, thirty-five thousand people in your country? Someone down there's bound to talk sooner or later, and—"

"You said someone's been arrested."

"Sorry. Yeah, a guy by name of . . ." She glanced down as if to consult some written notes. "Henry LeBeau, age twenty-three, native Dominican. Lives in a town called Saint Joseph, or at least that's where he was picked up. Seems that he got drunk in a bar and blabbed about the whole thing, and a police informer ratted him out. Lucky break."

"Very much indeed, yes." Toussaint's mind worked furiously. He didn't know any of the men who had been hired to stage the abduction, so there was no way he could be personally linked to the assault. And yet . . . "Have the police interrogated him yet?"

"Not only the police, but also the security specialists we hired to look into the case. Like I said, they're still trying to chase down leads in Dominica, and when this came up, they paid a visit to Mr. LeBeau in jail and had a talk with him. So they got the names of the other two guys, and the cops are searching for them now."

"That's good news," Jared said.

"Yes, it is," Helen Blanchard said, "but that's not the most interesting part. It appears that someone outside the country hired them."

Charles nervously ran a hand across his mouth. "That's sort of what we thought," Bartlett said. "At least I did . . . Doc thought it was just a local thing."

"Really?" The corners of Blanchard's mouth tucked down slightly as her brow furrowed. "Well, you were only half-right. These guys were local, but LeBeau says they were paid by a white Frenchman by name of . . ." Again, she consulted her notes. "Hilaire Benoit. And just to make things better, it turns out that Interpol has a file on him the size of the Bible. A mercenary. Specializes in kidnapping corporate types for ransom. Dirty deeds done dirt cheap, as the song goes, except Benoit doesn't work cheap. He's an expensive professional."

Hilaire Benoit. Charles felt his blood go cold at the sound of his name. A small man, very slender, yet with muscles under his short-sleeve polo shirt; tropical complexion, dark brown hair receding from the forehead, humorless black eyes. He enjoyed the port wine Mary had served him when he paid a visit to Charles's home in Roseau. Oh, dear God . . .

"So why would he want Doc?" Jared asked.

"Because he was hired by someone else," Blanchard replied. "Someone in Europe, we can safely assume, given Benoit's origins, and someone who can pay Benoit's tab. Dominican customs says that someone matching his general description entered the country twice in the last twelve months. He used a fake passport both times, but someone working at the airport must have a good memory for faces, because they got a positive ID on him. The first time he came to Dominica was several months back, but the second visit was only five days ago, when LeBeau says he first met him in Roseau. That's where things get even more interesting. According to LeBeau, Charles—hey, Doc, are you with me?"

Charles suddenly realized that he was staring blankly into space. Out of the corner of his eye, he saw that both Hilliard and Jacobi were watching him. "Sorry," he murmured. "Just . . . rather shocked by this, that's all."

This time Blanchard didn't smile. "Pay attention, please. This is why I'm calling." She checked her notes once more. "LeBeau says that once you'd been kidnapped, you were supposed to be taken off the island to a trawler. He doesn't know who owns it or where it was

going, but once that was done, he and his friends were
supposed to issue a communiqué stating that you had
been taken by a terrorist group called Caribbean Dawn.
Ransom, release of political prisoners, all that stuff . . .
but all that was a hoax, because there's no such organi-
zation. Benoit was taking you somewhere else. Follow
me so far?"

Charles folded his arms across his chest. "Yes, I follow you. Go on."

"Good. Because this is where it gets weird." Blanchard
raised a finger. "LeBeau says that he and his friends were
to wait for a phone call from Benoit, who would then tell
them where and when you were going to be placed in
their custody once more. He was under the impression
that it would be somewhere in Dominica—a village,
something like that—but wherever it was, you'd be released, they'd get paid off, and then they make like
ghosts."

"It sounds . . . very well organized," Charles said.

"At the very least." Blanchard's querying expression
reminded him of a dog who had chased a squirrel up a
tree, then lost her prey when it had leaped across high
limbs to another tree. "So why would anyone go to all
this trouble? That's what bothers me."

"What about Judith?" Bartlett asked. "I mean, she was
with Charles when—"

"Oh, yeah. Almost forgot." Blanchard consulted her
notes. "LeBeau says Benoit told him to ignore her entirely, not to do her any harm. In fact, she was supposed
to remain untouched and unharmed, no matter what." She
looked up once more. "So how does that figure? I mean,
if you go out to kidnap one scientist, why not get two
for the same bargain? Unless—"

"She was meant to supply an alibi," Jared said.

Helen nodded. "That's my feeling exactly."

There are two adjacent waterfalls nestled deep within the Dominican mountain rain forest: Mama Falls and Papa Falls. Mama gives cold water while Papa runs hot. They begin as two different rivers until they fall hundreds of feet from high rocky bluffs and converge at a fork farther downstream. At that moment Charles Toussaint remembered what it was like, as a young man, when he used to bathe in the clear, steaming water where the two streams came together.

"I . . . I have no idea," he murmured.

"Pardon me?" Helen Blanchard asked. "I didn't quite get that."

Charles cleared his throat. "I mean, this is quite interesting, but I have no idea what any of this is about. Why these people would want to . . . I mean, why this fellow Benoit would go to so much trouble . . ."

At a loss for words, his voice trailed off. For a few moments which seemed far longer, no one said anything. Charles stared straight into the camera lens, not blinking an eye, as Blanchard and Miles peered back at him. Although neither Jared nor Jacobi spoke, he could feel their silent gaze. His heart hammered against the walls of his chest.

"I haven't an explanation," he finished.

Blanchard's expression was unreadable. "I don't recall asking for one, Dr. Toussaint," she said at last. "I simply thought this may be of interest to you. If you think you know something, though . . ."

"I really don't. This is a mystery to me, too."

Blanchard slowly nodded. From the other half of the screen, Miles regarded him with what seemed to be cool appraisal. "If you think of anything, Charles," he said, "please call us. This is a serious issue, as I'm sure you well know."

"Please do," Blanchard added. "We can't let our people get threatened when they're out of the country."

"I'll keep that in mind." Charles pointedly glanced up at the wall clocks. "Now, if you don't mind . . ."

"I know, it's late," Miles said. "I think all of us would do better if we slept on it. Jared, I'll put it on you to radio the *Galatea* tomorrow."

"I'll do that." The operations manager scribbled something on a clipboard, then handed it to Jacobi. "I'll let you know what Mike says . . . but I can tell you already what the answer is going to be."

"Probably, but let's leave that up to him." Bartlett cupped a hand over his mouth to stifle a yawn. "Okay, that's it. See you guys tomorrow."

The screen went blank. Hilliard turned to Jacobi and nodded; the duty officer tapped a key on his touchpad, and a moment later the red light on the minicam went dark. "So what's this all about, Doc?" he asked quietly, not looking at Charles.

"I have no idea. Really." Charles pushed back his chair and rose. "As I told Ms. Blanchard—Helen—this is just as much of a mystery to me."

Jared swiveled around in his seat to gaze at him. For a moment he said nothing; he didn't have to, for the skepticism was plain in his eyes. Charles sensed that Jared knew he was lying; his denials made no difference.

"Good night, Charles," he said at last.

Charles nodded silently, then let himself out of the operations room. After the dimness of the compartment, the bright lights of the passageway dazzled him for a moment, yet he didn't stop to rub his eyes as he began walking down the vacant corridor to the hatch leading to Hab 3.

Then he stopped and briefly reconsidered. He turned around to head to Hab 2, the science deck. He opened the hatch and let himself into the access tunnel; it was not until he carefully shut the hatch behind him that he allowed himself to sag against its tubular concrete wall. His heart beat against his chest, and when he took a breath, it came with the deep rattle of fear.

He gave himself a moment to calm down as best he could, then he headed for his lab. It was time to send a message to Benoit.

W hen she came to him shortly after midnight, Peter wasn't surprised. Although he had gone to bed a couple of hours earlier, he had been unable to sleep; after a half hour of staring up at the low ceiling above his bunk, he finally switched on the reading lamp and picked up the paperback spy novel he had tucked into the niche behind his pillow. He was halfway through the scene where the OSS agent was making his way through night-time Berlin to meet the German interpreter when he heard the bunkroom door open and shut.

A pair of feet padded softly across the floor, then stopped just outside the closed curtains of his berth. For a moment he thought it might be Milkewski, the diver who presently occupied the bunk above his own, until he remembered that Rob was on shift right now, as indeed were most of the other rockhounds with whom he was sharing quarters on Deck 3A. When he heard her soft voice, the last bit of doubt evaporated.

"Peter? Are you awake?"

Of course, she knew he wasn't asleep. She could see light seeping around the edge of the heavy curtain . . . and hadn't he told her, ever so casually, his bunk number during dinner earlier that evening? For an instant he had an impulse to switch off the reading lamp, or at least play possum and pretend that he hadn't heard her. But . . .

"No," he said quietly. "I'm awake. Who's that?"

As if he didn't know already . . .

A hand pulled aside the heavy curtain, and there was Leslie. She wore a V-neck tee and a pair of cotton gym pants; for the first time since he had met her, she was wearing her hair loose, and it fell down around her shoulders. In her left hand, she held a coffee mug.

"Who did you think it was?" she whispered, grinning down at him. "The Big Bad Wolf?"

No, but the teeth were almost the same . . . "What's the matter?" he asked. "Couldn't sleep?"

"Insomnia. Happens all the time." Leslie sat down on the edge of the bunk. "Had a hunch you might have the same problem. Brought you a little treat." She held out the mug. "Here. Hot chocolate."

"Hot chocolate? Hey . . ." In truth, he wasn't very fond of the stuff, but there was no point in letting her know that. Peter marked his place in the book and sat up in bed, then accepted the warm mug from her hands and took a polite sip. Much to his surprise, it was better than he expected. "Where did you get this? The galley's closed."

"Didn't come from the galley. I always pack my own instant chocolate, and I use twice the usual amount. Terribly fattening, but it's great on a cold night." She took the mug from him and sipped it herself. "Nice to see the tap water runs hot enough to drink. Saves the hassle of having to boil it."

"Be glad that we have fresh water on tap. In the old undersea habs, it was rationed. Didn't you bring your own?"

"Only had one mug. Thought we'd share it." She shivered a bit. "Speaking of sharing, would you find moving over a bit? It's kinda chilly out here."

"Um . . ." He hesitated, and not because the bunk was barely large enough for one person. Yet the room was a bit cooler now that the ceiling lights were off, and she was rubbing her arms to stay warm. "Sure," he said as he pushed himself against the wall to make room for her. "Climb in."

"Thank you. Hold this a second, please." She passed the mug to him, then bent down and pulled off her mocs. Then, before Peter could protest, she pulled aside the top sheet and blanket and thrust her legs beneath the covers. "Oh, that's much better."

Peter was uncomfortably aware of just how close she was to him: her long legs nestled against his own, her hips touching his thighs, her left breast against the crook of his right elbow. She smiled as she propped herself up on her left arm and reached over to take the mug from him again; as she did, he couldn't help but look down the neck of her shirt. No, she wasn't wearing a bra.

"Your face is red," she said softly, smiling a little. "Something wrong?"

"Uh . . . well, now that you mention it . . ."

"Here, let me take care of that." Leslie twisted sideways to place the mug on the floor, then she grasped the edge of the curtain and pulled it across the bunk. "There," she said as she snuggled up to him again. "Problem solved. We're all alone now."

Which was exactly the problem. "Leslie . . . y'know, this might not be such a great idea . . ."

"Oh, really?" Her mouth turned downward in a pout. "And here I thought you were just being gallant. Maybe you have something else in mind."

"I did—no, I mean . . ."

Whatever he meant to say was frozen as she softly laid a hand on his bare chest. "That's good," she whispered, "because that's exactly what I had in mind, too."

Before he could stop her, she raised her face to his and, every so gently, kissed him. Her lips tasted faintly of chocolate. He raised a hand to her face, and although at first he meant to push her aside, he found his fingers slipping into her long, hair.

Before he knew it, she had eased him back against the foam pillow, her hair falling down around his face like a dark shroud. Beneath the covers, his hands found their way down her back until his fingers touched the swell of her buttocks. She sighed as his hands slipped beneath the waistband of her gym pants. She wasn't wearing any underwear, and that gave him a moment to wonder why, yet already his fingers were running along the cool cleft of her ass. She was warm, she was eager, and she was . . .

So terribly, terribly wrong.

"Wait," he murmured. "Hold on . . ."

"Sorry. A little cramped, isn't it? " Balancing herself on a hip and an elbow, she moved a little to one side. Her right hand moved the elastic top of his shorts. "Here, let me—"

"No. Please . . . no." As gently as he could, Peter brushed her hand away. As first she seemed to resist, and for a moment he felt an urge to succumb, to let the moment take him and the hell with his conscience . . .

"I'm sorry," he said, more reluctantly than she could ever know, "but I . . . we can't do this." Suddenly aware that his left hand still lingered on her rump, he slipped out from beneath her pants. "We just can't."

"Oh, c'mon . . . " She laid her hand on his chest once more. "Who's going to know?"

God help him, but he was tempted. There was no else in the compartment; there would be no witnesses. Judith was more than a thousand miles away. It would all be so easy, so effortless: a good, comfortable screw in the dark, and all he had to do . . .

Was lie to his wife, and to himself, for the rest of his life.

"I am," he said. "Sorry, but . . . I think you better get out of here."

He pushed himself up on his elbows. As he did, the top of her head struck the bunk ceiling. He hadn't meant to do that, but she yelped and winced in pain. Her hands left his body and reflexively flew to her scalp as her left knee came up and smacked his kidney. He grimaced, but said nothing.

"Goddammit!" she hissed. "It's because you're married, isn't it?"

The fury in her eyes was unmistakable. Peter wondered if this was the first time in her life someone had ever turned her down. Probably. She was an expert at the art of seduction, and a novice when it came to rejection.

"Yeah," he said flatly. "That's the way it is." He hesitated. "Sorry if I gave you the wrong signals, but . . . I'm not doing this. Sorry."

"Jesus H. Christ!" Whipping aside the covers, Leslie practically fell out of the bunk. She tipped over the mug; hot chocolate, now cold and resembling river mud, spilled out across the floor. She ignored the mess as she stood erect. "If you weren't going to . . . goddammit, why did you come on to me in the first place?"

"I didn't," he said quietly. "It was your idea."

She glared at him, her expression shadowed in the half-light cast from the reading lamp. At first it seemed as if she was going to say something, and he waited for the inevitable verbal abuse. Somehow, though, with her mouth agape and her hair a tousled mess, she seemed more absurd than alluring. He couldn't help but grin at her.

"You spilled your hot chocolate," he said.

"Go to hell," she said, then she hitched up her pants and turned to stalk across the compartment. A beam of light from the foyer outside outlined her figure as she opened the door; the compartment echoed when she slammed it shut again.

Peter let out his breath, then fell back against the pillow and stared at nothing for a few minutes. After a while he pushed aside the covers and climbed out of bed. He gathered some paper towels from the head and used them to sop up the spilled hot chocolate, then he found the empty mug and her mocs and, after some thought, threw them in the trash chute.

Then he returned to his bunk, stowed away the paperback he had been reading, and turned off the light. It took a few minutes for him to go to sleep, but when he finally did, it was without guilt.

FOURTH DAY

TUESDAY, JUNE 7, 2011

FIFTEEN

Genesis

"We copy, Tethys, and we'll take it under advisement." Cilantro released the mike's talk button, held it in his hand for a moment, then thumbed the switch again. "I'll get back to you after I speak with my people. *Galatea* out."

He shoved the mike back in its clip next to the UQC radio, then turned to look around the crowded control room. Everyone was jammed into the sub's forward compartment. Dale Schuster was seated in the pilot's chair next to him, with Joe Niedzwiecki squatting on the deck behind them; Jack Sheldon leaned against one of the racks in the sleep alcove, while Judith Lipscomb and Andie Lipscomb sat on the bunk. The compartment was quiet save for the ever-present engine noise.

"So there it is," Mike said. "Seems our vent field is a little more active than we thought. I don't think it makes that much difference, at least for what we're doing, but . . ." He shrugged. "Well, it's a first for me, too.

Every other vent I've ever dived has been pretty stable, relatively speaking."

The *Galatea* was hovering one hundred fathoms below the surface, keeping station by means of its lateral thrusters. An hour ago, upon its arrival at its dive spot at 33 degrees North, Schuster had launched the communication buoy from its bay within the sub's sail; after it floated to the surface, the buoy had automatically dropped its longline anchor. It had taken nearly an hour for the anchor to reach the seafloor, but once it was securely moored, Cilantro had tested the acoustic phone link to the buoy, then opened the satellite relay to Tethys. Within minutes he was speaking to Jared Hilliard at Tethys 2; that was when the operations manager informed him of the recent SOSUS data from the Mid-Atlantic Ridge.

"So what's your call, skipper?" Sheldon asked.

Cilantro shrugged. "My call is that we go ahead and make the dive . . . but I'm not going to commit us unless I've got a full consensus." He looked around at Niedzwiecki and Schuster. "Dale, you're going to be doing the driving until we get to the site. What's your opinion?"

The first mate ran a hand across the top of his shaved skull. "I can get us down, no problem. We probably won't pick up any chop until we're right on top of the thing. That's when we'll hit the hot water. After that, whatever happens next is your problem."

Everyone laughed out loud at this, save for Andie. For once, the teenager seemed inordinately nervous; sitting cross-legged on the bunk, she restlessly curled a lock of her hair between thumb and forefinger. "I dunno what you guys think so's funny," she murmured. "I mean, this is a fu—a friggin' volcano."

"Hey!" Cilantro glared at her and jabbed a finger in her direction. "No friggin' aboard my boat, young lady! That's an order!"

Andie's face turned scarlet as she glanced down at her lap, and Mike suddenly felt a twinge of regret. In hindsight, he realized that he really shouldn't have told her about the *Thresher* last night; now the girl was scared out of her wits, half believing that the same fate might befall her. Teenagers often try to disguise their fear by talking tough, but this morning she had barely touched her cereal, and shortly thereafter had rushed into the head and become seasick. Perfectly understandable; the first time he himself had made a deep-ocean dive, he had spent a half hour doubled over the railing of the Navy ship from which his DSRV was being launched. In this business, an attack of nerves was forgivable.

Nonetheless, he was beginning to wonder whether it had been wise to bring a kid along on this trip. Only once before had this girl ever been out on blue water, and then it was a fishing boat her dad had hired while on a family vacation to Key West. In fact, so far as he knew, no one had called Andie's parents to ask their permission. Of course, from what he had heard about her mother and father from Judith, they were probably more concerned about who was going to get the keys to the Mercedes, but still . . .

"It's not a volcano," Judith said. She cast Cilantro a cold look as she moved a little closer to her niece. "It's like a deep crack in the earth, that's all. The water gets superheated right around it, and there may be some lava, but that's about it."

"And believe me," Cilantro added gently, "I'm going to be real respectful of whatever we find down there. Besides, we're going to let the ROV do most of the work." He looked at Niedzwiecki. "That's your department, Joe. Think you can safely handle Fido?"

"Sure." Niedzwiecki gave him a dour nod of his head. "I imagine there might be some chop, but so long as it's working right, I don't think there's going to be a problem."

Cilantro absently drummed his fingers on the console. Three thousand meters below them was a brand-new, previously unexplored vent field. For deep-ocean sub drivers, this was better than sex; you got a chance to see something no other human had ever seen before, and bragging rights to go with the pictures. But there was always an element of risk in this sort of thing; the *Alvin* had once gotten wedged within a narrow fissure while exploring a different area of the MAR, and a Russian Mir submersible had come close to disaster when it got stuck while trying to penetrate the engine room of the *Titanic*. This far down, there was no way in hell a DSRV could come to your rescue; all you could do was slowly suffocate in the cold and dark.

"Okay," he said at last, "let's take a vote. All in favor, raise your hand. All opposed—"

"Raise your hand, too, " Sheldon said.

Again, laughter around the control room. Joe and Dale already had their palms in the air; Jack put up his own hand, and Judith's followed a moment later. The only person who seemed reluctant was Andie; she looked around at the others, and finally at her aunt. "It's going to be okay, sweetheart," Judith murmured, and Jack nodded encouragingly. Finally, Andie let out her breath and briefly raised a reluctant finger. She was in, but she clearly wasn't crazy about it.

Perhaps another skipper would have let the reluctance of one crew member sway the others, but Mike wasn't about to allow an anxious teenager to cancel an important dive. This wasn't a high-school field trip, after all. Judith would just have to hold Andie's hand.

"Okay, then. The ayes have it." Cilantro turned around and unclipped the acoustic radio mike. "I'll call Tethys

and give them the good news. Dale, rig for diving. Everyone else, stations please. We're going down."

The descent took just over three hours, and was as
smooth as riding an elevator. For a long time the only
sound within the sub was the metronomic ping of the
active sonar returning signals from the ocean floor, until
Schuster finally got tired of the silence and slipped an
Eric Clapton disc into the CD deck. The music seemed
to calm the passengers, particularly Andie; after a while
she and Jack Sheldon pulled out a deck of cards and sat
down for a game of gin in the sleep alcove. Judith played
a couple of losing hands, then went aft to make PB&J
sandwiches for the pilots.

As the sonar returns became more frequent, Mike
switched seats with Dale and sent everyone to their positions: Joe to the ROV station in the control room, Jack
back to the lab, Judith and Andie down into the blister.
This time, it was Andie who was the old pro; she showed
her aunt how to lie belly-down on the floor mats and
explained how all the switches worked, then picked up
her camcorder where she had left it from the previous
morning. The view through the porthole was even darker
than before, if such a thing were possible, even when the
forward searchlight was turned on. It took Judith a few
moments to realize what was different: the complete absence of life. No bioluminescent fish, no eels, no squid.
Just utter darkness, as black as the void in the timeless
moments before the Big Bang.

"Spooky, ain't it?" she murmured.

"Yeah. Unreal." Andie slipped a fresh disk into her
camcorder, checked the LED display, then pointed it out
the window. "Rats. Can't see a thing," she added, then
turned the camera toward her aunt. "Okay, that's better.

I think it's working. Say something, willya?"

Judith hated it when someone did that to her, and having a lens so close to her face made her even more self-conscious. "Hi," she said tersely and looked away. "That enough?"

"C'mon . . . something for posterity. 'This is the first historic dive to . . .'" Andie hesitated. "What do they call this place, anyway?"

"They don't. It doesn't have a name yet." Judith reached up and gently pushed the camcorder's lens aside. "Don't point that at me. I mean it. I don't like being on film."

Andie frowned at her, but pulled the instrument aside. "Jeez," she said, pushing the pause button, "how're you ever going to be famous with an attitude like that?"

"Believe it or not, Andie, but not everyone in the world wants to be famous." She cupped her chin in her hands and gazed out at the impenetrable darkness. "Science is like that, at least in its most pure form. It's not about making money or getting your picture in a magazine . . . it's about exploration, going somewhere no one has gone before. Like right now."

"Uh-huh." Andie was quiet for a moment. "So I guess that's why you don't like Leslie, huh?"

Judith felt a brief flash of anger. She had managed to put Leslie Sun out of her mind for a full twenty-four hours now, and she resented being reminded. No, she wanted to say, I don't like Leslie because she's interested in my damn husband! "Something like that," she replied, preferring to stick to the less truthful, albeit no less complicated, answer. "I don't think she had any business being down here. And I also don't like the way she tried to worm her way aboard—"

"Um . . . ladies?" Cilantro's voice came through the headset. "Hate to break up the tea party, but we're coming up on the bottom. Just thought you might be interested."

Goddammit! She had forgotten that the headsets they wore were on an open channel. She covered her face with her hands as she heard Andie snort with barely suppressed laughter. "Yeah, okay, Mike, we hear you," she said, and gave her niece a sour look. "We're ready down here."

"Okay, glad to hear it." A pause. "We're about forty feet from the ridge. You should see it any second now. Sing out when you spot it."

"Get your camera rolling," Judith said, pointing toward the porthole. She heard a muted electronic beep as Andie took the shutter control off pause; she muttered an obscenity, then reached up to kill the interior lights. The blister was plunged into darkness, save for the aquamarine glow of the searchlight outside the sub, and for an instant it felt as if they were floating alone in the abyss.

Then, all of a sudden, the edge of a long, stony crag appeared about thirty feet below them, resembling nothing more or less than the top of a river bluff. "We got it!" Judith snapped. "It's right below us!"

"Okay," Mike said calmly. "That's all I want to hear." A long, protracted shudder passed through the hull as the lateral thrusters kicked in, braking their descent. The sub seemed to groan as the ridgeline grew in size, and for a second Judith wondered if they were about to crash, but then the *Galatea* gradually stopped moving. It hovered above the crag, and everything became peaceful once more.

"All right," Mike said, "we're golden. Switching on the rest of the lights." Another pause, then the view outside the porthole brightened perceptibly as spotlights positioned on the port and starboard elevators turned on; the additional illumination was to help light the external

TV cameras the pilots would use to navigate the sub. "Okay, Dale's going to open the ROV bay. You might feel a little jolt, but don't worry about it."

"What's that mean?" Andie asked. For the first time in several hours the teenager looked nervous.

"They're opening Fido's hangar," Judith explained. "They flooded it while we were going down, but . . ." True to Mike's word, they felt a small kick. "There we go. That's the bay hatch. Nothing to worry about."

"So who's worrying?" Andie peered again through her viewfinder. "This is so cool."

Judith grinned. God, to be seventeen again . . .

Cilantro came back. "All right, we're ready to go into the rift valley. We're about fifteen miles south of the field. Judy, I've got Tethys linked. Doc Toussaint's on-line. You want to talk to him?"

"Please," Judith said. "Put him through."

She heard a strange, wallowing sort of static—background noise from the miles of water which separated the *Galatea* from the buoy on the surface—then Doc's voice came over the UQC. "Judith? Are you there?"

"Right here, Charles. Wish you were, too."

A long pause, broken by more of the same wavering acoustical static: prop noise from distant ships, she imagined. No wonder people worried about whales becoming deaf. Even this far below the ocean surface, the human presence on Earth was evident. "I'm glad you're there," Charles said at last. "You're my eyes and ears. Tell me what it looks like when you get there."

"I'll try, Charles. Keep your ears on."

No answer from Tethys, but she knew that her mentor was listening. Just the knowledge of his presence gave her some comfort. Judith cupped her cold hands together and blew into her moist palms. "We're ready to go," she said.

"Okay," Mike said. "Let's go get some vent action."

Another vibration passed through the hull as the main engine was engaged, then the *Galatea* slowly moved forward. The edge of the bluff passed beneath them, and now they saw a long, steep cliff yawning before them, with darkness falling away far below. For a second it seemed as if the sub was literally flying above the edge of the rift valley, then the *Galatea* began its descent into the heart of the Mid-Atlantic Ridge.

The floor of the valley lay only 114 feet below the surrounding bluffs, but its sloping walls were more than 300 feet apart; although the *Galatea*'s searchlight easily found the bottom, the sides disappeared beyond the edge of the beam. Yet as the sub began to move northeast through the narrow canyon, it walls began steadily to move closer together as, foot by foot, the floor dropped away.

Through the blister porthole, Judith watched as the valley weaved sinuously to the right and left, as if they were following an enormous furrow left by a drunken giant plowman, yet it was the walls which held her interest so much as the floor. While the walls were craggy and battered, the bottom of the trench seemed to be covered with vast, soft-looking black quilts which appeared to have been haphazardly laid one atop the other, their smoothly rounded edges overlapping the ones below them. As the searchlight passed over them, they reflected its beam like layers of thick melted glass

"Looks like . . . I dunno, lava flows or something," she said.

"That's it exactly." Jack Sheldon's voice spoke in her headset from the lab compartment; she reminded herself that he was monitoring the TV screens. "They're called lava pillows. Remnants of old vents, from way back when the ridge was formed umpteen million years ago. Pretty, aren't they?"

"Does this mean we're getting closer to the vent field?" Cilantro asked.

"Probably. Hard to tell. They might lead to—"

" Hey!" Andie yelled. "What's that? Look up ahead!"

Judith raised her eyes, and in that instant felt her heart stop. "Mike! Object dead ahead!"

Directly in front of the sub, less than fifty feet away, a rocky pinnacle loomed out of the darkness. Forty feet tall, it towered above the valley floor like a giant cave stalagmite. "Don't yell," Mike said calmly. "I saw it on sonar a long time ago. Hold on."

The sub slowed down and made a gradual turn to starboard, and the pinnacle began to move to their left. As they passed it, they saw another one, only slightly smaller, about fifty feet away. They tapered upward to ragged, broken tops, and their crusty, rust-hued flanks seemed to be covered with funguslike shelves, giving them the appearance of castles from a fantasy novel.

"Looks like Mordor," Andie murmured.

"What's that?" Mike asked. "Come again?"

"Mordor. Y'know . . . from *The Lord of the Rings*? Tolkien?"

"Sorry. Must have missed that one."

"Good name for the place, though," Sheldon said. "Those are smoker chimneys . . . extinct ones, from the looks of it. When minerals percolate up from the earth's mantle through the vents, they pile up one on top of the other, forming these things."

As the *Galatea* moved slowly away from the first pillar and past the second, more chimneys came into view. Not all were intact; some had crumbled, leaving piles of ash-colored talus heaped around jagged stumps. The sub flew over the destroyed ones and skirted the sides of those still standing, gradually winding its way back and forth across the valley. "Like driving a truck obstacle course," Mike mused. "Don't worry. Even if I hit one, it'd just collapse . . . But I really don't want to do that if I can help it."

"Please don't," Jack said. "These things were probably around when dinosaurs walked the earth. Maybe before then." He paused, then added in the hushed tone of reverence: "Genesis."

"Amen, brother," Cilantro said.

Judith nodded. Like the others, she was spellbound by this place; for a few moments no one said anything. "What do you mean by that?" Andie asked at last. She seemed to sense the mood within the vessel, for her voice was subdued. "Genesis, I mean."

"There's a theory that life on Earth may have originated here," Judith said. "Not necessarily right here, I mean, or even in the Mid-Atlantic Ridge . . . but down here, on the bottom of the ocean, with the first amino acids being formed by organic chemical processes within hydrothermal vents."

"I thought the first life evolved on the land," Andie said. "I mean, that's what they teach us in school. In tidal pools, that sort of thing."

"Jesus!" Sheldon laughed derisively. "When was the last time your school bought new textbooks? Maybe higher forms of life evolved that way, but what we're talking about are the molecular building blocks of life . . . the things microbes are made of. They may have come from black smokers. I swear, the state of public education these days . . ."

"Speaking of which, I don't see any smokers." Judith didn't want Sheldon to get started on one of his public-science policy rants. Once he got going, he could bore everyone for hours. "I think you're right, Jack. This field petered out a long time ago."

"I just think it's cool." Andie gaped at one of the larger chimneys as they passed it. Its base was at least twenty feet in diameter, and tall enough that its top disappeared above searchlight range. "How big can these things get?"

"There's one in the Pacific, on the Juan de Fuca Range, that's fifteen stories tall," Mike said. "It's called Godzilla." He paused. "Dale, mark this site on the chart as Mordor. The kid spotted it first, after all."

Judith smiled at her niece. "Congratulations. You've just named a vent field."

"Yeah, well . . ." Andie was grinning ear to ear as she recorded her discovery with the camcorder. "All in a day's work."

Mordor trailed off after another mile, and soon they left the last of the dead chimneys far behind. After a while the terrain became pitted and battered, with none of the lava pillows which had smoothed over the valley floor before *Galatea* entered the extinct vent field; apparently the lava from Mordor had flowed in a southerly direction. The floor rose upward a little as the valley broadened slightly, then it made a 30 degree turn to starboard, leading into a more narrow canyon.

"Sonar's picking up a hard contact," Cilantro said. "Metal source dead ahead. I'm going to take us down a little."

Andie peered through the porthole. "Another vent field?"

"Don't count on it. I bet I know what it is"

The searchlight drifted across rocks and silt-covered debris until, all at once, it glinted off a small, irregularly shaped mound. As the sub drifted closer, the light picked up a pile of small cylinders. Most of them were crushed flat as paper, but a few had remained intact. Several had managed to retain their original markings despite the years they had spent on the bottom of the ocean.

"Beer cans," Judith said in disgust.

"Yup," Cilantro said. "Probably tossed overboard by a cruise ship." He pulled back on the thrusters, slowing the sub down so they could take a closer look. "A tour group from St. Louis was aboard," he said after a moment.

"How can you tell?" Judith asked.

"They're all Budweiser cans."

For the life of her, Judith couldn't tell if he was kidding or not. Yet there was a certain black irony in this discovery; nearly two miles beneath the Atlantic, in one of the most remote places on the globe, the hand of man was still evident, in one of the least flattering ways. Beside her, Andie was shooting footage of the garbage dump. Judith hoped that whoever saw these particular shots would learn the proper lesson.

The *Galatea* moved on. Now the valley was becoming considerably more narrow; through the blister porthole, they could see steep rock walls looming on either side of them. "We're getting close to the Hayes Fracture Zone," Schuster said over the intercom. "The site's supposed to be located just south of there."

Andie peered through the porthole. "I don't see anything but—hey, wait a sec. I just saw something move!"

"Where?" Judith inched closer until her face was nearly against the Plexiglas. "Where are you looking?"

"Down there, on the ground." Andie pointed almost directly below the blister. For a moment neither woman could see anything except rubble and silt. "Aw, rats," she murmured, "we must have . . . No, there they are again! See 'em?"

Now Judith spotted what her niece had seen: a cluster

of spiny, gelatinous cylinders, almost transparent until the searchlight hit them directly, slowly creeping across the ocean floor. "Sea cucumbers," she breathed, astonished by the sight of something she had only previously viewed in photographs. "Mike, I've got a herd of sea cukes down here."

"Roger that," Cilantro said. "Which way are they headed?"

"Northeast. Straight up the valley."

Now they could see that the valley floor was dotted with dozens of invertebrates, all moving in the same direction. As the submersible flew over they, they caught the propwash from the thrusters and rolled out of the way. "They're animals, not plants," Judith explained to Andie. "Like most creatures down here, they tend to seek out heat sources. This herd looks like it's migrating."

"So you think they're heading toward the vent field?" Andie asked, and Judith nodded. "Guess that means we must be getting close."

"It's possible," Cilantro said. "I'm taking us down again."

The *Galatea* descended a little farther, until it was gliding less than ten feet above the rocky floor. Now the valley walls could easily be seen on either side of them; Judith guessed that the canyon was only about seventy feet wide at this point, less than the length of the sub itself. She wiped her sweaty palms on the cushion, and silently prayed that Cilantro's piloting skills were equal to his reputation.

Just ahead, the valley was making another narrow bend to the right. The *Galatea* had slowed down to a near crawl; it seemed as if its landing skids were about to drag in the mud. "C'mon," she heard Cilantro murmur. "You gotta be around here someplace. Just show me your ugly head . . ."

All at once, as the *Galatea* was about to go around the bend, Judith spotted what looked like another chimney: an opaque, apparently solid tower rising from a low mound in the center of the valley. Yet this shaft was visibly moving . . .

"Black smoker!" she snapped. "Dead ahead, thirty feet!"

"Holy . . . ! Hang on!"

A second later they heard the props thrum louder as Cilantro put the thrusters in reverse. The prow canted upward a couple of degrees, and Andie yelped in protest as she slid backward on her mat. The back of her head smacked the low ceiling, and she snarled an ugly curse. Judith slapped her hands flat against the cold deck; the friction of her palms was just enough to keep her from slamming against the blister's rear wall. Judging from the mingled protests she heard in her headset, Joe and Jack hadn't been nearly been so lucky.

Then the deck became level again, and the prop noise settled into its proper background hum. "Sorry about that, folks," Mike said after a moment. "I guess that woke y'all up."

"No shi—no kidding, Sherlock." Andie rubbed the bump she had sustained on the top of her head. "What did you do that for?"

"Hush. He knows what he's doing." Judith returned her attention to the porthole, and for an instant it seemed as if her heart had stopped beating. Only twenty feet away, the dark gray plume violently boiled up from a narrow fissure in the middle of a low mound, a thick cloud of particulate so dense that the searchlight couldn't penetrate it, so high that it rose out of sight.

"Hell," she whispered. Her throat was too dry to speak, and she forced herself to swallow. "This thing's a monster, Mike."

"Yeah. I see it. Oh, man . . ." A long pause. "Christ, this thing's too big to fly around, and it's right at the bend. Damn . . ."

Judith tore her eyes away from the porthole to glance back at Andie. The girl was still rubbing the back of her skull as she winced and muttered under her breath. "Andie!" she said sharply, then self-consciously clasped a hand over her headset mike. "Get your little ass up here! You gotta see this!"

"Aw, c'mon, why are you . . . ?" Andie crawled forward, pushing the mat in front of her. Whatever teenage invective she was about to issue against her aunt vanished when she looked out the porthole. "Whoa!"

"Yeah. Whoa." Judith found the camcorder where it had slid down the deck between them. She picked it up; nothing seemed to be broken, and the LED lamp was still lit. "Time for you to earn your keep," she murmured as she shoved the unit into her niece's hands. "Whatever you do now, don't fuck up."

Hearing her aunt use an obscenity seemed to make the teenager forget her pain and pay attention. She stared at Judith in amazement, then took the camcorder, gave it a brief inspection, and positioned herself so that it was cradled in her hands once more, her elbows firmly braced against the deck. "Okay," she said quietly as she squinted through the viewfinder. "Got it. What do you want me to catch?"

Everything, Judith almost said before she realized what Andie was asking. If Andie only filmed the smoker itself, they'd get footage that was little more useful than a home movie: interesting, but hardly useful for scientific purposes. "Okay . . . can you zoom in on the vent itself? Get me a close-up."

"Sure." Without looking for it, Andie's fingers found a recessed stud on the camera's housing. The lens

whirred softly as it telescoped to its full length. "Wow
... how weird. There's critters all around it."

Judith resisted an urge to grab the camera. "What do
you see? What do they look like?"

"Um ... sea cucumbers, some of them. But there's
also ..." She hesitated. "Shrimp? Does that make sense?"

"Sure does." Judith grinned. Blind albino shrimp commonly congregated around other hydrothermal vents in
the Mid-Atlantic Ridge. Before long, there would be
mussels, too, but the vent was probably too young for
that; it hadn't yet had a chance to build a substantial
chimney for them to colonize. "Get all that, then give me
a look at the plume. I want some idea of perspective, if
you can handle—"

"Judith?" Mike said. "We're going to go up a bit, to
get us above the plume. Joe's going to send out Fido to
get samples."

"Gimme a couple of minutes," she asked. "We're still
getting shots of the vent base." She prodded Andie with
her elbow. "Keep rolling," she murmured. "Get me as
much as you can. Jeez, this is great ..."

"Yeah. Sure." Andie carefully panned the camera back
and forth, filming the deep-ocean fauna clustered around
the vent. Watching her work, Judith felt vindicated for
having pulled strings to get her on the expedition. Leslie
Sun could never have done this ... "So why did Mike
put on the brakes?" she asked. "It's just stuff. We could
have gone right through it."

Judith hesitated. "See that?" she asked, pointing to the
center of the smoker. "The temperature in there is more
than seven hundred degrees." She gently tapped the nail
of her right forefinger against the porthole. "If we had
gone in, the heat would have shattered the glass like a
hammer. We'd be dead now."

Andie said nothing for a few seconds. When she

looked away from the viewfinder, though, her face was
ashen. Judith gravely nodded at her unspoken question,
and she seemed to swallow something acid in her throat.
"Mike?" she said at last. "I think I've got enough. Why
don't you take us up now . . . please?"

SIXTEEN

Lucifer

6.7.11—1702 AST

Cilantro took the *Galatea* up until it was about thirty feet above the valley floor, then carefully maneuvered the submersible until its prow was less than twenty feet from the black smoker. Now that they were looking at it from above, they could see that the hydrothermal vent actually had two plumes, one directly behind the other, their jets rising at right angles from the top of the mound. The mound itself was covered with the flaky, off-white particulate of a bacterial bloom, another indication that this was a new vent.

"Looks almost like horns," Judith murmured. She pointed to the twin plumes. "See? There's the head, see, and where the plumes are coming up, there's the horns."

"Oh, yeah. Weird." Andie moved the camcorder so that she could get a better shot through the small porthole. "Kind of looks like a devil's skull."

"Not a bad description," Mike said. "Dale, mark this site on the map as Lucifer. We ought to take you on more dives, kiddo. You've got a knack for names."

"Can't we just call it Andie?" she asked. "I think I like that better."

"Nope. Not in the protocol. Joe, are you ready with Fido?"

Up in the control room, Joe Niedzwiecki was squatting on a folding camp stool before the ROV station. "Coming right up, skipper," he said. He flipped a set of toggle switches on the main electrical panel; diodes flashed to red as several more lines of type ran down the small computer screen above the console. Joe studied the ROV's self-diagnostic report and nodded with satisfaction. "We're powered up and ready to go," he added. "Jack, are you linked back there?"

"Hold on a sec." In the small lab compartment in the back of the crew section, Jack Sheldon hastily typed a set of commands into the keypad. A moment later his CRT flashed STANDBY MOD. "Green for go," he murmured into his headset mike, then he glanced up at the TV monitor. The screen showed nothing but fuzzy gray static. "Can't see a damn thing," he said. "Are you sure the camera's on?"

"Oops. Sorry." Joe snapped a couple of switches on the TV control panel. An instant later the monitor above the swivel-mounted joysticks brightened to show the faint image of a smooth metal panel with a riveted seam running down the center: the interior of the ROV bay. "All right, we're on."

"Very good." Mike looked over at Schuster. "Dale, tell Tethys we're about to deploy Fido." Dale nodded, then switched his headset to the UQC frequency. Unnoticed by either of the women in the observation blister, Cilantro had quietly passed the responsibility of reporting back to Tethys to his first officer. He had needed Judith's eyes during the long journey through the rift valley, and didn't want her distracted by small talk with Charles Toussaint. Besides, the underwater acoustical phone was capable of handling only one voice channel at a time, and direct linkup with the ROV's cameras was impossible; if Tethys was going to monitor the dive via satellite, then it was best if someone in *Galatea's* control room delivered the play-by-play, in case something went wrong.

But nothing was going to go wrong, Cilantro sternly reminded himself. He was keeping the *Galatea* above the floor of the valley, just in case there was another violent eruption, and at safe distance from Lucifer's vent plumes. The ROV was designed to take risks, after all; it was nothing like the old days aboard *Alvin*, when he'd have to inch the tiny submersible so close to a vent that its ashtray-size portholes were only a couple of feet away from its smoking cauldron. White-knuckle flying, indeed . . .

"Tethys reports no major SOSUS activity," Dale said. "Hilliard says go ahead."

"Okay, let's do it, people." Cilantro glanced over his shoulder at Niedzwiecki. "Anytime you're ready."

"Let's go downtown." Joe rapidly snapped a half-dozen toggles. "Impellers on . . ." He gently pushed the left joystick forward, and the gray metal wall of the ROV bay disappeared as Fido's lights caught the snowlike flakes of sediment drifting against the inky blackness. "We're in the water . . ." Another nudge on the handcontroller; the TV image tilted sharply left, then right, capturing fleeting glimpses of the valley floor. "Umbilical free, no tangles, so far so good . . ." He brought the joystick back to center position; the image on the screen stabilized, showing the right plume of the vent. "Okay, we're clear. Which do you want first, the one on the right or the one on the left?"

"Judy, Jack . . . your call," Mike said.

Down in the blister, Judith gently pushed aside Andie's camera as she crawled closer to the porthole. She still couldn't see Fido, though; the robot remained hidden by the hull behind her. For the first time she regretted not being in the control room, where she could watch the action on the TV monitors. "Uh . . . go for the one on the right. The closer one."

"Works for me," Sheldon said. "Probably doesn't make any difference anyway."

Judith nodded. The twin plumes were rising from the same chute, most likely, and were being split in half by a lava wedge somewhere deep within the mound. In time, as the sediments began to build up, either a single large chimney would form above the mound, or two prongs would temporarily rise until gravity and pressure caused one to collapse. Or at least that was the way she figured it would occur; nature, of course, would have the final word.

"Okay, we're going for the one on the right." Joe carefully pulled the hand controller to the right as he watched the TV screen. It was a little like playing his kids' Nintendo machine at home; in fact, it helped his frame of mind if he pretended that was just the case. Yet he couldn't get away from the fact that this wasn't just a computer game, but a hand-built machine worth several million bucks. He had crashed one piece of expensive hardware only a few days ago, and he was damned if he was going to lose another.

"I see it," Judith said as Fido emerged from behind the blister. Approximately the size and shape of a small gas oven, its lights, cameras, and sensors protruded above a fragile-looking claw manipulator and a retracted sample arm; a pair of small skids were mounted beneath the open frame enclosing its boxlike main body. As the ROV moved forward, driven by six impellers mounted fore and aft of its fuselage, the long, serpentine coil of its umbilical cable trailed behind it.

Caught within the beam of *Galatea*'s searchlight, Fido slowly descended toward Lucifer, its twin lights drifting across the thick charcoal plume streaming up from the right vent. The ROV stayed clear of the plume until it had reached the mound, then it slowly moved in.

"Anyone want shrimp for dinner?" Joe asked. "There's a ton of 'em down here. Big ones, too. They're all over the place. I could try to bag a few."

"I don't think you'd like the taste," Judith said. "If you could smell the vent, it would stink like rotten eggs." It would probably also roar like a blast furnace, she added silently, although it was impossible to hear that through the *Galatea*'s thick titanium hull. Too bad; something as incredible as this should really be experienced by all five senses, yet even the creatures which had adapted to this environment were blind.

"Yuck. Forget it." He hesitated, undoubtedly to refocus his attention on driving the ROV. As they watched, Fido approached the right orifice as stealthily as a barnyard cat stalking a field mouse. "All right," he said after a few moments, "I'm almost on the mound. Ambient water temperature is thirty-two degrees."

"That's all?" Andie sounded incredulous. "I thought you said it was over seven hundred degrees."

"That's only within the smoker," Judith said quietly. "There's a sheath of cold water surrounding the plume, so the heat rises straight up, like in a chimney. You get a few hundred feet above the vent, though, and the heat dissipates. That's why it's impossible to locate these things by satellite."

"Joe, can you get a fix on the mound with the ion microbeam?" Jack asked. "I'd like to run a spectrographic analysis before you get the sample."

"Roger on that one." Another long pause. "Okay, you're locked in."

"Thank you." A few moments passed, then they heard a low chuckle from the lab; Sheldon was undoubtedly reading the raw data coming in from the ROV's electron probe microanalyzer. "Oh, this is cool . . . this is very, very cool . . ."

"Hey, I'm getting a kick from this thing," Joe said, his voice suddenly tense. "I dunno what it is, but Fido's beginning to buck a little. I don't—"

"Guys, I've got an incoming from Tethys." Dale's voice was sharp. "SOSUS reports major seismic activity in this area."

"Do they think it's an eruption?" Mike asked.

Andie looked up from her camcorder, glanced uncertainly at her aunt. She didn't say anything, but fear had reappeared in her eyes. "Don't worry," Judith murmured, clasping a hand over her mike. "It could just be a tremor."

"They don't know," Dale replied. "It might be, but they're not sure."

"Okay," Mike said, "let's make this short and sweet. Sorry, Jack, but I'm cutting short the microbeam probe. Joe, get ready to send in the bottles."

"I'm on it, skipper. Lemme move in a little closer."

Judith peered through the porthole. The ROV was right up against Lucifer, its umbilical almost lost in the thick, bubbling cloud of water churning from its aft impellers.

"Two feet from the vent," Joe said. "I'm telescoping the sample arm."

He gently bit the tip of his tongue as he carefully pushed the left joystick forward. On the TV monitor, he watched the sample arm slowly slide forward from beneath the ROV's body. Positioned at the end of the arm was a rack containing three metal bottles, about the same size and shape as test tubes yet made of titanium; just behind them were the studs and tubes of various sensors and chemical analyzers. The arm dully reflected the light cast from Fido's lamps as it entered the dense black liquid streaming out of the vent; in the next instant it disappeared from sight.

"Okay," he said, "it's in."

"Wow!" Sheldon exclaimed from the lab. "Temperature just jumped to 747 degrees!"

Joe was about to say something when he saw the TV image jar slightly. He moved the arm controller a little bit, and the image jostled again, as if something within the plume had kicked the sample arm. "Man, this thing's really fighting . . ."

Judith stared through the porthole. Was it her imagination, or was the plume getting thicker? "Better hurry up," she said. "I think something's happening down there."

"I'm on it," Joe said. "I'm opening the sample bottles now . . ."

"I'm getting a preliminary chemical readout," Jack said. "Major concentrations of iron, sulfur, zinc, potassium . . . this is some stinky brew we've got . . ."

All of a sudden, even as Joe watched the screen, it seemed as if a wave of inky smoke had washed out toward the ROV. The plume was expanding; in another second he couldn't see the sample arm at all.

"Holy shit!" he yelled. "It's erupting!"

"Get Fido out of there." Cilantro turned to gaze over Niedzwiecki's shoulder. "Close the bottles and retract the arm."

Through the porthole, Judith could see the umbilical going taut. The twin plumes jetting up from Lucifer had suddenly become larger, and *Galatea*'s lights caught a broad, black expanse flowing outward from the infant vent. The ROV had completely disappeared within the plumes, as if swallowed whole by Lucifer.

"I can't see Fido!" she shouted.

"Tethys says we're getting a major eruption!" Dale snapped.

Niedzwiecki grabbed both joysticks within his fists and hauled back on them, yet even as he watched in helpless astonishment, his TV screen was filled with black smoke. "I'm getting no response!" he yelled. "I can't—!"

Then the TV monitor went dark; an instant later the computer screen began flashing error codes. Joe let go of the left joystick and stabbed at toggle switches, fighting for control over the ROV. "Aw, shit, shit, shit!"

"I've lost telemetry!" Jack shouted. "Everything's down!"

"We've lost Fido!" Joe yelled.

In that instant he knew what had just happened. The ROV was sturdy enough to withstand the pressure of the deep ocean, but its instruments weren't designed to take the searing heat of a black smoker. Everything aboard Fido—camera lenses, sensors, wiring, circuit boards, microchips—had imploded or simply melted.

Judith was still staring at the place where Fido had vanished when she saw its cable jerk as tight as a fishing line. For a moment she thought Joe had managed to reassert some control over the ROV. Then the cable began to rise . . .

No. It wasn't the cable. It was Fido itself. The plume was throwing the dead ROV up and away from the vent.

The *Galatea* trembled beneath them, as if a strange wind had risen from the ocean bottom and caught the sub in its breeze, then it lurched to one side as Fido was pitched out of the smoker and hurled to the far side of Lucifer.

Andie screamed as she was thrown against the bulkhead, her camcorder falling from her hands. This time, Judith couldn't stop herself; she rolled across the narrow deck until she found herself pinning Andie against the side of the blister. Even so, she kept watching the porthole, and so she saw everything.

Fido was junk, yet its umbilical cable remained intact. Judith watched as it angled sharply downward, straight through the heart of the smoker. A cold wave of terror ran down her spine as she realized exactly what was happening. The dead ROV had landed on the far side of the vent mound, and now it was rolling down Lucifer's broad flank, wrapping its cable around itself as it went . . .

And dragging the *Galatea* along behind it. Straight into the smoker.

"Cut the cable!" she yelled. "Goddammit, cut the—!"

No tinny voices in her ears, only muffled noise from the deck above. Judith grabbed at her ears. Where the hell was her headset?

"What's going on?" Andie demanded, her voice now cartoonishly garbled. "Why . . . what's . . . ?"

"Shut up!" Judith scrabbled about on the tilted deck, searching for the lost headset. There was a deep groan from within the sub; the pilots were trying to use the thrusters to correct *Galatea*'s altitude, but they didn't know what was . . .

She glanced through the porthole, and felt her heart freeze. The plume was only a few dozen yards away, an oily mass of bubbling water coming closer with each passing second, the cable now stretched ahead of the Galatea. In another half minute or so the blister would be plunged straight into the superheated water. The porthole glass would shatter and . . .

The sub lurched again, this time forward. She heard a
long, dull scrape against the left side of the hull. The
Galatea had just hit something, probably an outcropping.
Judith closed her eyes, prayed that death would be
quick . . .

"Oh, my God! Oh, my God, oh, my God!" Andie was
hysterical, her face now only a few inches from Judith's.
"Someone, get us out of here! We're—!"

Who was she yelling at?

Judith twisted around, groped through the darkness for
her niece. Andie tried to grab for her, as if clutching for
comfort in her last moments of life, but Judith savagely
swatted the girl's hands aside.

There! Andie's headset!

Judith tore the headset from her niece's scalp—Andie
yelped as a few strands of hair came with it—then she
yanked its mike to her mouth.

"Cut the cable!" she yelled. "Joe, it's the umbilical!
It's dragging us down! Cut the ROV cable!"

She heard a swarm of indistinct voices through the
earphones, but she couldn't understand them. She
glanced again at the porthole, now canted sideways. All
she could see was black smoke. God, they were only a
few feet away . . .

"Joe!" she shouted again, her throat raw with terror.
"Mike! Joe! Cut the cable!"

The sub's prow violently pitched upward, so hard that
the back of her head slammed against the blister ceiling.
Judith yelped in pain as she was thrown away from Andie, and there was a sickening sensation in the pit of her
stomach as if she was in a runaway elevator which had
plunged two floors before being snagged by its safety
bars. Andie screamed again, and Judith had a moment to
wonder if this was the last sound she would ever hear . . .

Then the deck stabilized beneath them, became horizontal once more. Judith rolled away from her niece, collapsing in a heap on top of the forgotten camcorder. From somewhere above her, on the other side of the blister hatch, she detected the vague sound of raised voices. It sounded a little like they were cheering . . .

Christ, she thought as she let out her breath. Can't men do anything right?

M ike spent the next few minutes making sure the *Galatea* was intact and in good condition, a task rendered more difficult by the absence of Fido, without whom it was impossible to examine the sub's outer hull. Yet there was no sign of slow leakage and all major systems seemed to be operational, and once he was satisfied that everyone aboard was safe and, aside from a few bruises and minor abrasions, relatively uninjured, he traded seats with Schuster and told the first officer to take the *Galatea* out of the rift valley.

"Are you out of your mind?" Judith demanded. She had just crawled up from the observation blister, and now stood nearly face-to-face with the sub's skipper. "We have an accident, and now you're abandoning the dive?"

"Like we have another choice?" Grasping a ceiling hand rung as the deck gently moved beneath his feet, he regarded her with sublime astonishment, baffled by her outrage. "Maybe you weren't paying attention, so let me run it by you again. We lost the ROV, and—"

"I was paying attention," she said coldly. "I'm the one who told you guys to cut it loose, remember?"

"Yes, I do," he replied, remaining calm. "And since your memory's so clear, you'll recall that there's no way we can complete the mission without Fido."

She gaped at him. "That doesn't mean it's over. *Gal-*

atea's got its own lights and cameras. We can still explore the rest of the vent field."

"Sure we can, but only from a distance. There's no way we can take samples now, and that was the main reason for coming out here. Without the ROV, all we can do is take pictures."

"Then we take pictures! Isn't that enough reason to stay?"

Mike started to object, then thought better of it. He closed his eyes and slowly counted to ten, then looked at her again. "Judy," he said softly, "maybe you better take another look at your camera operator."

He nodded toward the rest alcove. Andie was seated cross-legged on Niedzwiecki's bunk, her arms tightly wrapped around herself as she stared dully down at the floor. Joe was sitting next to her, one arm cast around her shoulders; whatever he was saying was lost in the background noise. "Your girl's scared out of her mind," Mike continued, his voice barely above a whisper. "I mean, really scared. You saw the way she scrambled up here. I thought for a second we had a fire down there or something. Now, look at her and tell me she's ready to get anywhere near that smoker again."

Judith seemed to relent a bit as she regarded her niece. "Okay, you're right," she said quietly. "We can't count on her handling the camcorder." She hesitated. "But if we go back down there, we could still use the TV cameras to—"

"We could, maybe, yes. You're right." Yet he shook his head. "But we won't, because we don't know exactly what condition the boat is in. We hit something hard down there. You felt it, I felt it. Now, I don't know exactly where we got hit, but I'm willing to bet one of the skids took some damage. If that's the case, I don't want to get us into a situation where we might have to set down, because if that happens and that skid buckles, we're screwed but good."

"That's a lot of ifs."

"It sure is, and just one too many for my liking." He let out his breath. "Look, Judy, we got lucky back there. You just pointed it out yourself . . . if you hadn't yelled for us to cut the cable, we might have been pulled straight into the smoker, in which case we'd all be crab food by now."

"But we got out of it."

"Doesn't mean we should push our luck. Look, let me make this simple . . ." He dropped a hand from the ceiling to raise a forefinger. "One, we've lost Fido. Without an ROV, there's no way we can take samples. Two . . ." He raised another finger. "We're not one hundred percent certain of the condition of this boat. I have no doubt that we can make it safely back to Tethys . . . at very worst, we can surface, then gradually decompress while we send out an SOS and wait for someone to send out a sea-rescue team . . . but going down there again is foolhardy at the very least. And three . . ." He hesitated, not raising a third finger.

"Your third reason?" she asked.

Mike tucked his hand in the pocket of his jeans. "Third reason is that I'm in charge, and what I say goes. I say we go home. End of discussion."

He looked away from her, saw that everyone else in the compartment was tuned in on the argument. Only Schuster wasn't looking directly at them, for his gaze was concentrated on the controls. "This isn't a democracy," he said, a little more loudly now, "but if anyone else has any objections, I'm willing to hear them."

No one said anything for a moment. Everyone looked colorless and drained, as if all the courage had been sucked out of them. Then, very reluctantly, Andie raised a hand. "Uh . . . can I say something?"

Mike smiled broadly at her. "Sure you can, kiddo. Speak up."

"Uh . . . well, what I want to say is . . ." She glanced uncertainly at her aunt. "I mean, I think it sucks that we come all this way, just to go home empty-handed . . ."

"Thank you," Judith murmured.

Andie looked down at the deck again. "But I also think it's more important that we just get home, period." She swallowed. "Maybe, y'know, we can make a few zillion dollars by sticking around, but . . . I dunno, is that worth dying for?" She shrugged beneath Joe's arm. "I don't think so. I'd just like to . . . to see my mom and dad again. Even if they're a couple of assholes."

Everyone laughed out loud at this, even Judith. As Andie realized what she had just said, her face turned scarlet. "Sorry, skipper," she said, glancing at Mike. "Didn't mean to—"

"That's okay. You've earned the right to cuss like a sailor." Mike turned around, tapped Schuster on the shoulder. "Dale, drop weights and blow tanks one, two, four, and six. Take us up to a hundred fathoms. I'll reset the GPS for a return course." Schuster silently nodded as he reached up to flip switches on the ballast tank panels while Mike took the empty neat next to him. "I'll send a packet to Tethys, let them know we're—"

"You're going to have some trouble doing that," Dale said.

"How come?"

Dale shrugged. "I dunno, but we lost the fix on the buoy when everything went down." He pointed at one of the CRT screens. "See? Flat-lined. Maybe it's just the satellite uplink, but—"

"I'll work on it." Mike bent over the keyboard, began

tapping in commands. "When was the last time you had any voice contact with them?"

"About the time we lost Fido." Schuster hesitated. "They may think we're in trouble."

"Or they may figure that it's just a communications glitch." Mike studied the screen for moment, then entered another command, which opened a graphics window. "Okay, there it is. When we changed position, we lost the UQC pathway. Doesn't matter. When we get closer to the surface, we'll send a message on the ELF, let them know we're okay."

Judith watched in silence while the pilots worked, then turned away and walked over to where Andie was sitting. Joe waited until she sat down on the bunk across from them, then stood up. "I'm going to go back and help Jack clean up the mess in the lab," he murmured. "Want anything from the galley?"

Andie quietly shook her head. She didn't look up when Joe gave her shoulder a reassuring pat before he squeezed between her and Judith, and she seemed reluctant to meet her aunt's gaze. "Hey, kiddo . . ." Judith began.

"I wish everyone would stop calling me that," Andie said softly.

"Sorry. Didn't mean anything by it." Judith edged a little closer, gently touched the top of her head. "Feels like you got a little bump up there. Do you want anything for it? I could get a cold pack, maybe some Tylenol . . ."

"No thanks. I'm fine." Andie angrily jerked her head away. Their eyes met for a brief instant, and Judith was stunned to see naked hostility in her niece's glare. "Just leave me alone, okay? I'm not feeling well."

"Andie . . ."

Judith reached out for her, and the girl shoved her hands away, so hard that Judith fell back into the bunk.

For a moment it seemed as if Andie was going to say something, then she jumped up and moved as fast as she could to the hatch leading to the aft compartment. The hatch was half-shut; it banged loudly against the bulkhead as Andie impatiently threw it open. Out of the corner of her eye, Judith saw Mike and Dale looking over their shoulders at her. Then she stood up and followed her niece.

She found Andie in the head, doubled over the steel commode, noisily vomiting into the bowl. Niedzwiecki and Sheldon stood in the narrow passageway outside the lab, embarrassed and concerned. Joe started to come forward, but Judith waved him off. She stepped into the galley, gathered some paper towelettes and ran cold water over them, then wrung them out and walked back into the head.

Andie was collapsed on the floor next to the commode, one arm carelessly thrown across its filthy seat. Judith reached across her and flushed the toilet, then knelt in front of her and gently pressed the wadded towels against her clammy forehead. "Okay, just take it easy," she murmured softly. "It's all right. Everything's going to be fine. It's all over now."

"Oh, God . . ." Tears leaked from the corners of Andie's eyes, and her hand trembled when she reached up to take the compress from her aunt. "I'm sorry, I'm so . . . I'm . . ."

"Scared?" Judith asked, and the girl nodded weakly. "That's okay. So was everyone else."

Andie nodded again, her chin quivering. "I thought . . . I thought we were going to . . ."

"Shh," Judith whispered. "It's not going to happen." She took the towels back from her, used them to wipe her face and daub her mouth. "It's all over. Mike's taking us up. We're on the way home."

Andie nodded. She glanced at the toilet seat, then her arm. She winced in disgust, then pulled some toilet paper off the roll and self-consciously wiped her forearm clean. "I really . . . I really screwed things up for you, didn't I? I'm sorry . . ."

"Sorry? For what?" Judith stared at her niece in surprise. "You didn't screw up anything. You were great down there. You were a real pro. I couldn't have done it without you, really . . ."

"That's not what I mean." Andie snuffled as she pushed her hair away from her face. "I heard what Mike said. You could have gone back down there if I hadn't . . . I mean, if I hadn't . . ."

Damn. Now Judith understood why Andie had been so hostile a few minutes ago. The last thing she wanted to do was return to Lucifer, while her aunt had harangued the skipper to go back. For a teenager who had just come close to being plunged into an inferno, this was akin to a death sentence.

"No," Judith said quietly. "I'm the one who's supposed to be sorry, not you. I was being selfish. Mike was right, and I was wrong."

"Really?" For the first time since they had emerged from the blister, Andie looked her aunt straight in the eye. "You're not just saying that?"

Judith shook her head. "No, honey, I mean it. I just . . . I dunno, I just get carried away sometimes, and when I do, I forget the people around me." She managed a wan smile. "Just ask Uncle Pete. He's been putting up with me for years."

"Yeah, well . . ." Andie started to swallow, then made a face. She turned her head and spat some bile into the toilet. "Sorry . . . maybe you ought to pay more attention to him, and stop chasing sea monsters so much."

God. Out of the mouths of babes . . .

Judith abruptly realized that she had seldom thought of Peter since she had departed Tethys nearly two days ago, even though she had left him in the company of a woman who was clearly interested in him. Between fruitless searches for sea serpents and hyperthermophiles, she had given scarce thought to her own husband. Perhaps this was forgivable in an ambitious marine biologist, yet nonetheless the pursuit of science was no excuse for negligence.

"You're right," she whispered, more to herself than to Andie. "Damn, but you're right."

"Yeah, sure . . ." Andie looked around. "Hey, if it's okay with you, but . . . I'd like to get out of here. This is a toilet, y'know . . ."

"I hear you." Judith's knees cracked as she stood up. She offered Andie her hand, and helped the teenager to her feet. "You want some clean clothes?" she added as she backed out of the head. "I can get them from—"

"That'd be great, yeah. I could use that. I'll go change." Andie gestured to the wardroom. Through the open door, Judith saw DVDs and books scattered across the table, toppled from their shelves during the accident. "Maybe I'll watch a movie or something."

"Good idea," Judith said, then another thought occurred to her. "Hey, if I get your camera from the blister, you want to look at the disk you shot down there?" Andie hesitated, and for a moment Judith wondered if she had said the wrong thing. "Or maybe you just want to watch a *Star Wars* movie or something."

"No, no." Andie shook her head. "That's a good idea." Then she grinned. "What the hell. I shot it, didn't I? Maybe we'll learn something."

"We might," Judith said. "I know I have."

SEVENTEEN

Fearless

6.7.11—1911 EST

The Russian trawler was nearly a half century old, an iron-gray hulk constructed in the Murmansk shipyards of the former Union of Soviet Socialist Republics. During the height of the cold war, it had regularly prowled the American eastern seaboard just beyond the ten-mile territorial limit, the KGB officers aboard monitoring activity at U.S. Navy bases or observing NASA launches from Cape Canaveral, but eventually its usefulness had come to an end. When the USSR collapsed, the trawler was scheduled to make one last voyage to Africa's Ivory Coast, where shipbreakers would have dismantled its hull and sold it as scrap metal; at the last minute, though, the decrepit vessel was purchased by a shadowy group of European investors, who paid cash for the ship and bribed various Russian officials to alter the books so as to make it appear that it was no longer in service.

Now under Portuguese registry and rechristened the

Braga, the ship fulfilled other purposes. There are many things one can do with a decommissioned Soviet spy trawler, particularly one as uniquely equipped as the *Braga,* and the European businessmen who had purchased the ship were only too willing to lease it out with few questions asked. So it came to pass that the *Braga* made its way to the commercial port of Havana, where it took aboard a small group of French passengers, along with a certain piece of cargo which was loaded aboard at a certain hour just past midnight when it was known that *norte americano* spy satellites wouldn't be passing above Cuba.

Now the *Braga* rested at anchor off the northern coast of Florida, not far from where it had once conducted electronic surveillance against Jacksonville Naval Air Station. This time its mission was different, yet no less covert.

Twilight ocean breeze seeped through the open window of the cabin on the main deck, wafting away the smoke rising from Hilaire Benoit's cigarette. He lifted it from the glass ashtray next to his notebook computer, took a last drag from it, then stubbed out the butt as he read the next line appearing on the screen.

G. REPORTS ROV LOST AT MAR. TAQ SAMPLES LOST.
G. NOW RETURNING TO TETHYS. ETA 6/12 AT 2400.

Benoit frowned as he exhaled pale smoke through his aquiline nose. He wasn't a man given to violent outbursts, yet, at this moment, had he been any less self-controlled, he could have easily picked up the Sony computer and hurled it across the cabin. His employer had placed a considerable amount of funds at his disposal in order for him to achieve tangible results; he himself had invested nearly twelve months into setting up this operation, not the least part of which was recruiting the Dominican fool on the other end of this Internet conversation. All this way, all this time and money spent . . . and to what end?

Benoit impulsively reached for the half-empty cigarette pack on the table beside the ashtray, then deliberately stopped himself. Once the last of his Gitanes was gone, he'd have to smoke the wretched Marlboros favored by the Russian crew of this rustbucket. He absently rubbed a hand through his sparse beard, then laid his fingers on the keyboard again.

WHY WAS THE ROV LOST?

A simple question, he thought as he stabbed the enter button. It should produce a simple answer. A half minute went by, then he received his reply.

SEISMIC INSTABILITY AT MAR SITE. VENT
ERUPTION CAUSED LOSS OF
CONTROL OVER ROV WHILE IT WAS GATHERING
TAQ SAMPLE. G. FORCED
TO ABANDON DIVE.
UNFORESEEN OCCURRENCE. SORRY.

Benoit shut his eyes and murmured a Gallic curse under his breath. Sorry . . .

He barely understood the oceanographic science which went along with this assignment, nor did he particularly care to do so. He was a mercenary hired to do a relatively simple job: obtain a certain product from Company A and deliver it to Company B. The precise mechanics of this assignment held little interest for him; this was why he had gone to great trouble to hire experts. Most of the time this sort of compartmentalized operation worked out, if everyone involved did their jobs correctly. In this particular instance, though, one person in a long chain of individuals had fouled up . . .

And the best he could do was claim it was an unforeseen occurrence, and say he was sorry.

Benoit had just pulled another Gitane from his pack— screw it, he'd have to smoke those foul American cigarettes sooner or later—and was weighing his response when another message appeared on the screen.

    STILL HAVE FIRST SAMPLE. NEED TO DELIVER
    ASAP.
    UNDER SUSPICION. NEED TO CONCLUDE
    BUSINESS.

He lit the cigarette from the gold-plated lighter an old commanding officer had given him to commemorate a successful guerrilla operation in Zaire. Yes, of course the idiot wanted to wrap this up. He had emailed an urgent message only last night, to a drop box within the absurd pornographic web site Benoit had established to launder communications from everyone he had hired for this operation. The police had found one of the men whom Benoit had hired to make the faux abduction in Dominica, and now the trail was leading straight back to them.

Hilaire Benoit had less to lose than his contact aboard Tethys. While he could easily disappear, as he had so many times before, behind a smoke screen of forged passports and visas, his Dominican friend was stuck aboard an undersea laboratory over one hundred meters down and nearly thirty kilometers away. Yet the Caribbean scientist still had in his possession a sample of the sort of thing Benoit's current employers were so interested in obtaining; that alone would pay the costs of this rather expensive operation, along with a slightly more than marginal profit once it was delivered in Madrid.

And as for the scientist himself, and the services he offered . . . ?

Well, that was an entirely different issue, wasn't it? According to the last message received from his employer, they no longer believed that his talent was unique, particularly considering the amount of money he had recently demanded. In fact, they seemed to believe that his presence was a potential nuisance. Too many embarrassing questions if his role in this affair was discovered . . .

Benoit couldn't have agreed more. He laid his cigarette in the ashtray, then bent over the keyboard again.

```
HAVE ARRANGED PICKUP OF PRODUCT 1. MAKE
DELIVERY AT
```

When? He paused to check his watch and think for a moment before he typed the rest of the message. When it was sent, he lay back in his chair and regarded the tropical sunset through the porthole. He could get used to living in this climate. A few hurricanes now and then, to be sure, and sometimes the local currency was wildly inflated, but all the same . . .

A new message appeared on the screen:

```
WILL BE THERE WITH PRODUCT 1. WILL ACCEPT
PRIOR FIGURE.
```

Benoit laughed out loud when he read this. At least the man was honest! He had failed to deliver Product 2, so he had resorted to asking for the figure he had contracted for earlier. Yet somehow, despite all that had occurred over the last several hours, he hadn't grasped the fact that the terms of their agreement had changed.

"Idiot," he whispered.

Benoit closed the Internet connection and switched off the computer, then rose from his chair and left the cabin through the deck door. The sun was setting over the western horizon; he paused by the railing to finish his cigarette and admire the view, drinking in the cool evening breeze as it drifted in from the ocean, until he finally tired of the vista and flipped his cigarette overboard. He strode down the deck until he reached a hatch; opening it, he marched down a narrow flight of metal steps until he reached a ladder leading deep into the bowels of the *Braga*.

When the trawler had been used for spy missions, this part of the vessel was one of the KGB's most closely guarded secrets: a minisub hangar nestled within the ship's hull, concealed by a pair of double doors in the keel below the waterline. The sub it once contained had been used to locate the U.S. Navy's antisubmarine detection systems; it was long gone now, secretly sold to some third-world power with delusions of grandeur, but its hangar still remained, a rectangular pool surrounded by gridded catwalks, a bridge crane running along the low ceiling. On other occasions, it had been used to smuggle drugs into the United States, but now it was briefly being returned to its original purpose.

A small submersible was suspended by cables from the crane, its lower half submerged in the moon pool. The *Atlantida* was an unstreamlined, awkward-looking vehicle: a barrel-shaped afterbody with gimbal thrusters mounted on either side, mated to a transparent acrylic pilot sphere. A tubular frame beneath the hull contained ballast tanks, air bottles, and electrical batteries; a pair of landing skids were attached to the bottom of the frame. The sub held two independent, pressurized compartments; behind the pilot's sphere, within the cylindrical afterbody, was a "lock-out" chamber, designed to be pressurized with helium-oxygen up to twelve atmospheres. Divers within the rear compartment could therefore travel to extreme depths while simultaneously undergoing hyperbaric pressurization; once on the seafloor, they could safely leave the sub, then return again after their job was complete.

Built in France, the *Atlantida* was designed for deep-ocean salvage; like the *Braga*, it was owned by the same consortium which, on occasion, found itself needing to conduct illegal forms of business. Benoit strode around the catwalk until he reached the sub's aft end; through its hull, he saw a light gleaming from within a small porthole next to the divers' hatch. Benoit squatted on his haunches to peer through the porthole. Inside, he saw a young man in his late twenties wearing a neoprene scuba suit, sitting on the floor and calmly reading an American rock and roll magazine.

One of the Russian sailors who ran this part of the *Braga* walked over. "He's almost ready to go," he said in French, in response to Benoit's upraised eyebrow. "Thirty minutes more, and he'll be at pressure."

"May I speak to him?" Benoit asked, and the Russian silently handed him a radio handset. Benoit held it to his face. "René? You're going to lose that magazine, you know."

René Baptiste slyly looked up from his magazine, then smiled and held up a plastic freezer bag. Benoit chuckled; René was the type of person who never overlooked any detail, no matter how trivial. They had worked together before, and he had been one of the first men Benoit had sought out for this job, not least because of his qualifications as a professional diver. "How are you doing, my friend? Any ill effects?"

Baptiste laid down the magazine and picked up his radio. "None. I feel fine." His voice was distorted from the high helium content of the air he was breathing. "How much longer until we depart?"

"Not much longer. Let me check." Benoit stood up, whistled sharply between two fingers. On the other side of the pool, *Atlantida*'s pilot, Pierre Duval, glanced up from the bathymetric chart he was studying along with two of the Russians. Benoit silently pointed to his watch; Duval raised a single finger. Benoit nodded, then knelt on the catwalk and clicked the radio again. "Pierre says one hour," he said. "We're on schedule, don't worry."

Baptiste smiled. "Who's worrying? I'm catching up on my literature." He held up the magazine to show Benoit a full-page spread of an English diva. She wasn't wearing very much, and her eyes were as incredible as her body. "What do you think? Do I have a chance?"

"Only if she likes men who smell like seaweed," Benoit said, and the diver laughed out loud. René liked to pick up his girls at European rock concerts; the more famous they were, the more he desired them. With his blond good looks, easy touch, and money, he was seldom turned down. "Listen, my friend," he continued, "there's been a slight change of plan."

Baptiste stopped smiling. He marked his place in the magazine and laid it aside. "What we discussed earlier?" he asked solemnly. "The deal has gone sour?"

"I'm afraid so, yes," Benoit said.

The younger man shrugged. "Very well. I can do that." He hesitated. "But you still want the sample, correct?"

"By all means." Benoit nodded. "That's the first priority. Get the sample from him, then do what you must. No explanation is necessary. Just do it."

The diver nodded, then picked up his magazine again. "Not a problem," he said shortly. "Understood."

"Good luck," Benoit said. Baptiste nodded distractedly as he flipped back to the article about the rock singer who had caught his fancy. Probably already trying to figure out how to get a backstage pass for one of her concerts.

Benoit stood up and marched back down the catwalk, handing the radio back to the Russian who had loaned it to him. How remarkably easy it was to give a man his death sentence, he reflected as he headed for the ladder leading to the *Braga*'s upper decks. All you had to have was a complete lack of fear—of law, of God, of anything else that might stand in your way.

Hilaire Benoit had stopped being afraid a long time ago, not only because it interfered with his line of work, but also because he admired men who felt the same way as he did. He loved René like a brother because he was fearless.

It was only men like Dr. Charles Toussaint who deserved to die.

S tanding on the balcony outside MainOps, Miles Bartlett sipped a mug of hot tea as he gazed out over the ocean. It was a calm and moonless night, the sea as smooth as black glass; although there was a luminous haze above the western horizon where the lights of the mainland reflected off low clouds, the sky was pitch-black, the first stars only now beginning to come out. Off in the distance, he could make out a small cluster of lights on the water: a ship, probably a small freighter or a commercial fishing vessel, was anchored a few miles from Tethys. Perhaps its captain had given the crew the night off so they could catch a ball game on TV . . .

He heard the door open behind him, and looked

around to see one of the night duty officers stick his head
out. "Jared's on the line," he said.

Bartlett nodded. He'd been waiting for Hilliard to return his call; when Bartlett had tried calling him fifteen
minutes earlier, he'd been informed that the operations
manager was at dinner. Bartlett could have had Juan relay
the call to Hilliard's headset, but it was important that
they have some privacy, so he had the AI page him instead.

Bartlett stepped back into the operations center and
went to his desk, where he picked up the phone. "Jared?"
he said. "It's Miles. Sorry to drag you away from dinner."

"Not a problem," Hilliard said. "I'm in my quarters. I
take it this was something you don't want to talk about
on an open line."

In the voicemail message he had left with Juan, Bartlett had specified that Jared not call from Tethys 2's operations center. "No, it isn't. Are you alone?"

"All by myself. What's going on up there?"

Bartlett took a quick glance around MainOps. Three
men and two women were on duty just now, but none
seemed to be paying attention to him. He briefly considered having the call transferred to his office, but decided
that it wasn't necessary, so long as he kept his voice low.

"I got another call a little while ago from Helen Blanchard." He sat down in the desk chair and turned it
around so that he was facing away from the room. "She's
been in contact with the company's security consultants
in Dominica. The police have just arrested another one
of the guys who tried to abduct Charles. He was trying
to leave the country on a commercial flight to San Juan
when they busted him at the airport."

"Doc will be pleased to hear that."

Bartlett frowned. "I'm not so sure. Apparently this
person was the getaway driver, so he knew a little more

than the other guy did. Either that, or he was more co-operative with the cops. Either way, he . . . well, he knew something about the deal with this Hilaire Benoit character, the guy who set up the kidnapping."

"And?"

Bartlett looked over his shoulder once more to make sure no one was listening. "According to the driver, the whole thing was a hoax," he said as quietly as he could. "Charles himself helped set up his own kidnapping."

From the other end of the line, Bartlett heard the Hilliard take a long, deep breath. "You've gotta be kidding," he said at last. "I mean . . . look, someone's got to be putting us on."

"I know it sounds unbelievable," Bartlett said, "but that's what we're getting from the consultants, and Helen says they're working closely with the Dominican police. Benoit is still the guy everyone's looking for . . . and since the driver says he was running the operation out of Cuba, they can pretty much kiss off trying to bust him . . . but the driver claims that Charles knew someone was going to kidnap him at that particular place and time. He even called the driver himself to make the arrangements."

"Now, hold on a sec," Hilliard said. "That doesn't sound right. Judy told me that they decided to leave early because she got a call from Peter about the . . . y'know . . ."

"The *Doris* thing, yeah, right. I know. That was apparently a last-minute change of plan. The abduction was supposed to happen later the same day, when she and Charles went out for dinner. Same general idea, same place even, but at a different time. As before, Judy was to help provide the alibi. Only she screwed things up by deciding to catch the next flight out to P.R., so Doc had to move up the timetable. He called the driver and told him to swing by his place. That's why Doc didn't call a cab to his house . . . he insisted that they carry their bags several blocks to a taxi stand near a hotel. Follow me so far?"

"Yeah . . . no! I mean .. hell, it doesn't make any sense! Why would Doc . . . ?"

"That's what everyone wants to know." Bartlett rubbed his eyelids with his fingertips. "What's Charles been doing today?"

"He was here with me, keeping tabs on the *Galatea*. He was really tense . . . but, hey, y'know, so was everyone else, especially when they lost the ROV."

Bartlett nodded. Although he hadn't been directly patched into the satellite feed, he had monitored the operation from MainOps, and had helped relay the incoming SOSUS data to Tethys 2. There had been a long period there, after the *Galatea* had lost voice contact with Tethys, when everyone had been sweating blood; it wasn't until *Galatea* had come up from the Mid Atlantic Ridge and reestablished the satellite link with Tethys that he had breathed easy once more. "Since then, I mean. Where has he been?"

"I don't know. Went to the lab, I guess." A pause. "In fact, that's where he said he was going, right after we got *Galatea* back on line again. Said he needed to analyze the new data. I didn't see him at dinner."

"Well . . . yeah, okay." Bartlett picked up the mug; his tea had gone cold, and he placed it back on the desk again. "Helen wants to talk to him. She's waiting for one of the security consultants to fly up from Dominica. They're supposed to meet up in Jacksonville tonight and shuttle out here first thing tomorrow morning. I think they want Charles to come then."

"Tomorrow morning?" Hilliard whistled low under his breath. "I hope they're ready to wait."

Bartlett knew what he meant. Even after Charles Toussaint took a ride to the surface inside one of the diving bells, he'd have to spend three days gradually decompressing within the DDC belowdecks. But the hyperbaric dorm contained its own telephone, positioned next to the thick Plexiglas porthole; even if Helen Blanchard wouldn't be able to sit in the same room with Charles, she would nonetheless be able to look him straight in the eye when she questioned him about the Roseau incident.

"I think they've taken that into consideration," he said. "Look, Jared . . . I don't want to believe this either, but there's something screwy going on here and the company wants to get to the bottom of it. So sit tight and keep an eye on Charles. Okay?"

"Yeah, sure." A moment of hesitancy. "You want me to tell him about this?"

"No," Bartlett said flatly. "By all means, no. Not a peep until Helen gets here, and even then, say as little as you can before you get him aboard the bell. Just keep an eye on him . . . and one more thing. Lock out his communications with the surface. No phone, no email, nothing. Understand?"

"Christ, Miles . . . you make it sound like he's under arrest."

"Sorry. That's Helen's instructions. She's the company, so . . . well, there it is."

"Yeah. Okay. If that's what you say." Another sigh over the phone. "Jesus, man . . ."

"I know. I have a hard time with it, too." Bartlett let out his breath. "Look, we'll get this cleared up. There's probably just a misunderstanding, that's all. I'll check in with you later."

"All right. Over and out."

"Ditto." Bartlett hung up the phone, then gazed out the window. The ship he had spotted earlier was still lingering on the horizon, its running lights brilliant against the darkness. Sure, they'd get this straightened out, he mused. Charles must have an explanation for all this.

Peter found Charles in his lair, the top deck of the laboratory hab. Ever since the *Galatea* had left, Doc had the bio lab all to himself, and with few exceptions, he had rarely left it. Peter knew his old MIT professor to be rather reclusive at times, especially when he was working on an important project, but he had so seldom seen Doc over the last two days that he was beginning to worry about the old man. When he didn't show up for dinner, Peter decided it was time to pay him a visit.

Charles was seated at his computer when Peter came up the spiral steps from Deck 2B; gazing at the screen with his chin cupped in his right hand, he appeared to be lost in thought, and didn't seem to notice his former student until Peter cleared his throat. Then he jerked slightly, as if startled, and looked over his shoulder.

"Oh, Peter," he said. "I'm sorry. I didn't hear you come up."

"What's up, Doc?" Peter said. It was an old joke going back to their Cambridge days, when he and Judith had discovered, to their amazement, that their Dominican mentor had never seen a Bugs Bunny cartoon. Judith had invited the professor over for dinner at their apartment that next weekend, after which she slipped a Looney Tunes tape into the VCR. Dr. Toussaint had laughed uproariously for the next hour; ever since then, Peter had never missed a chance to throw that punch line at Charles.

This time, though, Doc didn't smile. In fact, his face looked haggard and drawn, his eyes shadowed from lack of sleep. "Didn't see you in the mess deck," Peter added, "so I kinda thought you might have forgotten dinner." He held up the covered tray he had brought with him. "It's meat loaf night. I know how you can't bear to miss that."

"Um . . . no, of course not." Charles peered at the tray as if not recognizing it for what it was, then gestured to the lab bench behind him. "Thank you, but I'm not very hungry just now. Go ahead and put it over there. I'm sure I'll enjoy it later."

"Not when it's cold," Peter said, but Doc simply shrugged and looked away. "Okay, whatever you want," he murmured as he carried the tray over to the island.

The top of the bench was nearly empty, but there was an item which Peter had to push out of the way to make room for the tray: a small plastic case, the kind an optician gives with a new pair of prescription glasses. Its hinged cover was open, yet within it lay not a pair of spectacles, but black foam padding, cut to securely hold a sealed glass test tube. It appeared to contain murky, brownish water, like that which might come from a polluted pond.

Peter started to ask what it was, but when he looked back at Doc, he saw that the scientist was staring at him in alarm. Whatever this was, it wasn't anything Charles wanted him to see.

"Haven't seen much of you lately," Peter said, instinctively changing the subject as he deliberately turned his back to the bench. "I mean, I saw you today in Operations, but . . . y'know, you've been keeping to yourself a lot."

"No . . . no . . . I've been up here most of the time." Charles nodded to the computer screen, and now Peter saw that it displayed the satellite map of the Mid-Atlantic Ridge. "Been trying to update Juan on the data we've received from Lucifer." He gazed pensively at the screen. "What precious little we got, that is," he added.

"I know. Damn shame it worked out the way it did."
When Doc looked away, Peter took the moment to steal
another glance at the test tube. Something was written in
black felt-tip on its frosted-glass label—GALAP.—but he
couldn't read the rest, for the tube was turned on its side.
"I'm just glad Judy got out of there safely. Sounds like
they had a few rough moments there."

"More than a few," Charles said softly. "They may
have come close to losing their lives." He sighed deeply
as shook his head. "I'm sorry, Peter. The last thing I
meant to do was put your wife and niece in harm's way."

Peter's mouth fell open. This was something he never,
ever would have expected Charles Toussaint to say. "You
didn't do anything, Doc. It was the company who wanted
to get to the site as soon as possible, not you. You just—"

"Yemaya wouldn't have sent out the *Galatea* if I
hadn't insisted." Charles removed his glasses to massage
the corners of his eyes. "And my reasons were entirely
selfish. Taq samples from a new vent . . . that's all I was
concerned about. It never occurred to me that Judith
might—"

"She wanted to go," Peter said quietly. "Nobody put
a gun to her head. Same for Andie."

Even as he said this, though, Peter knew he was sugar-
coating the truth. He had been in the control room when
Tethys had lost contact with the *Galatea;* the last thing
they heard was Joe Niedzwiecki yelling that they had lost
Fido, then a long silence that lasted almost two hours,
until the *Galatea* had come close enough to the surface
that it was able to transmit a brief ELF-band message to
Tethys. During that time Peter had managed to deny to
himself the notion that anything had happened to his
wife, yet there had always been the terrifying thought,
shoved to the back of his mind but nonetheless present,
that his wife could be dead.

Those two hours had been the longest of his life, made even more painful by the memory of what had almost happened the previous night.

"Perhaps." Charles shook his head again, then put his glasses back on. "And I'm glad everyone's safe and on their way home." He let out his breath as he turned to gaze at the screen once more. "But for what reason? It wasn't scientific knowledge, just . . . greed, I think."

As he spoke, Peter took advantage of Charles's distraction to half turn to the bench again. With his fingertip, he carefully rolled the test tube on its side. Now he could read the label: GALAP.TAQ . #311—7/18/10.

"Greed, materialism, call it what you will, but I—" Charles suddenly stopped, and Peter looked around to see that he was looking straight at him. "What are you . . ."

"Sorry. Just curious, that's all." Realizing that he had been caught, Peter's first impulse was to jerk his hand away from the tube—but what the hell was he afraid of? "Looks like a taq sample."

"Yes, it is . . . from the Galápagos vent Yemaya explored last year." Doc spoke quickly, his eyelids fluttering nervously. "I brought it here from Jacksonville so that I could compare it with the taq from the MAR."

Even as he said this, though, Peter knew Charles was lying. Doc had come straight to Tethys from Dominica; although he and Judith had changed planes in Jacksonville, no one had told him that they had enough time at Yemaya's corporate headquarters for Charles to visit its labs and remove a taq sample. Besides, wasn't this stuff kept under lock and key?

"I really wish you wouldn't bother with that. It's quite fragile." Doc stood up and hastily walked over to the bench; he snapped the case shut, then picked it up and moved it to the desk next to the computer. "I shouldn't have left it there."

"No," Peter murmured. "I guess not." What was going on here?

Doc sat down again. "I appreciate you looking in on me," he said, "but I really need to get back to work. Thanks for bringing up dinner. I'll return the tray when I'm done."

"Sure. No problem. Glad to oblige." Peter tucked his hands into his pockets, started walking toward the stairs. Doc had always been a little on the eccentric side, but even this...

"Peter?"

At the top of the stairs, Peter turned back again. Charles was staring at the computer once more, yet the haunted expression had returned to his face. "If you've done harm to someone," he asked, then he stopped as if gathering his thoughts. "Just as a rhetorical question, but... if you've betrayed someone's trust... how do you set things right?"

For an instant Peter felt his face grow warm. Did Charles know what had happened last night in his bunk, when Leslie had come to him? Throughout the day, particularly during the two-hour communications blackout from the Galatea, he had contemplated much the same question, although not in the same precise terms. For a few terrible moments he had come close to betraying Judith; although those moments had come and gone, he knew that this was something he was going to have to live with for the rest of his life.

Yet there was no way Charles could possibly be aware of this. The brief encounter with Leslie Sun had been witnessed by no one, so there was no way Doc could have heard about it. So what was he...?

"I don't know," he found himself saying. "I guess you try to make sure that it never happens again."

Charles slowly nodded. For a few seconds it seemed

as if he wanted to say something more; indeed, it appeared to Peter that he wanted to make a confession of some sort. But then Doc reached out and stabbed a button on the keyboard, changing the image on the screen.

"Thank you, Peter," he said, ever so quietly. "Good night."

" 'Night, Doc." Then Peter began walking down the stairs, his mind full of questions for which he had no answers, not the least of which was the one Doc had just posed.

EIGHTEEN
Intrusion

6.7.11—2156 EST

Leslie Sun waited until almost ten o'clock before she made her move.

It wasn't an arbitrary decision. She had spent most of the day thinking it over—not the deed itself, for that itself was a foregone conclusion, but rather the time when she would do it. She knew, from carefully asking questions among the divers who worked out at the nodule processing plant, that the evening shift would begin returning to the habitat between eleven and 11:30, and the graveyard shift would report to Deck CC around midnight to begin suit-up. Around ten o'clock, though, the wet room was likely to be deserted, and she had already observed that most of Tethys's personnel were either in bed or hanging around the rec room at that time. She could always wait until after twelve, of course, but if someone were to spot her walking through the habitat, she might have to explain herself, and that was the last thing she wanted to do.

So ten o'clock was the hour. Leslie had an early dinner by herself in the mess deck, then went back to her bunk and spent the rest of the evening curled up with her computer, working on the first draft of her article. She was about halfway through it already, and so far it was turning out to be a juicy little number: a financially questionable undersea facility, whose mining activities were potentially harmful to the deep-ocean environment and whose alleged "scientific research" seemed to consist mainly of chasing sea monsters. She'd have to wait until the *Galatea* returned before she got the full lowdown on that aspect of the story, but that would be worth a lengthy sidebar: a foolhardy decision to allow an inexperienced teenager to participate in a dangerous expedition, the loss of a costly ROV, the near loss of the *Galatea* itself (particularly alarming because it contained a nuclear reactor; that alone would make the fish-huggers howl). Once she transcribed the interviews she'd taken over the last few days, she'd have sufficient material to give the piece the necessary illusion of balanced objectivity, but she doubted that any reader with an IQ higher than room temperature would finish her article feeling anything less than moral outrage.

Granted, she was taking a risk. Her editors at *Millennium* hadn't sent her here to research an exposé; all they wanted was an in-depth profile of Tethys and the people who worked on her. Yet Leslie was tired of writing puff pieces about actors kayaking through Alaska. Other writers for the magazine had produced stories with some teeth in them; they were the ones whose names were listed as contributing editors in the masthead and who got the first call for all the best assignments. In order to join their ranks, Leslie knew that she had to write something that would put her on the map. This piece about Tethys—its working title was "Voyage to the Bottom of the Barrel," but she was trying to come up with something better—had the potential to do just that.

But the real clincher, the cherry for the whole sundae, was the experimental submersible hangared down in Deck CC.

From the moment Peter Lipscomb had refused to let her see the thing, Leslie knew that it was the key to a major scoop. There had been rumors in the Usenet newsgroups that the U.S. Navy was developing a one-man tactical attack sub; Leslie had picked up on the hearsay even before she left New York, but largely ignored it. Yet Lipscomb was a former SEAL, which meant that he must still have some Navy connections, and there was no question that something was berthed down in the wet room that everyone here was trying to keep secret. Getting the first look at a classified military project would be a journalistic coup.

But that wasn't all there was to it, was it?

As Leslie picked up the pocket-size digital camera she had smuggled down here—she had been careful not to allow anyone to search her bag, lest they find it—and tucked it in the pocket of the hooded sweatshirt she had pulled on over her T-shirt and jeans, she contemplated the fact that, deep down inside, she wanted to obtain pictures of the X-sub in order to get back at Peter.

Trying to seduce Lipscomb, however pleasurable it had been for a few minutes, was a mistake; she saw that now, and realized that she had let her gonads, so to speak, do the thinking. The guy was too much of a Boy Scout; great ass, nice hands, good mouth, but she should have known that he'd never fool around when that bitch he called a wife was away. The result was a humiliating near catastrophe; fortunately, Peter wasn't likely to tell anyone what had happened, even after the article was published and heads began to roll.

With any luck, his would be one of them. The Navy wouldn't be very pleased with him when they saw pictures of its top-secret sub in a national magazine. Peter, she thought, you shouldn't have thrown me out of bed. Not that sleeping with him would have made much difference, anyway ...

She smiled as she carefully slid back the curtains of her bunk and slipped her legs out. The VIP deck was dark now, save for a couple of lights glimmering behind curtains around her: a couple of visiting Euro-scientists, catching up on a little late-night reading before they sacked out. Totally self-absorbed in their work, they hadn't paid much attention to her earlier; no reason for them to start now.

Leslie tiptoed across the compartment and managed to open and shut the door without causing anyone to so much as stir. She paused for a moment at the top of the stairs to let her eyes adjust to the harsh light of the ceiling tubes, and to listen for movement below. Hearing nothing, she started for the stairs ...

One deck below, the faint, metallic grind of the access tunnel hatch being opened.

Leslie froze, then stepped back away from the stairs, trying to melt into the shadows.

Two sets of footsteps on the narrow landing outside the mess deck; two men murmuring to each other, their words unintelligible beneath the constant background noise.Their footsteps clattered on the spiral staircase, and for a moment Leslie believed that they were coming up, then the footsteps began to recede, echoing against one another up the empty shaft between Hab 1's three levels.

They were heading down to the rec room on the bottom deck. She relaxed and allowed herself to take a deep breath; after a few seconds she no longer heard their footsteps. A door opened, and for an instant she heard a snatch of an old Johnny Cash song before the door slammed shut and the vertical passageway was vacant once again.

Leslie reached up to push back her hair, and her fingers fell against the wand of her headset. Damn! She had become so accustomed to wearing this thing over the last three days, she instinctively put it on every time she got dressed. Of course it allowed her to understand what people were saying to her; that was why she always wore it, as did everyone else. But it also enabled Juan to track her through the base; if anyone wanted to know where she was, all they had to do was ask the AI.

She considered returning to her bunk and dropping it there. Yet she had just managed to leave the VIP quarters without anyone noticing; going back in and leaving again so quickly was bound to rouse someone's curiosity. She could ditch the headset somewhere, but what would happen if someone found it? Questions might be raised. And if someone spotted her walking around without it? Same problem.

No. Better keep it on. And . . . wasn't there a trick she had seen Judith Lipscomb pull a couple of days ago? Oh, yeah . . .

"Juan," she whispered, "take Leslie Sun off-line, please."

"Leslie Sun is now off-line," Juan replied immediately, then she heard a soft double beep in her headset.

Leslie smiled. Problem fixed. Time to go spying. She hesitated for another moment, then began walking down the stairs.

When the lock-out chamber was flooded, René Baptiste reached up and undogged the diver exit hatch, then pushed it open. A ray of light washed out through the hatch, illuminating the darkness outside; Baptiste swam out of the chamber, then paused outside the minisub to shut the hatch behind him. He let himself drop to the sea floor next to the *Atlantida,* then paused for a moment to check his bearings against the illuminated compass of his wrist-mounted dive computer.

Duval had landed the sub about a half kilometer east of Tethys 2, only a hundred meters or so from the edge of the Florida-Hatteras Slope. The descent had been slow and painstaking; in order to ensure that they wouldn't be detected by the base or its divers working nearby, the pilot had switched off the submersible's lights and active sonar, relying only on compass and charts to guide them to this point. Duval deliberately selected a touchdown point on the opposite side of Tethys from the *Braga,* near the long horizontal pipeline of the OTEC intake shaft. If for some reason they had to make a quick escape, it would better to head out to deep ocean than go back toward shore, where they might be easily found in more shallow water by any pursuit craft.

Looking around, Baptiste had no trouble locating the base: a large off-white structure only a few hundred meters away, surrounded by a nimbus of blue light. With only an hour of mixed gas in his tanks, he would have to hurry in order to make it safely to Tethys and back again. And he'd have to make the swim in almost complete darkness; although he had a flashlight strapped next to his right thigh, using it might tip off one of the divers at the mining facility. He'd have to follow the pipeline. With luck, he wouldn't run into any sharks or barracuda.

Well, so be it. Once this mission was accomplished, he'd be more wealthy by a hundred thousand francs: not bad for a single night's work. Breathing steadily through his regulator, Baptiste kicked off from the sandy floor and, tucking his arms next to his body, began the long swim toward Tethys.

L eslie didn't encounter anyone on her way through the access tunnel, although she heard the faint murmur of men's voices as she carefully walked past the door of the operations center. As she expected, the main hab was deserted at this time of night; the midnight dive shift was probably still asleep, and the scientists were tucked into bed, visions of mollusks dancing in their heads.

She found the manhole leading to the hab's bottom level and managed to open its hatch without making too much noise. She briefly considered leaving it open, then decided it wouldn't be a good idea; if someone happened to walk by, they might get curious. So she paused on the ladder to lower the hatch cover behind her, then she clambered the rest of the way down to Deck CC.

The wet room was vacant, silent except for the faint mechanical noise of the airtank compressor and the slow, eerie drip of seawater from some unseen source. The surface of the moon pool rippled with blue light from below; it vaguely reminded her of a hotel swimming pool in Las Vegas where she had once gone midnight skinny-dipping with a German student, back when she was just young enough to do such things. She smiled at this sweet recollection; if this worked out, perhaps one day soon she'd have enough money to have a pool of her own, along with a house in Connecticut behind which to build it . . .

Enough.

On the other side of the moon pool was the hatch leading to the minisub bay. She quickly moved across the wet room, being careful to avoid the slippery areas near the pool. The hatch was shut, but not locked. Taking one last look over her shoulder, she gently pushed it open and, ducking her head a little, stepped inside.

The bay was a small, cylindrical chamber, dimly lit by caged sodium bulbs along its curving walls, with grated drains in the concrete floor. On the far wall was a broad metal hatch. And in the center of the bay, suspended above the floor by steel chains, was the object of her desire.

The Navy submersible was smaller than she had imagined, hardly much larger than the torpedo it vaguely resembled, yet with short winglike elevators poking out from the forward fuselage and stubby, fin-shaped rudders in the aft section. The transparent canopy was recessed into its streamlined, silver-blue hull; although it was shut, Leslie could easily peer into the cockpit. A reclined couch surrounded by waterproofed keypads and buttons, with what seemed to be a small periscope folded against the canopy ceiling; the interior made a two-seater sports car look roomy.

Forgetting for a moment why she was here, Leslie slowly walked around the craft, admiring its elegance. No props, no ungainly thrusters; just a pair of elongated intake vents tucked into the hull beneath the elevators; behind the aft fins were larger exhaust vents, nestled close against the hull like the engines of a Stealth fighter. Apparently this thing operated much like an underwater jet. And these little recessed hatches here, on either side of the elevators? Weapons systems, perhaps?

God. No wonder Lipscomb wanted to keep her from seeing this thing. It was a killer, a man-made shark. She smiled as the thought ran through her mind. The readers ought to know what Uncle Sam was doing with their tax money.

Right. And so they would, once the pictures were published in *Millennium*.

Leslie reached into the pocket of her sweatshirt, pulled

out the tiny camera. She flipped open its tiny strobe light; a tinny electronic whine and a quick beep, and the flash was ready. She needed better equipment for something like this, really, but . . .

Outside the bay, beyond the hatch, she heard something.

She froze, and caught her breath as she listened.

There. A soft, echoing sound, like . . .

Footsteps on the ladder.

She thrust the camera into her sweatshirt, looked around in panic. No way to get out of here without being spotted . . . and, goddammit, she had left the hatch half-open!

The footsteps stopped at the bottom of the ladder, then began slowly walking across the wet room. Directly toward the minisub bay.

Leslie's heart beat against her chest. The sub offered no place for easy concealment; even if she stood directly behind it, someone could still see her, even if she ducked below one of the vertical fins.

The footsteps were coming closer. Whoever they belonged to, he or she was nearly at the moon pool.

If she hugged the wall next to the inner hatch, lay flat against it, there was a chance she might not be seen. Maybe they would just take a quick look inside, see the bay was empty, and shut the hatch. Once the coast was clear . . .

Leslie held her breath as she scampered on tiptoe across the room. Halfway to where she wanted to be, she almost slipped on the wet concrete. The footsteps seemed to hesitate for a moment as she regained her balance; there was a long moment of silence, and for a few seconds she thought she was caught, but when she put her back against the wall, she heard only the grumble of the air compressor, the slow drip of water.

The footsteps had stopped near the moon pool.

Someone was waiting out there.

Leslie hesitated, then slowly turned her head to peer, ever so cautiously, through the hatch.

Hearing a faint sound from somewhere behind him, Charles Toussaint turned away from the moon pool to look over his shoulder. There was no one else in the wet room. The hatch to the minisub bay was half-open, and through it he could see the experimental craft Judith had told him Peter was testing for the Navy.

The chamber was apparently empty. Nonetheless, he had the oddest feeling that he wasn't alone . . .

Nerves. He had made his way down here without anyone seeing him, and he knew that the wet room would be deserted at this hour. It was just his nerves.

Toussaint let out his breath, checked his watch again: 10:30, and no sign of the man Benoit had instructed him to meet here at this time. The room was cold; he rubbed his arms briskly, trying to warm himself, as he turned back toward the pool. Yet something he had just seen bothered him, something he couldn't quite . . .

Why was the minisub bay open? Shouldn't its hatch be shut?

He glanced over his shoulder again; for an instant, just out of the corner of his eye, he thought he saw a shadow move within the bay.

"Hello?" he called softly. "Is someone there?"

No response. If someone was hiding in the minisub bay, though, would they surrender so easily? "Is someone there?" Charles said again, taking a tentative step toward the chamber. "Don't be alarmed. I won't—"

He heard a wet splash from the moon pool, and turned to see a diver surfacing from below. For a moment he thought it might be one of the rockhounds returning early from his shift, until he realized that his gear was different: black military-style dry suit, hood and face mask instead of a helmet, air tanks instead of a rebreather pack.

The diver stared up at him, then paddled over to the ladder. Forgetting about the mysterious sound he had heard from the minisub bay, Charles hurried to the pool. He offered his hand to the diver, but the stranger ignored him. Charles lowered his hand and stepped aside to watch the diver as he slowly climbed up the ladder.

Once he was on the concrete apron, he deflated his PC vest before pulling the regulator from his mouth and raising his mask. The diver was young, handsome in a disarmingly boyish way; he glanced suspiciously around the wet room, then returned his cool blue eyes to Charles.

"M'sser Toussaint?" he asked, and despite the high-pitched helium garble, there was no mistaking the French accent in his voice.

"*Oui,*" Charles replied in the same language. "Hilaire sent you?"

"He did indeed." The diver smiled charmingly. "My name's René. A pleasure to meet you."

W hat the hell was going on here?
     Leslie kept her back flat against the wall as she peered around the edge of the hatchway at the two men near the moon pool. Toussaint, of course, she recognized, but the guy who had just come up . . . she knew the instant he emerged from the pool that he wasn't a Yemaya employee. His equipment wasn't company standard issue, and besides, he spoke French.

She had taken French for a couple of years in high school, but that was a long time ago. Her language skills were sufficient only for understanding the menu in a good

Parisian-style Manhattan restaurant and the occasional
sexy double entendre. Yet she needed to know what they
were saying. If only . . .

Of course. She carefully raised her headset mike to
her lips. "Juan, this is Leslie Sun," she whispered. "Put
me back online."

A double beep in her earphones. "You're back online,
Ms. Sun."

So far, so good. Now if she remembered how that
computer glitch worked . . . "Juan, put Charles Toussaint
online," she whispered.

A second passed, then she heard another double beep.
"Charles Toussaint is online," Juan said.

Now she heard Charles's voice. All right, that was
what she was hoping for; since they were technically in
the same room, Juan was allowing her to eavesdrop on
his conversation. Yet he was speaking French, and she
could barely understand what he was saying.

"Juan," she murmured, "can you translate what
Charles Toussaint is saying?"

She had no idea whether this could be done, but it was
worth a shot. After all, if the AI was programmed to
reinterpret helium-distorted voices so that others could
understand them, wouldn't it stand to reason that it had
also been programmed to interpret foreign languages?

A pause, then: "I'm sorry, Ms. Sun. I'm unable to
translate the language Charles Toussaint is presently
speaking."

Damn! Leslie closed her eyes. Well, she'd just have
to get by on her own.

"Pardon me, but I'm in a bit of rush," René said. "Do
you have the package for Hilaire?"

The diver seemed relaxed, almost as if they were

meeting at a taxi stand. His blue eyes regarded Charles with Gallic humor; just a quick business transaction among friends, and then off to other pressing appointments. Yet there was something behind that vanilla gaze . . .

"Of course," Charles replied as easily as he could. "But first, we need to conclude the rest of our business." He hesitated. "I believe you have a certain number for me."

The easy smile faded from René's face. He stared at Charles for a long moment, as if sizing up a potential adversary, before his expression relaxed once more.

"Certainly." Shifting his weight from one hip to another, he turned slightly and reached for a sealed pocket on the right thigh of his bulky suit. "I'd appreciate it, of course," he added as he unzipped the pocket, "if you showed me the goods."

Charles hesitated, then reached into his trouser pocket and pulled out the eyeglass case he had modified to smuggle the Galápagos taq sample through Dominican customs. He held up the case to René; the diver regarded it with unimpressed interest, then silently nodded.

Charles opened the case and pulled out the sealed test tube. "This is the material," he said softly, trying to control the tremor of his hand as he held it up for René to inspect. "In two weeks, I'll be able to board a flight to Paris. Then I'll help your people—"

"Of course," René said, with just a touch of impatience. "They're expecting that." He fished a small, plastic-wrapped pouch from his pocket, extended it with his right hand to Charles. "Here is the number. The money is there, as you've requested."

The pouch was transparent; within it lay a slip of paper which Charles knew to contain the secret number of an offshore bank account in the Caymans. All he had to do was take the number, hand over the sample, and their business was done. In one well-executed moment he'd become a rich man . . .

And no friends left in the world with whom to share his wealth.

"Is there a problem?" René seemed to notice his reticence. He peered closely at Charles, as if trying to read his mind through his icy-blue eyes. "Here's the money. Our deal is done. Take it, please, and let's be on our way."

Charles sighed, and took the pouch from the diver's hand. He regarded it for a moment, not bothering to open it, then dropped it into the pool.

"I'm sorry," he said, shaking his head, "but I'm afraid the deal's off."

Then he opened his hand and let the vial drop to the floor.

Yet it didn't break, as he expected it would. Instead, it landed on its solid glass end, bouncing once before it landed intact on its side and began to roll across the concrete floor.

Charles swore beneath his breath, uttering an uncharacteristic word he had so often heard his American friends use. Then he stepped forward to stamp down on the tube with his left foot. It shattered beneath the heel of his sneaker; rank brownish liquid, older than creation, splattered across the cement along with frail shards of sharp glass, and for a moment he smelled a pungent odor, like chicken eggs left out in the sun for too long.

"There, well, you see," he said as he lifted his foot, intending to apologize to the young French diver, "I'm afraid you'll have to—"

Then the long, serrated blade of a diver's knife plunged into his stomach, and ripped up into his chest.

NINETEEN

Canyon

6.7.11—2236 EST

F eeling death's hand, Judith screamed.

Thrashing within the bedsheets, she pitched upward out of the nightmare which had held her in its grip until, all of a sudden, she found herself wide awake and gasping for breath.

The rest alcove was dark, with only narrow bands of light seeping around the edges of the curtains separating it from the *Galatea*'s control room. The submarine murmured to itself as it cruised beneath the Atlantic. From the bunk below hers, she heard Andie turn restlessly in her sleep.

"Hey, something wrong?" Across the aisle, Joe Niedzwiecki spoke to her from the darkness. He alone had awakened; Dale Schuster was still snoring in the bunk below his.

"No . . . nothing." Her chest and the back of her neck were clammy with sweat. Judith pulled up the top sheet of her bed, used it to mop her face. "Bad dream. Sorry."

"Hmmph . . . okay." His bunk creaked heavily as he rolled over. "G'night."

Judith slowly let out her breath, then lay back in bed, her heart still thudding deep within her chest. She seldom remembered her dreams, even those she had just left behind, and this one was no exception. Yet she couldn't escape the notion that, somewhere far away, something terrible had just happened to someone she loved . . .

P eter Lipscomb slammed open the access tunnel hatch and, not bothering to close it behind him, sprinted down the main hab's central passageway. A crewman was emerging from the operations center; he saw Peter coming and quickly stepped aside, barely avoiding a collision. "What the hell are you—?"

"Get Jared down here!" Peter snapped as he rushed past. "Wet room, now!"

He found the hatch leading to Deck CC, yanked it open, and hastily clambered down the manhole. "Leslie!" he shouted. "Where are—?"

"Here." Her voice, uncharacteristically harsh, echoed through the cold room. She was on the other side of the moon pool, huddled over a dark form which lay near the ladder. "Over here . . . oh, God, Peter . . ."

For a moment he didn't recognize the shape on the floor as a body. It lay within a small pond of blood, its dark redness diluted with salt water and running freely into a nearby drain. Leslie knelt beside the body, her jeans soaked scarlet, her hands clutching a limp, upraised arm.

"Oh, God . . . oh, my Christ . . ." she kept saying as he dashed over to her, and it was then, and only then, that Peter recognized the man on the floor as Charles Toussaint.

For a long, timeless second all he could do was stare down at him, not willing to believe that this was his former professor. Then he was on the floor next to Doc, shoving Leslie away as he bent over him, slipping his right hand beneath the back of his head to raise it slightly.

"Doc?" he said softly. "Doc, can you hear me?"

No response. Charles's dark face had become pallid; his eyes remained shut, his mouth slack. Although the blood which had soaked into his hair remained lukewarm, the skin beneath Peter's fingers was cool. He looked down, saw the long, deep gash which started in the middle of his stomach and went all the way up to the middle of his chest.

Doc was dead.

Next to him, Leslie wept hysterically, her shoulders quaking with each ragged sob. "Oh, God . . . oh, my God, Peter . . ."

"What . . . what happened here?" Unable to take his eyes away from Charles, his voice came as a whisper. "Who did this?"

"Oh . . . Christ, Peter, I . . . I don't . . . I . . ."

"Leslie, stop it," he said, trying to remain calm. "Tell me what happened to Doc." When she didn't respond, he gently laid Doc's head back down, then he reached around and grabbed her shoulders. "What happened?" he demanded, shaking her hard. "Tell me what you saw!"

"I was . . . I was . . ." She looked at him for a moment, then she winced and glanced away. "Oh, God, Peter, I didn't mean to, but . . . I was down here, and . . . I know I shouldn't have been, but . . ."

Past her, Peter caught a glimpse of the open hatch of the minisub bay. Goddammit, she had been sneaking a look at the Barracuda! He fought a sudden urge to slap her across the face. "Okay, so you were in there," he said. "Never mind that now . . . what did you see, Leslie? Tell me."

From behind him, he heard footfalls against the manhole ladder, the muffled voices of men. He didn't look over his shoulder; instead, he grasped Leslie's face with his bloodstained hand, forced her to look straight at him. "C'mon, dammit," he snapped, less gently now. "You called me, told me to get down here . . . now tell me what you saw!"

"He . . ." She took a deep, rattling breath. "Doc came down here . . . I was hiding in there, but he didn't see me . . . and he was waiting for someone, and then a guy in scuba gear came up . . . they were talking about something . . . it was in French, I couldn't understand them . . . but then the guy, the new guy, handed Doc a piece of paper, and—"

"Holy Christ!" From the other side of the wet room, Jared's voice. "Peter, what . . . ?"

"Doc's dead." Keeping his attention focused Leslie, he barely glanced over his shoulder. "Okay, c'mon . . . the guy in the scuba gear . . . what happened then?"

Leslie took another deep breath. "He . . . they seemed to be talking normally, but then . . . I dunno, Doc pulled something out of his pocket." She gestured vaguely behind her. "That case . . . it had a glass tube in it . . ."

Peter looked where she pointed. A couple of feet away, a small pile of broken glass lay on the concrete. Some of the larger fragments retained the curved surface of a Pyrex test tube, and suddenly he remembered the sample of Galápagos taq he had seen in the bio lab a couple of hours earlier. And only a few inches from Doc's body lay the eyeglass case within which it had been contained.

"Okay, I understand," he said quietly. "Did Doc give him the tube?"

Leslie shook her head. "No . . . no, he dropped it, then he broke it under his foot. Then the other guy pulled a knife and . . ." She looked away again. "Oh, God, Peter . . . he didn't even scream, he just . . . he just had this . . . this look on his face and then he . . . he fell over and—"

"What happened to the diver?" Jared asked from behind Peter. His voice was subdued, yet cold. "Did he go back in the water?"

Without looking up, Leslie quickly jerked her chin up and down. "He didn't know I was there. I . . . I stayed quiet until he . . . till I knew he was gone, then I—"

"That's when she called me." Peter let go of her, stood up, and turned around. Jared was staring down at the two crewmen kneeling beside Charles's corpse. "Someone came up from the moon pool, a diver. He—"

"I caught that. Jesus . . ." Hilliard absently rubbed the back of his neck with his hand. "I got word from topside a few hours ago. Seems that the whole thing in Dominica was a setup of some kind. Doc was playing both sides of the fence. We were supposed to keep an eye on him until tomorrow, when—"

"Tell me later." Peter turned back to Leslie. "When did this happen? How long did you wait till you called me?"

For a second she looked confused. "I . . . only a couple of minutes, I think. He was . . . the diver, I mean . . . he was gone as soon as . . . oh, Peter, I was so scared . . ."

Peter glanced at his watch, trying to figure out how much time had passed since he had received her panic-stricken call through the comlink. Fifteen minutes, maybe twenty . . . "He had diving gear," he murmured to Jared, "but there's no way he could have come from the surface. Ascent time is too long . . ."

"Not unless he's got a boat up there," Jared said.

Peter shook his head. "If he does, it would have to be

parked right next to topside, with an ascent line with pony bottles all the way down. Counting the decompression stops, it would take him take hours to rise, and someone up there would have seen the boat."

"You're right. Doesn't make sense. So he must have come from . . ." He looked up sharply. " A submersible. A minisub with a lock-out chamber."

"It's the only way." Peter didn't think twice about it; no other explanation made sense. He snapped his fingers at the two crewmen kneeling beside Charles. "You and you!" he rapped, pointing first at them, then at the Barracuda. "Get in there and prep that thing for diving!"

They stared at him in surprise. "Uh, Pete," one of them said hesitantly, "I don't how—"

"Jared'll show you. Move!" Already he was running for the wetsuit lockers. He wouldn't need to put all the gear on; he only needed to change from his shorts and T-shirt. Behind him, Jared was leading the two men into the minisub bay. Getting the Barracuda ready for EVA would be simple; when he had checked on it yesterday, its batteries were charged, its fuel tanks topped off. All they had to do was turn it around on its chains so that it faced the outer hatch and lower it to the deck. Once he was in the sub, all they had to do was close the inside hatch and flood the bay.

Yet the diver already had a head start of at least fifteen minutes, probably more. Not only that, but there was no telling where his ride was parked. Close enough to swim to, but far enough away that it wouldn't been seen by anyone within the station. And where the hell did it come from, anyway?

No time to worry about that now. Peter yanked open one of the lockers, pulled out a one-piece neoprene suit, then ripped off his T-shirt. If they hurried, he could be out of there in five minutes.

Charles's killer was out there. And he was damned if he was going to let him get away.

Following the luminescent dial of his compass, René Baptiste swam alongside the OTEC pipeline, kicking as hard as he could as he backtracked toward the *Atlantida*. He still couldn't make out the submersible through the darkness—according to plan, Duval was keeping its lights extinguished—yet Baptiste was certain that he wasn't lost. Before he had left the sub, he had programmed its position into his suit's dive computer, and the pipeline served as an adequate landmark.

He glanced again at the digital readout, saw that he was only a couple of dozen meters away. It had been almost twenty-five minutes since he left Tethys 2. He would be there soon enough; once he was safely aboard, he and Pierre would make their way back to the *Braga*.

And then he'd have to explain to Benoit what went wrong . . .

Once again, he silently swore at Toussaint. Damn the bastard! Who would have ever expected him to break the test tube he was supposed to hand over? Baptiste was no stranger to murder—he had committed it several times already, first as a SDECE deep-cover operative, then as a mercenary following his forced resignation from French intelligence—but this was one of those rare occasions when killing had almost been a pleasure. He had no idea what was in the vial, for Benoit had withheld that information from him, yet the entire point of this operation had been its successful recovery; eliminating Toussaint had been necessary only to cover their tracks. Without the vial, no one would get paid—not him, not Pierre, not the Russians, not even Benoit.

Toussaint, you pig! Gutting you was almost a mercy!

In Angola, you would have spent several days dying!

Baptiste shoved those angry thoughts to the back of his mind. Although he still couldn't see it, he knew that he was almost on top of the *Atlantida*. He found the heavy flashlight strapped to his left thigh, unclipped it, and switched it on. Just as he anticipated, the submersible lay only a few meters away. Baptiste aimed the flashlight beam toward the transparent pilot sphere, saw Duval staring back at him; he switched the light off and on twice, his identification signal, then swam toward the lock-out chamber.

Duval was already powering up the fore and aft thrusters as Baptiste closed the hatch behind him. He pulled the regulator from his mouth, unclipped the air mask leading to the sub's internal air supply, and quickly shoved it against his face, then found the telephone cable and plugged it into the socket on the side of the mask, pushing an earphone through the left side of his hood.

"Get us out of here," Baptiste said. "I didn't get the vial."

"What?" Duval's voice, tinny in the earphone, was nonetheless outraged. "You idiot! How could you—?"

"Don't call me an idiot!" Baptiste snapped. "It was the scientist! He broke the vial just when I thought he was going to give it to me!"

"Why did he—?"

"I don't know! I'll explain later! God damn it, Pierre, just get us out of here!"

An angry silence, then Baptiste heard a sullen rumble from somewhere deep within the vessel. A low vibration passed through the hull as electric pumps began discharging the water within the lock-out chamber. *Atlantida* wouldn't be able to ascend until the aft compartment was dry; otherwise, all that water was another liquid ton of unwanted ballast.

Baptiste sighed, then began to wrestle out of his diving gear. It would take a little while for the lock-out chamber to repressurize, and his ears would pop painfully a few times before then. Might as well make himself as comfortable as possible; and he could use a few extra minutes to think of how he would explain what happened to Benoit.

Until now, he had never taken the Barracuda this far below the surface. All previous test dives had been from the shore or from Tethys 1, but never before at operational depth; that was supposed to be one of the next major tests, previously scheduled for two days from now. Its hull creaked ominously while the bay was being flooded, and for a few seconds Peter wondered whether this was such a wise idea, but by then it was much too late to reconsider: the bay was full of seawater, the outer hatch opened like a pair of barn doors, and the midnight darkness of the ocean lay before him.

"Okay, Tethys," Peter murmured, "I'm on the loose." The he pushed the yoke forward and stamped down his left foot, and the Barracuda shot out of the bay.

Startled by his lights, a school of fish hovering outside the hatch scattered in either direction. Peter caught a glimpse of one of the mooring cables, crusted with zebra mussels and taut against the massive round shoe of its anchor, dead ahead of him; he twisted the yoke hard to the right and the cable shot past, disappearing from the left side of his canopy.

"We copy, Pete." Jared's voice in his headset was calm. Just before Peter had climbed into the Barracuda, he had returned to the operations center, where he was now handling home plate. "Looking good here. You're clear for your run."

For all intents and purposes, this jaunt was being officially logged as the next Navy test; he and Jared had simply taken the liberty of moving it up a couple of days. "Copy that," Peter said. "I'll keep you posted."

Now to find the target submersible. Leaving the radio on, he tapped a command into the keypad, and the canopy heads-up lit to display a translucent bathymetric map of this area of seafloor surrounding Tethys 2. If he had this figured right, the sub must have set down somewhere reasonably close . . .

But where did the sub itself come from? Most submersibles with lock-out chambers tended to be salvage craft; if that was the case, then it wouldn't have had sufficient fuel to come all the way from the shore. Which meant that there had to be a mother ship anchored somewhere nearby. "Jared?" he said. "Get me someone in MainOps topside."

"Miles is up there," Jared replied. "I've informed him of the situation. Gimme a sec and I'll patch you through."

"Thanks." Peter switched on the side-scan sonar, then turned the Barracuda to the east, following a bearing of 90 degrees. He'd start his search at the edge of the shelf, out toward deep ocean, then make a wide, slow sweep around the station. With any luck, he might—

"What do you got, Peter?" Bartlett's voice was scratchy with radio static; Lipscomb suddenly realized that if he continued his orbit as planned, he would soon be out of UHF range from the station. No time to deal with that now, though.

"I think the sub we're looking for came from a ship," he said, turning the yoke slowly as he kept an eye on the compass. The sonar beeped as it caught something; he quickly glanced at the grid, saw a long line leading straight to the edge of the shelf. That would be the OTEC intake pipe. "Is there any surface traffic up there? Something near Tethys?"

A short pause. He heard voices in the background, then Miles came back. "There's a trawler anchored a couple of miles out, due west of us. I spotted it earlier tonight. Radar shows nothing else except an oil tanker about fifteen miles northeast of us."

A trawler? It sounded unlikely, but . . .

"Contact the Coast Guard, get them to send a boat out there to check it out. It might be nothing, but—"

The sonar beeped loudly, registering a hard contact. He glanced at the heads-up. A large metallic object on the ocean floor, bearing 92.5 degrees, less than a half mile from his position. Besides the OTEC shaft, there was nothing out this way that belonged to Tethys.

"Hold on," he said. "I think I got something."

"S hit!" Duval yelled.

Baptiste looked up. The lock-out chamber was half-full of water, yet for the sake of caution he was still wearing his air mask; through its earphones he could hear the pilot's alarmed voice. "What's going on?" he demanded.

"Sonar contact!"

What the hell . . . ? Baptiste felt a surge of fear colder than the water around him. "Where's it coming from? What's its bearing?"

"West 269, from the station! Closing at fifteen knots!"

Damn it! Someone must have sent out a submersible. "Take us up!" Baptiste shouted. "Get us out of here!"

"Idiot! What do you think I'm doing?"

There was a hard, sudden lurch that nearly threw Baptiste headfirst into the water; he grabbed a rack for support and cursed under his breath as the *Atlantida* began to rise. Yet through the hull he could hear the dull groan of the fore and aft thrusters, as if the submersible was a heavy truck stuck in a ditch, its tires spinning wildly against the mud.

"Damn it!" Duval yelled. "We haven't lost enough ballast!"

Baptiste understood. With the lock-out chamber still half-full, the *Atlantida* was weighed down by its own mass. "Drop the lead!" he shouted.

"Shut up!" Duval snarled, but then a instant later Baptiste felt another lurch as the pilot jettisoned the lead ballast bars from the submersible's undercarriage. The sound of the thrusters subtly changed pitch, and now there was the sensation of rising.

"It's locked on us." Duval's voice was a little more calm now, yet nonetheless tense. "We're not going to be able to make it back to the *Braga* without him following us. God damn it . . ."

"Think! Work it out!" Baptiste resisted an urge to pound a fist against the bulkhead separating him from the pilot's compartment. "If you can't outrun them, then lose them!"

The submersible from Tethys must be one of the DSVs they used for exploration. Either that, or a shuttle. Either way, it probably didn't have much more power than their own craft; at fifteen knots, it was probably running at top speed. And Pierre was an experienced pilot. He would know this; he would find a way of—

"Hold on," Duval said tightly. "I'm taking us down."

Hearing this, Baptiste was confused. Down? Where could he possibly . . . ?

Then he realized what the pilot meant. "Christ," he whispered.

● ● ●

T he object was in motion.

No doubt about it, the sonar acquisition was a submersible parked only a few hundred yards from the edge
of the long, steep slope leading down to the Blake Plateau. Yet, even as Peter steadied the yoke and kicked the
waterjets up to twenty knots, the vehicle began moving
away, slowly at first, yet gaining speed. And it appeared
to heading straight away from him . . . not to the west,
toward the shore and the trawler he suspected was its
mother ship, but out to deep ocean.

"Peter . . . do you . . . contact . . . ?" Bartlett's voice
was breaking up, overwhelmed by static. The Barracuda
was rapidly moving out of radio range, and there wasn't
enough time to find another clear channel.

"Breaking up, Tethys, breaking up." Peter reached to
the com panel, twisted the UHF knob to maximum gain.
"I've acquired a moving sonar contact. Repeat, moving
sonar contact. In pursuit. Repeat, in pursuit."

There was a reply, but it was completely lost in the
angry fuzz. Peter impatiently turned down the volume as
he nudged more power to the Barracuda's main engines.
He switched on the forward lights, but all he could see
through the canopy were snowy flakes of sediment. The
heads-up showed a hard object less than a five hundred
feet away, yet there were no visible lights ahead of him.

So it was running dark, trying to remain unseen. It
didn't matter. Peter smiled grimly. The Barracuda was
faster than any half-ass salvage sub in the water. He could
chase this lame bastard across the ocean if he . . .

Then the object disappeared from the grid.

One moment, it was there. The next, it had vanished
like a ghost.

"What the . . . ?" Peter gaped at the heads-up. Nothing.
But there was no way it could have disappeared so sud-

denly. There was nothing out there for it to hide behind, except . . .

"Shit!" he snapped, and punched another command into the keypad. The heads-up display changed again, showing now a false red-blue ceiling of thermoclimes painted over the bathymetric chart. Yes, right there! A sharp rise of cold water just above the edge of the Florida-Hatteras Slope, where the continental shelf ended and the sea bottom fell sharply away into the narrow, troughlike canyon separating the shelf from the Blake Plateau.

The pilot of the other submersible knew his business; he was aware that the thermoclime would shield him from the Barracuda's sonar. So he had taken his craft over the edge of the shelf, then dived sharply into the canyon. So long as he remained below the layer of warmer water and above his boat's crush depth, he might be able to escape.

"Oh, no, you asshole," Peter muttered. "You're not getting away that easy."

He throttled back to fifteen knots and pushed the yoke forward until the Barracuda was skimming only a few feet above the seafloor. Within the lights, he saw rocks and muddy silt; crabs kicked up sand as they scuttled out of the way. Then, all at once, the seafloor sloped sharply downward, and now there was only darkness below.

Peter sucked in his breath, then shoved the yoke forward, and the Barracuda plunged into the perpetual midnight.

For a couple of blessed minutes Duval believed that he had lost the craft behind him. Diving into the canyon past the edge of the continental shelf was a risk; *Atlantida* was a sturdy vessel, built to withstand pressures where only divers wearing armored JIM suits could exit its aft compartment, yet its hull was rated to only six hundred meters, and the floor of the submarine canyon fell away to eight hundred meters at some points.

He was counting on the thermoclime to protect him from the pursuing sub. He had no idea what the pursuing craft was, only that it was much faster than his own. Escape within the canyon was his only hope.

"Pierre!" Baptiste's voice was an anxious rasp in his headset. "What are you doing? Where are you?"

Duval grabbed the headset cable, angrily jerked it out of its socket. Fool! It was bad enough that he had somehow fouled up, but he had also come back empty-handed. If it were possible to do so, he could have jettisoned the diver then and there. The last thing he needed right then was to have him yapping in his ear.

He reached up to the control panel above his head, flipped a couple of toggle switches. Two searchlights arrayed below the sphere flashed on, illuminating the vast wall of the continental slope with their greenish glow. He hugged the wall as he descended, carefully keeping an eye on the depth gauge as he studied the chart spread out across his lap, trying to figure out where to go.

There. A few kilometers to the northeast, on the opposite side of the trench, lay a small archipelago of seamounts on the edge of the Blake Plateau, just west of Stetson Mesa. At an average depth of seven hundred meters, the seamounts were far too deep for the *Atlantida,* yet he could count on the ocean currents which swept around them to produce thermoclimes which would help him evade the enemy's sonar. Once he was sure that he had lost his pursuer, he could jettison more ballast, rise closer to the surface again, and double back to where the *Braga* was anchored.

Duval glanced again at his sonar screen. No sign of

the other craft, but he had no doubt that it was still searching for him. Yet the depth gauge read 560 meters; he was getting perilously close to crush depth, and through the bulkhead behind him he could hear the aluminum hull creaking ominously.

Duval pulled back on the stick, rotating the thrusters to level the sub off at 570 meters. A deep current caught the submersible, caused it to fishtail around. Duval grabbed the stick with his hands, gritted his teeth as he muscled the diving planes back into proper trim. Through the sphere, he saw the canyon wall loom dangerously close; he swore as he pitched the sub to the right, and let out his breath as it moved away, yet so close to the canyon that the port skid nearly connected with a large boulder.

Duval muttered an angry curse. He needed more light! He switched on the rest of the searchlights, and the threatening wall was brightly illuminated.

Good, now he could see a little better. Now all he had to do was find his way up the canyon. Turning the stick a few degrees to the right, he began moving northeast, heading for the sea mounts.

For a few minutes Peter thought he had lost the other submersible. Its abrupt dive into the narrow trench separating the Florida-Hatteras Slope from the Blake Plateau had fooled him just long enough for its pilot to lengthen his head start. Yet once he was below the thermoclime, he picked up the other craft once more when its pilot switched on its lights.

He cautiously followed the submersible from above, tracking it through sonar and visual contact while maintaining a vertical distance of only a thousand feet, watching as the other craft hugged the canyon wall. He was still well above the Barracuda's maximum depth, yet he doubted that his quarry could dive any deeper than he could. Nonetheless, his palms were slick with sweat, and he was all too conscious of the occasional creak he heard from the hull surrounding him.

For the first time Peter found himself wishing that the Navy had armed the Barracuda before it had given it to him for testing, for he would have dearly loved to blow a torpedo up their ass. Yet even then, he knew that this was only his rage speaking; this was an unarmed craft, after all, and although they were playing much the same hunt-and-seek game which submarine captains had practiced since World War I, there was no way he could consciously destroy an unarmed enemy vessel, and the sort of electronic warfare he had performed against the pirate whaler a few days ago was an unavailable option at this depth.

No. All he could do was follow the sub back to its mother ship, whether it was the trawler Bartlett had spotted earlier or not. He'd work it out from there. Right now his major task was keeping track of the submersible.

At 570 meters, the other craft abruptly leveled off its descent. As he figured, it was probably near crush depth. Peter hauled back the yoke, watched as the red spot painted on the heads-up display made an abrupt northeast turn, then started heading up the canyon on a 19-degree bearing. Through the translucent heads-up, he saw the submersible's lights brighten sharply, and he smiled to himself. Must be getting a little too dark down here for the other guy's taste; from the look of things, he had come close to hitting the canyon's west wall.

So what was he doing now? Peter studied the heads-up. The sub seemed to be heading diagonally across the canyon, directly across from a thumb-shaped spur of the its west wall. On the opposite side of the spur, past the deepest part of the trench where the slope fell away to 780 meters, was a cluster of small, teardrop-shaped sea mounts on the eastern edge of the Blake Plateau. They lay much too deep for anything except an exploration DSV, but perhaps . . .

Of course. The bastard was trying to evade him this way. "Oh, no, you don't," Peter murmured. "Not on my watch, motherfucker."

He pushed the yoke forward, coaxing the Barracuda up to twenty-five knots. Now the chase was getting serious.

D uval was almost halfway across the canyon, above the deepest part of the trench, when his sonar caught something below him.

For a few seconds he believed it to be an uncharted seamount. The NOAA chart he used was more than ten years old, after all, and the ocean floor was always changing. Duval made a turn, a few degrees starboard, to clear the obstruction.

The sonar stopped pinging, and he relaxed a little. He was in a narrow part of the canyon now, a little closer to the west wall than he cared to be, above a point where the trench threatened to close in on him. Yet the seamounts lay to his right, and already he could feel ocean currents pushing him from behind. If he was still being pursued, he might be able to—

Then the sonar pinged again.

Much louder this time. He blinked, glanced at his screen.

Ping . . . ping . . . ping-ping . . . ping-ping-ping . . .

Something was moving down there. On the screen, he saw a twisting, S-shaped form, about a hundred meters below him.

Ping-ping-ping-ping . . .

Now it was eighty meters away. What the hell? Duval twisted the stick to the left, then hard to the right. Yet the object wasn't leaving him. In fact, it seemed . . .

Ping-ping-ping-ping-ping . . .

P eter watched in confusion as the lights of the submersible below and in front of him weaved back and forth.

What the hell was that guy doing? Maybe he was trying to evade him . . . but there was no way he could have seen him. He was above and behind the bastard. There was no way he could see him . . .

Then, all of a sudden, his sonar captured another target. Something was moving beneath the other sub.

G oddammit! Seventy meters and still closing!

Staring in bewilderment at the sonar, Duval shoved the stick to the left. And still it was coming closer, as if tracking his movements. Distracted, he gaped at the screen . . .

Fifty meters, and . . . the fucking thing was changing shape! "What in . . . ?

Ping-ping-ping-ping-ping-ping . . .

A long shadow, backwashed from his searchlights, fell across him. Duval glanced up, saw the west wall of the canyon hurtling straight toward him.

T he other submersible veered sharply to the left.

"You dumb son of a bitch!" Peter yelled. "You're getting too—"

• • •

"S hit!" Duval shoved the stick to the right. For an instant he thought he was going to clear it, yet the current had caught the side of his boat, and now he was being propelled bow-first into the vast rocky mass.

He was still screaming when the *Atlantida* slammed straight into the canyon wall.

The lights below him flashed once, very briefly, as the submersible collided with the western wall of the trench. Peter couldn't hear the impact, but when he reached up to snap on the external floodlights, he caught a swarm of oxygenated bubbles surging up from below.

Horrified, he watched on sonar as a large, metallic object fell away, rolling down the wall of the slope into the black depths of the canyon. Long before it hit the ocean floor three hundred meters down, he knew that whoever was aboard was dead.

Yet that wasn't all that the sonar picked up. For a few brief seconds he saw an elongated, serpentine form moving less than eighty feet beneath the sub's point of impact. It seemed to hover there for a half a minute, then it quickly moved away, until it vanished off his screen.

Peter waited long after the other sub hit the bottom of the trench. He waited for the source of the ghost contact to reappear, yet it never did. For a little while he considered investigating further.

But then he decided that this might not be very wise. Instead, he switched off his lights, discharged ballast, and began to head home.

SEVENTH DAY

FRIDAY, JUNE 10, 2011

TWENTY
Mystery

6.10.11—1857 EST

There was a hollow clunk within the steel hatch as heavy bolts were withdrawn, then the lock wheel spun like a bank vault being opened. A faint hiss of air escaping past the rubber gaskets which lined the frame, then the hatch swung open from outside.

"Welcome back to the world,", said the crewman standing just outside. "Be careful. Watch your head."

Judith was the first to leave. Picking up her duffel bag and slinging it over her shoulder, she ducked her head as she stepped through the hatch. She let the crewman help her down the short ladder, then she stopped and took a long, deep breath.

Yes. Despite the hyperbaric facility being on the lowest level of Tethys 1, she could taste salt in the air. It wasn't the first time she had endured the fifty-six-hour decompression period, but never before had she been so eager to return to the surface again.

She turned to watch the others as they emerged from

the chamber. Andie was next; as restless as she had been over the two and a half days, especially during those long stretches when she had to lie still on her bed, breathing pure oxygen through a face mask, Judith would have thought the teenager would now be turning handsprings. Yet instead she seemed almost withdrawn; carrying her bag and camcorder case, she quietly walked down the ladder, glanced incuriously around the room, then looked at her aunt.

"Well, what now?" she murmured, setting the case down on the floor.

What now indeed? Judith didn't have an answer for that.

Peter was behind her, carrying his own bag over his shoulder. "I think I like going down better," he said when he joined them . . . then, for no reason that Judith could think of, he dropped his bag and wrapped his arms around her, giving her a hug as if he hadn't seen her in several days.

He seemed to want to do that a lot lately, beginning with the moment she emerged from the *Galatea* after it returned to Tethys 2 three days ago. Judith didn't mind, although she had a sneaking suspicion as to why he had become so affectionate. Yet she had decided not to probe too deeply; if he ever wanted to tell her, he eventually would, and if he never told her, perhaps it was just as well.

There was a long pause, then Leslie Sun exited the chamber, carrying her flight bag in one hand, her computer case in the other. As she had done for the last three days, she avoided making eye contact with either Peter or Judith, although once more she tried to give Andie a friendly smile. Yet Andie still didn't want to have anything to do with her, although for reasons Judith couldn't quite understand. Rebuffed, the journalist's expression relapsed into that cool, professional mask she had worn the entire time they had spent together in decompression; she walked stiffly down the ladder, then strode past them without saying a word.

"Jerk," Andie murmured.

"I wonder if she knows where she's going?" Judith whispered as she watched her walk across the deck. There were no exit signs, although she knew from past experience that she was headed in the right direction for the stairs that would lead her to the station's upper levels. If she bothered to stop and ask someone for help, that is; as Judith watched, Leslie silently marched past a crewman who could have easily pointed out the right way.

"Nope. She doesn't." Peter's voice was condescendingly amused. "But that won't stop her."

Judith looked at her husband, caught a glimpse of a vague smile that quickly vanished. Yes, there was something there. Two and half days together in a sealed dormitory not much larger than a low-rent city apartment, yet he and Leslie had spoken barely five words to each other the entire time. Indeed, she had spent her waking hours sitting on her bunk, the curtains shut, typing away at her keyboard. Meanwhile Peter had been his usual self, although perhaps a little more playful than at any time in recent memory; Judith kept having to swat his hands off her, although had it not been for the utter lack of privacy, she would have jumped him in a split second.

She decided once more to ask no questions. If she didn't, then she'd receive no lies.

She heard another set of footsteps coming down the ladder, and for an instant they sounded just familiar enough to make her look over her shoulder. Yet it was only the crewman who had opened the chamber. Judith looked away quickly; once again, she felt her eyes swelling. For a second there, it sounded just like Charles . . .

Peter must have sensed this, because he slipped his arm around her, pulled her closer. "C'mon," he murmured. "Let's go see Miles."

The briefing room where they had met only six days before was unchanged: same walls, same chairs, same table. Yet somehow it seemed different, as if it was a stage set which had been hastily placed back together again for a final scene, although with some of the players missing. Indeed, when Judith came in, she almost sat down in the nearest available chair . . . then, remembering that this was where Charles had been seated the last time they were here, she moved to the next chair.

It was going to take a long time for her to get over the loss of her friend. It wouldn't be made any easier by what Bartlett was telling them.

"Charles was working for a French pharmaceutical company." Sitting at his accustomed place at the end of the table, Miles stared at his hands, folded together on the table. "He agreed to sell them taq samples from the Galápagos site. That was the original bargain, which is why the phony kidnapping in Dominica was arranged, but when that fell through, he tried to keep the deal alive by offering to sell them taq from Lucifer as well."

"For how much?" Judith found herself asking, although she really didn't want to know.

Bartlett started to answer, but then he glanced at Leslie Sun. The journalist wasn't taking notes, yet the general manager apparently didn't want to divulge any more details than necessary. "It was a lot of money," he replied. "Let's just leave it at that. But then our people caught on to what he was doing, and when the people he was dealing with got wise to that, they decided . . ." He cleared his throat. "Well, you know the rest."

"I saw the Galápagos sample in his lab, just before he died." As he spoke, Peter slid his hand beneath the table to grasp Judith's, offering comfort. "I don't know, but I think he was having second thoughts about giving it to them." He looked across the table at Leslie. "You said he smashed the tube."

Leslie reluctantly looked his way as she nodded. "No, he didn't give it to the diver," she said quietly. "I saw him drop it, break it under his foot. That's when . . ."

For the first time in several days, her eyes briefly met Judith's. There was apology in her gaze, and perhaps not only for the things they were discussing. Judith stared back at her, and Leslie glanced away once more.

Miles cleared his throat again. "At any rate, we're getting the remaining details from the feds. The Coast Guard has the *Braga* impounded in Jacksonville . . . seems it used to be a Russian spy trawler, if you can believe it . . . and everyone aboard is in lockup down in Miami. The FBI and Interpol are really happy about this. They've been trying to nail this Benoit character for a long time, and now they've got a murder conspiracy rap on him."

"Hip, hip, hooray," Andie murmured. "Hope they fry the bastard."

Sitting between Peter and Miles, Andie was uncommonly cynical, a shadow of the teenager who had been seated in this very same room six days earlier. Judith understood. Her niece had grown up a bit over the last week, but becoming an adult wasn't always pleasant. Was it ever?

"I'm sure they will." Miles looked at Judith. "Judy, I can't tell you how sorry I am."

"I know." She forcefully shook her head. "I can't get over it either, but . . . I dunno. I guess Charles must have had his reasons." She let out her breath. "You've got his body, right?"

Miles nodded. "It's in a morgue in Jacksonville." He hesitated. "Does he have any next of kin in Dominica?"

"No, but he's quite well known down there." Feeling the tears coming again, she hastily snuffled them back. "Peter and I are flying his body back to Dominica tomorrow morning. He's going to be buried outside Roseau, in the mountains. He loved to . . ."

Remembering the hike they had taken together only a week ago, the place where he had shown her exotic plants and mineral springs, she was ready to burst into tears again. But she had already wept so much over the last few days; for a few minutes she had to be strong, for there was one last thing which had to be settled.

She gazed across the table at Leslie Sun. "You're not putting this in your story, are you? I'd like to give Charles a little dignity."

The journalist moved restlessly in her seat. "I'm sorry, Judith, but I have to. It's part of—"

"No, you're not." Bartlett shook his head. "In fact, nothing you've seen or heard this week is going to leave the room. We made an agreement, remember?"

Leslie stared at him in surprise. "Oh, come on now. You don't really expect me to abide by that, do you?" When Bartlett slowly nodded, it seemed as if she was almost about to laugh out loud. "Sorry, but that was an informal agreement. It isn't legally binding. I'm under no obligation to—"

"You know, I rather thought you were going to say that." Bartlett stood up and walked to the door. Opening it, he thrust his head out into the hallway. "You can come in now."

Three people walked into the conference room: two men in business suits, along with a middle-aged woman.

"These gentlemen are U.S. federal marshals," Bartlett said as he stepped aside. "Mr. Williamson and Mr. Pohl, I believe." They nodded perfunctorily. "And this is Helen Blanchard, the company's chief of security. I believe they have something they wish to discuss with you."

Leslie gaped at them in astonishment. "You can't be serious!"

"I'm afraid we are, ma'am," Williamson replied. "We have reason to believe that you have certain notes and photographs pertaining to classified Navy material."

"What?" She blinked in confusion before quickly recovering her poise. "I have no idea what you're talking about."

"They're talking about the minisub, Leslie." Peter regarded her coolly from across the table. "I asked you not to look at it. Did you think I was kidding?"

"You're also a potential eyewitness to a major felony," Pohl added. He pulled a folded sheaf of papers from the inside pocket of his jacket, extended them to Leslie. "This is a subpoena for you to appear before a federal grand jury. I must warn you that any attempt to publish any information you may have would be considered contempt of court."

Leslie stared at the subpoena without taking it, then glared at Bartlett. "You set me up. If you think I'm going to let—"

"Ma'am, we're authorized to place you under arrest, if necessary." Williamson folded his hands in front of him. "It would be much easier for all of us if you'd cooperate."

"Ms. Sun, if you'll come with us, please?" Helen Blanchard gestured to the door. "I believe we should discuss this in private."

Her face scarlet with barely suppressed rage, Leslie glanced around the table. Finding no sympathy from anyone in the room, she shoved back her chair, stood up, and turned toward the door.

"Don't forget your stuff," Peter murmured.

For a moment it seemed as if she was going to say something, then she caught a glimpse of the expression on Judith's face, and wisely decided to remain silent. She picked up her bags and started toward the door.

"Hey, Leslie?" Andie said, and Leslie paused to turn to her. "Thanks for teaching me what it's like to be a professional," she said, utterly stone-faced. "I'll always remember your example."

For a second Leslie actually smiled. "You're welcome. I hope you . . ." Then she caught the irony behind what the girl had just said, and her face darkened again. "Go to hell," she finished, then she stalked out the door, followed closely by the federal marshals.

"Sorry to disturb you," Blanchard said, then she closed the door behind her.

A long moment, then everyone let out a collective sigh of relief. "She might try to put all that in her story, you know," Peter murmured. "It could be embarrassing."

"Not if she's smart, she won't." Sitting down once more, Bartlett leaned back in his chair and folded his arms across his chest. "And if she isn't smart, then her editors will be. Helen's already been in touch with *Millennium*. I don't believe they're very pleased with Ms. Sun's conduct." He glanced at Andie and smiled. "I hope you meant what you said . . . or at least the way I think you meant what you said."

"I meant it." Andie rolled her eyes in disgust. "If I grow up to be her, please do me a favor, and kill me."

Peter reached around to give his niece a quick hug. "I don't think that'll be necessary."

Miles shook his head. "If we're looking for a happy ending to all this, I'm afraid that's it." He sighed. "Seven days, and what do we have to show for it?"

No one said anything for a few moments, for it seemed as if no one had anything left to say. A disastrous expedition. A betrayal of trust. The loss of a friend . . .

"We're still alive," Judith murmured after a while. "We're still alive, and we've got each other. That's got to count for something."

Bartlett nodded reflectively. "I suppose it does. It should, at any rate." He stood up again, stepped toward the door. "Anyway, you guys have a flight to catch. The VTOL to Jacksonville will be landing in about a half hour. Judy, if you can send me your report . . . ?"

"I'll email it tomorrow." She glanced at Peter. "Maybe the day after. Got some things to take care of first."

"Whatever. I'm in no rush." Bartlett opened the door, walked out into the corridor. "I'll catch up with y'all before you leave."

They were walking down the passageway, almost at the ladder leading up to the top deck, when one of federal marshals stepped out of MainOps. "Mr. Lipscomb?" Pohl asked quietly. "Could I speak with you for a moment?"

Alarmed by his abrupt reappearance, Judith and Andie glanced uncertainly at him, then at Peter. "It's nothing very important," Pohl quickly added. "Just a couple of questions. It shouldn't take more than a minute."

Peter nodded, then looked at the two women. "Go on ahead. I'll be right there." He waited until they climbed the ladder, then he turned to the officer. "How can I help you?"

"I read the report you submitted . . . about how the *Atlantida* was lost." Somehow, Pohl seemed less menacing than earlier; leaning against the ladder, he reached into his coat pocket and pulled out a stick of gum. "It covers all the bases, but there's just one thing I'm wondering about . . . unofficially, I mean."

"Unofficially?" Peter raised an eyebrow.

"Just out of curiosity." The federal marshal smiled. "It won't be in my final report."

Peter shrugged. "Sure. What do you want to know?"

Pohl played with the gum wrapper. "You stated that the pilot of the *Atlantida* appeared to get distracted just before he slammed into the canyon wall. But you didn't say what distracted him."

"Yes," Peter replied, "that's what I wrote."

"So . . . ?" Pohl regarded him with sharp gray eyes. "What do you think distracted him so much that he would crash his sub? You were down there, after all. You must have a clue."

Peter was silent for a moment, Pohl patiently awaiting his answer. "I have no idea," he said at last. "I didn't see anything."

Pohl slowly nodded. "You mean you didn't see anything, period, or you didn't see anything people would believe?"

"Something like that, yeah."

The marshal grinned, then turned to walk away. "Call me sometime when your memory gets better. I think I'd love to hear about this." Then he paused to glance at Peter over his shoulder. "You'd be surprised at some of the things I've heard."

The summer sun was setting behind the western horizon, out where the land met the water. From here on Tethys's top deck, looking to the east, they could only see the vast expanse of the Atlantic. The sea seemed to have been painted gold, its gentle waves gilded as if by some master artisan. The breeze was cool and fragrant with salt; above the wispy purple clouds, the first stars were beginning to appear in the night sky. It was a beautiful evening.

"God, I love this place." Hands cupped together, Judith leaned against the railing, taking in the majesty. "Doc and I used to come up here all the time, just before we'd go home. It was always something special."

Andie nodded. The two of them were alone on the balcony behind MainOps. Peter was at the chopper pad, minding their bags while he chatted with Bartlett. The company VTOL was due to arrive in just a few minutes, but her aunt wanted to come out here while they waited.

"Nice place for a sunset," she said quietly. A moment of hesitation, then: "You really loved him, didn't you? Doc, I mean."

Judith thought about it for a second. "Yeah ... yeah, I really did. He was sort of like a father, but not ..." She sighed, pulled her windblown hair from her eyes. "Well, if you're lucky, one day you'll get to know someone like him. Then you'll understand."

"A teacher, you mean," Andie said, and Judith nodded. "Yeah, well ... maybe I already have."

Judith turned her head, saw her niece staring out at the twilight sea. "I'm never going to look at this place the same way again," she said. "Thanks, Aunt Judy ... I really mean it. Thanks."

For a moment Judith thought she was about to cry. No, perhaps it hadn't been a complete loss after all.

"You're welcome," she whispered. "Come back anytime."

She started to reach for Andie, to put her arm around the girl's shoulder, draw her close the way Charles never had, when her niece suddenly froze, her mouth dropping open as she stared in blank astonishment at something in the distance.

"Aunt Judy . . ."

Judith turned, followed Andie's gaze.

Out on the water, barely a hundred yards from the station, something raised its elongated head from the water.

Barely visible against the evening light, it hovered for half a minute, then plunged back into the sea once more. For an instant it seemed as if a great serpentine form moved across the surface, hidden just beneath the waves.

"Should I get my camera?" Andie asked quietly. "It might come back."

"Nope. Too late." Judith smiled. "Maybe if we wait, though . . ."

They stood together for a while longer, until night fell across the water and they heard the sound of the approaching aircraft. Yet whatever they saw, or thought they had seen, never reappeared.

As always, the ocean retained its mysteries.

ACKNOWLEDGMENTS

'm greatly indebted to a number of individuals who gave me assistance during the research and development of this novel. They include:

J. W. "Buzz" Ryan, U.S. Navy master parachutist, for suggestions and technical assistance; John Wyatt, Professor of Electrical Engineering, MIT, and Jim Lynch, Senior Scientist, Woods Hole Oceanographic Institution, for reviewing the manuscript; Linda Lotto, Woods Hole Oceanographic Institution, for providing bathymetric charts of the Blake Plateau and refering me to published research about hydrothermal vents in the Mid-Atlantic Ridge; Barbara Haase, my diving instructor at the Castaways Hotel in Dominica, for teaching me the basics of scuba; Chris Alyott, the proprietor of the Space-Crime Continuum Bookstore in Northampton, Massachusetts, for recommending that I take diving lessons; Daniel Didier and Cornel Semper, my guides in Dominica, for escorting me around the island; Janice Murphy, the creator of my web site (http//www.sfwa.org/authors/allen), for providing me with the name of Yemaya; and my sister, Genevive Edwards, for connecting me with Dr. Wyatt and telling me about the *Alvin* mockup at Woods Hole.

As always, my deepest appreciation to my agent, Martha Millard, and my editor, Ginjer Buchanan, for their continued support, and to my wife Linda, for her endurance.

—"Highgate"
Whately, Massachusetts
December 1997–November 1998

SOURCES

Anonymous, *The Encyclopedia of Recreational Diving* (International PADI, 1996).

Ballard, Robert D., Ph.D, and McConnell, Malcolm, *Explorations* (Hyperion, 1995).

—— "Research Submersibles: Explorers of the Ocean Depths," *1979 Yearbook of Science and the Future* (Encyclopedia Britannica, 1978).

Borgese, Elisabeth Mann, *The Mines of Neptune* (Abrams, 1985).

Burns, Robert E.; "Mining the Ocean," *1980 Yearbook of Science and the Future* (Encyclopedia Britannica, 1979).

Broad, William J., *The Universe Below* (Simon and Schuster, 1997).

—— "Swift Growth Found in Ocean Depths," *The New York Times,* Oct. 20, 1994.

—— "Secret Sub to Scan Sea Floor for Roman Wrecks," *The New York Times,* Feb. 7, 1995.

—— "First Move Made to Mine Mineral Riches of Seabed," *The New York Times,* Dec. 21, 1997.

—— "Undersea Treasure and Its Odd Guardians," *The New York Times,* Dec. 30, 1997.

Clancy, Tom, *Submarine* (Berkley, 1993).

Cousteau, J. Y., *World Without Sun* (Harper & Row, 1964).

Cousteau, Jacques, *The Ocean World* (Times-Mirror, 1979; Abrams, 1993).

Darby, Ray and Patricia, *Conquering the Deep Sea Frontier* (David McKay Company, 1971).

Dillon, William P., and Popenoe, Peter, "The Blake Plateau and Carolina Trough," *The Geology of North America* (The Geological Society of America, 1988).

Egan, Timothy, "Salmon 'Pirates' in Pacific Assailed," *The New York Times,* May 14, 1991.

Ellis, Richard, *Deep Atlantic* (Alfred A. Knopf, 1996).

Evans, J. Harvey, and Adamchack, John C., *Ocean Engineering Structures* (MIT Press, 1969).

Hawkes. Graham S., "Microsubs Go to Sea," *Scientific American,* Oct. 1997.

Hendrickson, Robert, *The Ocean Almanac* (Doubleday, 1984).

Horsfield, Brenda, and Stone, Peter Bennet, *The Great Ocean Business* (Coward, McCann & Geoghan, 1972).

Idyll, C. P., *Abyss* (Thomas Y. Crowell, 1976).

Langmuir, C., *et al,* "Hydrothermal Vents near a Mantle Hot Spot: The Lucky Strike Vent Field at 37°N on the Mid-Atlantic Ridge," *Earth and Planetary Science Letters* 148 (1997).

Ley, Willy, *Exotic Zoology* (Capricorn, 1966).

Pellegrino, Charles, *Her Name, Titanic* (McGraw-Hill, 1988).

Pernetta, Dr. John, *Atlas of the Oceans* (Rand McNally, 1994).

Polmar, Norman, *Death of the Thresher* (Chilton, 1964).

Rona, P. A. *et al,* "Black Smokers, Massive Sulphides and Vent Biota at the Mid-Atlantic Ridge," *Nature,* May 1, 1996.

Rona, Peter, "Direct Observation of Atlantic Black Smokers," *Eos,* Nov. 18, 1986.

Safina, Carl, "The World's Imperiled Fish," *The Oceans: Scientific American Quarterly,* Summer 1998.

Sweeney, James B., *A Pictorial History of Sea Monsters* (Bonanza, 1972).

Van Dover, Cindy Lee, *Deep-Ocean Journeys* (Addison-Wesley, 1996).

Wilford, John Noble, "Sea Chimneys Hold Clues on Life in Harsh Habitats," *The New York Times,* July 20, 1998.